BEST BRITISH HORROR 2014

JOHNNY MAINS IS an award-winning editor, author and horror historian. He has written for *Illustrators Quarterly*, *SFX* and *The Paperback Fanatic*. He was project editor to Pan Macmillan's critically acclaimed 2010 re-issue of *The Pan Book of Horror* and is currently co-editing *Dead Funny* with multi-award winning comedian Robin Ince. Mains has also written the introduction to Stephen King's 30th Anniversary edition of *Thinner*. He is the author of two short story collections and editor of five anthologies.

Also by Johnny Mains:

EDITED

Back From The Dead: The Legacy of the Pan Book of Horror Stories

The Pan Book of Horror Stories (2010 re-issue, Project Editor)

The Mask and Other Stories by Herbert van Thal

Bite-Sized Horror

Party Pieces: The Horror Fiction of Mary Danby

The Screaming Book of Horror

The Burning Circus

The Sorcerers: The Original Screenplay by John Burke

WRITTEN

With Deepest Sympathy

Lest You Should Suffer Nightmares: A Biography of Herbert van Thal

Frightfully Cosy and Mild Stories For Nervous Types

BEST BRITISH HORROR 2014

SERIES EDITED BY

JOHNNY MAINS

CROMER

PUBLISHED BY SALT PUBLISHING
12 Norwich Road, Cromer, Norfolk NR27 0AX

All rights reserved

Selection and introduction © Johnny Mains, 2014
Individual contributions © the contributors, 2014

The right of Johnny Mains to be identified as the editor of this work has been asserted by him in accordance with Section 77 of the Copyright, Designs and Patents Act 1988.

This book is in copyright. Subject to statutory exception and to provisions of relevant collective licensing agreements, no reproduction of any part may take place without the written permission of Salt Publishing.

First published by Salt Publishing, 2014

Printed in Great Britain by Clays Ltd, St Ives plc

Typeset in Paperback 9/12

This book is sold subject to the conditions that it shall not, by way of trade or otherwise, be lent, re-sold, hired out, or otherwise circulated without the publisher's prior consent in any form of binding or cover other than that in which it is published and without a similar condition including this condition being imposed on the subsequent purchaser.

ISBN 978 1 907773 64 8 paperback

1 3 5 7 9 8 6 4 2

This book would not have happened without

Charles Birkin, Christine Campbell Thompson, Dennis Wheatley, Herbert van Thal, Christine Bernard, Mary Danby, Ronald Chetwynd Hayes, Robert Aickman, John Burke, Peter Haining, James Dickie, Hugh Lamb, Michel Parry, Rosemary Timperley, Cynthia Asquith, Richard Dalby, David Sutton, Mike Ashley, Ramsey Campbell, Nicholas Royle and Stephen Jones.

I am honoured to be following in the footsteps of these great editors.

CONTENTS

CREDITS

All stories are copyright their respective author

'When Charlie Sleeps' by Laura Mauro was originally published in *Black Static* (Issue 37)

'Exploding Raphaelesque Heads' by Ian Hunter was originally published in *The Tenth Black Book of Horror*

The Bloody Tower by Anna Taborska was originally published in *Terror Tales of London*

'Behind the Doors' by Ramsey Campbell was originally published in *Holes for Faces*

'The Secondary Host' by John Llewellyn Probert was originally published in *Exotic Gothic Volume 5, Part 2*

'The Garscube Creative Writing Group' by Muriel Gray was originally published in *The Burning Circus*

'Biofeedback' by Gary Fry was originally published in *Shades of Nothingness*

'Doll Hands' by Adam Nevill was originally published in *The Burning Circus*

'Guinea Pig Girl' by Thana Niveau was originally published in *The Tenth Black Book of Horror*

'Touch Me With Your Cold, Hard Fingers' by Elizabeth Stott was originally published as a stand alone chapbook.

'Dad Dancing' by Kate Farrell was originally published in *The Tenth Black Book of Horror*

'The Arse-Licker' by Stephen Volk was originally published in *Anatomy of Death*

'Doll Re Mi' by Tanith Lee was originally published in *Nightmare Magazine*

'Laudate Dominum (For Many Voices)' by D.P. Watt was originally published in *Shadows and Tall Trees (Issue 5)*

'Someone To Watch Over You' by Marie O'Regan originally published in *Terror Tales of London*

'Namesake' by V.H. Leslie was originally published in *Black Static* (Issue 31)

'Come into my Parlour' by Reggie Oliver was originally published in *Dark World: Ghost Stories*

'The Red Door' by Mark Morris was originally published in *Terror Tales of London*

'Author of the Death' by Michael Marshall Smith was originally published in *Everything You Need*

'The Magician Kelso Dennett' by Stephen Volk was originally published in *Terror Tales of the Seaside*

'That Tiny Flutter Of The Heart I Used To Call Love' by Robert Shearman was originally published in *Psycho-mania!*

INTRODUCTION

horror
Pronunciation: /ˈhɒrə/
noun
[MASS NOUN] an intense feeling of fear, shock, or disgust.
Origin:
Middle English: via Old French from Latin *horror*, from *horrere*: 'tremble, shudder'.

Welcome to a new strand (or should that be strain?) of Salt's 'Best' series. It's always nice to be asked to do things, rather than ask to do them, so when the people who run Salt approached and broached the idea of me becoming the series editor of 'Best British Horror', it wasn't a request taken lightly. Of all the genres out there at the moment, I think that fans of the horror genre are the most passionate and are not scared to wear hearts on sleeves. And they deserve to be treated with respect, not to be taken for fools. So from one passionate fan to another, this book is for you. Yes, it's a completely subjective list and your idea or definition of horror may be wildly different to mine, but I think the following stories will slake your thirst, whether you like your horror bloody, psychological, tied to the everyday, quiet, or hidden under a layer or two of obscurity.

I'm also excited by the prospect of bringing to you names you may not have heard of before and setting you on the path to discovering other works by them. And that was part of my selection process; I was adamant in wanting a book in which there were authors I was unfamiliar with, and 'discovering' Laura Mauro, Ian Hunter, Elizabeth Stott, and D.P. Watt's work were amongst the true highlights of 2013.

We must not, of course, forget names who are familiar on the high street bookshelves or in popular culture and it is indeed an honour to use stories from Ramsey Campbell, Muriel Gray, Adam Nevill, Michael Marshall Smith, Mark Morris and Robert Shearman. The depth and range of stories, not just from these authors, but from everyone in the book have blown me away; 2013 was indeed an embarrassment of riches.

Sadly, 2013 also saw the untimely death of Joel Lane, a fellow editor and author whose body of work will be talked about in the same breath as Robert Aickman and M.R. James. Joel's legacy is honoured at the end of this gathering of stories.

I am incredibly proud of this selection, I think it's a strong and challenging one, and would love to hear what you think. We now live in the days where social media is king, so leave your reviews (good and bad) on Amazon and Goodreads, spread the word on Facebook and Twitter; it helps other fans discover the book and its authors, and the more people this volume reaches the better. There are not enough horror stories on the high street, but if we all shout loud enough, we might be able to change that for the good.

JOHNNY MAINS

BEST BRITISH HORROR 2014

LAURA MAURO

WHEN CHARLIE SLEEPS

Propped against the bathroom door, clutching an old guitar, Hanna sings Charlie another lullaby.

Go to sleep, Charlie.

He's awake in there, still. The black beetles that come from under the bathroom door are his messengers. They walk ponderous circuits, antennae trembling, moving jerkily like windup toys.

Sleep, Charlie, sleep.

The guitar is held together by duct-tape and willpower. It belongs to Mercy, who can coax delicate music from the four remaining strings. Hanna strums nonsense chords and sings old pop songs, though she is not much good at either of these things. Charlie doesn't seem to mind.

The flickering of the lights is slow now, the blinking of a single sleepy eye. It's a good sign. An agitated Charlie is quite a thing to behold; every light in the squat flashes wildly, though they were disconnected years ago. Stella says Charlie creates his own energy. As she sits in the hall, breathing white in the dark, Hanna wishes he'd channel a little of it into the central heating.

Even more than that, she wishes he'd *go to fucking sleep*.

So Hanna sings. And when the song finishes, after what feels like hours, Hanna holds her breath, and her heart sinks when she hears Charlie's insectile nonsense-chatter emanate from the keyhole. She knows, by now, what this means: *Another*.

She starts anew. The back of her skull beats a steady rhythm against the door and outside, as the sun struggles over the horizon, London stirs.

The previous night – the night Mercy brought her to the squat – Hanna woke with a violent start. She sat up, heart hammering, tongue thick in her dry mouth. She searched in the dark but Steve wasn't there, his space in the bed was cold as a bone, and Hanna wanted to scream for him but then she remembered. She wasn't at home anymore. There was no home, at least not one she could go back to. No doubt there'd be another woman in their bed tonight. Stupid girl, Hanna thought, fingers trailing up her forearms, tracing old bruises in the shape of Steve's fingers. Her swollen nose throbbed in the dark.

She needed the toilet. She got up, wrapping the sleeping bag around her like a shawl. She wore only an old T-shirt, one Mercy lent her, several sizes too large. The bathroom was next door. When Mercy first showed her around, she'd mentioned in passing that the upstairs bathroom was off-limits. Something about rotten floorboards, but Hanna was disorientated and rattled and by the time she remembered, the door was already open and the black expanse of the bathroom revealed. For a moment, Hanna thought she'd opened the wrong door; that this was no room but a void, and then something had risen above the rim of the bath, slowly, eyes glowing like embers in the dark.

It wasn't as if Hanna woke Charlie on purpose. She hadn't even known he was there. She tells Mercy this, over and over until Mercy is sick with it, threatening to lock her in with Charlie and throw away the key. That shuts Hanna up. Subdued, she stares at Mercy, wanting to ask how she could have let her sleep next door to a monster.

Stella comes down the stairs, finger pressed to her lips. She has accomplished what Hanna could not. It stands to reason; she has had prior experience with Charlie, has spent long, sleepless nights reading him stories and coaxing him to sleep. She and Mercy, working shifts.

Neither of them seems outwardly angry at her, although Hanna thinks they'd have a right to be; she is an accidental guest, after all. She's here only out of kindness. The squat is theirs. Actually, it's *his*: an Edwardian townhouse in the heart of Lambeth, imposing even in its neglect. The windows are scabbed over with sun-bleached newspaper. The front garden is a snarl of bindweed. The neighbours don't notice them. Nobody knocks at the door. Hanna suspects that this is not a coincidence.

'He's napping. He'll be awake again soon,' Mercy says. She's a stout Filipina, an ex-nurse; she had found Hanna dazed and bleeding in a Southwark underpass, clinging desperately to a tattered rucksack as if her entire life were within it and begging to be taken home to the man who'd relieved her of several teeth. Mercy had brought Hanna back to the squat instead, let her sleep next door to Charlie. Just for one night, supposedly.

'You'll have to change his water when he wakes up again,' Stella tells Hanna. She doesn't bother to hide how put-out she is by it all. She piles her thick hair beneath a bandana in lieu of washing it, rubs her tired eyes with the back of her hand. 'You woke him up. You do your bit.'

Nobody shows Hanna what to do, but it seems like common sense. She takes the bucket into the back garden and, hidden by snarls of overgrown foliage, quietly siphons water from the neighbour's hosepipe. Like changing a litter tray, or cleaning a fish tank, except Charlie's no pet. Hanna pushes the back door open with one foot, clutching the full bucket to her chest. Who'd want a pet like Charlie?

It's hot in the bathroom. A thick, tropical heat like the inside of a vivarium. Hanna closes the door behind her with a click. Across the room is a cast-iron bathtub, the enamel stained yellow like old bones. The tiles are furry with black mildew, the windows obscured by newspaper. She breathes deep, easing her nerves, and heaves the bucket onto the counter.

'Hello, Charlie,' she says.

The tinkle of displaced water indicates his acknowledgement. She sees him as she approaches, a dark smudge beneath the surface. His form is distorted but recognisable. Red eyes stare up at her, unblinking. She doesn't know if he's holding his breath under there; Charlie, neither man nor frog but something else, something *other*. It wouldn't surprise Hanna if he didn't breathe at all.

Hanna sits on the lip of the bath and Charlie rises with slow grace; his skin is the glossy grey of a wet paving slab. He smells like an underpass, the ammoniac stench of week-old piss and gutter mulch. Clubbed fingers splay towards her, grasping. She leaps to her feet, backing quickly away. He is ugly, and alien, and although she senses nothing but benign curiosity, she keeps her distance.

'I've come to change your water,' she says, trying to hide the quiver in her voice. Charlie regards her with what she interprets as disappointment. His features are primitive; dull, Neanderthal jaw, empty black slit-mouth, heavy brow. Clicks and whirrs emanate from the depths of his pulsating throat. The glut of mucus obstructing the plughole comes away with a thick sucking sound. Clots of stinking matter streak the bathtub as the water drains. He stares up at her, awaiting her approach.

Hanna fetches the bucket from the counter. Her sweat-damp hair sticks to the back of her neck.

'Ready?' she asks – why is she talking to him? If he understands, he doesn't care to answer. As the water spatters against his skin the clogged-sewer stink of him rolls up into the air. Hanna presses her sleeve to her mouth until the water settles, already stained a pale sepia. Charlie chitters in what might be joy. It's so unexpected, such an innocent sound that Hanna almost smiles. Almost forgets he's a monster.

The water is barely enough to cover his feet. She'll have to make several more trips. Charlie reclines in his puddle, heavy skull resting against the slope of the bath. The fleshy rope of his umbilical cord floats in the shallow water. Hanna follows its trajectory. One end joins seamlessly with the concavity of his abdomen, coiling up and around and sinking once again, pallid as a cave fish, into the open black mouth of the plug hole. Down into the sewers, the guts of the city off which Charlie feeds.

When she returns, Mercy and Stella sit Hanna down and explain, as well as they can, what Charlie is.

'Stella named it Charlie,' Mercy says. 'It's been here longer than we have. Possibly even longer than this house. We think it's taken several forms over its lifetime. It keeps us off the radar here, which gives us a safe place to stay. I suppose we're meant to be his caretakers, but we mostly try to keep him asleep. It's safer when he is.'

'What happens when he's awake?' Hanna asks.

Stella indicates the squat with a sweep of her arm. The water has calmed Charlie temporarily, but it's not enough; the lights still flicker like a faulty flashbulb. The taps in the downstairs bathroom gush brown water in sudden bursts. Hanna sits, cross-legged, sleeping bag wrapped around her shoulders. It is imperative, Mercy explains, that they return Charlie to a state of hibernation, because the longer he stays awake the greater his agitation will grow, and the more extreme the manifestations will become.

'There was a time, two years ago, when we couldn't get him back to sleep for over two weeks,' Stella says. 'By the time we wore him down, almost the entire borough was in a blackout, and a massive hole opened up just off the high street. Nothing but black all the way down. The Imperial War Museum was infested with giant rats. There was an outbreak of leptospirosis. They shut it down for months.'

'Maybe it was a coincidence?' Hanna suggests, although she's not convinced. Mercy shoots Stella a wry look and it occurs to Hanna that they must have had this conversation many times over. And the more Hanna thinks about it, the more ridiculous it seems; how can she even try to apply an idea as quaint as 'coincidence' to a sexless grey monster living in a bathtub in an abandoned London townhouse?

'It's a parasite,' Mercy says, like they're discussing someone's problematic cousin. 'A malignancy. It feeds off the city. You saw the plughole, right? That's how it communicates with London. It's a two-way thing: if Charlie's unhappy, the city suffers. The worse its temper, the worse things get. It's only when Charlie's asleep that London becomes autonomous again. When he's awake, it's chaos. And that's why Stella and I try to keep him asleep.' Implicit in her glance is the accusation – *you fucked this up. I never should've brought you here.* She's probably too polite to say it out loud.

Hanna looks away. 'How do you know all this?' she asks.

'She doesn't,' Stella says. 'We don't know a bloody thing. What Mercy's telling you, she learned from the people before us. The rest is educated guesswork.' She pauses, rifling through a pile of mouldering books to find Charlie a bedtime story. 'This goes back longer than you can imagine. We won't be the last of his keepers.'

It's nonsense, the stuff of feverish fantasy. And yet, as Hanna looks from Mercy to Stella, at the grim lines of their mouths, a cold sensation creeps into the pit of her stomach and coils there, tight; maybe it *is* nonsense, but it's happening all the same.

The next day, a swarm of beetles pour from the rotten space inside the walls and take up residence in the dark spaces. Hanna has spent her second night acting parent to their communal monster-child, and she is heavy-limbed with exhaustion. She comes into the living room, sinks into the futon. Already, this is too much. She hadn't wanted to be a part of this. She didn't choose to come here. When she tells Stella this the other woman just smiles, a mirthless flash of teeth.

'Nobody *wants* to be here,' Stella says. 'But someone has to take care of him. Mercy and I have no family, no life to go back to. We might as well do what we can.'

'You could kill him,' Hanna says.

Stella regards her silently for a while.

'Charlie didn't choose to be the way he is,' Stella says – Mercy calls Charlie 'it', but with Stella, it's always 'he' – I don't know much about him, but I know he was here before London was even a little twinkle in man's eye. By accident or design, the city was built around him, and now he's a part of it, and it's part of him. You say we could kill him.' She shakes her head. 'The truth is, we're afraid of what will happen if we do. Charlie's bond with this city is strong. In a sense, Charlie *is* London. If Mercy's right about him transmitting his moods – if there is some weird psychic bond – what kind of chaos would killing him create?'

'You've thought about it,' Hanna says.

'Mercy has.' A beetle crawls up her thigh, coming to rest in the crook of her knee. She doesn't seem bothered. It's probably not the first time. 'We've always managed to calm him down. But yes, she's talked about it more than once, when things get bad.'

'And you?'

Stella plucks the beetle from her leg and holds it between her thumb and forefinger. Black eyelash legs skitter frantically in mid-air. She lifts the struggling insect slowly up until it's level with her mouth.

'You have to understand,' she says. 'When Charlie sleeps, his dreams stay in his head. But he never stops dreaming. And when he's awake, the visions leak out. That's what you see here. All of it. This is what's in Charlie's head.'

Hanna's stomach twists into a knot as Stella's lips part, a slow, thoughtful motion, and Hanna desperately tries not to retch, but Stella purses her lips and blows, gently, as if extinguishing a birthday candle. The beetle disintegrates, scattering gently outwards in a shower of black dust.

'He didn't choose to be this way,' she says, brushing the dust from her hands. 'He doesn't mean any harm. I know you think he's a monster, and you're probably right. But this is the only life he knows.'

Hanna thinks of Steve. She thinks of the rage bright in his eyes, the scrape of his knuckles against her cheek. She hadn't been able to change him, or even warn the next girl. Not that she'd have listened. She can't change Charlie either, but maybe she can make things better. Maybe she can stop him doing any harm.

Besides. It's her fault he's awake to begin with.

She talks to Charlie a little more after that. Not much. Day to day things, the kind she'd usually talk to Steve about. Things she can't tell the others, because they don't seem to want to know anything about her. So she talks to Charlie, and although he doesn't seem to understand, she swears he's listening.

It seems fitting to Hanna that when Mercy finally cracks, it's during Stella's shift.

The back door slams; every other door in the squat rattles on its hinges. Hanna is pulled violently from sleep, legs tangled in her sleeping bag. There is a thunder of boots as someone storms upstairs. It's Steve, she thinks, huddling beneath the blanket. It's Steve and he's angry about something and he's coming up the stairs, towards her. It's only when Stella starts screaming that she remembers where she is.

She rolls over. Someone is in the bathroom, stomping hard on the rotting floorboards. Hanna scrambles to her feet, shedding the sleeping bag as she goes. Stella stands at the bathroom door, blocking the way with arms outstretched. Her book lies forgotten at her feet, her torch a black shape on the periphery. Mercy stands before her, wielding a mud-caked pickaxe in both hands like a spear.

'Riots,' she says. 'There've been riots up in London. It's all over the papers. Buildings burnt to the ground. People cracking each other's heads open. It's fucking insane out there. Nobody knows what's sparked it.' Her fingers tighten around the pickaxe. 'But we know, don't we Stella?'

'You can't be sure,' Stella says, but she's shaking, and before she can react Mercy bulldozes through her, shoving her aside. Stella stumbles out onto the landing. She stares at Hanna for a moment, looking small and powerless. Hanna dashes into the bathroom. Mercy stands over Charlie, the pickaxe raised. It would be comical were it not for Charlie's high, keening cries, and Hanna feels a sharp pain somewhere in the vicinity of her heart at the sound. She hadn't been convinced he was capable of emotion, but his fear is unmistakable.

'People are *hurting* one another,' Mercy says, indicating Charlie with a jut of her chin. 'Don't tell me it's coincidence.

Don't you dare insult my intelligence like that. This has gone as far as I'm going to let it.'

'Mercy,' Hanna says, and the woman turns for a moment; there is doubt in her eyes, and Hanna realises she has a choice. For the first time in a long time, she has a choice. 'Calm down. Let's talk about it. That's how you get things done here, isn't it?' She raises both hands, a placating gesture. 'You've got him to sleep so many times before. You can do it again. We'll work together.' She swallows hard. 'This is my fault, Mercy. Not his. I should never have gone into the bathroom. I'm so sorry.'

Mercy looks uncertain, but she steels herself all the same, raises the pickaxe high in both hands like a wooden stake.

'Mercy, *please*,' Hanna says.

The axe-head is clotted with old earth, but it glints in the guttering light, and Hanna barely has time to wonder what Charlie sees when Mercy brings it down hard. The blunt metal pierces Charlie's skull like a knife through paper. Black spills out into the bath water. Charlie chokes, gurgles. The axe descends again, faster this time, cracking brittle bones, and the stink rising from the bathtub is rich and thick and rotten. Mercy raises her weapon again, but looks up at the bathroom light, dead at last. Her T-shirt is spattered with black. Charlie floats in the dark water.

Hanna looks over her shoulder, away from Charlie's ruined body. His fearful wailing still echoes in her ears. Charlie is dead, and she's too stunned to feel anything. Stella sits against the bathroom door, knees drawn to her chest, staring numbly at her.

'There,' Mercy says, wiping sweat from her cheeks. 'He's gone. You fucking cowards.' The shovel clatters to the floor. For a long moment, the only sounds are Mercy's ragged breathing and the slow drip of spilled water over the edge of the bath. 'It's over,' she says, after a time. She wipes her hands on her T-shirt.

'For both our sakes,' Stella replies, 'I hope you're right.'

Stella and Hanna wrap Charlie's body in black bags and haul it into the boot of Stella's old Ford Mondeo. The neighbours peer at them through a gap in the curtain as they leave the squat, narrow-eyed and suspicious. Charlie is gone; the dreamlike ignorance with which the neighbours had previously regarded them is gone too. They are exposed.

Hanna goes with Stella because it feels like the right thing to do. To see that Charlie's death does not go unremarked. Helpless Charlie, the heart of a city, though he never had a say in the matter. Who asked for nothing but a safe space. Hanna understands that longing perhaps better than any of them. Mercy had called him a malignancy. As they wrestled his sad little body from the bathtub and onto the floor, severing the umbilical cord, Mercy told them she'd saved the city, cut it free from Charlie's greedy, suckling influence. Neither of them had argued. Mercy wouldn't have understood.

Mercy's door was shut when they left the squat. 'She got what she wanted,' Stella says bitterly, staring out of the window at the passing houses, the skyline still shrouded in early morning mist. Everything is calm. Debris from last night's rioting lies in the gutter, undisturbed. Nothing is burning. Nothing is crumbling. 'Give it time,' Stella tells her, adamant, although there is doubt in her eyes, and the frown lines around her mouth speak volumes. Whatever Stella had been afraid of should have happened by now. The idea that Mercy might have been right all along must stick in her throat.

They drive to the dump ('Recycling Centre', the sign insists) and hide his body among a sea of broken furniture and wet, yellowing weeds. Hanna looks to Stella, and she shakes her head. There's nothing to be said. Charlie is dead, and the city carries on without him, at least for now. Hanna wonders what they'll make of his body, if anyone ever finds it; if they'll think him a strange, awful sculpture abandoned by its creator. She knows nobody ever will.

They get back into the car. The lush, rotten smell of Charlie still lingers. There is a heaviness in Hanna's chest. Without Charlie's protection, the squat is no longer a safe haven. She will have to move on. Perhaps back to Birmingham, where her mother will undoubtedly greet this new failure with glee. If Stella is right – and Hanna is increasingly uncertain of this – then it's probably best to leave London altogether, before the last of Charlie's influence dissipates and the cracks start to show. *If* they start to show.

They pull up to the squat. The neighbours' curtains are wide open, their windows empty. Perhaps they've given up watching for now. Stella pushes the door open. A scattering of tiny black beetles emerge, pouring out into the sunlight where they disintegrate. Hanna looks sharply at Stella, who shakes her head. 'Remnants of a dream,' she says. 'I don't know. This is new to me, too.'

'Maybe.' They haven't spoken much since Charlie was killed. Neither of them quite know what to make of it. There's a sense that an injustice has been done – Stella still won't accept Charlie's part in the rioting, although the streets are ominously quiet this morning. Still, though, Hanna can't help but blame herself. If only she'd never woken him. If only she'd calmed him in time . . .

Inside, everything is as they left it. The squat has not yet fallen apart without Charlie's protection. The smell of damp plaster and lemongrass incense still presides. They mill at the bottom of the stairs, uneasy, none of them willing to be the first to ascend into the black hallway above. What lurks there now Charlie is gone? Finally, Hanna takes the lead, hoping her nerves don't show. Stella brings up the rear. Hanna suspects she might have gone first if she hadn't been trying to make a point. Better the devil you know, even when that devil is a grey-skinned, bathtub-dwelling parasite.

Stella strides past Mercy's open door and is about to ascend the stairs to her attic room when there is a sudden pulse of light from the overhead bulb. A momentary flicker, gone almost as soon as it appears. Hanna looks from Stella to Mercy and waits for one of them to comment, but neither does. For a moment, she wonders if she saw anything at all.

She waits for Stella to disappear into the attic and veers sharply towards the bathroom. It takes everything in her power to stop her from running, and yet as she approaches the bathtub in the centre of the room, she's filled with equal parts joy and trepidation; what if there's nothing? Remnants of a dream, Stella said, traces of Charlie lingering like old blood at a crime scene. As she leans over the rim of the bath, she hears her own sharp intake of breath, her wide eyes reflected in the shallow pool at the bottom of the bath.

The bathroom light buzzes.

There he is. Charlie in miniature, a grey bud bursting from the remains of the discarded umbilical cord. Of course. They should have destroyed it, but in their haste, they simply severed it and left the remainder to rot. He is tiny, this new Charlie, the size of a child's fist, a glistening grey maquette wallowing in a stagnant puddle still stained with his predecessor's black blood. His eyes are tiny rubies. She slips her hand into the water, cups the newborn Charlie in her palm. He stares up at her, unblinking, chittering faintly like a faraway insect. Talking to her in whatever primitive language he speaks. Like he's telling her it'll be different this time. And maybe it will.

'I'm sorry about what happened,' she says. 'But we're going to do it properly this time. No more bad dreams. No more riots. I'll keep you safe.' His skin is leathery, and not unpleasant. 'Go back to sleep, Charlie.'

His eyes slip shut. And as he rests there in the warm concavity of her hand, Hanna swears she sees the black slit of his mouth contort into a smile.

IAN HUNTER

EXPLODING RAPHAELESQUE HEADS

IT WAS IN Scotland of all places that I saw the painting; those few months when I was rattling around Europe, cramming in as much culture as I could as if it was about to be rationed to us Americans, or the world was coming to an end and this would all be rubble, while we were dust. It was in the Scottish National Gallery in Edinburgh, a big grey, temple-like building with imposing pillars, which sat at the bottom of a small hill they called the Mound, below the old houses that stretched up and down the Royal Mile from the castle to the palace down at the other end.

I came round the corner, eyes drifting between the brochure in my hand and the paintings on the wall, when suddenly there it was, a section devoted to Salvador Dali. Although they didn't have much in the way of exhibits and things started with various black and white photographs of the man himself taken at different times during his life, but all seemed to show him with wide eyes and eyebrows raised, either in a questioning or condescending pose. In many his moustache was tapered to two deadly points. One photograph showed those points skewering two flowers, in another they were curled upwards, climbing over his cheeks, ready to impale his eyes. In some photographs, he was standing beside famous people. I recognised Harpo Marx, Alfred Hitchcock, Sonny Bono, John Lennon, even Raquel Welch, and Alice Cooper. It was obviously a bit of a thing to have your picture taken with Dali, but I have to confess that I didn't recognise Coco Chanel, although the little card below the photograph told me her name anyway. Sadly, the rhino Dali was almost kissing in one photo seemed to go unnamed, like the headless manikin he carried in another shot, as if the jointed dummy was his dead, robot bride from a bad 50's B-movie. My kind of stuff.

Walking on, the blizzard of photographs ended and the small exhibition started with his painting *Oiseau*, or *Bird* to you and me. What was it about? It looked like the skeletal remains of a dead bird, almost prehistoric, decaying on a beach, with part of the body missing to reveal the corpse of a young bird inside. Then there were a couple of sketches of things that looked like skeletons adorned with various pieces of meat.

Entrails and sausages, steaks and cuts. Next came a storyboard for a proposed film on surrealism and a proper painting called *Le Signal de l'angoisee – The Signal of Anguish* – depicting a woman who was naked, except for a pair of stockings, standing in a strange landscape being watched by someone you couldn't really see through the square window of the building behind her. It was disconcerting, it was creepy, it made you stop and look back at the painting to see if the watcher had stepped forward, revealing themselves, but, no, they always stayed in the shadows. And that was good, that was something out of left field, which couldn't be topped, or so I thought, but I was wrong. They had kept the best for last. Kept it for me, because it changed my life forever.

~

Tête Raphaëlesque éclatée.
Exploding Raphaelesque Head.

If you don't know it, Dali's painting was inspired by the bombing of Hiroshima and uses a classic Madonna-like pose typical of the Renaissance artist, Raphael, but has the head fragmenting. Some of these fragments looked like pieces of twisted silver. Flesh turned to metal, possibly transformed by the alchemy of nuclear forces, while the splitting parts around her neck are darker, almost stone-like, but in strange, sharp, conical, wriggling shapes that resemble shapes seen in some of Dali's other work. This may be a painting depicting the instant after the explosion, still head-like before it shatters in a thousand different directions, as the woman looks down, demurely, almost in prayer.

I couldn't take my eyes off it. I stood staring, oblivious to the other people who flowed behind me, tried to get in front of me for a better look, but I denied them with my closeness to the canvas. Eventually, after several minutes had passed and my eyes had finished taking in every square centimetre of the canvas, I snapped out of my reverie and spoke to a member of the gallery staff. I made some vague, rambling enquiries about buying the painting, which were instantly laughed off, until I insisted that I had the money to buy it if they named their price. That received a more hesitant, less certain laugh, which attracted the attention of some security staff who stood in the corners, hands behind their backs, watching my every move until I went to the shop in the Gallery. There I bought all the books I could find with Dali's work in them. They even had a few tacky products inspired by the very painting that dominated my thoughts. A jigsaw, a tea towel, various notebooks, a shopping bag. I've added a few tacky products of my own over the years, all with a production run of one. Some I've commissioned from other artists, some I've made myself. If you ever come to my house, which is admittedly highly unlikely, you will see two walls covered in a reproduction of that exploding head. It also adorns my bedroom ceiling. I try to make it the last thing I see at night and the first thing I see in the morning keeping my eyes firmly closed until I am in position to gaze up at it.

But all of these things, they are never enough.

After I had made my mind up, after I had foolishly thought I was ready, my first subject was male, in his thirties, found sleeping rough beneath the pier – what was I thinking about? I almost died. He spat at me as soon as I took the tape off his mouth, struggling violently in the chair I had tied him to, trying to rock from side to side before he fell over. I've seen enough movies to know if that happened he would break the chair and be on me. I thought I could get the grenade into his mouth when he was shouting. It wouldn't fit, and I had already pulled the pin. We both had about five seconds. I dropped the grenade under his chair and dived behind one of the blast walls I had constructed in my special studio. There wasn't much left of him, and what was left, wasn't pretty, and was, well, everywhere. Wrong, wrong, wrong and I thought my ear drums had burst with the noise.

My second subject was a homeless man and this time things went slightly better. I drugged him and took out all his teeth with the help of a hammer and some pliers, and managed to squeeze the grenade into his ruined mouth in plenty of time, especially with the pin protruding outwards. Still, what a mess. Grenades were clearly not the answer, but at least the money I splashed on state of the art earplugs, connected to a digital processor, was money well spent.

My third subject was a male hitchhiker. I killed him first – how? Well, that doesn't matter, but it was better he was dead as I had started to experiment with different kinds of explosives and wanted to make things as simple as possible.

This time I used ammonia gelatine, placed in the mouth. Again, messy, but not without potential.

The fourth subject was an old beggar, and an old boozer too. I used Semtex this time, obtained from shadowy contacts of a guerrilla artist I know. This time I tried a different, more ambitious place to put the explosive, namely inside the skull. I should have been a surgeon, instead of the third waster son of a logging tycoon. I'm good at this. I shaved some of the old man's hair off, before peeling back the scalp, and sawing through the bone, and then again and again at different angles until I was able to pull out a rough circle of skull before removing part of the brain. Too much Semtex was an obvious, beginner's mistake and I also noted that I needed to remove more of the brain in future.

By now, I'd learned all I could from the men. I didn't need them anyway; they were just practice. Dali's painting is the fragmenting head of a woman. Killing these male subjects first had made things easier from a planning and preparation point of view, but from now on, it was going to be women only, and they would all be dead if possible. At peace, serene. Madonna-like.

The fifth subject was my first female, and my brilliant idea was to try and take the top of her skull out from inside her head, and make it easier to explode and come apart. It took hours to achieve anything like the desired effect, leaving me exhausted with another mess on my bloody, gloved hands. What was there before the explosion didn't even resemble a head very much, so you can imagine what was left afterwards.

From now on, the skull would have to stay.

My sixth subject was a drug addict, and I went back to basics with the hole in the top of her head and a slightly lower amount of plastic explosive. Not enough for the desired effect, but getting there.

A woman possibly in her early thirties was my seventh subject. It was hard to tell her age. She'd clearly had it tough by the state of her, so in a way I was doing her a favour. I picked her up by the old bus station. Sadly, I over compensated with the explosive charge, and her head sort of imploded, collapsed in on itself, totally the wrong result, possibly due to where I placed it within her skull, I would need to do much better next time.

Now it was time to go up a gear, time to find a different sort of woman. Three at most, I hoped. Two to practise on and the third would be the charm. Sad, but true, and I'm not being insincere, not really, but none of my female test subjects so far could be classified as 'lookers', not after the drugs and the booze and the abuse have worn them down. Two out of three have had broken noses and all have cheeks riddled with broken blood vessels.

Victim number eight was a high-school beauty and a real test of my mettle. Her youth and good looks gave her some of the qualities of the subject in the Dali Painting, which was strangely off-putting. What a set of lungs she had as well, constantly screaming the place down. Even though my place is out in the country and my studio well hidden within the depths of the estate, I still kept her drugged at the end. Glued her eyes shut, and puffed up her lips slightly with collagen filler. She was almost perfect, almost.

Ninth victim was me being really stupid and acting on impulse after finding a woman at the side of the road, trying to get her car to start. Anyone could have come along and seen me. Seen us. Anyone. What an idiot I can be at times, although I did take care to push her car down one of the old forest tracks and saw it tumbling between the trees towards the old lake where it should be rusting at the bottom. I was also pleased to note the similarities to the Dali painting when I slowed down the film I have been taking of all my explosions, slowed it down to almost frame by frame, the incandescent Hiroshima moment.

For my tenth victim I scoured a lot of online model agencies until I found the ideal woman to hire, being very careful to cover my tracks for when she was inevitably reported as missing. That face. That nose. Those lips, they hardly needed filler at all. As for the curve of her eyebrows? Well it was divine. The hair wasn't, of course, but still, you can't have everything. Crucially, her hair was longer than I needed it to be, but I still had to be very careful when I cut it, very careful when I styled it. I wasn't even really sure if she needed to be alive when I did all that. Not being sure, I thought it better to drug her then wash and cut her hair. Shame I had to cut into her scalp to plant my little charges.

Now it is perfect. She is perfect. Head and neck severed from her body and carefully mounted. Drained of blood. Lips perfectly full. Eyes closed, head angled downwards, Hole cut out of the top of the head with an angled light source shining down from above. I know the angle isn't going to mirror Dali's exactly, but I don't want anyone to see the Semtex placed inside her. Now there are six cameras pointing at the head. One from each side. One from above. One slightly below, looking up as she looks down.

Dali would be proud of me.

ANNA TABORSKA

THE BLOODY TOWER

SHAKIL HAD MORE in common with Jim Morrison than Osama bin Laden, so it came as something of a surprise to his family when the front door splintered with an ear-rending crash at four o'clock one Sunday morning, and a naked Shakil was dragged out of bed, handcuffed and pulled out into the darkness.

It was a year since the Prime Minister had given his speech in Parliament to accompany his new anti-terrorism legislation, and a year since the ravens had flown the Tower.

The birds had been restless all morning. The Raven Master tried in vain to persuade Thor the talking raven to say 'good morning'. At around midday, about the time that the Prime Minister sat down amidst a deathly silence a little over two miles away, Thor croaked something that might have been construed as sounding rather like 'Nevermore!' and took off – half flying, half hopping, taking the other ravens with him.

'Thor! Thor, come back!' The Raven Master ran as far as he could after the departing birds. Another Yeoman Warder joined him, disturbed by the desperation in the older man's voice.

'Don't worry mate, you know they won't get far with their feathers clipped'. But the Raven Master wasn't convinced.

A year later and the ravens weren't back, the Crown Jewels had been removed, the tourist attractions ousted, the Yeoman Warders sacked, and the Prime Minister had his own little Guantanamo right here on British soil – in the heart of the capital.

The Tower – in reality a collection of twenty-four towers and various other structures – was nothing if not perfect for the job at hand. It was as if the ancient buildings had been waiting for seventy-five years for blood to flow down their walls once more. The Tower's last victim had been shot on 15th August 1941: a hapless German spy who broke his right ankle while parachuting into Ramsey Hollow, Huntingdonshire, and was duly court-martialled and executed before he had managed to do any spying. Josef Jacobs's executioners had been considerate enough to allow him to sit before the eight-man firing squad – made up of members of the Holding Battalion, Scots Guards – as his injured leg made standing difficult. The coroner noted during the autopsy that Josef had been shot once in the head and seven times around the white lint target that had been pinned over his heart. The poor man was buried in an unmarked grave at St. Mary's Roman Catholic Cemetery in Kensal Green, Northwest London, and, to add insult to injury, earth was later thrown over his grave, allowing for the cadavers of total strangers to be buried on top of him.

Shakil had enjoyed history at school, and under different circumstances would perhaps have been interested to know that he was being driven into the Tower of London complex, but by the time the tear-stained blindfold was removed from the eighteen-year-old's eyes, he was already in a damp, dark cell, and his only thought was one of fear for his life.

He spent his first half hour shouting for help and looking for a way out, then footsteps resounded and three guards appeared.

'Shut up, you piece of shit! And stand up for The Warden.'

The Warden was dressed in an Armani suit and very shiny shoes. His accent was an uneasy fusion of public school and East End wide boy, explainable by the fact that his daddy had paid for him to go to public school, but the boy had not been bright enough to get into university, and had instead used his financial leverage to hang out with bankers, gangsters and aspiring politicians. His money and dubious connections had finally landed him his current position, and he intended to abuse every inch of his power.

'Congratulations,' the Warden intoned sarcastically to the frightened teenager on the other side of the bars. 'It is my duty as Warden to welcome you here. You are officially the first detainee of the Tower of London Detention and Concentration Facility.'

'I didn't do nothing!'

'Shut up when the Warden's speaking!'

The Warden continued by assuring Shakil that during his stay he would not only give up his terror cell, but would also help them to fine-tune the system they were creating.

'But I didn't do nothing!'

'I am referring, of course, to the Government's new anti-terror system.'

'But I didn't do nothing.'

The Warden laughed. 'Get him scrubbed up,' he told the guards.

Even as Shakil was told where he was, his family had no idea whatsoever. It was seven in the morning and they had already been waiting two hours at the local police station to speak to someone who might know something. The duty officer told them to come back at nine, when the chief superintendent would be in, but they refused to leave. It took all of Mr Malik's diplomatic skills to stop his wife and daughter ending up in the holding cells, as panic for Shakil made it impossible for the women to sit still and wait in silence.

When the chief superintendent finally turned up at half past nine, he tried to go straight into a meeting, and this time it was Mr Malik whose nerves gave way.

'What have you done with my son?' he shouted repeatedly at the top of his voice. The police station was filling up with other distressed members of the public by now, and the chief superintendent decided that in the interests of public relations it would be best to assist the Malik family rather than incarcerate them. He made a couple of phone calls, and finally informed the Maliks that their son was being held on terrorist charges at an undisclosed location.

'Terrorist charges! Shakil? Do you even know what you're talking about?' Shakil's sixteen-year-old sister Adara yelled at the chief superintendent, while Mrs Malik suddenly felt faint and her husband had to hold her up.

'Calm down, Miss Malik.' The chief was starting to seriously consider locking up the lot of them – public relations or not. If the son was a terrorist, then there was a good chance that the rest of the family were as well.

'Shakil – a terrorist? Look, my brother's greatest ambition is to strip at hen parties. How on earth could he be a terrorist?' Adara was hysterical, and Mr Malik tried to calm her down, while holding onto her sobbing mother.

'Mr Malik,' the chief superintendent put on his most professional smile. 'Why don't you all go home and once we know something more about your son, we'll contact you.'

Eventually Mr Malik decided to take the remains of his family home, to regroup and think where to appeal for help. On the way home, Adara replayed the events of the previous night in her mind, and tried to think of anything that could have contributed to her brother's abduction by the Met's Anti-Terror Squad.

Shakil and Adara had been invited to a party. There had been a long discussion with their dad, who hadn't wanted Adara to go. Shakil argued that if his father trusted him with the keys to his car and to his explosives warehouse, then surely he could trust him to bring his sister home safely.

'Your sister's not a car.' But Mr Malik lost the argument, as his wife joined in on the side of the children, and the siblings went to their friend's party.

After about half an hour of chatting to each other and the hostess, a blonde girl had come up to Shakil and asked him where he was from.

'East End,' Shakil gave the girl his sexy smile.

'No, I mean, where's your family from? You're not English.'

'I'm Pakistani.'

'Oh . . . Are you a terrorist?'

'Maddy!' Their hostess's embarrassment was painful to see.

'My dad says that all Pakis are terrorists,' explained Maddy. Adara and the hostess exchanged glances, wondering which one of them was going to deck her first, but Shakil merely thought hard for a moment, then said, 'I don't know about anyone else, but I *am* a terrorist – a terrorist of the heart.'

The girl processed the information for a while, then laughed. Adara rolled her eyes, while Shakil explained to Maddy that his name meant 'sexy' in Arabic. Adara caught Shakil's eye and put her finger in her mouth, making like she was about to vomit. Shakil got that mischievous glint in his eye, and added, 'Lots of Pakistani names have Arabic origins, and most of them mean something. For example, "Adara" means "virgin".' Everyone looked at Adara and laughed.

'Does not!' Adara stuck her middle finger up at Shakil,

eliciting more hilarity. The blonde whispered something in Shakil's ear, 'Let's see what you got then, Mr Terrorist,' and went to kiss him, her hand straying downwards towards the boy's crotch. But just then Shakil's favourite Doors song came on the stereo. 'I love that song!' and he was off – leaving Maddy to wonder whether her low-cut top was showing enough cleavage.

As Adara recalled her brother dancing to 'Light My Fire' in front of a room of admiring girls and jealous boys, his shoulder-length black hair glistening under the dim lighting, Shakil was hosed down with freezing water and his fine locks were shaved off by a brute of a guard who doubled as the prison's 'hairdresser'. Shakil had been very proud of his hair, and the sight of it falling on the stone floor, and the bald, bleeding reflection staring out at him from a mirror that was shoved in front of his face with the words 'Who's a pretty boy, then?', broke him. What with the fluorescent yellow jumpsuit he'd been forced to don after his 'shower', in place of his customary jeans, Nirvana T-shirt and leather jacket, the old Shakil was no more.

Then Adara remembered that a couple of the boys at the party had started a conversation about making bombs. One of the boys said that it would be easy to make a home-made bomb, while the other disagreed. Shakil had piped up, saying that you could make a detonator really easily out of just about anything – even a mobile phone. Shakil knew a lot about explosives, as his father was an engineer, specialising in demolitions, who was often asked by the council to demolish traditional areas of the East End so that developers could turn them into car parks or high-rise hell holes for the underprivileged.

'You see, son,' Adara had heard her father say to Shakil more than once, 'You could be blowing things up too, just like your old man, if you just went to college and studied engineering, instead of playing guitar and thinking about girls all day.'

Maybe someone had reported Shakil's stupid teenage conversation to the authorities. How sick would that be? What kind of a world were they living in if you couldn't even chat at a party without being kidnapped by the police several hours later?

'Mum, we gotta go back . . . Dad . . .'

'What is it, sweetheart?'

'There was some stupid conversation at the party last night about making bombs.'

'Oh God.' Mrs Malik was starting to feel light-headed again.

'We have to go back and explain that no way would Shakil make a bomb; he just knows about explosives because of Dad's job.'

'Okay, sweetheart, we'll go back and tell them,' said her father.

'But what if they take your father away as well?' Mrs Malik had aged ten years in the last few hours. 'What if they don't give us Shakil back, but take away your father too?'

'We have to try,' Mr Malik was adamant.

So Adara and her parents went back to the police station – that day, as they would every day in the weeks that followed.

The interrogation had not lasted long, as after several pelts around the back, chest, face and head, Shakil was already unconscious.

'We'll have to do something about your technique,' the Warden told the interrogating officer. 'This isn't going to work. I'm seriously thinking we need to look at the equipment we have at our disposal, starting with that weird looking thing in the basement.'

The weird looking thing in the basement was a Scavenger's Daughter – the one claim to fame of one Leonard Skeffington,

Lieutenant of the Tower of London during the reign of King Henry VIII. Mr Skeffington must have been either a very bored or a very unpleasant man – perhaps both – for it would have taken him no small amount of time to come up with a device that matched the infamous rack, both in terms of the pain and the damage it caused its victims. And having a day job at the Tower of London, Mr Skeffington would have had ample opportunity to observe both instruments in practice. While the rack stretched people until their limbs were dislocated and then torn from their sockets, the Scavenger's Daughter compressed them – in a foetal position – until they bled from their orifices and their bones broke.

Had the Warden displayed any interest in the Tower's rich history, or had he taken the time to speak to the former Chief Yeoman Warder of the Tower or any of his staff before having them thrown out of the complex, he would have known all about the Scavenger's Daughter, but – perhaps luckily for Shakil – he hadn't and he didn't.

Now a breeze with no discernible source stirred in the torture chamber. The ropes on the rack creaked and shadows flitted uneasily around Mr Skeffington's invention. Eddies of dust formed and whirled out into the corridor, swirling around the feet of a guard who'd been trailing slightly behind the Warden's guided tour of the Tower complex. Bob shivered as the temperature suddenly dropped, and hurried to join the others.

It had been a long tour, but the Warden was still going strong and was just now explaining to the Home Secretary and the heads of MI5 and MI6 his plans for the redevelopment of the Tower.

'As you know, the Prime Minister has informed me that the war on terror will require the detention and interrogation of many more suspects than previously thought.' The Warden was positively beaming at the attention he was getting from some of the country's most important men. 'So I am having plans drawn up for a large number of holding cells with bunks. We are now about to enter phase one of the project, but once all the work is complete, the Tower will hold more inmates per square metre than any other prison in Europe.'

'And how much time do you think you'll need to finish the project, Warden?' asked the Home Secretary.

Several hours later, and the cold wind that had started in the torture chamber now stirred the ropes on the row of gallows outside the White Tower, causing them to creak and swing. Had an observer chanced upon the scene, he or she might have had the impression that something heavy, yet unseen, was dangling from them.

Bob was on guard duty, patrolling the southern part of the Tower complex. He was in the basement of the Wakefield Tower, consciously avoiding the torture chamber and trying not to spend too long gazing into any of the dark corners, when he heard a child crying – a boy.

Bob froze, listening intently. 'Hello?' The sobbing came again and Bob moved cautiously towards the sound. 'Hello?' A second boy called out something – Bob couldn't make out what. 'Who's there?' Bob walked towards the voices, but as he did so they seemed to move away. 'Wait!' A flurry of footsteps and Bob followed, determined to find the boys. He couldn't understand for the life of him what they were doing in the Tower, and in the middle of the night as well.

Bob followed the crying up the stairs to the ground floor and out of the building. As he stepped outside, he saw two small figures ahead of him. He hurried after them, calling to them. They disappeared into the Bloody Tower, and Bob went in after them. He didn't see them again, but followed their voices up to a room on the first floor, where all trace of them disappeared. Confused and disconcerted, Bob was searching the room when he heard a blood-curdling scream in one of the adjoining chambers. He rushed next door and stopped short as he saw something coming rapidly towards him from the far end of the room. It was like a mist emerging from the darkness – a mist that transformed into solid matter, as a screaming woman, dressed in what to Bob looked like a ball gown, came running in his direction.

Bob shouted at the woman to stop, but she kept running at him and kept screaming. The guard drew his weapon. 'Stop or I'll shoot!' The woman kept coming and Bob panicked, shooting at her a couple of times. As she reached him, the woman finally dropped – facedown – right in front of the shaking guard. Bob closed his eyes for a moment and sucked in air through his mouth; in his fear he had forgotten to breathe. He bent down and checked the woman's pulse – nothing. That was when he noticed the gashes on her back; fragments of whitish backbone protruding from all the blood. He'd only had time to discharge two rounds at the woman, so why was her back slashed a dozen times? Bob looked at his gun, puzzled. Perhaps the new ammo they'd been issued splintered inside a person? He felt bad about killing the woman. He put his weapon away and went to report the incident.

Back in the White Tower, Bob was hurrying to see the Warden, when he bumped into the Head Guard.

'What's wrong, mate?' Pete looked concerned. 'You look like you've seen a ghost.'

'I just killed a woman.'

'What?'

'I just shot a woman. She was coming at me. I told her to stop, but she wouldn't listen. I think she was crazy.'

'Bob, what the hell are you on about?'

'I killed someone. I have to go report it.'

'Whoa, whoa. Hang on a sec there, mate. Look, don't take this the wrong way, but . . . have you been drinking?'

'No. No, I haven't.' Bob tried to get past the older man, but Pete was having none of it.

'Look, if you killed someone, then there's a body, right?'

'Right . . . Now let me past. I need to see the Warden.'

'Let's go and check that there's definitely a body. You don't want to bother the Warden and get yourself sacked if this is all just in your head.'

Pete wouldn't let it go and eventually Bob found himself on his way back to the Bloody Tower.

'This is a strange place,' Pete was saying. 'Sometimes people see things. My brother knew someone who was a Yeoman Warder here when it was still a tourist attraction. And he said that one of the other Warders left after something tried to strangle him in the Salt Tower – something nobody could see.'

'Well, I definitely saw someone,' Bob was getting upset again, 'and I shot her.' But when they got back to the Bloody Tower, there was no dead woman anywhere to be found.

A couple of hours later, around two in the morning, Crewes and Hampel were on guard duty in the White Tower. Crewes decided to check out the armoury. It was like Christmas come early. The gun in his holster forgotten, Crewes was soon happily swinging a poleaxe around the chamber.

'What the fuck are you doing, man?' But five minutes later Hampel too had a large grin on his face and a poleaxe in his hands, and the two of them were giggling like schoolboys and re-enacting some light-sabre battle or other from an early episode of *Star Wars*.

Neither of them noticed the shadow that fell across the threshold, nor the huge masked figure that entered the room, nor the massive axe it was holding. Crewes didn't even have time to discharge his gun or swing his poleaxe, but neither did he see what was coming. Hampel was less fortune for, although he got to fight briefly for his life, he also got to stare death right in the eyes and see the scant light glint for one blinding moment on the axe's head before it came down and sideways.

As the masked figure strode back to the hell from which it had come, axe in one hand and the fruits of the night's labours in the other, Shakil was lying shackled on the floor of his cell. He was running a fever, slipping in and out of consciousness. In one of his lucid moments, he became aware of a delicate scent, quite out of sorts with the damp, musty chamber that was his new home. He shouldn't have smelled anything, as he could hardly breathe through his pulverised, blood-encrusted nostrils, and yet he did. The scent was sweet and floral – like a woman's perfume, but weak and distant.

Shakil's swollen, cracked lips moved incoherently as he found himself trying to hum a tune: 'Sweet Jane. Sweet, sweet Jane'. Shakil knew the song so well, but in his present delirious state he couldn't remember who it was by. His failure to remember distressed him and he wanted to cry, but then that scent wafted by again, closer this time. The Velvet Underground, Shakil remembered and smiled.

Just then the air in his cell stirred slightly and eddies of dust started to rise and twist. Shakil tried to change position, but only succeeded in causing a fresh stab of pain in his head and chest. He lost consciousness for a moment, then regained it as a soft, cool hand tenderly stroked his face.

'Mum?' he whispered before drifting off into a gentle sleep. But the woman who knelt beside him was not his mother.

The boy could not have been much older than her. His skin, dark compared to the pale young men of the court that she had been used to, made a stark and fascinating contrast with the whiteness of her own hand. There were even darker patches on his skin, where they had hit him, and bloody marks on his face and body.

The girl with the heavy embroidered dress and the long, reddish-golden hair continued to stroke Shakil's face, gazing at him with sadness and compassion. A tear fell from her eye onto the boy's cheek, and he stirred for a moment, then fell asleep once more.

As the grey light of dawn filtered in through the tiny barred window at the top of the cell, a gaping wound opened up in the girl's neck and started to bleed profusely. She grimaced in pain and put her hand up to her neck. Her already pale complexion turned white as a sheet and she faded away to nothing. A tear rolled down Shakil's cheek, but he slept on.

The following morning Shakil woke up to his cell door slamming open, and freezing cold water under pressure forced him against the wall of his cell. He was thrown a bowl of slop to eat, and he crawled over to it, stiff and feverish.

While Shakil tried to eat, his family were down at the police station again, being told that if they persisted in asking questions about him, they would be arrested as well. They followed their visit to the police with a trip to the offices of *The Guardian*. After a long wait, a sympathetic journalist informed them that if Shakil was being held on terror charges, then it was probably at the new detention centre in the Tower of London. This being the case, there was nothing *The Guardian* or any other newspaper could do, as there was a Government injunction against reporting on the Tower. Any journalist caught investigating issues relating to the complex would be imprisoned, and there would be repercussions against the editor and other staff at his or her newspaper.

'I am very, very sorry for your son and for your family. But the only help I can give you is to tell you to forget about your son, or you will end up in prison yourselves, along with your daughter.'

'I will not forget about my son!' raged Mrs Malik as her husband and daughter escorted her out of the building – just as they would escort her out of various newspaper, police, human rights organisation and government buildings every day in the weeks that followed.

Shakil's second interrogation was even shorter than the first. The boy only just managed to reiterate that all he'd done was to take part in a general drunken discussion about explosives at the party, that he wasn't part of a terror cell, and that during his summer trip to Pakistan his uncle had taken him sight-seeing with his aunt and cousins and not to a terror training camp, when Pete came in to report that the bodies of two guards who had been on duty late last night had been found in the Armoury.

'What?' For the first time since anyone in the room could remember, the Warden looked shaken.

'Crewes and Hampel, sir. We found their bodies.' Pete's face was ashen, and he seemed unsteady on his feet. 'At least, we think it's them.'

'What do you mean, you think it's them?'

'The heads sir . . .'

'What about their heads?'

'They're missing, sir.'

'What?'

'I said . . .'

'I know what you said, man!' The Warden pushed his seat away from the table so violently that it toppled over, and the interrogating officer dived to pick it up. 'Take me to the bodies, and organise a search for the heads at once. Use the dogs.'

As the Warden swept out of the room with Pete in tow, the interrogating officer piped up in a feeble little voice, 'Excuse me, sir . . .' Despite his fear, pain and confusion, Shakil couldn't believe how the interrogator's whole demeanour changed when he spoke to the Warden.

'What is it?'

'What shall I do with *him*?' The interrogator nodded in Shakil's direction.

'Take him back to his cell. We'll continue this later.'

Shakil was thrown back in his cell, amidst his usual protestations that he hadn't done anything, that they'd made a mistake and that he wanted to call his parents; and guards with dogs were dispatched to look for the missing heads.

The search came to an abortive end when the dogs were taken to the Salt Tower. As soon as the shadow of the tower fell on the two Alsatians, they started to whimper like puppies. And as their handler dragged them towards the threshold, they bayed and jumped about, trying to pull away from the building.

'Come on, you little bastards, we're going in!' But Jeffries didn't stand a chance. Max dropped into a crouch and started backing away, eyes fixed on the dark entrance to the Salt Tower, while Theo let out a plaintive howl, bit Jeffries on the hand and, when the shocked handler let go of his leash, ran in the opposite direction like the hounds of hell had been loosed on his fine black pedigree tail – now tucked between his legs, right under his belly, and fleeing for its dear fluffy life.

While Jeffries led the disgraced Max back to the kennels, then rounded up Theo and gave him a good hiding, the other guards entered the Salt Tower and searched it top to bottom, but found nothing. By dusk the heads still hadn't turned up. A discussion flared up as to whether police and crime scene investigation teams should be brought in from the outside, but the Warden categorically refused, on the general rule of thumb that 'What goes down in the Tower, stays in the Tower.' The search for the heads would resume in the morning. For now, all guards were to be extra cautious and patrol only in pairs. The guards grumbled amongst themselves that Crewes and Hampel were in a pair when they were murdered, but nobody dared contradict the Warden. And so night fell.

Bob was patrolling the Wakefield Tower with Pete. There were only ten minutes left until the end of the shift, but Pete couldn't wait that long.

'I need to take a leak, mate. Wait for me, won't you?'

'Sure.' But as soon as Pete disappeared around the corner, Bob heard the heartbreaking sobbing of a child – the little boy from the night before. 'Pete? Pete!' But Pete couldn't hear him and Bob couldn't wait, as the child's crying receded down the corridor, joined by the voice of the older boy. Bob threw one last, undecided glance in the direction of the toilets, then took off after the boys.

Bob followed the voices and footsteps, calling out to the children as he spotted them heading out of the building. He couldn't see them clearly in the darkness, but the little one looked about ten, and the older one couldn't be more than twelve or thirteen. What the hell were they doing here, and where were they hiding during the day? It wasn't that much of a surprise that the dogs hadn't found them – Max and Theo seemed to be about as much use as his late aunt's toy poodle – but the massive hunt for Crewes's and Hampel's heads should have unearthed the boys' hiding place. Then again, the heads hadn't turned up, so perhaps where the heads were so too were the boys . . . what a horrible thought. And speaking of Crewes's and Hampel's heads . . . as Bob followed the boys into the Bloody Tower, he suddenly realised the folly of what he was doing. He stopped for a moment and thought about turning back and rejoining Pete, but then the little boy cried out somewhere in the darkness ahead of him, so he drew his gun and hurried inside.

Pete came out of the toilet and returned to the place where he'd left the younger guard. He called out to his colleague, then glanced at his watch and figured that Bob must have gone back to the guards' quarters. 'Thanks for waiting,' he muttered under his breath, and followed suit.

The boys were gone. By the time Bob realised that he was in the same chamber as he'd shot the woman in, it was too late – the woman was running at him from the far end of the room, shrieking. Bob's brain stalled, but his automatic pilot engaged and he pointed his weapon at the woman, shouting for her to stop. This time he did not fire and, as the woman drew closer to him, Bob noticed that she was not looking at him – she was running in his direction, but not actually at him. Now she was close enough for Bob to see the terror and madness in her eyes. As the screaming woman reached Bob, he jumped back, weapon raised, ready to let her pass, but she fell bleeding to the floor, exactly as she had the other night when he'd thought he'd shot her.

When Bob recovered enough to lower his weapon and think rationally, he bent down and studied the gashes in the woman's back. It was obvious now that he wasn't responsible for them. It was as if someone had hacked into her from behind, over and over, while she was running away. Bob looked in the direction from which the woman had come, and that was when he heard the footsteps – heavy and getting closer. Then a sight more monstrous than anything he could have imagined appeared at the far end of the chamber. Striding rapidly towards the guard, giant axe in hand, was a mountain of a man, with a black hood-like mask over his head, holes cut out for the eyes – and the eyes unblinking, deathlike, yet burning with a malevolence that could only have come from Hell itself.

Bob fought to keep a hold of himself. 'Stop or I'll shoot!' The monster paused for the briefest moment, looking directly at the guard. Bob could have sworn that the fiend smiled beneath his mask, before moving forward again with added determination. As he approached Bob, he raised his axe. 'Stay back!' Bob took aim and squeezed the trigger, but his gun jammed. He tried not to panic; he managed to unblock the gun, and discharged several shots at the approaching giant. He kept shooting, but the monster kept coming. Bob was still shooting as the axe came down. The last thing he saw was the room spinning over and over, and then his own headless body slumping to the ground, then receding in the distance, as his head was picked up and carried off into the darkness.

Shakil had fallen into a restless sleep. He dreamed that he was in a different cell. There was a window at eye level and he looked out of it onto the patch of land known as Tower Green. A scaffold had been erected there and Shakil could see a small crowd gathering. Then he saw a procession of people walking from the White Tower in the direction of the scaffold. Among them was an elderly man, leading the most gorgeous girl Shakil had ever seen. She was slim and petite, with a beautiful face, rendered very pale against her jet black dress. Her hair was hidden by a silk scarf, but a lock of it had escaped, and shone once reddish, once golden in the cold February sun. She held a small book in her hand, and walked like a goddess or a queen might walk.

As Shakil watched, the girl was led towards the scaffold. Shakil expected her to take a place among the crowd, but the elderly man led her up the steps, onto the wooden structure itself. That's when Shakil noticed the large block of wood, and the huge, monstrous-looking, hooded man who stood in the shadows at the side of the scaffold, holding a massive axe. Shakil looked at the girl, who addressed the crowd and read something out of her book, and then the reality of what was going to happen dawned on the boy and he felt sick. As he watched, the girl removed her scarf and coat, and handed them to one of the women attending her. Then she took a handkerchief and tied it around her eyes. Shakil tried to open the window, but it was stuck. He rattled it in a desperate attempt to get it open, but to no avail. He shouted, but nobody could hear him. He was forced to watch helplessly as the beautiful girl kneeled, then panicked as she couldn't locate the block by touch alone. Shakil watched in horror as someone from the crowd scaled the scaffold, and guided the girl's hands to the chopping block. She calmed down, and lay her head upon it. The masked man stepped out of the shadows and raised his axe.

As the axe came down, Shakil cried out and woke up. His relief that it had only been a dream dissipated as soon as he realised where he was. As his eyes adjusted to the dark, he saw a figure watching him from a corner of his cell. He pulled back, frightened, but then he recognised the girl from his dream. The gentleness emanating from her dispelled Shakil's fear in an instant. Confused, but unafraid, he watched the girl draw closer. He could smell her perfume, and wondered why it was familiar. The girl touched his face and Shakil closed his sore eyes for a moment, then opened them again and gazed into the girl's sad face. He reached out and touched her reddish-gold hair, smiling back when she smiled at him.

The first light of dawn crept into the cell. Pain clouded the girl's delicate features and a thin red line appeared on her pale neck. Shakil watched in horror as the girl put a hand up to her neck, and blood oozed out between her fingers. Shakil started to panic, and the girl held out her free hand to him, trying to reassure him even as she fought to stem the flow of her own blood with her other hand. As she bled, the girl's features became soft and blurred, and she faded away, leaving only a pool of blood on the floor; a second later that too was gone.

Shakil pushed himself back against the cold damp wall of his cell and sat there, shaking. He was still sitting there when the guards came to hose him down.

'We're going back upstairs now,' said the Warden, 'but bear in mind that this is where we'll be having our little chats from now on if you don't tell us what we want to know.'

Shakil's hands were handcuffed behind his back and his ankles loosely chained together. He was speechless following the interrogating officer's demonstration of the rack, unable even to protest his innocence, which he'd done at every given opportunity up until now. The Warden took Shakil's silence to be an admission of guilt, and congratulated himself silently on his first small victory over the youth. The interrogating officer, on the other hand, was still miffed that the plaques about the torture instruments had been removed – along with all the other tourist information – as his urge to try out the Scavenger's Daughter was growing daily, but he couldn't for the life of him figure out how the damned thing worked. If only someone had told him about Google.

Back in the interrogating room, the officer ordered Shakil to name the other people in his terror cell. Shakil was still unable to speak, and the Warden thought that perhaps he'd been wrong: the stubborn little shit was not on the verge of spilling the beans after all; his silence was merely a new and irritating resistance tactic. The Warden nodded to the interrogating officer to get physical. The interrogator grinned and was about to take a swipe at Shakil when Pete appeared, and informed them in a trembling voice that the body of Bob Dawson had been found in the Bloody Tower – the body, but not the head. The Warden had no choice but to order Shakil to be taken back to his cell.

'You are one lucky son of a bitch,' the interrogating officer hissed in Shakil's ear as Pete led the boy out of the room.

Shakil was left alone for the rest of the day, as everyone in the Tower complex was preoccupied with the search for a psycho killer and three missing heads. The boy spent much of the day lying on the hard stone floor. At night he couldn't get to sleep, and when he finally did, he dreamed about the execution again. This time he was right there, standing among the small group of people at the foot of the scaffold. As the executioner moved towards the girl and raised his axe, Shakil started screaming, 'Stop! Let her go!'

The hooded monster turned away from the girl and headed towards Shakil.

'Run! Go! Now!' The girl's voice rang out over the agitated whispers of the crowd. She had raised her head from the block and, the blindfold still over her eyes, moved her head around, as if trying to locate Shakil through sound alone. 'You can't stop what will happen to me. It will go on happening over and over – as long as the Tower stands.'

The executioner went to descend the scaffold, axe raised, eyes on Shakil.

'Run! Please go! Now!' So urgent was the plea in the girl's voice that Shakil ran.

He woke up to the familiar sound of his cell door slamming open. As Shakil was hosed down, his family were preparing to see a woman from Amnesty International. By the time they had arrived at the Amnesty office, and the woman had said that she would try to help them, but it would be a slow and difficult process, Shakil was already strapped to the rack in the basement of the Wakefield Tower.

'I don't know!' he half screamed, half pleaded.

'You don't know their names?' asked the Warden, as the interrogating officer got ready to tighten the ropes one more time. Shakil was stretched out on the iron frame, his feet secured at one end, his hands at the other. The replica of the sixteenth century original worked just fine. The lever on the central wooden roller allowed the interrogating officer to turn the rollers at the head and foot of the rack simultaneously, pulling the ropes that secured Shakil's hands and feet in opposite directions.

'I don't know what you're talking about!'

The interrogating officer was about to turn the roller again, when Pete came running in and informed the Warden that Jeffries was missing. If looks could kill, the filthy look that the interrogator gave Shakil would have dispatched the boy to the next life for sure.

'What shall I do with him?' the interrogator asked the Warden.

'Leave him where he is.'

Luckily for Shakil, the ropes on the rack were not stretched tight enough to do any serious damage, but as the day wore on, the agony of having his arms pulled taught over his head grew. At lunchtime a fly found its way into the basement, and tortured the sweating, suffering boy by buzzing round his head and sitting on him, again and again; every time he managed to move enough to dislodge it, it would be back. This carried on for about an hour until the fly grew bored and flew off to find some dog shit to feed on. Half an hour later Shakil's nose started to itch for no apparent reason, and the boy squirmed, tried to blow on his nose and did whatever he could to alleviate the itch, but it persisted for a good forty minutes, driving him crazy, and then suddenly it eased. By teatime his muscles began to cramp painfully and Shakil cried out in pain and fear.

As darkness fell, the chamber changed. Shadows moved around Shakil, and he could hear whispers and moans in the dark corners. Despite his great discomfort, exhaustion overcame him and he almost dozed off, but the approach of heavy footsteps brought him wide awake. The night was at its darkest now, and Shakil peered into the gloom near the chamber door with growing trepidation. The footsteps grew louder, the shadows and whispers around Shakil stilled, and a terrible silence fell on the chamber.

Shakil struggled against his bonds as the footsteps came closer. Then the chamber door swung open, and in the scant light from the corridor Shakil saw the silhouette of a massive man. As the giant entered the chamber, Shakil recognised him: it was the hooded monster that had cut off the girl's head in his nightmare – it was the executioner, and he had seen Shakil, and was advancing towards him, raising his axe.

Shakil thrashed about on the rack, crying out and twisting madly from side to side. An image of his parents and his sister flashed into Shakil's head, and he was sure he was going to die. When a white mist formed before his eyes, he thought he was passing out, but the mist quickly solidified and took on human form. It was the girl from Shakil's dreams – the girl who had visited him in his cell – and she now stood between the boy and the executioner, small and slender, but more corporeal and stronger than the other night.

The executioner went for the girl immediately, but she ducked his blow and fled from the chamber, leading him away from Shakil. The boy shouted out in protest, but the executioner and the girl were gone. Shakil struggled on the rack again, terrified for the girl. Eventually he exhausted himself and gave up. Tears for the girl welled up in his eyes, and he closed them. Then all of a sudden there was that perfume again, and a gentle, soothing presence was in the room.

The girl was back. She touched Shakil's face and chest; she touched his hands and studied his bonds closely.

Ever since the presence of people in the Tower at night had disrupted the fine balance between the living and the dead, the girl had found herself increasingly able to interact with the physical world. For many years those who walked in the Tower during the day and those who walked there at night had been separate. Now the order was destroyed, and the girl, and the realm of nightmare in which she resided, had entered the waking world. And she had fallen in love again – and again her love was doomed.

Jane Grey had been fifteen when she was bullied into marrying a young man she hardly knew, but she had grown to love him. Nine months after their wedding, she had watched from her confines in the Tower as he was taken for execution and brought back a while later – his rag-covered head rattling around beside his headless body in the horse-drawn cart. An hour later, Jane suffered the same fate. Her crime: being too young to withstand the machinations of her ambitious parents and powerful in-laws, who had made her queen of England for nine days, incurring the wrath of the rightful heir to the throne.

Jane loosened Shakil's bonds and let him down. The boy's body slumped, his arms temporarily useless, and he fell into the girl's arms. Drawing on his life-force to give her strength, Jane led Shakil out of the dark building.

Jones was checking the area west of the White Tower when he spotted the prisoner whose head he'd shaved leaving the Wakefield Tower with a girl in an old-fashioned dress. He raised his weapon, shouting for them to stop, then gave chase.

Jane and Shakil fled towards Traitor's Gate and the River Thames beyond. The only obstacle in their way was the portcullis on the south side of the Bloody Tower. The pins-and-needles had eased, and Shakil had enough feeling back in his arms to work the ancient mechanism that pulled up the seven hundred and fifty year old spiked gate. He and Jane ran under the portcullis just as Jones was catching up with them. The guard paused for a moment, taking aim at Shakil's back. There was a loud creaking noise as the mechanism holding up the portcullis gave way, and the two and a half tonne structure came crashing down, its spikes impaling the guard through his head and his shoulders. He held onto his weapon a moment longer, and then it fell from his hand. His body remained upright, fixed by the iron spikes, surprised eyes staring ahead.

Jane and Shakil ran down the steps leading to the water-logged Traitor's Gate. Water levels had risen in the last few years, the river's tides had increased in strength, and the land beneath the water-gate had been worn away. The bottom of the gate no longer sat on the mud beneath the water, but hung free in the water itself, the gate now held up by the solid walls on either side of it. As Shakil inspected the bottom of the gate, he understood why the girl had brought him to this spot.

'We just have to swim under it,' he said to her. 'I'll go first, then I'll help pull you under the gate.'

Shakil lowered himself into the freezing water and went under, using the bars to pull himself down one side, then up the other side of the gate. He came up, gasping for breath, and stood chest-high in water, shaking from the cold. He reached out to Jane through the bars.

'You just have to get down and under the bars, and I'll help pull you up,' he told her.

Jane gazed at Shakil, sadness and longing in her eyes. As Shakil watched, her features began to soften and fade. She turned from the boy and fled back towards the Bloody Tower, disappearing before she reached the top of the steps.

'I'll come back for you,' Shakil called out to the night.

~

The Warden and the interrogating officer were returning from the site where Jeffries's headless body had been found. The multiple lacerations on the dead guard's back and the lengthy blood trail leading up to the body suggested that Jeffries had managed to run a fair distance before succumbing to the killer's axe.

'I'm going to have to get the police involved.' The Warden looked defeated.

'We'd better get the prisoner off the rack,' the interrogator reminded him.

'Christ, I forgot all about him. Let's go and get him ourselves. There are hardly any guards left, for God's sake.' The two of them went down to the torture chamber, but Shakil was nowhere to be found.

'Goddammit! Goddammit!' The Warden's vocabulary – never huge – shrank to one word.

After a final search of the Tower complex by what was left of his staff, the Warden finally called the police and admitted to having a terror suspect on the loose and a bunch of dead guards with missing heads.

The executioner was not happy. The pathetic slip of a girl had outfoxed him, robbing him of the head of the traitor on the rack. It was his duty to collect as many heads for the Queen as possible – and he would have to hurry if he was to get a decent quota before daybreak.

Shakil made it back home before dawn. His luminous yellow jumpsuit was almost dry, but he had to ditch it as soon as possible. He used the last of his strength to scale a tree at the back of the house, and quietly opened his sister's bedroom window. He gazed at Adara, longing to hug her, but what was the point of waking her up? Things would never be the same again, and it was best not to get her hopes up. He looked in on his parents, also sound asleep. Then he went to his room and changed his clothes. He noticed an old history book from school and quickly flipped through the pages, looking for something. And there it was: a reproduction of Paul Delaroche's painting of the execution of Lady Jane Grey. Recognition and sadness crept into Shakil's eyes. 'Jane.'

Shakil moved swiftly and silently to his father's study, opened a drawer and took out the keys to his father's office and warehouse. He put on a long, loose-fitting coat, and tucked the jumpsuit under it – he would dispose of it later, away from the house, preventing any repercussions against his family. He took a final look at his sleeping parents, then went into Adara's bedroom and left quietly through her window.

Adara woke up, looked around her room and shivered. For a moment she had the vague feeling that something wasn't right, but sleep quickly reclaimed her and she sank back onto her pillow.

Shakil disappeared around the corner just as the first police cars pulled up.

The Warden and the interrogating officer were on their way to the Warden's office in the White Tower, when their path was cut off by a brick shithouse of a man, carrying an axe in one hand and Jeffries's head in the other.

'Shit!' The Warden froze for a moment, and the interrogating officer was first to draw his gun.

'Drop the axe!' But the giant didn't drop the axe; he raised it and ran at the interrogator. The interrogating officer emptied his gun into the giant's chest, then turned and ran towards the Wakefield Tower. The Warden paused long enough to ascertain that the killer was following the interrogator, then ran as fast as he could in the opposite direction.

~

The interrogating officer ran down the stairs to the basement. Before he knew it, he found himself in the torture chamber, cowering behind the Scavenger's Daughter and listening to the heavy footsteps coming closer. He'd barely had time to reload his gun when the heavy door of the chamber swung open, its hinges breaking, and the executioner strode in, Jeffries's head still swinging by one side and the axe held firmly on the other.

The guard emptied his gun into the advancing giant's head and chest, then fell to his knees and started to pray. The executioner raised his axe over the guard's head, and then thought better of it. He placed the axe and Jeffries's head carefully on the ground. Then he grabbed the sobbing interrogator by the back of his neck and the seat of his pants, squeezed his head down towards his knees, and thrust him into the Scavenger's Daughter, fastening the iron bonds with ease.

'So that's how it works.' The ridiculously inappropriate thought slipped into the interrogator's head before the monster tightened his bonds, forcing blood from his nose and mouth, and cracking his spine.

The executioner contemplated his handiwork for a moment, then picked up his axe and cut the man's head off.

The Warden had locked himself in his office and was calling the police again when he heard heavy footsteps approaching. He put the phone down and stood very still, hoping the footsteps wouldn't stop outside his office door, but they did. There was a moment's silence, and then an ear-splitting thud as the axe came splintering through the thick wood of the door. The Warden thought he was going to have a heart attack. For some reason all he could think of was Jack Nicholson breaking down the bathroom door in *The Shining*. Then he remembered that the door on the far side of his office led to an adjoining chamber, which in turn led back round to the stairs.

When the executioner burst in, the Warden was already leaving through the back and heading downstairs. As he ran for the main entrance leading out of the Tower, the Warden ran straight into the escaped prisoner.

'You're back!'

'Yes, I'm back.' And Shakil opened his jacket, revealing the vast amount of explosives strapped around his waist, and the detonator in his other hand. The Warden turned around, planning to go back the way he'd just come, but the executioner was striding towards him, axe in one hand, Jeffries's and the interrogator's heads in the other.

The Warden turned back to Shakil.

'We can make a deal. I can get you released from here.' Shakil looked the Warden in the eye and raised the detonator in front of the man's face. 'No!' The Warden raised a hand in protest and backed away as Shakil placed his thumb over the detonating button. 'Please, don't. I have a wife and kids.' The Warden didn't have a wife or kids. In fact he hated both kids and women, only using the latter sporadically when his urges got the better of him. But Shakil wasn't to know. The Warden sensed the boy's hesitation. 'I have two kids, and a third on the way.' Shakil's thumb wavered over the detonator.

The Warden held the boy's gaze. He didn't see the axe rise behind his head; nor did he see it swing down and round. But he felt the sharp pain in his neck, and then the world spun and became red and orange, as the Warden's head went one way and his body went another, flailing arms lashing out in reflex action and grabbing Shakil's hand, pushing the boy's thumb down on the detonator.

Debris flew everywhere: stone, timber, metal, body parts and shards of glass. Among the body parts were severed heads, which fell – some of them burning, all of them thudding – to the ground.

Had there been any witnesses at that early time of the morning, and had those witnesses looked closely, they might have noticed orbs of light and strange wisps of mist rising from the burning ruins and merging with the dawn sky.

Police, fire trucks and ambulances were on the scene within minutes; news vans not much later.

Adara woke up to the sound of the news on her television.

'Police are puzzled by the disproportionate number of heads among the remains . . .'

She sat up, startled, convinced that she'd switched her TV off the night before, and saw her brother standing before her. He wore his favourite leather jacket and smiled at her, pushing a thick lock of shiny black hair away from his eyes. Adara's grogginess was instantly replaced by astonishment, then pure joy. She smiled back at Shakil and reached towards him, but he faded away, revealing the television with the newsman still reporting on the explosion.

Adara cried out and burst into tears.

'The authorities believe that the explosion was an act of terror. Many will no doubt be saying that the Prime Minister's new anti-terror legislation has already been justified; some that it is still not enough.'

As Adara stared at the television uncomprehendingly, several ravens hopped past the reporter's back and perched on a nearby wall, overlooking the burning wreckage.

RAMSEY CAMPBELL

BEHIND THE DOORS

As Adam ran to the school gates he cried, 'Look what the teacher gave me, Grandad.'

It was an Advent calendar, too large to fit in his satchel. Each of the little cardboard doors had the same jolly bearded countenance, with a bigger one for Christmas Day. 'Well,' Summers said as the mid-December air turned his breath pale, 'that's a bit late.'

The ten-year-old's small plump face flushed while his eyes grew wider and moister. 'He gave me it because I did best in the class.'

'Then hurrah for you, Adam.' Summers would have ruffled the boy's hair if it hadn't been too clipped to respond. 'Don't scoff all the chocolates you should have had already,' he said as Adam poked at a door with an inky finger. 'We don't want your mum and dad telling me off for letting you spoil your dinner.'

'I was going to give you one,' the boy protested, shoving the calendar under one arm before he tramped across the road.

Summers kept a sigh to himself as he followed Adam into the park opposite Park Junior. He didn't want to upset the boy, especially when he recalled how sensitive he'd been at Adam's age. He caught up with him on the gravel path along an avenue of leafless trees, above which the sky resembled an untrodden snowfield. 'How did you earn the prize, Adam?'

'The maths teacher says I should be called Add 'Em.'

'Ha,' said Summers. 'Who's the witty teacher?'

'Mr Smart,' Adam said and glanced back to see why Summers had fallen behind. 'He's come to our school because Miss Logan's having a baby.'

Summers overtook him beside the playground, a rubbery expanse where swings hung inert above abandoned cans of lager. 'What else can you tell me about him?'

'I expect he was teaching when you were at school.' With some pride in the observation Adam said, 'He must be as older than you than I'm old.'

'Does he always give his pupils calendars like that?'

'I don't know. Shall I ask him?'

'No, don't do that. Don't mention me, or say anything I said.'

'Didn't you ever get one?'

Summers attempted to swallow a sour stale taste, 'Not that I could tell you.'

Adam considered this while his expression grew more sympathetic, and then he said, 'You can have mine if you like.'

Summers was touched by the offer but disconcerted by the prospect. 'I tell you what,' he said, 'you give me that and I'll buy you another.'

He was glad for Adam as soon as the boy handed him the calendar. Even if only the winter day made the cardboard feel cold and damp, the corners were scuffed and the colours looked faded. The jovial faces were almost as white as their beards, and the floppy red hats had turned so brown that they resembled mounds of earth perched on the heads. Summers thrust the calendar under his arm to avoid handling it further. 'Let's get you home,' he said.

Beyond a bowling green torn up by bicycles, a Frugo Corner supermarket had replaced a small parade of shops that used to face the park. As the automatic doors let out the thin strains of a carol from the overhead loudspeakers, Summers wondered if it was too late for Advent calendars to be on sale. He couldn't bring the date to mind, and trying to add up the spent days of December made his head feel raw. But there were calendars beside the tills, and Adam chose one swarming with creatures from outer space, though Summers was unclear what this had to do with Christmas.

His old house was half a mile away across the suburb. Along the wide quiet streets the trees looked frozen to the sky. He saw Adam to the antique door that Paul and Tina had installed within their stained-glass wrought-iron porch. 'Will you be all right now?'

The boy gave the elderly formula an old-fashioned look. 'I always am,' he reminded Summers and slipped his key into the lock.

The streets narrowed as Summers made his way home. The houses grew shabbier and their doorbells multiplied, while the gardens were occupied by seedy cars and parts of cars. Each floor of the concrete block where he lived was six apartments long, with a view of an identical block. Once Elaine left him he'd found the house too large, and might have given it to his son even if Paul hadn't moved in with a partner.

The apartment was something like halfway along the middle balcony, two doors distant from the only other number with a tail, but Summers knew it by the green door between the red pair. He marched down the hall to the kitchen, where he stopped short of the bin. If the sweets in the calendar weren't past their edible date, why shouldn't he finish them off?

He stood it on the mantelpiece in the main room, beneath Christmas cards pinned to the nondescript wallpaper. As he searched for the first cardboard door he heard an object shift within the calendar, a sound emphasised by the silence of the hi-fi and the television and the empty suite that faced them. At last he located the door in the midst of the haphazard dates and pried it open with a fingernail. The dark chocolate behind the door was shaped like the number. 'One up for me,' he declared, biting it in half.

The sweet wasn't stale after all. He levered the second door open as soon as he found it, remarking 'Two's not for you,' as he put the number in his mouth. How many did he mean to see off? He ought to heed the warning he'd given Adam about dinner. 'Three's a crowd,' he commented once he managed to locate the number. That had certainly felt like the case when, having decided that Paul was old enough for her to own up, Elaine had told Summers about the other man. The taste in his mouth was growing bitter yet sickly as well, and any more of it might put him off his dinner. Perhaps it already had, but since taking early retirement he'd gained weight that he could do with losing. There was no point in eating much when he was by himself.

For a while he watched the teachers' channel, which seemed to be the only sign of intelligence on television. An hour or two of folk music on the hi-fi with the sound turned low out of consideration for the neighbours left him readier for bed. He brushed his teeth until the only flavour in his mouth was toothpaste, and then he did his best to be amused by having to count a multitude of Santas in the dark before he could fall asleep.

At least his skull wasn't crawling with thoughts of tomorrow's lessons and more lessons yet to plan, and tests to set, and conflicts to resolve or at any rate address, both among the children and within themselves. However badly he might sleep, he no longer had to set the alarm clock, never mind lying awake for hours before it went off or struggling to doze until it did. Since it was Friday he needn't bother with breakfast; he would be meeting some of his old colleagues from Dockside Primary – and then he realised he'd lost count of the weeks. His friends would be preparing for tonight's Christmas play at the school, and they'd cancelled their usual Friday lunch.

He could still do without breakfast, given the stale sweetish taste in his mouth. He brushed his teeth at length and used mouthwash before swallowing his various pills. Once he was dressed heavily enough to switch off the heating he wandered into the living room to feed himself today's date from the Advent calendar. When at last he put his finger on the eighteenth he felt he'd earned a walk in the park.

In spring he'd liked to take his classes to the one near Dockside Primary – to imagine that their minds were budding like the trees. That was before teaching had turned into a business of filling in forms and conforming to prescribed notions as narrow as the boxes on the documents. Now he could think that the children in the schoolyard of Park Junior were caged not just by the railings but by the educational system. He couldn't see Adam, but if he ventured closer the boy might be embarrassed by his presence. What was Summers doing there at all? The children's uninhibited shouts must prove that Smart was nowhere near.

Summers watched the school until he saw teachers trooping back from lunch, but none of them looked familiar. Once the yard was empty he stood up from the bench. Ambling around the park used up some time, and then he strolled to the Dockside library, where he might have found work if the job had involved fewer numbers. People even older than he was or just as unemployed were reading the papers, and he had to content himself with a tabloid. Perhaps the prose as terse as the bitten-off headlines was all that some people could read. That was a failure of education, like the young and even younger criminals who figured in many of the reports. The paper took him a very few minutes to read, and then he hurried back to the school. He wanted to be there before anyone emerged.

Some teachers did in the midst of the flood of children, but he recognised none of them, and Adam was impatient to question him. 'How many did you have?'

Summers was thrown by the irrational notion that it could have been a problem set by Smart. 'Not as many as you, I expect,' he retorted.

'I just had one and then we had some after dinner.'

'Good boy.' Summers felt a little sly for adding ,'Did your teacher say anything about it?'

'He wanted me to add up all the days till today in my head.'

'Just this month, you mean. And did you?'

'I got it right. He said everyone should be like me.'

'It wouldn't be much of a world if we were all the same, do you think?' Summers sensed that the boy had more to tell. 'Is that all he did?'

'Jimmy was next to top in class, but he got the answer wrong.'

'What happened, Adam?'

'Mr Smart gave him a calendar as well, but now Jimmy has to give it back.'

'I knew he couldn't change. He's the shit he always was.'

Summers had done his best to lower his voice, but Adam giggled with delight. 'What did you say, Grandad?'

'You didn't hear it, and don't tell your parents, all right? There's no need for language like that.'

'I don't mind. Some of the boys in my class say worse, and the girls.'

'Then they shouldn't, even about –' Although Summers had already said too much, his nerves were prompting him. 'Just so long as your teacher never tries anything like that with you,' he said. 'He'll have me to deal with. I've got the calendar.'

'He won't, Grandad. He says he wishes all the summers were like me.'

Summers recalled Smart's jokes about his name, but they'd been vicious. 'So long as you are, Adam,' he said, and nothing more until they reached the house. 'I'll see you all tomorrow,' he said, which meant once a week.

He brought dinner home from the Doner Burger Pizzeria, and ate nearly half of the fish and some of the chips before thoughts of Smart stole his appetite. He'd prove he deserved to have the prize. He cleared the kitchen table and laid the calendar face up on it. The open doors stood more or less erect, and he totted up their numbers while he looked for the fourth. There it eventually was, and he rewarded himself with the contents as he added to the total in his head and carried on the search. Ten became fifteen, and he swallowed to make room for the five in his mouth. He needn't eat any more chocolates; he certainly shouldn't see off however many led to today's, even if it would feel like saving Adam from any reason to be grateful to the teacher. Twenty-what, twenty-one, twenty-more . . . At the eighth he lost count and had to start again. The relentless glare of the fluorescent tube overhead intensified his sense of sitting an examination, but it was only a mock one. One, three, six, ten . . . This time he progressed as far as the eleventh, and then searching through the numerical maze drove the total out of his head. He did his best to add up the numbers without looking for them, but he'd tallied fewer than many when he found he had to see them. He tried saying them aloud as he found them and repeating the latest total over and over while he searched for the next number, though he had to keep raising his voice to hold the count in his head. At last he arrived at the date and shouted the total, not loud enough to bother the neighbours, he hoped. He was about to feed himself one more sweet when he wondered if he'd arrived at the right answer.

He added all the numbers up again, and the total was even louder than the process. It was a shout of frustration, because the amount was twenty-two less than his previous answer, which couldn't even mean he'd missed a number out. He tried another count, though his throat was raw with shouting before he came to the end. Figuring out the difference aggravated the headache that was already making his vision throb. The total was nineteen more than the last one, which meant it was three less than he'd added up in the first place, but why did he need to know any of this? His head felt as if it was hatching numbers, a sensation that exacerbated a greasy sweetish sickness in his mouth. He stumbled to the bathroom to gulp water and splash some on his face. When none of this seemed to help he groped his way into the bedroom, but his thoughts came to bed with him. The year Smart had taken him for mathematics had been one of the worst of his life.

'I'm here to make you smart like me,' the teacher had informed the class. 'If I don't do it one way I'll do it another.' With his plump petulant constantly flushed face he'd resembled an overgrown schoolboy, and he'd revealed a schoolboy's ingenuity at inventing tortures, tweaking a tuft of hair at the nape of the neck to lift his victim on tiptoe and hold them there until he'd delivered a lecture to them or about them. He'd called his favourite victim Summer because, he'd said in anything but praise, the boy was so singular. Before long Summers had spent every school night lying awake in terror of the next day, but he'd been too ashamed to tell his parents and afraid that any intervention would only make the situation worse. He'd lost count of how often he'd been singled out before the first of December, when Smart asked him to add up the days of the month.

Everyone had found his bewilderment hilarious. He'd had to risk answering at last, and Smart had given him a round of dry applause. When he'd produced an Advent calendar from his briefcase Summers had felt encouraged until he was called to the front of the class to find the date. Long before he did, the teacher was declaring, 'Summer means to keep us all here till next summer.' After that every mathematics lesson began with Summers on his feet to announce the total to date. He'd succeeded for over a week, having lost even more sleep to be sure of the answers, but he'd gone wrong on the ninth and on every school day for the rest of December. He'd still had to find the day's sweet as he stood on tiptoe, raised ever higher by the agonising drag at his neck, and then he'd had to drop the chocolate into the bin.

His anger at the memory kept him awake. Counting Father Christmases no longer helped, and he tried adding up punches to Smart's cruel smug face. That was satisfying enough to let Summers doze, only to waken in a rage, having realised that he didn't need to find the numbers on the calendar to count them. He turned it on its face and listed all the dates in a column on a pad – if he hadn't felt that mobile phones involved too many numbers he would have had a calculator to use now. He tapped each date with the pen as he picked his way down the column. A smell of paint threatened to revive his headache, but eventually he had a number to write at the foot of the last row and another to add at the top of the next one. At last he had the full amount, and muttered something like a prayer before adding up the dates again. He did the sum a third time to be certain, and then he rewarded himself with a bath. Three times in a row he'd arrived at the same answer.

He oughtn't to have tried to prove he could repeat the calculation in his head. By the time he succeeded, the water was too cold to stay in. He meant only to glance at the bedside clock to see how soon he ought to leave for Paul's and Tina's, but he was already late. He almost snagged the padding of his jacket with the zip as he hurried out, to be hindered by tins of paint on the balcony. His left-hand neighbour's door had turned green. 'Just brightening the place up for you,' the over-alled workman said, sounding rather too much like a nurse in a sickroom.

Summers had scarcely rung the bell in the wrought-iron porch when Adam ran to open the door. 'I said Grandad said he was coming.'

Paul emerged in a chef's apron from the kitchen as Tina appeared from the dining room with an electric corkscrew. 'I didn't mean to keep you waiting,' Summers said.

'Don't give it a thought.' To his wife, Paul said, 'I told you he'd never mistake the date.'

'He's just being silly, Teddy,' Tina assured Summers, which only made him wonder what else she'd said about him. 'Take your grandfather's coat, Adam,' she said and blinked at Summers. 'Haven't you been well?'

'Perfectly,' Summers said, feeling too defensive to be truthful. 'What makes you ask?'

'You look as if you could do with feeding,' Paul said.

'You can have one of my chocolates if you like,' said Adam.

'I hope you thanked Grandpa for the calendar,' Paul said. 'I never had one at your age.'

'I gave Grandad one as well.'

'Poor mite,' Tina said to Paul, and less satirically, 'That was kind of you, Adam.'

'He gave me mine so he could have the one the teacher gave me.'

'I don't think I understand.'

She was gazing at Paul, but Summers felt interrogated. 'Perhaps we could discuss it later,' he said.

'Adam, you can set the table,' Tina said as if it were a treat, and gestured the adults into the lounge. Once the door was shut she said, 'What's the situation?'

'I shouldn't really think there is one,' Summers tried saying.

'It sounds like one to us,' Tina said without glancing at Paul. 'Why did you want Adam's present?'

'I just took it off him because it looked a bit ancient. Exactly like his grandfather, you could say.'

'You mean you binned it.'

Summers might have said so, but suppose Adam learned of it? 'I didn't do that, no. I've still got most of it.'

'Most,' Paul said like some kind of rebuke.

'I ate a few chocolates.' Summers felt driven to come up with the number. 'Five of them,' he said with an effort. 'I'm sure they're nowhere near as good as the ones I gave Adam.'

'They can't be so bad,' Tina said, 'if you saw five of them off.'

'All right, it wasn't only that. I just didn't want Adam taking anything from that man.'

'Which man?' Tina demanded as Paul said even more sharply, 'Why?'

'The maths man. I hope he won't be there much longer. Smart,' Summers made himself add and wiped his lips. 'I wouldn't trust him with a dog, never mind children.'

'What are you saying?' Tina cried as Paul opened his mouth.

'I had him for a year at Adam's age. It felt like the rest of my life.' Summers saw he had to be specific so that they wouldn't imagine worse. 'He loved hurting people,' he said.

'He'd never get away with that these days at school,' Paul protested.

'There are more ways than physical. Let's just hope Adam stays his favourite.'

Tina gave Summers a long look before enquiring, 'Have you said any of this to Adam?'

'I wouldn't put him under any pressure, but I do think you should keep a close eye on the situation.'

'I thought you said there wasn't one,' Tina said and opened the door to the hall. 'We'll be discussing it further.'

Summers gathered that he wouldn't be involved, and

couldn't argue while Adam might hear. He offered to help but was sent into the dining room, where Tina served him a glass of wine while his son and grandson brought in dinner. He saw they meant to make him feel at home, but every Saturday he felt as if he'd returned to find the house almost wholly unfamiliar, scattered with a few token items to remind him he'd once lived there – mostly photographs with Elaine in them. At least he could enthuse about Paul's casserole, but this gave Adam an excuse to ask, 'Do you know what it's called, Grandad?'

'Adam,' his mother warned him.

'It's not called Adam.' Perhaps the boy was misbehaving because he'd been excluded from the conversation in the lounge. 'It's cock off, Ann,' he said.

'That's very rude,' Tina said, 'and not at all clever.'

'Maybe it's cocker fan.'

'That's rude too.' Apparently in case it wasn't, Tina insisted, 'And silly as well.'

'Then I expect it's cock – '

'Now, Adam, you've already impressed us with your schoolwork,' Summers said as he thought a grandparent should. 'You're an example to us all. You're even one to me.'

'How am I, grandad?'

'I've been doing some sums of my own. I can tell you what the month adds up to so far.' When nobody asked for the answer Summers felt not much better than distrusted, but he'd repeated the amount to himself all the way to the house. 'One hundred and eighty-one,' he said with some defiance.

Adam squeezed his eyes shut for a moment. 'No it isn't, Grandad.'

'I'm sure it is, you know.' On the way to growing desperate Summers said, 'Hang on, I've left today out, haven't I?'

'That's not it, Grandad. One hundred and ninety, you should have said.'

'I don't think that can be right,' Summers said to the boy's parents as well. 'That's ten times whatever it's ten times, nineteen, isn't it, of course.'

'I should have thought the last thing you'd want to do,' Tina said, 'is undermine his confidence.'

'He's undermining mine,' Summers complained, but not aloud. He was silent while he tried to make the days add up to Adam's total. They either fell short or overshot it, and the need to carry on some sort of conversation didn't help, any more than the drinks during and after the meal did.

The streets were full of numbers – on the doors of houses and the gates, on the front and back of every car and, if they were for sale, in their windows too. There were just three digits to each registration plate, and he tried to add up each group as it came in sight. He was absurdly grateful to reach home, although the orange lights on the balcony had turned his door and its neighbours identically black. 'Nine,' he repeated, 'nine, nine,' and felt as if he were calling for aid by the time he managed to identify the door.

The Advent calendar was still lying on its numbers, and he hoped that would keep them out of his head – but they were only waiting for him to try to sleep, and started awake whenever he did. They got out of bed with him in the morning and followed him into the bath. Couldn't he just add today to Adam's total? That seemed too much like copying an answer in an examination, and in any case he wanted to learn how Adam had arrived at the result. When it continued to elude him he floundered out of the bath.

He did his best to linger over dressing, then listed all the numbers on a new sheet of the pad, pronouncing them aloud to make certain he missed none. Today's date could be added once he'd written down the total. He poked each number with the ballpoint as the amount swelled in his head, only for the pen to hover above the space beneath the line he'd drawn at the foot of the column. He went down the list of figures again and again, jabbing at them until they looked as though they'd contracted a disease. He announced every amount on the way to the total – he might almost have been uttering some kind of Sunday prayer – but none of this was much use. One hundred and seventy-nine, one hundred and ninety-three, one hundred and eighty-seven . . . He hadn't hit upon the same amount twice, let alone the one Adam had told him, when somebody rang the raucous doorbell.

He thought they might have come to complain about his noise, especially once he noticed it was dark. He couldn't leave the table until the sum was done. 'One hundred and ninety,' he said, but that wasn't the whole of the total. 'Seven,' he yelled in a rage, 'one hundred and ninety-seven,' and shoved back his chair to tramp along the hall.

He was preparing to apologise, if hardly to explain, but Tina was outside. 'Well, this is a surprise,' he said. 'Come in.'

'I won't, thanks, Teddy. I just came to tell you –' With a frown that Summers felt was aimed to some extent at him, she turned to say, 'Adam, I told you to wait in the car.'

'I wanted to say goodbye to Grandad.'

'Why,' Summers said in bewilderment, 'where's anybody going?'

'Adam will be going home with a friend next week.' Apparently in recompense, Tina added, 'You'll still be coming to us for Christmas.'

'You mean, I'm not wanted for picking up Adam from school.'

'I've explained the situation.'

As Summers managed not to retort that he suspected the opposite, Adam said, 'Grandad, did you go to school when you were a baby?'

'I wasn't quite that young. Why do you ask?'

'Grandma said you were a baby when Mr Smart had you at school.'

Elaine had been in the same class – Summers used to thank their schooldays for bringing them together. Now he was almost too enraged to ask, 'What else did she say about me?'

'We won't talk about it now, if you don't mind,' Tina said, 'and I hope it won't spoil Christmas either. Just say goodbye to your grandfather till then, Adam.'

'Bye, Grandad,' the boy said. 'You got something nice from Mr Smart, didn't you? All the chocolates.'

'I won't argue,' Summers said and watched Tina shoo Adam back to the car. When he returned to the kitchen the clamour of numbers and emotions in his head robbed him of the ability to think. Turning the calendar over didn't help, especially since every open door had been flattened shut. He stared at however many identical idiotically grinning faces there were, and the pad swarming with diseased amounts, and all at once his mind seemed to clear. Had Tina freed him? Now that he wouldn't be associated with Adam, surely he could deal with the teacher.

He didn't feel beset by numbers once he went to bed. He slept, and in the morning he was able to ignore the calculations on the pad. He listened to symphonies on the radio until it was time to head for Park Junior, and was in a shelter with a view of the school several minutes before the last bell. When the children streamed out under the grey sky, the explosion of colours and chatter felt like a promise of spring. He was cut off from it, skulking in a corner so that Adam wouldn't notice him. Soon he saw his grandson with another boy, and they set about kicking a ball as they followed a young woman into the park.

As Summers turned his face to the wall to make sure he wasn't recognised, he felt like a schoolboy sent to stand in the corner. Surely Adam hadn't looked happier than he did when his grandfather met him. As soon as the thumps of the football passed the shelter Summers peered towards the school. Suppose the teacher had sneaked away unobserved? Summers hurried to the railings opposite the school but could see nobody he knew. The doors let out some teachers and then even more he didn't recognise, and he was clenching his shaky fists in frustration by the time a man emerged into the deserted schoolyard.

He was thin and bent, and as grey as the sky – his suit, his thinning hair, the smoke of the cigarette he lit before stalking to the gates. For a moment Summers wondered if the teacher was too old to bother with – even old enough to be given some grudging respect – and then he saw that Smart had become the vicious old man he'd resembled forty years ago. Any hesitation felt too much like fear, and he barely managed to unclench his fists as he strode out of the park. 'Mr Smart,' he said in triumph. 'Can I ask you a question?'

The teacher stared at him with no more interest than emotion. 'Are you a parent?'

'That and a lot more.' Summers was determined to relish the confrontation. 'Can you tell me what December adds up to so far?' he said.

'Are you asking for one of my pupils?'

'No, I'm speaking for myself. I've learned to do that.' Summers struggled to contain his rage as he enquired, 'Can you do it in your head?'

'Quite obviously I can.' Smart took a measured puff at the cigarette and exhaled smoke, disturbing a stained hair in his left nostril. 'It's two hundred and thirty-one,' he said, 'if that's of any consequence to you.'

'Not so sure of yourself for a bit there, were you? That's a taste of what it feels like.'

'I fear you have the advantage of me,' Smart said and made to step around him.

'You bet I have. It's taken long enough but it was worth the wait.' Summers sidestepped to block his way. 'Don't you know me yet?' he demanded. 'Tortured so many youngsters you've lost count, have you?'

'What on earth do you imagine you're referring to?' Smart narrowed his already pinched eyes at a clatter of cans in the park, where Summers had seen teenagers drinking lager on the swings. 'That's what comes of undermining discipline in school,' Smart said. 'They'd never behave like that if we were still allowed to touch them.'

'It's your sort who undermined it. Made everyone who suffered from the likes of you want to make sure nobody ever does again. It's your fault it's so hard to keep discipline now. It's swine like you that lost teachers their respect.'

Smart lifted the cigarette towards his face but seemed uncertain where his mouth was. 'Did I have you at school?'

'Recognised one of your victims at last, have you? One of the ones you could touch. Do you dream about touching children, you filthy shit? I've often thought that's what your sort wanted to get up to. You took out on children because they made you want to fiddle with them. I bet having them at your mercy worked you up as well.' Was Smart's face turning grey just with the winter twilight? 'Just remember, I know where you are now,' Summers murmured. 'If I even think you're mistreating anyone I'll make it my business to lose you your job. What are you going to do with your fag? Thinking of using it on me, are you? Just try and I'll stick it somewhere that'll make you scream.'

Smart's mouth had begun to work soundlessly, and Summers was reminded of a masticating animal. The cigarette looked close to dropping from the man's fingers, which were shaking the ash loose. Had Summers gone too far? Not unless Smart could identify him, and surely the man would have done so aloud. 'Have the Christmas you deserve,' Summers told him and turned away from him.

When he glanced back from the park he saw the teacher standing just where he'd left him. Smart raised his hand as though bidding him some kind of farewell, but he was finding his mouth with the cigarette. 'Who's the baby now?' Summers muttered. 'Go on, suck your dummy. Suck yourself to death.'

He felt exhilarated as a schoolboy who'd got away with a prank. He might almost have boasted to the teenage drinkers on the swings. If he had any doubts about how he'd spoken to the teacher, they left him as soon as he saw his old house. It was Smart's fault that he wasn't trusted to bring Adam home, and when he reached the apartment block he might have thought the teacher had played another trick. The glare of the declining sun showed him that both doors flanking his had turned green, so that every door on the balcony was the same colour.

'It's nine, you swine,' he said, he hoped not too loud, and let himself in once he was sure of the number on the door. Smart couldn't undermine his confidence any longer, and so he tore the calculations off the pad and flung the spotty wad of paper in the bin. The calendar was a trophy, all the more so since Smart didn't know he had it. He microwaved a cottage pie and a packet of vegetables, and gobbled the lot like a growing boy. He could have thought he was growing up at last, having dealt with the teacher.

How many doors had he already opened on the calendar? He wasn't going to reopen them; taking chocolates at random was one more way to taunt the teacher. 'Unlucky for you,' he mumbled as he crunched the thirteenth sweet, and 'That's how old you like them, is it?' on prising open the tenth door. He might have finished all the chocolates except for not wanting to make himself sick. The best celebration would be a good night's sleep.

At first he didn't understand why it kept being interrupted. Whenever he jerked awake he felt as if he'd heard a sound, unless he'd had a thought. He stayed in bed late; he couldn't be seen with Adam at the school in case Smart took some revenge. What if he'd simply made the teacher even more vindictive? Suppose Smart had recognised him after all and meant to take it out on Adam? A sour stale taste urged Summers to the bathroom. Water didn't rid him of the taste, and he stumbled to the kitchen, only to falter in the doorway. More compartments than he'd opened on the calendar last night stood open now – six doors, no, seven. Those that had reopened were the five he'd previously emptied. With its upright tabs the calendar resembled a miniature graveyard.

'I wish it was yours, you swine,' Summers muttered. He was growing more anxious, and once he was dressed he headed for Park Junior. Soon he saw Adam, though not soon enough for his nerves. The boy was chasing other boys in the schoolyard and being chased, and looked entirely carefree, but had he encountered Smart yet? For a moment Summers had the irrational notion that the teacher was not merely hiding like himself but skulking at his back. There was nothing in the corner of the shelter except a scattering of cigarette butts on the floor and on the end of the bench.

Once the schoolyard was deserted Summers lingered in the shelter, listening for Smart's cold high voice – straining his ears so hard that he thought he heard it amid the scrape of windblown leaves on gravel. The idea that Smart was still at large in the school made him want to storm into the school and report the swine to the headmistress – to say whatever would get rid of him. To overcome the compulsion he had to retreat out of sight of the school. Long before the final bell he was back in the shelter. He hadn't counted the cigarette ends, and so he couldn't tell if they'd multiplied or even whether they'd been rearranged like an aid to a child's arithmetic. He spied on the schoolyard until he saw Adam, who looked happier than ever. Summers hid his face in the corner while the boys and their football clamoured past, and then he turned back to the school. He watched until the doors finished swinging at last, but there was no sign of Smart in the secretive dusk.

Had he been moved to another school? 'So long as you're safe, Adam,' Summers murmured, but the comment seemed to sum up how little he'd achieved. He was so preoccupied that he nearly tried to let himself into the wrong flat. Of course the number on the door was upside down. He shut his door and tramped along the hall to stare at the Advent calendar as if it might inspire him. The shadows of the cardboard markers appeared to deepen the empty compartments, and he was seeing them as trenches when the doorbell rang.

Paul's expression was oddly constrained. 'Well, you'll be pleased,' he said.

'You're trusting me with Adam again.'

Paul took a breath but didn't speak at once. 'The teacher you had trouble with,' he said, 'you can forget about him.'

'Why would I want to do that?'

'He's no longer with us.' Since Summers didn't react Paul added, 'He's dead.'

'Good heavens,' Summers said, although he hoped those weren't involved. 'When did that come about?'

'He had some kind of stroke when he was driving home yesterday. People saw him lose control and his car went into the front of a bus.'

'That's unexpected.' Summers did his best to control his face but thought it prudent to admit, 'I can't say I'm too distressed.'

'I wasn't expecting you to be.'

'So I'll be collecting Adam from school tomorrow, yes?'

Paul made another breath apparent on the way to saying,

'Let's leave it for this week, shall we? We'll sort it out after Christmas.'

'Is it you who doesn't want me looking after him?' When Paul was silent Summers said, 'I didn't know I'd raised you not to stand up for yourself.'

His son paused but said, 'Mum makes it sound as if you didn't for yourself at school.'

'Then she'd better know I've changed. Just hope you never find out how much, like –' Summers' rage was close to robbing him of discretion. 'Go home to your family. I'll leave you all alone till Christmas,' he said and shut the door.

Any qualms he might have suffered over causing Smart's demise were swallowed by his fury with Elaine and Tina and, yes, Paul. He stalked into the kitchen to bare his teeth at the calendar. 'I wish I'd been there,' he said in a voice that wasn't far from Smart's. 'Did you count the seconds when you saw what was coming? It'd just about sum you up.' Talking wasn't enough, and he poked a door open at random. 'Revenge is sweet, don't you think? Revenge is a sweet,' he said and shoved the pair of digits he'd uncovered into his mouth.

Perhaps it was too sweet, the chocolate plaque bulging with numbers. He didn't much care for the taste that filled his mouth once the unexpectedly brittle object crumbled like a lump of ash. As the sweetness immediately grew stale he had the impression that it masked a less palatable flavour. He grabbed a bottle of brandy still half full from last Christmas and poured some into the Greatest Grandad mug Adam had given him. A mouthful seared away part of the tastes, and another did more of the job, but he still felt as if some unpleasant sensation lay in wait for him. Perhaps he was exhausted, both emotionally and by insomnia. He could celebrate the end of Smart with a good night's sleep.

His nerves didn't let him. He kept thinking he'd heard a sound, unless he was about to hear one, or was it too stealthy to be audible? He didn't know how often he'd opened his aching eyes to confront the cluttered darkness before he saw a pair of red eyes staring back at him. They were two of the digits on the bedside clock until one pinched into a single line. It was a minute after midnight, and a day closer to Christmas.

The thought sent him out of bed. While he wouldn't be putting any of the contents of the calendar anywhere near his mouth, perhaps he could relax once he'd located the date and opened the door. As the fluorescent tube jittered alight he could have imagined he glimpsed a flap staggering upright on the calendar. He peered at the swarm of identically mirthful faces in search of the date. How many of the doors were open? Seven, or there should be, and he prodded them while counting them aloud. However often he added them up there was one more, and it was today's.

Could he have opened the door and forgotten? Was that a blurred fingerprint on the chocolate? He grabbed the calendar and shook the sweet into the bin. He was tempted to stuff the calendar in as well, if that wouldn't have felt too much like continuing to fear the teacher. 'Do your worst,' he mumbled, still not entirely awake. Throwing the calendar on the table, he sat down to watch.

Before long the lids of some of the compartments began to twitch. It was his debilitated vision or the shaking of the table, if not both. Whenever his head lurched more or less upright, having slid off his fists that were propping it up, he had to force his eyes wide and count the open doors afresh. 'Eight,' he kept declaring, even when someone thumped on the wall of the kitchen. 'Had enough for one day, have you?' he retorted, though he wasn't sure to whom. He didn't notice when the fluorescent glow merged with pallid sunlight, but it seemed to be an excuse for retreating into bed.

It was almost dark by the time he gave up dozing. He had

enough food to last until Christmas – enough that he needn't be troubled by the identical doors on the balcony. He ate some of a bowl of cereal while he glared a raw-eyed challenge at the calendar, and then he listened to a carol concert on the radio – it was many years since he'd heard carollers at his or anybody's door. The music lulled him almost to sleep until the choir set about amassing the twelve days of Christmas and all that they brought. Even after he switched off the radio, the numbers kept demanding to be totalled in his head.

Well before midnight he was at the kitchen table, where he stood the bedside clock next to the calendar. The digits twitched into various shapes on their way to turning into eyes, which he could have imagined were refusing to blink because they were determined to watch him, even without pupils. At last – it seemed much longer than a minute – the final digit shrank, but nothing else moved. Didn't that last number look more like an I than a 1? Summers was attempting to ignore it when it crumbled into segments, but he mustn't feel compelled to count them; he had to catch the calendar opening today's door, or see whatever happened. He gripped his temples and dug his thumbs into his cheeks, feeling the bones of his skull. His face began to ache, but not enough to keep him alert, though he didn't know he'd dozed until his head jerked up. 'Eight,' he said when at last he thought he was sure of the number. He oughtn't to start bothering the neighbours again, and there was a way to avoid it – by tearing all the open doors off the calendar. They and the boxy holes they left put him in mind of a vandalised graveyard, an idea that felt capable of shrinking Smart no larger than an insect. 'That's all you are. That's all you ever were,' Summers muttered as his head drooped.

When had he eaten last? No wonder he was weak. At least he didn't need to leave the table to find food. He dragged the calendar to him and fumbled a door open. Some instinct must have guided him, since it was the first unopened one – the number of his flat. As he bit the chocolate, the coiled object on the little slab writhed into life. Its tail slithered from between his teeth, and it wormed down his throat as though it had rediscovered its burrow in the earth.

His head wavered up, and he clapped a hand over his mouth. No more doors were open after all – only eight, he was able to believe once he'd counted the gaping compartments several times. The calendar wasn't as close to him as he'd imagined, and he might have been sure he'd dreamed the grisly incident except for an odd taste in his mouth. Perhaps it was merely stale and sweetish, or was there an underlying earthiness? It sent him to gulp brandy straight from the bottle, and he turned back to the table just in time to glimpse a movement. A lid had been lifted, although it was instantly still.

'Caught you,' Summers cried. It bore today's date. The prize it had exposed was marked with scratches, as if someone had been clawing at it for want of a better victim. He shook the chocolate into the bin and tore off the date. 'Finished for today?' he demanded, but couldn't interpret the lack of an answer. He was sinking shakily onto the chair when he glanced at the clock. The number beside the blind red eyes was his apartments. No, it was upside down with its tail in the air, but it still showed he'd spent the night in front of the calendar.

He felt as if Smart had robbed him of all sense of time as well as any confidence about numbers. He would be no fun on Christmas Day if he'd had so little sleep. 'You won't spoil this Christmas as well,' he vowed. Suppose the presents for his family and Tina were ruined somehow? He threw the calendar on its face and pinned it down with a saucepan so heavy that his arms shook. Once he'd returned the clock to the bedside table he fetched the presents from the living room and lined them up in bed before he joined them.

He had to keep reminding himself that the muffled rustling came from the presents, especially whenever it wakened him after dark. His lurches into consciousness were too reminiscent of the Christmas he'd spent dreading next year's days with Smart, far too many to count – shivering awake to realise the worst nightmare wasn't in his sleep. The nights leading up to his retirement had been just as bad, and Smart's fault too. He saw the eyes blink wide to stare towards him, and managed to name the digits next to them. 'One and two, that's three to you,' he mouthed, and, 'Happy Christmas,' when the right eye narrowed to a slit. He didn't need to go and look at the calendar; surely he would hear if anything happened. He lay awake listening, and tried not to move in case that disturbed the wrappings of the presents, though why should he fear being heard? It was almost dawn by the time he went to look.

The light in the fluorescent tube buzzed and fluttered like an insect and eventually grew still. Summers used both hands to remove the saucepan and then turned over the calendar. It put him in mind of lifting a slab – one from beneath which something might scuttle or crawl. Nothing else stirred, however. That wasn't why he let the calendar fall on its back with a hollow flimsy sound. All the numbers on the remaining doors were blurred beyond any possibility of recognition, while the festive faces were no more than blotches with misshapen blobs for eyes. Had age overtaken the calendar? Summers only needed to open today's door to finish celebrating his triumph. He could open all of them to find it if he had to – but prising one open revealed that the sweet was as unrecognisably deformed as the number on the door. The next was the same, and its neighbour, and he felt as if they were showing how deranged Smart had always been or was now. At last Summers wakened enough to realise that he didn't have to try every door; today's was larger. As soon as he located it he dug his fingertip under the lid.

His nail sank into a substance too firm for chocolate but in another way not firm enough, and then the object moved beneath his finger. As he recoiled, the door sprang up, exposing a greyish piebald surface in which a rounded lump bulged. He was trying to grasp the sight when the lump into which he'd poked his finger blinked again and glared at him. Even though it had already begun to wither and grow discoloured, he knew it all too well.

He swept the calendar onto the floor and trampled on it, feeling more than cardboard give way underfoot. He might have been stamping on a mask, but not an empty one. Once it was crushed absolutely flat he watched to be sure that nothing crept from beneath it, not even a stain, and then he retreated to the bedroom.

Suppose he'd set the madness free? He didn't like to keep the presents so close to the remains of the calendar. In any case it might be wise to set off for his old house – he was afraid it could take him some time to find. At least he hadn't undressed for bed. He clutched the presents to his chest and hurried onto the balcony, beyond which a greyish light was starting to take hold of the world. He gazed at his door until he succeeded in fixing at least the shape of the number in his mind. 'You're the one with your tail hanging down,' he said.

It was daylight now, however grey, and he did his best to hasten through the streets. He shouldn't be distracted by trying to count Christmas trees in windows, let alone Christmas lights. Today's date ought to be enough for him. 'Two and five and you're alive,' he told some children before they fled across the road. He mustn't frighten anyone. Among the reasons he'd retired had been the fear of needing to resemble Smart so as to teach.

He came to his old road at last, only to feel as if someone had gone ahead of him to jumble all the numbers. He just had to locate his old home, not remember which number it was.

He didn't have to count his way to it, and he was surprised how soon he found the wrought-iron porch. He hugged the presents – one, two and another – as he thumbed the bell push. 'Two and five and you're alive,' he carolled until the boy ran to open the door. Summers was about to hand him the presents when the boy turned his back. 'I don't know what he wants,' he called. 'It's some old man.'

JOHN LLEWELLYN PROBERT

THE SECONDARY HOST

THERE ISN'T MUCH time. Blood is already spattering the paper on which I am writing. I have no idea how many minutes I have left and yet there is so much to say, so much I need to warn people about. Already the pain that sears my face distracts me from setting down this account. Perhaps it would be better if the world did not know. It would be simpler if I just lay here and allowed myself to die. I am finding it difficult to focus, both because of the burning agony and the other thing that I cannot talk about . . . yet. I must begin at the beginning, or as close to it as I feel is relevant. There – the morphine has made the pain a little more bearable, for the moment at least.

'To travel is better than to arrive.' I seem to remember being quoted that somewhere. Whether or not that was the author's intended meaning doesn't matter. Words and phrases corrupt with the passing of time, but until I came to Zanzibar I would never have known that words themselves can be corrupting and destructive, when formed by the right kind of tongue, issued from the right kind of lips.

Torn from the right kind of throat.

I stood there on Stone Town dock, pondering that phrase with regard to cancelled flights, missed connections, and numbers of days lost in innumerable sleepover hotel rooms and figured that I hadn't done too badly in taking just under three days to get here from England. At my feet were two suitcases. The pale blue Samsonite was filled with personal possessions. The other, a battered black affair I was intending to leave behind, was filled with medical supplies I had brought from my hospital – items which could still be put to good use in a country where venous cannulas and suture materials a few months past their expiry date could still be used to administer drugs and stitch wounds when the alternative was no treatment at all.

I took a deep breath. The air was redolent with spices from the markets across the way, but tainted with the stink of petrol from the motor boats moored nearby, the musky odour of the flavourings a veneer for the grim functionality, the gritty ugliness that lay beneath. To my left, along the seafront of the island's west coast, lay the strip of bars and nightclubs that they had still been in the process of building during my last visit over ten years ago. I had taken the first ferry across from Dar Es Salaam that morning, having been stranded there late last night after delays to my connecting flight from Kilimanjaro. I was tired and fed up and could have used a drink. In fact under the circumstances it was probably a good thing that the bars were closed.

A battered pickup truck with the works 'Amir's Cabs' unprofessionally stencilled on the side took me the short distance through the winding streets of the old part of Stone Town to my hotel. On my way there I saw several of the large, intricate, and ornately carved wooden doors that are unique to the country. The beggars crouched beside them (there were so many more now than last time), a grim modern-day contrast to their old world elegance. Again I experienced the same feeling as I had on the jetty – that mixture of beauty nestling beside the grim reminders of everyday life.

With so much having changed it was a delight to discover

Mazson's Hotel pretty much the same as it had been ten years ago. Tucked away within an unobtrusive courtyard, it was an unassuming older brother to the vast modern constructs where most of the holidaymakers stayed. The whitewashed walls and varnished boards of it veranda were the first welcoming thing I had encountered since my arrival. I was given an upstairs room, from the doorway of which I could look onto the courtyard. As soon as I had unpacked I lay on the bed, intending to spend my first days back on the island asleep, with possibly a break for food and scotch a little later in the day.

It was not to be.

The trilling of the bedside telephone shook me from a troubled sleep filled with nightmare imagery no doubt influenced by my journey. I looked at my watch to see it was only nine am – I had been asleep for just two hours.

'Hello?' My voice was a dry croak but I ignored the water in the decanter at my bedside. I had learned before to my cost that when in these climes it is best to stick to the bottled stuff.

'Dr Kendrick?'

I nodded and then rasped an acknowledgement.

'You are here at last, then?'

I resisted the urge to reply that no, I was still stuck in Dar, but from the man's tone I couldn't tell if he had much of a sense of humour. Instead I explained I had just arrived.

'Good!' The voice brightened considerably. 'Can you come to the hospital this morning?'

'I'm not really awake,' I replied.

'But there is someone here who wants to meet you,' the voice continued. 'Come as soon as you can.'

It didn't sound as if I had much choice. I asked who was speaking only to be rewarded with the click of a disconnected line. I knew from past experience that 'someone' could mean the island's president and his entourage, complete with television crew to ensure the event of an English doctor coming to the island was as widely publicised as possible, and so I rang room service and asked for lots of coffee as I prepared to survive on raw energy for yet another day.

The Mnazi Mmoja Hospital ('It means One Coconut Tree,' Mohammed Makinde, the hospital's director, had explained to me on my previous visit) had been built in the early 1960s, and was as forbidding a block of communist concrete as one might expect for a building that had, until the relinquishing of power, been named after Lenin. The main building's grim oblong stood flanked by the sea on one side and the buildings of Old Stone Town on the other. If anything, the passage of time had made it look like more of an anachronism than ever.

The cool interior still stank of a familiar mixture – the raw antiseptic of carbolic mingled with the sickly sweet odour of infected wounds and rotting flesh. Many of the patients here had suffered trauma that had been sufficient to disable but not severe enough to kill, and open wounds, even with the best surgical care, often did not do well in a climate where heat and humidity could cause infection to run riot.

I stood in the hospital's foyer, the walls the same sickly shade of dark green, the fluorescent strip lighting still insufficient to cast away the shadows. There were plenty of windows but even on a bright morning like this the building was still good at scaring away sunshine.

'Dr Kendrick?' A broad-faced African man, whose smudge of black moustache on his upper lip was the only hair on his otherwise gleaming head, emerged from the door to my left, gave me the widest if not the most sincere of smiles, and clasped my hand a little too hard for comfort. 'I am Zuberi Amadi, the director of Mnazi Mmoja.'

I frowned. 'But where's Mohammed Makinde?' I asked.

Amadi's face fell. 'I am sorry to have to tell you this when you have only just arrived, but Mohammed has become very unwell. Under the circumstances it was thought best that he be allowed to rest, far away from the job that had been causing him too many worries.'

I looked behind me. Across the street was Mohammed's house. I hadn't noticed on my way here but it looked locked up. 'He's not at home then?'

Amadi shook his head. 'He has gone to the north of the island to recuperate.' He put a meaty hand around my shoulders, causing me to tense. 'Relax my friend! Everything else here is much the same.' He eyed my suitcase. 'I see you have brought us fresh supplies – good! Let me relieve you of them.' He snapped his fingers and a beautiful young woman appeared. She brushed past me to get to the battered black bag, and as she did so my senses were momentarily swept away by a the aromas of cinnamon and sandalwood; a subtle mixture that seemed uniquely hers and made me want to follow her. She gave me the kind of look men have been known to kill for, then took the case and went off somewhere upstairs with it. 'Now,' he said, leading me firmly and not so gently, 'I have someone for you to meet waiting in my office.'

Mohammed had never had an office, and as Amadi led me into the room he had emerged from earlier I recognised it as the old X-Ray suite. Not anymore. The ageing fluoroscopy equipment had been moved out and a large, chipped wooden desk moved in. Several chairs, their worn blue plastic coverings ripped in places and leaking yellow foam completed this untidy collection of furniture. The man who had been sitting on the one closest to the desk got to his feet as I entered.

'May I present Mr Andreas van der Merwe.' Amadi's eyes seemed to glitter with pride as he introduced me.

Whoever I had been expecting, it had most certainly not been a Caucasian man in a crumpled white linen suit. His open-necked shirt bore a little grime around the inside of the collar, but the hand he held out to greet me with was clean, the nails manicured.

'I have heard a lot about you,' he said, his voice betraying the slightest hint of a South African accent, 'and I am pleased to meet you at last.'

'It's a pleasure,' I replied, returning his brisk handshake, 'although I must confess I'm surprised that you've heard anything about me at all.'

'Mohammed spoke very highly of you before he became... ill,' said Amadi from behind me.

I looked from one man to the other, trying to work out the politest way of finding out what I needed to know. 'So if Mohammed is no longer here,' I said, 'which of you is now the acting director of this hospital?'

'Oh that would be Zuberi,' replied van der Merwe with a laugh. 'I'm not medical. I wouldn't have a rat's chance in hell of knowing how to run this place.'

Somehow the way he said that suggested it wasn't exactly true. 'And what is your profession, Mr van de Merwe?' I asked.

'I'm an anthropologist,' was his reply. 'I've been coming here on and off for a couple of years now, studying local culture, history.'

'From the way Stone Town has changed since I was last here I'd say the local culture consists mainly of cheap bars and desperate nightclubs,' I said with a grin.

It was not returned. 'My studies have been confined to the inner part of Zanzibar, Dr Kendrick. The very centre, in fact. I believe you have some familiarity with Eusi Ngome?'

I had been taken on a tour of the island by Mohammed on my last visit here, and it only took a moment to recall the place van der Merwe was talking about.

Eusi Ngome – the Black Castle.

Actually, Mohammed had explained, it had most likely been a temple in aeons past, but the locals had given it that name anyway. I remembered the crumbling masonry and teetering towers of the place he had taken me to, buried deep in the forest at the centre of the island. When I had asked him why it had acquired such a name he had merely shrugged. 'Probably mothers keeping their children away from a dangerous building,' he had said.

'You spent some time there yourself, I understand,' van der Merwe persisted, bringing me back into the present.

I nodded. It was all coming back to me now. I had wanted to see something of Zanzibar's past, something from way before the involvement of communism, even before Muslim rule if possible. 'Have you nothing really ancient for me to look at?' I had asked, citing the medieval castles of my own country as examples.

It had taken some time before Mohammed had finally admitted to the temple's existence, citing as his reason for hesitation that it was difficult to get to, and that the place itself was risky. The huge, weathered masonry blocks were apt to shift at any time, he had said, and throughout the ground there were said to be sinkholes down which people had fallen to their deaths.

But I had insisted and so we had gone, leaving Mohammed's pickup truck on one of the narrow dirt tracks that wound their way through the forest, and making the rest of the trip on foot. It took us nearly an hour of following tiny paths through increasingly thick jungle before we reached our goal.

And what a goal it had turned out to be.

I found it difficult to believe that such a place was not described in the guidebooks, but Mohammed had explained that it was considered too much of a deathtrap by the authorities for its whereabouts to be too well known.

I had expected the crumbling stone ruins to be overgrown with creepers and vines from the surrounding jungle, the almost obsidian rock to be obscured with a thousand years' worth of gradual encroachment from the surrounding foliage, but that was not the case at all.

'The forest does not like it,' Mohammed had said, his voice deadly serious. 'It stays away.'

The remains of the Black Castle covered an area about the size of a football field. But this was no playground. I was about to begin exploring when Mohammed stopped me and reminded me about the sinkholes.

I regarded the stretch of bare hard-packed earth before me. 'It looks safe enough to me,' I said.

Mohammed had shaken his head, taking a stone from nearby and tossing it into the clearing. It hit the earth with a dull thud. I watched expectantly for something to happen.

'See?' I said when nothing did. 'This bit seems to be safe enough.'

I had taken three paces when I felt the ground give way beneath me.

It occurred with such frightening rapidity that I had no time to leap free. I threw myself forward, scrabbling at the edges of the pit that had opened up as I began to slide down. As my fingers finally gained purchase a little way inside and I almost cried with relief, I also noticed a very curious thing.

The pit into which I had fallen was lined with black bricks.

'Are you OK?' Mohammed's face appeared at the rim, his worried expression turning to relief as he realised I was just inside. I reassured him that I was but that I wasn't sure how long I would be able to hang on.

I could hear Mohammed rushing around outside, hopefully looking for a vine strong enough to cast down and help pull me out. I was only a few feet inside and so there was enough daylight for me to see that I appeared to be hanging in an artificially constructed shaft, lined with moss-encrusted brown stone. Below me the pit swiftly disappeared into blackness.

What on earth could the purpose of something like this have been?

There was a noise from beneath me.

I can't begin to describe it, and remembering it now still turns my insides to water the way it did then. It was not a natural noise, by which I mean it wasn't the crashing of waves or the grinding of rocks, and yet somehow there were elements of those two things in it, and so much more besides. As if some vast and ancient slumbering beast that both lived in the rock and was part of it had been disturbed by my actions.

It felt as if the depths of the earth were growling at me.

And it was coming closer.

'Mohammed!' I screamed. 'Get me out!'

I began to kick at the sides of the pit to try and lever myself up, but my thrashing just made me slide down further.

'Hurry, Mohammed!' I cried as I clung to the damp brick, the tearing growls from beneath growing ever louder.

I looked down and for a second caught a glimpse of flailing suckered tendrils reaching up to ensnare me, tiny barbs on their wriggling tips ready to plunge into my skin. I cannot possibly describe the sense of relief I felt as I saw the vine drop beside me. My sheer terror of the thing below meant that I didn't stop to think whether or not the vine would hold my weight as I grabbed it and felt myself being pulled to safety, my bare arms scraping across the stone and leaving streaks of blood behind.

Once I was out Mohammed looked at my bloodied arms and hands with horror but I assured him I was all right as I dragged him away from the place, urging him to run.

'There's something down there!' I screamed as he followed me. 'I don't know what it is, but it's huge!'

And then the strangest thing of all happened. Mohammed looked at me with something approaching awe, and when he spoke it was with reverence rather than horror.

'You woke Him up,' he said. 'He wanted you.'

At least, that's what I thought he said. Mohammed refused to be drawn on the matter further, and by the time we got back to Stone Town he was behaving as if nothing had happened.

'It is good to have you back here,' said van der Merwe, Amadi nodding behind him. The two of them seemed almost excessively enthusiastic about my presence but at the time I put my impressions down to exhaustion. 'Will you be lecturing at all while you are here?'

I nodded. 'I gave a talk on Bilharzia last time that went down quite well,' I replied, 'so I thought I would give a presentation on some of the latest research into it.'

Van der Merwe's eyes lit up at the mention of that particular tropical infection. 'Ah, yes,' he said, '*Schistosomiasis haematobium* is the organism which causes it, isn't that right?' I nodded, wondering why someone non-medical would be sufficiently interested in it to be able to reel off its Latin name. And that wasn't all he seemed to know. 'An organism that begins its life as an egg shed from the lining of the human bladder, passing into fresh water where it hatches and enters the body of a specific type of snail.'

'*Bulinus globosus*,' I interjected, determined not to be outdone in the Latin stakes.

'I forget,' said van der Merwe. 'But what I do remember is that while it lives inside the snail it completes the first stage of its life cycle, becoming a form which can then infect humans. Remind me,' he said in a way that suggested he didn't need reminding at all, 'how long does one need to be in contact with infected water for the organism to penetrate the skin?'

'About ten seconds,' I replied.

'Ten seconds – yes, of course. I've always found that life cycle fascinating. Without the snail – known as the secondary host, I believe?' I nodded. 'Without the secondary host this creature would not be able to infect humans and it would die. Quite, quite fascinating.'

I yawned and apologised, explaining how tired I was. Despite that, van de Merwe was insistent that I come to dinner at his house that evening. I blurted an acceptance, bade farewell to both him and Amadi, and made my way back along the dusty street to my hotel, wondering quite what was going on. I had found nothing so far to be as I had been expecting it and my disorientation continued when I took out the key to my room only to find the door standing open and someone sitting on the bed within.

It was the girl who had taken the suitcase from me in the hospital.

I had thought she was attractive before, but now I could see that she was quite beautiful. Luxuriously rich, long, black hair framed a face whose olive skin suggested her origin was west of here. Far west. Perhaps Brazil or Argentina. Despite the fact that it was still morning I needed sleep, and most of all I needed time to myself, but there was something in those eyes that prevented me from acting indignant at her presence. Besides, I have always found that, when in doubt, it is best to be polite and charming.

She told me her name was Aeliya. I ventured a hello and when it looked as if she was about to say more I added, 'I'm afraid I'm not really in the mood for any more talking just now.'

She crossed legs that were barely concealed beneath the simple white linen skirt she wore that was fashionably slashed to mid-thigh.

'I know that,' she said. 'But I couldn't let you just walk into the trap they're setting for you tonight.'

That woke me up. 'Trap?' Under normal circumstances I would have thought the idea ridiculous, but right now anything seemed possible.

'They want you,' she said, getting to her feet. 'You're special.'

'Why?'

She was close to me now, almost thrillingly so. 'I don't know,' she said. 'But I heard them talking, and it has something to do with what you did when you were here before. More than that I cannot say.'

'And why are you warning me?'

She smiled and it lit up the room better than the sunshine trying to bleed its way through the half-drawn blind. 'Because I like you, and because I liked your friend – the one who hurt himself so horribly.'

I frowned. 'Mohammed?' she nodded. 'How did he hurt himself? Why is he no longer the director?'

'He is no longer the director because of what happened to him,' she replied.

'You mean his injury?'

'I mean he was tested and he was found wanting.' Now she was glaring at me. 'And they will do the same to you, and if you are found wanting you will end up like him.'

'What do you mean?' I said, gripping her by the wrist as she tried to leave. 'Where is he?'

She looked at me and now the sunshine in her eyes had been replaced with fear. 'Believe me,' she said, 'you do not want to know.'

'Believe me,' I said, my grip tightening, 'I do.'

I wasn't expecting her to kiss me, and thinking back now it was probably the desperate act of a woman who cared about what might happen to me and didn't know what else to do. In the end it was I who broke it off, knowing full well that any longer and we would be doing more than just kissing. I was still savouring the sweet taste of her on my lips as she wrote the address down for me and, at my insistence, drew a map as well. As her footsteps echoed down the stairs I studied the scrap of paper and wondered why on earth my old friend had decided to take up residence on the northernmost tip of the island.

To say that my first impressions of Mohammed Makinde's new home were worrying would be a vast understatement.

I'm sure it didn't help that during the twenty mile journey from Stone Town to Ras Nungwi it had begun to rain – great gouts of water that quickly reduced the road to mud and visibility to almost nil. I shook my head and looked at the darkening sky. I was already regretting having set out so late but I wanted to know what had happened to the friend I had made all those years ago. I had also been desperate for sleep, and something told me I would need all my wits about me for van de Merwe's dinner party. Now, looking at my watch, I wondered if I would make it at all.

'You could try using the windscreen wipers,' I suggested to my driver, only to be rewarded with a shake of his head.

'Don't work,' he said. 'Been meaning to get them fixed.'

This didn't seem to deter him, however, and the final five miles was the most terrifying road journey I have ever experienced. I was just able to make out the beach huts at Ras Nungwi as we rattled past it, travelling on until we reached a modern-looking complex that didn't look like a house at all.

'You sure you want to go in there?' my driver asked as I handed him his fee.

'Yes,' I replied, as if it was any business of his. 'My friend is staying there.'

The driver looked concerned. 'You mean he is an inmate?'

That made me pause. I looked up at the imposing white walls and the tiny windows which would admit light but which were too small to allow a fully grown man to escape. 'Is it a prison?' I asked.

The driver shook his head and then tapped a finger against his temple. 'For the sick – you know?'

I did, just as I understood how much Zanzibar had changed since my last visit, when this building hadn't even existed. 'How long has it been here?' I asked.

'A couple of years,' was the reply, which could have meant anything. My attempts to find out just how long was met with a shrug of the shoulders that didn't really surprise me. The car drove away in the pouring rain as I rushed to the door, only to realise it was more like a gate, the heavy vertical bars presumably operated by whoever could be contacted by the intercom to the right.

I explained who I was and held up my ID to the camera, wondering all the time where the money had come from to build such a place. When all I got was an angry dismissal I pressed the buzzer again and this time held up my UK passport.

There was a pause, and then a clunk as the gate was unlocked. Once I had passed through it slammed behind me and there was another clunk as the gate was locked again.

I found myself in a courtyard surrounded by white walls. A concrete path stretched across a patch of dry earth on which a few withered plants obviously intended to flourish had resolutely failed to do so. On the opposite side a door was standing open and an unhappy-looking nurse who must have weighed close to eighteen stone was blocking the way.

'What do you want?' she asked.

'I've come from Mnazi Mmoja to see Mohammed Makinde,' I said. 'I understand he is now resident here.' I hoped mention of the hospital would gain me access.

'He is fine,' said the nurse. 'He does not need any visitors.'

'Nevertheless, I would appreciate it if you would take me to him,' I said in my most authoritative tones, raising my head at a slight angle along with a brow. 'Now, if you please.'

The nurse looked taken aback as she fingered the ring of keys attached to her belt. I began to stride purposefully towards her, half expecting the door to be slammed in my face. Instead I found myself following her down a dark corridor, the only light coming from a narrow window at its far end. At regular intervals along this corridor I could see white doors, featureless except for the Judas holes that had been set into them at eye level. The nurse didn't stop until we reached the last one on the left.

'How long?' she asked as she rattled a key in the lock.

'Twenty minutes,' I replied, my expression impassive while inside I was wondering just what the hell was going on. Any sign of my true feelings would, I knew, result in my immediate eviction, and so I did my best to keep calm as I was allowed entry to what turned out to be Mohammed's cell.

It did not escape my notice that the door was locked behind me once I had entered. The cell was narrow, its walls as white as the rest of the place, and there was a tiny window at the far end, beneath which someone was sitting, their back to me. It was much colder here than outside, but I couldn't tell if it was the air temperature or merely my own fear that had caused the sudden chill. The click of the key in the lock distracted me momentarily before my attention returned to the figure seated at the bare desk.

'Mohammed?' I breathed, taking a step forward.

Click . . . click.

His hands were still, clasped on the desk in front of him, but still that strange noise seemed to be coming from him. I came closer and called his name again.

Click . . . tap . . . tap . . . click.

Where was that noise coming from? My mounting concern led me to lay a hand on his shoulder, and when that had little effect I shook him and then turned him to face me.

My God I wish I hadn't.

Click . . . click . . . tap . . . tap . . . click.

My eyes filled with tears as I beheld what was left of the face of my friend. Because the poor demented soul I saw before me was Mohammed Makinde, or rather what remained of him.

Someone – I dread to think that it was he who had perpetrated this atrocity upon himself – had cut away his lips, had in fact removed all the skin and muscle from the lower half of his face so that all that now remained was hardened scar tissue. When he opened his mouth I could see that his tongue was gone, too.

The only way he could communicate was by clicking his teeth.

It took him a few moments to realise who I was, and when he did his eyes filled with tears. He began to push me away, towards the door, all the time making that awful clicking sound, his teeth chattering faster and faster and so vigorously I was worried he was going to break off the few that still remained in their sockets.

This commotion was loud enough to attract the attention of the nurse who must have been waiting outside for me. I heard the rattle of keys again and as the door swung open I glared at her.

'What's happened to him?' I demanded. This time she refused to even acknowledge me, instead motioning to the two men who had accompanied her. I recognised one as the driver who had brought me to this place as they manhandled me out of there.

'What are you doing?' I shouted as they dragged me back the way I had come.

From behind me the nurse was speaking now, but what she said made little sense. 'I was wrong. Forgive me. You have not yet seen Him,' she said.

I shouted more protests but the grip on my arms was firm. As they took me through the gate she said one more thing that at the time made even less sense.

'He waits for you to save us.'

~

It wasn't long before I realised where they were taking me. Deeper and deeper into the forest we drove, until the path became so narrow that the truck had to be abandoned and we continued on foot. There was no question of my escaping, I thought, as I eyed the machete my driver had rescued from the vehicle's back seat.

Eventually we came to the clearing, to the temple, to Eusi Ngome, where Andreas van der Merwe as waiting for me.

He was not alone.

'I'm sorry I missed the dinner party,' I said. 'But I presume I would have ended up here anyway.'

'The mountain would not go to Mohammed,' he said with a trace of a smile, 'and so we have brought you to us.'

I looked around me. Now, in the twilight, I could see that we were surrounded by a circle of people standing shoulder to shoulder around the perimeter of the clearing. And they were not just ordinary people. From their general appearance I could see that van de Merwe had recruited the derelicts and beggars of Zanzibar to his cause. I even thought I recognised some of them from the dock this morning.

'Always the easy ones to bring into any cult,' I said, gesturing around me.

Van de Merwe's eyes narrowed. 'Let me assure you, Dr Kendrick, that this is not just any cult. Besides, they wanted to meet you, and who am I to deny the wishes of my followers?'

It was true. As I looked around now I could see the assembled multitude regarding me with some kind of holy awe. There were so many of them that I was grateful they kept their distance.

I only started to get scared when they began to shuffle towards me.

'Enough!' Their leader held up a hand and to my relief they

stopped. 'Dr Kendrick is here for a purpose – to meet that which he awoke during his previous visit here.'

Now the group fell back, its members whispering and muttering to themselves and not taking their eyes off me for a moment. Van de Merwe stepped to one side to reveal the black hole in the ground behind him. It was the pit I had fallen into all those years ago.

'You woke Him,' he said. 'You were the one He had been waiting for. Now He wishes to make peace with you and through you with all humankind. He wishes you to take His message to the world.'

I took a step back, only to feel the strong grip of the men who had brought me here force me forward until the toes of my shoes were at the rim of the pit. A hand in my hair forced me to look downward.

To see a thing of horror.

Even now I cannot describe it accurately. It must have lived down there a very long time and fed a great deal to be the size that it was – a size that prevented it from ever making its way up the brick-lined passage.

'It was once a tower,' said van de Merwe, as if that explained anything, 'but that was a long time ago, and He has been waiting even longer than that for the right one. For his secondary host.'

I continued to stare at the mass of undulating colours, at the amorphous shape that extended fronds and tendrils towards me and then almost immediately snatched them back again into its bulk.

Then its eye opened.

At that moment, as it beheld me with that awful ochre pupil, I felt something pass between us. Something powerful and ancient and hungry. Hungry not for food, but for souls, for belief.

For faith.

I closed my eyes but by then it was already too late. Its power was in me now, and was a part of me as sure as if I had been born with it.

When I looked again the creature had gone.

'He is pleased!' van de Merwe turned to his congregation and made his announcement with arms raised, to be rewarded by a sea of beatific obeisance. He turned back to me. 'And now the Chosen One must see what he is capable of!'

He pointed at a young man who couldn't have been more than twenty and beckoned him towards us. The rest of the crowd stayed still, held by the power of van de Merwe's words. When the young man was six feet away, van der Merwe ordered him to stop.

'Talk to him.'

I frowned. 'What?'

Van Der Merwe pointed at the boy. 'Talk to him. Say something. Anything.'

The situation was becoming increasingly absurd. I faced the young man and said the first thing that came into my head.

'Mary had a little lamb,' I recited – slowly, deliberately, and very sardonically.

The effect of my words on the young man was instantaneous, startling, and horrifying. He smiled, and his eyes glazed over so that he assumed the expression of someone under deep hypnosis. He swayed a little, and when he spoke it was in a serene monotone that was far more frightening than if he had screamed.

'I show my face to you, my Lord,' he said.

I snorted. What was going on? Had he been drugged? Did it matter that all he wanted to do was just look at me?

Then the boy raised his hands to his face, and I saw that the nails of both thumbs, allowed to grow long for weeks, had been fashioned into barbed hooks. With little ceremony he dug both thumbnails into the soft tissue beneath his chin, raking them across the skin so that for one horrific moment I thought he was trying to cut his throat.

But it was not his throat that he wished to mutilate.

Slowly, and with some difficulty, the young man tore the skin from his face, peeling it upwards until he reached his scalp. Then, with a final gouge of those awful nails what he had ripped away was thrown to the ground.

'My face for you, my Lord,' he hissed through lipless teeth as his shining eyeballs looked towards the opening of the pit.

Now the others were coming forward and making supplication, and I could see that they, too, had grown their nails long. Some had encouraged the growth on every finger. All of them were smiling, all were raising those terrible claws to their faces, and all of them wanted me to talk to them.

I began to look for some means of escape.

'It doesn't matter where you go,' said van der Merwe, 'and it doesn't matter what you say. All anyone will hear is the Call. You are the Messiah. Or, if you prefer a more medical analogy,' and here his voice became a sneer, 'you are the secondary host – unaffected by the disease that you spread but helpless to do anything but allow it to achieve its goal. I tried with Mohammed because he was here with you that day. I tried with others, but they were abject failures. The Call needed you and now that you are finally here, the whole world will listen to its cry.'

'Who are you?' I gasped, trying my best to ignore the horrifying self-mutilation that was taking place all around me with every word I spoke.

Van der Merwe glanced back at the pit. 'I am the Call made flesh,' he said. 'I am part of that which you awoke all those years ago. But the Call cannot work directly. It needs a conduit, a catalyst, a means of making humankind understand and see its shining light of purity.' He was smiling now. 'It needs you.'

I ran. At the time I thought I was swift enough to outwit them, that it was sheer good fortune that allowed me to make my way unimpeded to the car to find the keys in the ignition. I drove back to my hotel, ignoring the concierge's quizzical look as I dashed in and took the stairs two at a time. I had no idea what I was going to do but I needed time to think.

When I got to my room Aeliya was waiting for me.

'Are you all right?' she asked.

'No,' I replied, closing the door behind me. 'I'm not. I don't know what I've just seen but I do know that I need to get away from here as quickly as possible. Can you help me?'

But Aeliya was no longer listening. As soon as I had started to speak her expression had changed to one of total serenity. She picked up my bedside alarm clock and smashed it against the wall. Then she brought one of the fragments of fractured plastic up to her chin.

'So I may see you better, my Lord,' she said, before digging the point of it into her face.

I tried to stop her cutting away those beautiful lips that had only all too recently been pressed to mine, but she was surprisingly strong, and very determined. By the time she had finished there were blood blotches on the bed and scraps of her beautiful skin smeared across the wall.

She gave me one last, lidless look with those lovely bloodstained eyes of hers, and then left, no doubt to join those gathered around the pit.

Which brings me almost up to date in my writing of this account. Except of course for the part where I took a scalpel from my medical bag and, in front of the mirror and with great care, removed my lips. Mohammed must have done something similar to himself and I now realise that the clicking and tapping of the man's teeth was his way of trying to communicate with me by Morse code.

But I couldn't allow myself to communicate, even like that. Anything that came out of my mouth would cause whoever heard it to act the way Aeliya had, and those wretched souls in the forest. That is why once I had cut the flesh away I took a length of strong non-absorbable suture material on a hand-held needle and, bracing myself as I held the curved pointed steel in my right hand, proceeded to sew shut what remained of my mouth.

I pray that it will be enough.

I am the secondary host, van der Merwe said, the way by which this disease, religion, or whatever it is, can spread to the rest of humankind, just like the tiny schistosomes need a freshwater snail to complete part of their life cycle before they can infect humans.

Let this, then, be my final testament. I cannot allow myself to live, for if some reason the sutures should break or God forbid someone should come here and cut them free then humanity is lost. At least it seems to be only through speech that I communicate this pestilence and I thank God that it is not through the Call is love the Call is truth show your true face to the Call the Call is love show your true face show your face for love show your face SHOW YOUR FACE SHOW YOUR FACE SH—

MURIEL GRAY

THE GARSCUBE CREATIVE WRITING GROUP

THE ENDING WAS good. The wrestler finds his slut mother in bed with the two men from the bar, and smashes one against the wall before throttling the other. Yes, it worked just fine. Graham admitted to himself that perhaps the prose required a little more elegance, maybe some subtle recalibration of pace, but on the whole it was satisfactory.

He picked up the three laden bin bags and swung them into the back of the Polaris Ranger, its idling engine chugging in the dark like a fishing boat, and pulled his work gauntlets back up over his wrists. The smell from the bags was gruesome. What new, inventive suffering had today's veterinary students inflicted on their helpless, animal captives? The bags were heavy. Whole bodies perhaps, as well as organs. Graham climbed onto the bench seat, coughed once against the stench, pushed the truck into gear and trundled slowly towards the incinerator building. Maybe the wrestler should kill the mother too. Smother her. Crush her. Silence her. Punish her. But then again, maybe not. The strength of the story demanded that she's kept alive to suffer. Enough. The ending was good. Best left.

Graham always wore a tie for the group. As the furnace fired up behind the metal boxing he mused on which one from the dozen he owned he would favour tonight. The tartan one was useful. Looked casual. Not too dressy. But this evening his mind was steering more towards the lilac daisies. He celebrated the fact that men could now wear pinks and pastels and flowered shirts, without being considered homosexual. It was fashionable. It felt good. It felt free. Being the only man in the group already rendered him self-conscious each time he took his seat. Dressing smartly steeled his nerves against those often deathly stares of indifference that met him on entering and scraping his chair into the tight half circle. Tonight, however, he felt strong. He'd noted Sonia's contempt last week that he hadn't finished his chapter, and now he had it. An ending. A good one. She could scowl all she liked but he was going to read it out with confidence and be justifiably proud. He threw the last bag into the hatch and pressed the button.

Professor Hanson raised an apologetic hand through the window as Graham stood at the open lab block door and rattled the keys in his boiler suit pocket. The lecturer's face suggested guilt that the janitor was once again being kept waiting to lock up, and Graham watched pitilessly as the man fumbled with papers, scattering them as he hurried to make his tardy exit. Graham used the time to hone his Booker prize acceptance speech. He would be gracious. He would thank all those who deserved it, and then surprise the audience with introducing a political edge. It would depend on the events of the day of course, but he'd have an opinion that would make the front pages of all the broadsheets. 'Kearney uses prize to plea for striking firemen.' Or maybe 'Bestselling author of *Slammed* scorns government u turn on debt.' Something like that. Something that would touch people. Make them realise that not only was he the finest writer of his generation, but also the boldest, the most controversial.

Hanson exploded from the swing doors, nearly dropping his folder. Graham held the door for him.

'Thanks Graham. Sorry, sorry, sorry. Lost track of time.'

'Not a problem Professor.'

He scurried away then stopped, remembering.

'The lights have gone in the male student changing rooms.'

Graham remained impassive. He enjoyed keeping Hanson guessing as to whether he was annoyed or not. He was good at it.

'Not a problem.'

'Good night then.'

'Night.'

The gangly, awkward man waved a hand and crashed on through the fading light to his car. Graham watched him go, then peered into the building. He weighed up the time it would take to replace the lights and decided the chore could wait until tomorrow. It was group night. He flicked the mains switch off at the door and locked up.

It didn't matter how many times he'd been through this, it never seemed to change. They were silent when he entered. All four of them. He knew they'd been discussing him, could see it in their eyes.

A brief muttered hello as he adjusted his tie and seated himself in the usual place at the end. There was seldom any preamble. The Garscube Creative Writing Group took itself very seriously indeed. Graham waited patiently as the others ran through their work. He listened politely, nodding, cupping his chin in his hands as they droned out their dreary, stale ideas, his mind drifting as their voices merged into one low background hum of mediocrity. He clapped at the end of Fiona's piece, if only for something to do until it was his turn.

It didn't deserve applause. Both her story, and the self-consciously arch reading of it were lame. He, on the other hand, would dazzle. He would make them see this week that he was better than all of them. Cleverer. Funnier. More astute in his observations and original in his style. Shereen finished off with some tiresome cliché about pre-partition India that made him press his fingernails into his palm in irritation, and suddenly there was an expectant silence. It was his turn at last. All eyes on him.

Graham cleared his throat, took the pages from his satchel, and calmly, slowly, began to read.

As he knew she would, the girl was in her usual seat on the bus. Graham watched her in the reflection of the glass, a ploy to make her think he was looking away from her, out of the window, instead of studying her closely as he was now. He watched as she pushed the spectacles up her squat, shiny nose each time she turned a page. He followed her hand as she lowered it to scratch at one of her generous thighs, pushing against the tight fabric of leggings that looked a size too small. He delighted in the tiny, almost imperceptible motions her small, cupid bow mouth made in its plump face as something in the book moved her. She always got on at Maryhill Road, and off again at Anniesland, so there was little time. He knew she sometimes stole a look at him. She had a furtive glance from beneath her glasses, tiny and fast, but not too fast for him. He'd worked hard to make sure his book, the one that was always ostentatiously laid on his lap, was interesting, something she wouldn't have heard of but might look up later. Last week it had been Thomas Pynchon. The week before, R. Chetwynd-Hayes. But tonight the graft he'd put in watching her in the library had been fruitful, and as anticipated she was reading the Henry James she'd borrowed. His own copy of *Portrait of a Lady* was placed casually on his lap. He watched her carefully, trying not to smile with satisfaction as her small eyes flicked to him, to the book on his knee, then back up to his face with interest.

Her stop was three away. He waited as the bus pulled up, poured some passengers onto the pavement, then moved off. It had to be now. He stood, rising to get off. It was one stop before hers. No looking back. He tucked his book under his arm and walked casually to the front of the bus. Graham felt her behind him before he saw her. Her hand was on the metal pole beneath his. He could feel its warmth.

He walked no more than fifty yards before she caught up. Impressive. How was she going to do this he wondered? Her pace quickened and she overtook him, nonchalant, though the fast pace had taken its toll on her heavy frame and she was already a little out of breath. She dropped her book. Graham almost laughed out loud. Was she living in some Victorian fantasy? What next? A dropped hanky?

He picked up the Henry James and wiped the mud gently from the cover.

She ordered cappuccino. He ordered tea and a pastry. As the waitress set it down with clumsy clattering Graham regarded his reflection in the darkened cafe window. He was handsome. A catch. Look how beautiful his jaw line was, with its dusting of carefully trimmed stubble. Look at his deep set brown eyes and heavily lashed lids, his gently curling dark brown hair that he'd fashioned down the nape of his neck to accentuate its sinewy strength. Actually, maybe he was more than handsome. Maybe he was beautiful. Think how that face would look on the cover of *The Observer* magazine, looking back over one shoulder, wearing his loose denim shirt, and a fine silver chain round his neck. So what if she was plain and heavy? Maybe this time she'd be the one. The girl who would understand him. See past his physical beauty to the genius in him. Really know him.

Her name was Moira, and she loved historical fiction as well as modern. She wanted to be a writer. Of course she did. Why did she think she was here? She lit up when he told her he was one too. He talked of the ecstasy of plotting, the temporary schizophrenia of living in another character, of the task of keeping the reader looking in one direction while you, the author, snuck up on them from another direction and sprung the ending.

She laughed, she listened, she argued. She liked to know where a story was going. Enjoyed the familiarity of a well told tale where everything came out as you'd hoped. He listened politely, admiring the whiteness of her small even teeth that transformed her face when she laughed or smiled.

They discussed Dickens and Eyre, Shelley and Le Fanu, then he asked her what exactly it was that she wanted to write.

Moira's eyes shone with pleasure as she took off her pink rimmed spectacles, wiped them on the corner of her shirt and placed them carefully back on her nose. Graham guessed few people, if any at all, had asked her this. Bullseye. He settled in his chair and waited.

It was a huge tale. Epic, yet focussing in on the detail of love, endeavour, suffering and longing, it was both exciting and heartbreaking. Graham felt his mouth dry as she described the setting, the vast Canadian tundra, where two 19th century settler families vied for trapping rights in the beautiful and most ferocious of landscapes. He could understand the resolve of the stiff, formal father, feel the frustration of the young, wilderness-savvy tomboy daughter and the wickedness of the boy from the rival family, using his charm and sex to woo, deceive and ruin. It was familiar territory, yet not clichéd. It was wonderful.

His turn. She leant forward, eager to hear. He mustered his courage, scared yet excited, and began to tell her of his masterpiece. The Mexican wrestler was famous, strong and universally celebrated. There were plastic action figures made in his image. Posters printed of his photograph. But his mother was the dark secret he dared not reveal to his adoring public. A feckless drug addict and whore. He had worked hard to escape her home made hell, a secret childhood of obscenity, physical brutality and deprivation. His fame, on having broken free of these satanic chains, was all his own doing and he was proud. But pushed too far, he kills two men and collapses in remorse, begging his mother's forgiveness. It ends as they drag him from her hovel and she screams in agony that he, her child is the real obscenity, the stain on humanity and the darkness that engulfed her when he was born. The unwanted product of some violent coupling with a client, her son makes her sick every time she looks at him. His murderous instinct, which she has driven him to, is simply the squaring of the circle. Her final admission of her visceral hatred is his spiritual salvation.

Moira blinked at him and swallowed. Graham waited. She looked at him through the thick lenses of her spectacles and cleared her throat.

'I think that's one of the most remarkable stories I've ever heard.'

'Really?'

'Yes. Really. It's dark, and terrible, of course, but, well the sheer boldness of it. The pain. The forging of a soul through such torment. It's . . . absolutely amazing.'

He looked closely at her earnest, slightly sweaty face.

She was lying.

Moira felt lighter than air. She'd been aware of him for weeks of course. The beautiful boy on the bus. Once, her fevered passion had made her imagine she'd glimpsed him in her local library, and the possibility had made her heart beat faster. And now she had a date. A real date with this wonderful stranger. A brainy, bookish, gorgeous man. A mature vet student, it turned out, and even better, if such a thing was possible, a budding writer. So here she was, trying to select exactly the right outfit, the perfect look to go on not some routine trip to the cinema, or an awkward meal at a restaurant, but an evening at a creative writing group. An intellectual tussle. Something they shared and could talk about. That too was perfect. Moira was so happy she wanted to sing. Even the writer in her wouldn't have dared to conjure an evening as faultless as this, this dazzling break from her small life, a receptionist in a commercial law firm, her confinement to a one roomed flat, nearly five hundred miles from her quiet, doting parents, the only two people in the world who loved her. It was a life with few friends and even fewer adventures. Now, the prospect that she might have both a boyfriend and a group of new and interesting acquaintances made her dizzy with joy. People who shared her love of storytelling and the frank exchange of ideas. It was impossibly thrilling.

Graham had apologised that the group was all female except for him, which only made her adore him more. How manly he was, to make women his friends, to be so confident and assured of himself that such a group wouldn't intimidate him. She guessed that all the women were secretly in love with him. Why wouldn't they be? It was a rare and exotic thing, a man enjoying the easy company of women, but then he was obviously a very special man.

She held up her tight and shiny green blouse to her chin and admired herself in the mirror. Yes. It was just right. A daring top but twinned with carefully demure trousers and low heels. She wanted Graham to notice the girl, discover she was more than just a friend who had reading in common. A passionate, tender, loyal, warm-blooded woman. Almost as important, she didn't want the girls in the group to hate her. If they were Graham's friends it was important they liked like her too. Moira put down the blouse and flicked nervously through the ten printed pages of 'Frost That Binds the Boughs', checking again that there was no dialogue. Attempting a Canadian accent would be humiliating, but these pages were free of speech and rich in description. She could read them aloud with pride, making him recognise that she had talent, that she was a person of worth. She moved aside, with some tenderness, a tribe of watchful soft toys on her bed laid her clothes carefully on the centre of the duvet, and went to run a bath.

It was a night for the tartan tie. He wasn't quite certain yet if Moira was sufficiently modern in spirit to understand that his favourite pastel flowers and swirls were an expression of manliness. Best play safe. He fastened it neatly and adjusted the cuffs of his jacket. His instincts had been proved right. She was a nice girl. Very nice. Almost pretty under the flab. Darting intelligent blue eyes, and a smile that was all gratitude and expectancy. He was pleased they'd finally made contact. He suspected the group members would be resistant at first but knew that eventually they'd accept her as one of their own. There was no question she had talent. More talent than Irene and her steam punk drivel, that was for sure. Heaven preserve them all from another deathly chapter of post-apocalyptic urban decay, mumbled from underneath a flop of badly dyed, raven black hair. His stock would rise tonight in The Garscube Creative Writing Group. He was bringing them new, exciting ideas. He was bringing them fresh meat.

'Lightly dusting the northern sides of the bone-white aspen boles, the snow merely hinted at its relentless mission to smother the land in a soft, quiet death. Winter would come. And it would come soon. The slate grey sky weighed in on her, pushed her deep in to herself. Under its pressure, beneath the unstoppable nature of matter giving way to force, her hot heart leant against her ribs and ignited the fuse that was a forbidden love for Arnold Crane.'

Moira pushed her spectacles up her nose and blinked across the table at Graham. He put his hand over hers. She flushed, pink and hot.

'Beautiful.'

She smiled, immediately trying to hide it with the back of her free hand.

'Really?'

'Yes.'

Graham held her gaze until she was compelled to look away.

The moment was broken as the waitress arrived and cleared their cups with a clatter that had a point.

'Anything else?'

Graham glanced up at her with irritation. He scanned the pinch-faced, sassy, forty-something woman, all attitude and confidence, and committed her foundation-smothered features to memory. He knew she drove the silver Nissan Micra that was always parked outside under the street light and only had seven and half thousand miles on the clock, which meant she lived very close, had a husband who had a real job and paid for her new, barely used car. For later. Right now, the moment was all Moira's.

'No. Nothing.'

The waitress read his face and left. Graham turned to his new author.

'They're going to love this.'

Moira turned her sweating palm up and squeezed his hand. She looked at the floor and flushed again.

She looked so pretty. So humble. So vulnerable. Graham felt an unfamiliar tumble in his chest.

Moira gazed around the campus

'Oh this is . . . lovely!'

Graham smiled, shrugged as though it was all his.

'It was the Garscube estate before the vet college bought it. Some of the trees are nearly a hundred and fifty years old.'

She craned her neck up at the silhouetted branches of ancient chestnuts, oaks and beeches, lit from beneath by the pure white glare of the halogen lighting.

'They're like watchers. Like guards. I can see why they kept them.'

Graham stopped. He looked at Moira and she caught disquiet in his eyes. Without warning, she moved quickly, held his face and kissed him. Taken by surprise, his arms held back like a diver about to plunge, he closed his eyes. It was sublime. Her surprisingly soft lips enveloped his in the cold air, a night air enlivened by the oxygen leaching from the last leaves of ancient creatures crowding around them, breathing, living, and dropping their fruit at their feet like messages from the Gods.

She stepped back. He drew breath, like a drowning man breaking the surface of a cold lake.

Moira smiled, folded herself in to her coat, hugging herself. They stood awkwardly, shifting and shuffling for a beat, then she stooped and picked up a conker, carefully managing its spiky shell.

She pushed her specs up her nose and her face lit up.

'Look at it. Isn't it perfect?'

She handed it to him. He extended his hand and took the armoured chestnut in his hand.

He felt the tiny spikes prick his skin, and beneath the smoothness of a perfect globe containing the seed that could grow a giant.

'Yes. It's perfect.'

Moira walked on. Hands deep in her coat pockets.

'Are we near? Which one is the meeting in?'

In the darkness a handful of modern buildings showed

randomly lit windows, offices and labs still occupied by stragglers, each square of light a tableau like an advent calendar. She was excited, trying to guess which one hosted the group.

Graham watched her scanning. He tightened his grip on the spiky conker until it hurt and then dropped it.

They stopped outside the incinerator building. He gathered his courage and turned to her.

'I don't think we should go. Not tonight.'

Moira blinked, pulling her coat around her shoulders.

'Why not?'

Graham shrugged, looking at his shoes.

'I don't know. Let's just do something else. Something where we can talk. You know. Alone.'

He looked up again.

'I like you Moira. You're kind.'

She moved forward and took his hand.

'Let's go in. Show them how good we are.'

Graham stood, head bowed, his free hand clenched. He stamped his feet, as if against the cold.

'No.'

He looked like a child.

Moira had never felt so confident. She was in control. Here was the man of her dreams, unsure of himself, nervous, small, and she had to take charge.

'What are you afraid of?'

He shook his head, shrugged, then looked up.

'Can I ask you something?'

She nodded, waited, heart racing.

'What do you really think of my story?'

So that was it. He wanted honesty. She should have known better than to have flattered him earlier. Silly mistake. Lesson learned. Every relationship has honesty at its heart and she had nearly blown this one before it began.

Moira looked him in the eye.

'I think that it needs work.'

Graham's gaze was steady, unflinching. No trace of hurt or disappointment. It emboldened her.

'The premise is weak at the moment because there's no real motivation in either character. If we're to understand why a man would survive such abuse to become a success, and then oddly ruin it all by what seems no more than a fit of temper, then we need to know why he's suddenly so out of control. Why he ends up still being the loser. It's not that it's simply unpleasant. It's more that it's . . . well . . . just not plausible.'

Graham let go the breath he'd been holding and touched her face.

'Thank you.'

She flushed with pleasure. He took keys from his pocket and started to un-padlock the heavy door.

She examined the industrial facade with curiosity.

'In here?'

He laughed.

'No. We meet in the refectory. I just need my manuscript. Left it in the back labs. You can wait out here if you want.'

Moira glanced at the warm, distant buildings across the broad plains of the campus, and for a fraction of a second she hesitated. He turned to her as the door swung open. A smile like an angel. His dark hair curling around a perfect neck. She smiled back.

'No. I'll come with you.'

Graham looked at his watch as surreptitiously as he could. No need to offend while someone was reading, even if it was appalling. So he was wrong about Moira. She was as stupid as the rest of them. Her reading had been embarrassing. Romantic, standard soap opera trash, masquerading as literature by forcing it into a predictable historical setting. He was already regretting having introduced her. Why had he thought she would be different? He lowered his eyes and picked at his finger nails, barely trying to hide his despondency. Sonia's moronic chic lit shopping romp was worse than usual tonight, and the desire to read his own few chapters was fast receding.

One day, it would happen. He'd find the girl who could recognise a genius. She'd be the one sitting next to him at the awards dinner table, who would leap to her feet and clap as he rose to collect his prize, who would kiss him and cheer and wipe away a tear of pride. He would single her out for her unending support and the cameras would swing to her, catch her laughing through her tears as she blew him a kiss. She wouldn't criticize, or tell him what was wrong with his work. She would be clever, and brilliant of course, yet desperate to learn from him, hanging on his every word, and analysing every brilliant turn of his unique and celebrated prose. She would be the one.

The room grew silent. Graham looked up. He realised he'd been drifting while they read and now they were waiting, expectant, judgmental, their eyes as hard as coals. Waiting to tear his perfect story to bits.

He stood up, pulse racing, fists clenched and kicked his chair away.

'Fuck you. Fuck you all.'

He turned and left. There was work to do at home. He was going to start from chapter one and polish it until it shone.

The rats were getting bolder. Less than three minutes after Graham Kearney had switched off the lights and locked the bolts on the long forgotten basement store beneath the furnace, they scuttled from beneath the plaster board. Fiona Hardy was mostly gone, but then she had been the first. Her jaw had been eaten down to the back teeth, the eye sockets empty and black. The tape that had bound her hands to the chair was frayed and bitten and any day now she would tumble to the side, like Shereen Kholi had done, and would require to be propped back up.

But tonight the rats were not interested in the four bone-dry corpses. There was new meat. Fresh meat. Warm, bruised, bloody and soft. Still warm. They pricked up their flattened ears only once, as the sound of thick metal doors slammed shut in the far distance, and then got to work.

GARY FRY

BIOFEEDBACK

THE FOLLOWING AUTHOR biographies have been extracted from selected editions of the annual anthology *Year's Best Spooks*, edited by Simon Jackson. They are presented here with no editorial modifications.

Extract from *Year's Best Spooks, 2012*

Gordon Franklyn lives in Leeds with his wife, Harriet, and their two young children, Nadia and Toby. Fans of ghostly fiction need little introduction to Franklyn's work. His frightening first novel *Truth Twice Removed* was a supernatural treat and won a stack of awards the world over. And so we're delighted to welcome him to this, his first appearance in *Year's Best Spooks*. Despite the nature of his work, Franklyn claims to be a sceptic about the 'other side'. He writes: 'I find the supernatural genre imaginatively appealing in an emotional sense, but it's certainly vulnerable to intellectual analysis. Its power, I think, derives from its ability, when done well, to peel away rationality. Under its surface, life is disconnected fragments, and that frightens us. And ghosts can serve as a powerful symbol for that fundamental uncertainty.' What follows is a creepy tale some might say lays waste to the author's scepticism. The story came to Franklyn, as often the case, in the form of a playful idea: 'I've long been drawn to the notion that a living man can become a ghost to others on the basis of negligence, or perhaps as a result of detached tyranny. That forms the core of this story. The absentee factory owner haunting his staff is based loosely on a guy I used to work for, before my writing became successful. Christ, never let it be said I haven't earned my right to make some money out of this game!' In his mid-thirties, Franklyn likes cigarettes, fine food, drink, and – when he's not writing – walks with his family.

Extract from *Year's Best Spooks, 2013*

Gordon Franklyn lives in Leeds with his wife, Harriet, and their two young children, Nadia and Toby. Franklyn's second supernatural novel – *Lott's Mirror* – more than fulfilled the promise of his first, the genre-defining *Truth Twice Removed*. Indeed, we at *Year's Best Spooks* predict big things for this author, and that's why we're delighted to see him back in our annual anthology. Another reason is that he tells one helluva scary story . . . and the one you're about to read is no exception. Franklyn writes: 'On the strength of sales of my novels, I recently quit the day job – Lord, never put me in a classroom again! – and moved into what me and the family consider our dream home: a lovely, secluded 17th Century property in North Yorkshire. And does this place have ghosts, I hear readers ask? Well, I'm afraid to say that, despite my wife and kids reporting a few spooky incidents, I've personally encountered nothing that cannot be accounted for by reason. Which is not to say the house isn't a source of inspiration. Solitary walks in the surrounding countryside have done much to stir my creative juices, and I now have enough dark material under development to inform years of work.' I think fans of supernatural fiction will agree that, in the tale that follows, Franklyn shows little sign of losing of his touch. Its ruthless narrative about a man haunted by a former owner of his new home with a penchant for liquor is incongruously powerful in its brief span, and hints at more of the novel length fiction we crave from this sterling new master of terror.

Extract from *Year's Best Spooks, 2016*

Gordon Franklyn lives in North Yorkshire with his wife, Harriet, and their two children, Nadia and Toby. It's been a while since we welcomed him to the pages of *Year's Best Spooks*, and that's because he's been writing a number of increasingly popular supernatural novels. After showing early promise in *Truth Twice Removed* and *Lott's Mirror*, Franklyn has published *Still Waters, The Family Man*, and *Nothing Changes,* all well received by readers and critics alike. Nevertheless, it troubles him that certain sections of the supernatural community, originally defenders of his work, have recently accused him of selling out. Franklyn writes: 'Any fool knows that commercial success involves concessions to markets that pre-exist the artist. Hell, I worked long enough in the real world to realise that life is often about compromise, especially when economic survival remains so challenging. It's my working class background, much of it spent in the mean streets of Leeds, that makes me fond of fast cars. I also have a family to clothe and feed. So come on, guys, give me a break here.' Fighting words, we must surely agree. Indeed, Franklyn has lost little of the boozy rage that fuelled his early fiction; by way of illustration, witness the following tale. 'On doctor's advice, I recently quit smoking,' Franklyn explains, 'and that involved a month of hell for me and others. I found myself feeling intolerant of many things, even my wife's belief – unsuspected until this stage of our marriage – in the supernatural. This got me thinking about psychological demons. Imagine a guy who so vehemently denies the existence of a ghost haunting his partner that it shifts its attention to him . . .' The tale you're about to read, dear readers, shows that commercial success has done little to dull Franklyn's sinister disposition. He remains as exquisitely warped as ever.

Extract from *Year's Best Spooks, 2019*

Gordon Franklyn lives in North Yorkshire with his wife, Harriet, and their two children, Nadia and Toby. Since his last appearance in *Year's Best Spooks* three years ago, Franklyn has moved away from the supernatural genre, writing crime novels in an attempt, he candidly admits, to 'remain afloat in a market unsympathetic to [his] previous fictional focus.' Nevertheless, despite rumours of its death, we at this annual anthology believe that our field is in rude health, and we offer this latest collection as proof. Unsurprisingly, Franklyn's story is one of its strongest offerings. We can only assume that the tale, a harrowing depiction of marital and paternal abuse, is based on Franklyn's childhood, which he's alluded to in many frank media interviews. His depiction of a husband and father haunted by a brutal, ale-enraged ancestor is a bold attempt to understand an abuser's behaviour from the outside. Perhaps it's time for Franklyn to address these issues; we know from public statements that his father – from whom he'd been estranged since teen-hood – died recently. In an interview earlier this year, Franklyn said, 'Despite my contractual commitments with the novels – they alone pay for petrol and put food on the table – I've never lost my love for short stories. They offer me the opportunity to take risks, to dig a bit deeper into life.' When asked about his infamous scepticism concerning the afterlife, he added, 'As I get older, I become less certain about many things, and the supernatural is one of them. Let's just say I'm more open-minded now than I was even a decade ago.'

Extract from *Year's Best Spooks, 2021*

Gordon Franklyn lives in North Yorkshire with his wife,

Harriet. Fans of genre fiction will realise that this has been a demanding one for the author, and we at *Year's Best Spooks* don't intend to add to media speculation about the challenges he and his wife have faced. Needless to say, we wish them both well during this period of recovery, and hope inclusion of a new story by Franklyn in our latest anthology is a way of supporting them. Not that the tale doesn't earn its modest fee. It's often said that writers' best work comes from duress, and that certainly holds true here. One wonders whether Franklyn's latest novels, alluded to in rare interviews, have also returned to the frightening territory of his early work. We can only hope a publisher snaps them up soon. In the meantime, we have this treat to savour, and it's one that seems more autobiographical than Franklyn's usual portraits of haunted men whose circumstances are quite removed from his own (formerly) idyllic lifestyle in North Yorkshire. The central character likes fast cars, hard liquor and even psychotherapy. One might say he's racing from his past, and his sudden shift from gad-about-town to a cripple's carer is certainly disturbing. Perhaps the cocky ghost of a man killed in the same crash that disabled the carer's wife serves as Franklyn's attempt to castigate the person he once was: arrogant, rash, intolerant . . . Understandably, Franklyn didn't reply to emails asking for comments about this piece, but he made a telling statement in the last interview he gave before suffering his familial tragedy: 'All of us haunt; we haunt everyone around us and the places we occupy. We're all ghosts.'

Extract from *Year's Best Spooks, 2026*

Gordon Franklyn lives in Leeds with his wife, Harriet. Life hasn't been kind to the author, especially when, half a decade ago, his two children were killed in a car accident that also involved his wife. Franklyn alone, driving the fast vehicle, escaped the flaming melee. Unpublished for several years, the author now lives back in his native West Yorkshire, caring for his disabled wife on a full-time basis. It's a tragic story as unsettlingly heart-breaking as those with which he once thrilled a generation of genre fans. Nevertheless, this forgotten man of supernatural fiction has never been less than surprising, and imagine our delight at *Year's Best Spooks* when, during our 25th Anniversary, we received a brand new submission from this living legend. And if it isn't one of the most horrifying pieces we've ever had the pleasure to read. As usual in Franklyn's last few contributions to this anthology, the author was unavailable for commentary, and so we must let the tale speak for itself. One thing that will strike readers familiar with his work is the shift from his characteristic third-person narrative to the more intimate first-person. We think this lends the fiction much more power. But Franklyn's depiction of a drinking man haunted by past shadows that darken his path is as subconsciously accurate, analytically dispassionate, and unwittingly illuminating as anything he wrote during his all-too-brief professional career. The demons on the fringes of consciousness now take centre stage, in what the author might once have described as the nebulous mind. And so let us raise the spotlight of our mind's eye: unblinking, obsessive, moist with unquenchable grief. Behold . . .

Extract from *Year's Best Spooks, 2029*

Gordon Franklyn lives in Leeds. That's pretty much all we now know about this reclusive author. The return address for e-payment that accompanied the story you're about to read was of a street full of tenements in a rundown area. We understand that the author's wife has recently died, following medical complications. The only other clue about Franklyn's circumstances on the note attached to the following tale was a single, enigmatic message: 'I was wrong – about many things. But wrong about *this*, especially.' And does he refer here to the *supernatural*? That certainly seems plausible, particularly after reading the following piece, Franklyn's first fictional output since his last contribution to *Year's Best Spooks* . . . But *is* this fiction? That's the question readers will surely ask themselves. The setting seems authentic: the house the author once occupied in the splendid Yorkshire countryside. But the time is all wrong, because the spooks that haunt this latest abusive, alcoholic in a Franklyn tale could never have existed there. That was once a happy, family home. And this is no happy family. We speculate that Franklyn, struggling as a result of hard experience, regular drink, and a twisted state of mind, could be planning an autobiography and has simply got some details wrong. The ghosts surely belong elsewhere: where the author now lives, in a dilapidated city. Nevertheless, these creatures are no less frightening for their tranquil rural location. They make one believe – as we at *Year's Best Spooks* have always believed; as even Gordon Franklyn, once such a wry sceptic, has possibly come to believe – that the supernatural is *real*. We hope that you, dear readers, also share this sentiment. And so turn the page and lapse again into Franklyn's world. He might never have been more frightening, nor have created such potent beings. The vicious behaviour of the two vengeful children, and perhaps worse, the hideously mangled wife, contain an element of autobiography, of unforgiving accuracy, of experienced *horror* . . . Gordon Franklyn is a haunting and haunted man. And we hope he gets by.

ADAM NEVILL

DOLL HANDS

I AM THE one with the big white head and the doll hands. I work behind the desk in the West block of Gruut Huis. When I'm not taking delivered medicines upstairs to the residents who slowly die in their beds, I watch the greenish screens of the security monitors that cover every inch of Gruut Huis's big red brick walls and its empty tarmac forecourt.

I watch out for deliveries and for intruders. Deliveries come every day. Intruders not so much anymore. They have mostly died out there in the draughty buildings of the dead city, or are lying still on the dark stones before The Church of Our Lady. In Brugge the dying shuffle and crawl to the church. It's like they have lost everything but a memory of where to go.

Last Christmas I was sent out with two porters to find the baboon child of Mr Hussain who lives in the east wing. The baboon boy escaped from his cage and blinded his carer. And as I searched for the boy in Guido Gezelleplein, I saw all of the wet stiff bodies beneath the tower, lying down in the mist.

One of the day porters, Vinegar Irish, beat the baboon boy when we found him feeding amongst the bodies. Like the residents, the baboon boy had grown tired of the yeast from the tanks in the basement. He wanted meat.

At ten in the morning, there is movement on the monitor screens. Someone has arrived at the GOODS AND SERVICES entrance of Gruut Huis. Out of the mist the squarish front of a white truck appears and waits by the roller gate. It's the caterers. Inside my stomach I feel a sickish skitter.

With my teeny fingers I press the buttons on the security console and open Door Eight. On the screen I watch the metal grill rise. The truck passes into the central court of Gruut Huis and parks the rear doors by the utility door of the service area. Behind this utility door are the storage cages for the resident's old possessions, as well as the porter's dormitory, the staff room, the stock cupboards, the boiler room, the workshop, the staff washroom, and the yeast tanks that feed us with their yellow softness. Today, the caterers will need to use the staff washroom for their work.

Yesterday, we were told a delivery of food was arriving for the Head Resident's Annual Banquet. Mrs Van den Broeck, the Head Resident of the building, also informed us that our showers were to be cancelled and that we were not allowed into the staff room all day because the caterers needed to use these areas to prepare the banquet. But none of the staff ever want to go into the washroom anyway if the caterers are on-site. Despite the sleepiness of the White Ape, who is nightwatchman, and the drunkenness of Vinegar Irish, and the slow movements of Les Spider, handyman, and the merry giggles of the two cleaning girls, we can all remember the other times when the little white truck came to Gruut Huis for the banquets. None of the staff talk about the days of the General Meetings and Annual Banquets. We all pretend they're normal days, but Vinegar Irish drinks more cleaning fluid than usual.

Using the desk phone I call Vinegar Irish who is the porter on duty in the East wing. He takes a long time to answer the phone. On the security console, I switch to the camera above his reception desk to see what he is doing. Slowly, like his pants are full of shit and he can't walk straight, I see him stumble into the green underwater world of the monitor screen. Even on camera I can see the bulgy veins under his strawberry face. He's been in the key cupboard drinking fluids and not beside his monitors like he is supposed to be at all times. If he was behind his desk he would have heard the alarm sound when I opened the outer gate, and he would have known a delivery had arrived. His barking voice is slurred. 'What you want?'

'Delivery,' I say. 'Watch my side. I'm going down.'

'Aye. Aye. Trucks come. What you need to do –' I put the phone down while he is speaking. It will make him go shaky with rage in the east wing. He'll call me a bastard and swear to punch his trembly hands at my big head, while spit flies out of his vinegar mouth. But he won't remember the altercation tonight when we finish the day shift, and I have no time right now for a slurred lecture about all the things I already know about our duties that he cannot manage to do.

As I walk across the lobby to the porter's door, with my sack-cloth mask in my doll hands, the phone rings behind my desk. I know it is Vinegar Irish in a spitting rage. All the residents are still asleep. Those that can still walk never come down before noon.

Smiling to myself, at this little way I get revenge on Vinegar Irish, I stretch the brownish mask over my head. Then I open the airlock and duck through the escape hatch to the metal staircase outside. As I trot down the stairs, the mist rushes in to cover my little shiny shoes. Even with the mask pulled over my fat Octopus head, I can smell the sulphur-rust of the chemical air.

At the bottom of the staircase, I enter the courtyard. The courtyard is right in the middle of all four blocks of flats. The resident's can look down and into the courtyard from their kitchen windows. I bet their mouths fill with water when they see the white van parked by the utility door. What the Head Residents don't eat, we porters deliver up to their flats in white plastic bags.

Seeing the caterer's truck makes my stomach turn over with a wallop. The two caterers who came in the white truck are standing by the driver's door, talking, and waiting for me to open the utility area. Both of them are wearing rubber hoods shaped into pig faces. The pig faces are supposed to be smiling, but they look like the faces in dreams that wake you up with a scream.

The caterers are wearing rubber boots to their knees too, and stripy trousers tucked into the tops of their boots. Over their stripy trousers and white smocks they wear long black rubber aprons. They are both putting on gloves made from wire mesh.

'Christ. Would you look at the cunt's head,' the older caterer says. His son giggles inside his rubber pig mask.

I clench my tiny hands into marble hammers.

'Awright?' the father says to me. Under the mask I know he is laughing at my big white head and stick body. The father gives me a clipboard. There is a plastic pen under the metal clasp that holds the pink delivery note to the clipboard. With my doll hands I take the pen and sign and print my name, then date the slip: 10/04/2152. They watch my hands in silence. The world goes quiet when my hands go to work like no one can believe they have any use.

On the *Grote and Sons Fine Foods and Gourmet Catering* sales slip, I see I am signing for: *2 livestock. Extra lean, premium fresh. 120 kilos.*

The caterers go into the cabin of their truck and drag their equipment out. 'Let's get set up. Give us hand,' the father says to me.

From behind the two seats in the dirty cabin that smells

of metal and floor bleach, they pass two big grey sacks to me. They are heavy with dark stains at the bottom and around the top are little brass holes for chains to pass through. Touching the sacks makes my legs shake. I tuck them under my arm. In my other hand I am given a metal box to carry. It has little red numbers by the lock. The box is cold to touch and is patterned with black and yellow stripes.

'Careful with that,' the fat father says as I take the cold box in my small hand. 'Is for the hearts and livers. We sell them, see. They is worth more than you are.'

The son hangs heavy chains over one arm and grabs a black cloth bag. As he walks, the black cloth sack makes a hollow knocking sound as the wooden clubs inside bang together. The father carries two small steel cases the size of small suitcases in one hand, and two big white plastic buckets in the other that are reddish-grubby inside. 'Same place as before?' he asks me.

'Follow me,' I say, and walk to the utility door of the basement. We go inside and pass the iron storage cages and are watched by the rocking horse with the big blue eyes and lady lashes. We go through the white door with the STAFF ONLY sign on it, and the floor changes from cement to tiles. In the white tiled corridor I take them to the washroom where they will work. In here it always smells of the bleach used by the whispering cleaners. The cleaners sleep in the cupboard with all the bottles, mops and cloths and are not allowed to use the staff room. When the white ape catches them in there smiling at the television, he roars.

I take the caterers into the big washroom that is tiled to the ceiling and divided in two by a metal rail and shower curtain. There is a sink and toilet on one side and the other half has a floor that slopes to the plug grate under the big round shower head. Against the wall in the shower section is a wooden bench, bolted to the wall. The father drops his cases and mask on to the bench. His head is round and pink as the flavoured yeast the residents eat from square ration tins.

The son coils his chains on the bench and removes his hood too. He has a weasel face with many pimples among the scruffy whiskers on his chin. His tiny black eyes flit about and his thin lips curl away from long gums and two sharp teeth like he is about to laugh.

'Luvverly,' the father says, looking around the wash room. I notice the father has no neck.

'Perfek,' the weasel son adds, grinning and sniffing.

'Your night boy asleep?' the father asks. His fat body sweats under his smock and apron. His sweat smells of beef powder. Small and yellow and sharp, his two snaggle teeth are the same as the son's. When he squints, his tiny red eyes sink into his face.

I nod.

'Not for long,' the weasel says, and then shuffles about, giggling. They both smell of sweat and old blood.

I shuffle towards the door.

'Hang on. Hang on,' the father says. 'We need you to open that friggin' door when we bring the meat in.'

'Yeah,' Weasel agrees, while he threads the chains through the brass eyes in the top of the sacks.

The father opens the cases on the bench. Stainless steel gleams under the yellow lights. His tools are carefully fitted into little trays. In his world of dirty trucks, old sacks, rusty chains and snaggle teeth, it surprises me to see his fat fingers become gentle on the steel of his tools.

With eyes full of glee, the weasel son watches his father remove the two biggest knives from a metal case. Weasel then unties the ribbon of the last sack with the hollow wooden sounds inside, and pulls out two thick clubs. He stands with a club in each hand, staring at me. He is pleased to see the horror on my little face. At the bottom of the clubs the wood is stained a dark colour and some bits have chipped off.

'Go fetch 'em in,' the father says, while he lays two cleavers with black handles on an oily cloth.

'Right,' the weasel son says.

We go back down the tiled corridor. I walk slowly because I am in no hurry to see the livestock. When Mrs Van den Broeck, the Director of Residents, announced the banquet, I decided I would show the livestock a friendly face before they were taken into the washroom; otherwise, the fat father and the weasel son would be the last people they would see in this world, before they were stuffed inside the sacks and chained up.

When we reach the courtyard, I remember what the fat father told me last time, about how the meat tastes better with bruises under the skin. That's why they use the clubs. To tenderise the meat and get blood into the flesh. When he told me that, I wanted to escape from Gruut Huis and keep running into the poisonous mist until I fell down, until no one in the building could ever find me again. The residents don't need to eat the fresh meats. Like the staff they can eat the soft yellow yeast from the tanks, but the residents are rich and can afford variety.

We go back into the courtyard. Above us some lights have come on in the flats. I can see the dark lumps of the resident's heads watching from kitchen windows. And suddenly, from the East wing, the baboon child of Mr Hussein screams. It rips the smoky air apart. Weasel boy flinches. You never get used to the sound of the baboon child in the cage.

The weasel son rattles keys in his chain-mail hand. 'We done a wedding last week. St Jan in de Meers.'

I can't speak with all the churning in my tummy.

'We done eight livestock for the barbecue. Da girl's farver was loaded. Had a tent built and everything. Ya know, a

Marquee. All in this garden, under a glass roof. Me and dad was up at five. They had fifty guests, like. We filled four ice-chests with fillets. Done the sausages the day before. For the kids, like.'

He finds the correct key and unlocks the back doors of the truck. Under his pig mask I know he is smiling. 'We made a few shillings. There's a few shillings to be made at weddings in this part of town.'

When Weasel opens the back doors, I feel the hot air puff out of the truck. With it comes the smell of pee and sweat to mix with the chemical stink of the swirly air. Two small shapes are huddled at the far end of the truck, near the engine where it is warmer.

I walk away from the open doors of the truck and look up at the vapours. They drift and show little pieces of grey sky. There is a smudgy yellow stain where the sun must be. But you can never tell with the cloud so low. I wish I was in heaven.

'C'mon ya shit-brains,' Weasel shouts from inside the truck. He's climbed in to get the livestock out. They never want to come out.

I cringe as if he is about to pull a lion out of the back. Through the white sides of the truck comes a bumping of bare feet on metal and then the *chinka, chinka, chinka* of a chain.

Weasel boy jumps out of the truck, holding a rope in both hands. 'They as dumb as shit, but it's like they know when this day is coming. Get outta there. Git! Git!'

Out of the back of the truck two pale yellowish figures stumble and then drop onto the misty slabs of the courtyard. They fall down and are yanked back to their feet by the weasel.

The livestock is skinny and completely shaven. Their elbows are tied together and their hands are tucked under their chins. They are young males with big eyes. They look like each other. Like angels with pretty faces and slender bodies. They start to cough in the acid-stinging air.

Shivering against each other, the smaller one starts to cry and hides behind the taller one, who is too frightened to cry, but pee's instead, down the inside of his thighs. It steams in the cold air.

'Dirty bastards. They'll piss anywhere. Trucks full of it. Yous'll have to wash that corridor down after we're gone.' Weasel Boy pulls the rope taut. Each male wears a thick iron collar that looks loose on his yellowish neck. A rope is attached to the short chains welded to the collars. In his metal hands Weasel Boy holds the slack rope.

As Weasel Boy pulls them across the courtyard, the livestock jogs and jostles together for warmth in the cold air. I run ahead to open the utility door, but can't feel my legs properly, even when my knees bang together.

Inside the corridor I take off my mask and walk behind the livestock. Weasel boy leads the way to the washroom. The livestock peer about at the storage cages. The small one stops crying, distracted by the paintings and furniture and boxes inside the cages. The taller one looks over his shoulder at me. He smiles. His eyes are full of water. I try to smile back at him, but my jaw is numb. So I just stare at him. His face is scared, but trusting and wanting a friend who smiles on this day when he is frightened.

I think what I think every time the caterers come to Gruut Huis, that there must be some kind of mistake. Livestock is supposed to be dumb. It has no feelings we're told. But in these eyes I can see a frightened boy.

'No,' I say, before I even know I am speaking.

Weasel Boy turns around and stares at me. 'You what?'

'This can't be right.'

Weasel Boy laughs under his pig mask. 'Don't you believe it. They got human faces, but they is shit-brains. Pretty as pitchers, but dead in the head. They ain't like us.'

There is so much I want to say, but all the words vanish off my tongue and my head is filled with wind. A big lump chokes my sparrow throat shut.

'Git! Git!' Weasel snarls at the livestock, who cringe at the sound of his voice. On the back of each livestock-boy I see the scars. Long pinkish scars with little holes around the slits, where the stitches once were, after things had been taken out of their thin bodies for the sick. 'Best meat in town,' Weasel says to me, grinning. 'They cook up lovely like. Thousand euro a kilo, they cost. More than fruit in them tins, like. Think of that. *More than fruit in tins.*'

Weasel Boy is pleased I am feeling dizzy and sick. And, like most people in this building, he likes to tell me things I don't want to hear. 'These two, we been feeding for months. Shut it!' He straps the smaller one, who has started to cry again, on the backside with the end of the rope. The little one suddenly stops crying when the rope makes a wet sound on his yellow buttock. The mark goes white. Then back to yellow again. The force of the blow makes him trip over the feet of the taller boy, who is still looking at me with watery eyes, wanting a smile from me. They have long toenails.

'Where . . .'

Weasel Boy stops dragging the livestock and looks at me. 'Aye?'

I clear my throat. 'Where they from?'

'Nuns.'

'What?'

'Nuns. Them old nuns up in Brussels all died of the milk-leg. So all there shit-brains went to auction. These two were like strips of piss when me and me dad looked at them. No meat on them. All they got fed from them nuns was yeast and water. No good for the meat, see. So we been feeding them for months. Who's they for, like?'

'Head Residents.' My voice is a whisper.

'Aye?'

'The Head Residents of the building. For the Annual Banquet.'

'They gonna love them.' Weasel boy rips his mask off and points his septic muzzle at the livestock in a grimace to frighten them. They both try and hide behind each other, but get tangled.

The weasel's bristle hair is wet with sweat. I wondered if the salt stings his pimples. They go down his neck and on to his back. I can smell the sickish vinegar of his boils.

'Are . . . Are . . . Are you sure it's OK?' I know the answers to all of my stupid questions, asked in my stupid voice, but I have to keep speaking to hold my panic back. The livestock starts to giggle.

'Like I said, don't be fooled. They's useless. Was nothing but pets to them nuns. Only me and me dad make them worth anything. They is worth more than the organs in you and me put together.' He tugs the rope hard so the livestock make chokey noises and their naked bodies slap against his rubber apron. Their eyes are watering. The little one looks up into the Weasel Boy's rat eyes and tries to hug him.

But the livestock go quiet when the washroom door is opened. Weasel Boy shoves them inside. Through the gap in the door, I can see his fat dad holding a sack open. 'Get in here,' he growls at the big one. Both livestocks start to cry.

'I have to get back to my desk,' I say, even though I can't feel my jaw.

'Fair enough,' Weasel says, with a smirk. 'We need you to open the doors when we finished the first one. Me mam is coming at three. She's the cook. Me dad'll bring her later. We'll *do* the second one in the morning.'

He closes the door. Behind me the livestock is crying in the washroom. The Fat Dad is shouting and the Weasel Son is laughing. I can hear it all through the white tiled walls. I put my fingers inside my ears as I run away.

~

Follow me through the dark house. Watch me kill the old lady. It won't take long.

My little brass clock says it's three in the morning, so I'll go and put a pillow over Mrs Van den Broeck's bird mouth until she stops breathing. It'll be all right as long as I pretend it's just an ordinary thing that I'm doing. I know because I've done this before.

Above my bunk, Vinegar Irish is asleep and snoring in his bed. He won't see me leave the dormitory room. After drinking so much this evening – the cleaning liquid with the wet paint smell that I stole from the stores for him – he climbed into bed on his hands and knees with eyes looking at nothing in particular. Most mornings it takes me over twenty minutes to wake him for our work upstairs behind the reception desks. He drinks all day, can remember nothing and needs his sleep. His face is purple with veins and his lumpy nose smells of bad yeast.

I go out of the dormitory with the bunk beds and I follow the cement path through the big store room. There are no lights on in the store because we are forbidden to come here at night, but I know my way around in the dark. Sometimes at night I go into the cages with a torch and the master keys to poke around the boxes, trunks and cases full of things that used to matter in the world. But nothing you can eat or sell for food so it has no value now. Sometimes, as I walk through the store, I feel I'm being watched from inside the cages.

Slowly, I unlock the air-tight door that opens into the courtyard. Already, since I have worked here, five residents have jumped from the sixth floor and smashed themselves on the tarmac below. They had the lunger disease and were choking on red brine. At night you could hear their voices in the cold courtyard, drifting out of windows and spanking off all the brick walls as they drowned in bed. *Whuff, whuff, whuff* they went.

I go out from the store and step into the mist. The door shuts behind me with a wheeze. Cold out here and the rain sizzles through the fog to sting the thin skin over my skull. Then the air gets inside my nose and mouth too and it feels like I am sucking a battery. No one is permitted to go outdoors without a mask because of the poison in the air, but the porter's masks are only sacks with plastic cups sown over the mouth-part. My face stings just as much with a mask on and I sweat too much inside the linen, so when no one is watching I go out without a mask over my big white head. I'm not too worried about dying. At the boy's home I came from, the nurses told me 'people in your condition never see their teens'. I'm eighteen so I should be dead soon. Inside my see-through chest one of the little grey pumps or blackish lumps will just stop working. Maybe I'll go greyish first like most of the residents dying upstairs inside the flats.

Crouching down, my shoulder in the night-gown slides against the red brick walls. A special coating to stop the air dissolving the whole place has made the bricks smooth. Taking shallow stinging breaths, I look up. Most of the apartments are dark, but a few yellowy kitchens shine like little boxes, high up in the vapours that fill the world outside our airlocks and sealed doors.

I go up the giant black metal fire escape to the airlock that will get me into the west wing reception. If there was a fire here, and the thought of it makes me grin, where could the residents be evacuated to? They would stand in the courtyard and watch the building blaze around them until the air in their masks ran out. This is the last place they can retreat to in the city. There's nowhere left to hide from the mist in the world. At night, when I stand on the roof by the big satellite dishes, I see fewer lights out there in the city. Like the people, the lights are all being turned off one by one.

Outside the little back door of the west wing, I wait for the dizzies in my head to stop. I'm so scared now my dolly hands and puppet legs have gone all shaky. Closing my eyes, I tell myself this is going to be easy, it's just an ordinary thing that I'm about to do.

I think of the two little boys that came here inside the white truck. I will always see their frightened faces as they are pulled by the caterer's ropes. Mrs Van den Broeck wanted them. She brought them here. So now I am going to her.

Feeling stronger after the attack of the dizzies passes, I tap the code into the steel number pad on the wall beside the little back door: 1, 2, 3, 4. An easy sequence to remember so Vinegar Irish can always get inside. The door unlocks with a click and hiss. I push it open.

Yellow corridor light, the smell of cleaned carpets and polished wood comes out the door to die in the mist. Ducking my head, I climb through quickly. If any of the doors of the building are open for longer than five seconds a buzzer will go off behind the reception desk and wake the night porter.

Blinking my black button eyes I get rid of the outside mist in my tears. The corridor becomes clear. It's empty. Only thing I can hear is the sound of the ceiling lights as they buzz inside their glass shades. My thin feet go warm on the red carpet. This corridor will take me down to reception.

Creeping and sneaking, I go grinning down the passage and stop at the end where it opens into the reception. Listening hard with my eyes-closed I try to hear the squeak of the porter's chair. But there is only silence down there behind the reception desk. Good.

Going down to my hands and knees I peek the top half of my head around the corner. I smile. Leaning back in his chair with his red face pointed at the ceiling, the white ape sleeps tonight. Big purple tongue and one brown tooth, hot with shit-breath, swallowing the clean air. He is supposed to be watching the monitor screens on his desk. But he has even taken his glasses and shoes off. I can see his black socks full of white hair and yellow claws on top of the desk.

I go into reception on my dolly hands and bony knees and I crawl to the staircase that will take me up to *her*. Even if the white ape's eyes open now, he won't see me because of the desk's high front. He would have to stand up and put his glasses on to catch sight of my thin bones in the night-gown and my swollen skull going up the stairs like a spider.

I go up the stairs to the second floor and stand outside the door marked number five. Her smell is strong up here, perfume and medicine. When I think of Mrs Van den Broeck's grey bird head on a fat silk pillow, sleeping somewhere on the other side of this wooden door, my slit-mouth trembles.

All day long I run up and down these stairs on errands for the residents, they who cannot be argued with at any time. But now I am up here in a flappy night shirt with a stolen key because I mean to drown one of them in pillow softness. A big part of me wants to run back down the stairs, go through the building and across the courtyard to my little warm bunk in the dormitory where Vinegar Irish snores and wheezes above me.

Resting on my ankles, I put my head between my knees and screw my eyes shut. All of this – the building of old brick, the shiny wooden doors, the marble skirting boards, the wall mirrors and brass lights, the rich people and Mrs Van den Broeck with her white gloves and pecking face – are so much bigger than me. I am a grain of seed that cannot escape her yellow teeth. In my left doll hand I squeeze the key until it hurts.

Today, two pale boys with pee on their hairless legs, stepped about on cold toes in the back of the caterer's truck. They held each other with small hands, crying and smiling, and making throaty sounds to each other. They were marched by the caterers to the wash room with the white tiles and the big plug in the middle. And then the smaller one had to watch his brother put in a sack . . .

Inside my slit-mouth my squarish milk teeth grind together. Inside my fists my long nails make red half-moons on my palms. She brought them here. Mrs Van den Broeck called for the white truck that had the bumping sounds of boys inside. My stomach makes squirly sounds as the rage makes me shake and go the pink colour of the blind things that no chemicals can kill, who flit deep in the hot oceans, so far down they cannot be caught and eaten.

With a snarl, I stand up. Into the brass lock of her front door goes the key. The thunk of the lock opening feels good within the china bones of my dollish hand. My fingers look so small against the brown wood. I push the heavy door. A sigh of air escapes. The whisper of her apartment's air runs over my face: medicine, dusty silk, old lady sour smell.

Inside it is dark. The door closes behind me with a tired sound.

Waiting for my eyes to get used to the place, the outlines of vases, dry flowers, picture frames, a hat-stand and mirror appear out of the gloom. Then I notice a faint bluish light spilling from the kitchen. It comes from the electric panel with the warning lights about leaks and gases and fires; all the flats have them. In the kitchen is where I usually take yeast tins and put them on the blue table for the maid Gemima to unpack. Gemima is the tiny woman who wears rubber sandals and who never speaks. But after tonight, Gemima will also be free of Mrs Van den Broeck, and there will be no more journeys up here for me with the wet meats inside the plastic bags. No more feeling like my body is made of glass that will shatter when she shouts. No more poking from her bird claws. No more squinting from her tiny pink eyes when she teeters out of the elevator in the afternoon and sees my big head behind the reception desk.

I look down the hallway and see her bedroom door at the end. I pass the living room where she sits in the long silk gown and scolds us porters down the house phone. Then I tippy-toe past the bathroom where Gemima scrubs Mrs Van den Broeck's spiny back and rinses her shrunken chest.

I stand outside the two bedrooms. Gemima sleeps in the left one. Now she will be resting for a few hours until her mistress's sharp voice begins another day for her. But part of Gemima never sleeps. The part of Gemima that must listen for the sound of Mrs Van den Broeck's bird feet on the marble tiles and the scratch of her voice, calling out for attention from among the crystals and china cups and photos of smiling men with big teeth and thick hair in her room. This part of Gemima I must be careful of.

Mrs Van den Broeck sleeps behind the right door in a big bed. I go in on legs I cannot feel. In here there is no light, the curtains are thick and fall to the floor. There is complete darkness . . . and a voice. It crackles in my ears. 'Who's there?'

I stop moving and feel like I am underwater and trying to gulp a breath that will never come. Taking a step back, I want to run from here. Then I am about to say my own name, like I do on the house phone when the residents call down from upstairs. *Hello, Bobby speaking. How may I help?* I stop myself before my lips form the shape of the first word.

'Is that you, Gemima?'

Has my heart stopped beating inside its cage of thin bone and see-through skin?

'What's the time? Where are my glasses?'

I listen out for Gemima and imagine her rising without thought or choice from her cot next door. The other room stays silent, but it won't for long if Van den Broeck keeps talking.

Somewhere in front of me I hear a rustling. Out there in the dark I know a birdie claw is reaching for the switch of a table lamp. It the light comes on there might be a scream.

I cannot move.

'Who is there?' she says, her voice deeper. I can imagine the squinty eyes and pointy mouth with no lips. Again, I hear her long claws rake across the wooden surface of the side-table by the bed. The light cannot come on or I am finished. I race to the sound of her voice.

Something hard and cold hits my shine bones and blue streaks of pain enter my head. It is the end of her metal bed-frame that I have run into, so I am not in the part of the room I thought I was.

Greenish light explodes through the glass shade of the table lamp and makes me flinch. Propped-up among fat pillows with shiny cases is Mrs Van den Broeck. I can see her pointy shoulders and satin night gown where the bedclothes have slipped down. Collarbones stick through skin. She must sleep with her head raised and ready to snap at Gemima when she comes in with the breakfast.

Small red eyes watch me. Her face is surprised, but not afraid. For a while she cannot speak and I stand dizzy before her with pinpricks of sweat growing out of my whole head.

'What are you doing in my room?' There is no sleepiness in her voice, she has been awake for a long time. Not even her hair is mussed-up or flat at the back. Her voice gets sharper. It fills the room. 'I knew it was you. I always knew you were not to be trusted. You've been taking things. Jewellery. I suspected you from the start.'

'No. It wasn't me.' I feel like I'm five again, before the desk of the director at the boy's home.

'I'll have you executed in the morning. You disgust me.' Her face has begun to shake and she pulls her bed sheets up to her chin, as if to stop me looking at her bird body in the shiny nighty. 'People will thank me for having you put down. You should have been smothered in the cradle. Why do they let things like you live?' All this I have heard before when she is in a spiteful mood. But the thing that makes me so angry is her suspicion that I want to look at her skeleton body in the silk gown.

At any moment I expect Gemima to come in and start wailing. Then the white ape will be up here too and I will have a few hours to live. I stare at the bird-face with the plume of grey hair. Never have I hated anything so much. A little gargle comes out of my throat and I am at her bedside before she can say another word.

She looks up at me with surprise in her eyes. Neither of us can believe we are facing each other like this in her bedroom. This is not how I imagined it would be: the light on, me in my night gown, and Mrs Van Den Broeck's dry-stick body sitting upright and supported by pillows.

She opens her mouth to speak, but no spiky words come out to hurt my ears. It is my time to speak. 'You,' I say. 'The boys. The boys in the truck. You brought them here.'

'What are you talking about? Have you lost your mind?'

I take one of the pillows from behind her back. Mrs Van den Broeck never liked to see my china-doll hands poking from the sleeves of my uniform, so it is only right they are the last things she sees before I put the pillow over her face.

'Oh,' she says in a little girl voice. Her frown is still asking me a question when I put her in the dark and take away the thin streams of air that must whistle through her beak holes. I grin the wild grin I cannot control that makes my whole face shake. This bully-bird can't peck me now.

Her pigeon skull fidgets under the pressing pillow. Twiggish legs with brown spots on the skin kick out inside the sheets, but only make whispers like mice behind the skirting boards. Claws open, claws close, claws open, claws stop moving.

I put my big onion skull against the pillow to add weight to my late-night pressings. Now our faces are closer together than they have ever been before, but we can't see each other. A few feathers and some silk is the only thing between us. The pillow smells of perfume and old lady. Squalls and squirts of excitement start in my belly. Triumph makes me want to take a shit.

I whisper words through the veil between us. I send her on her way with mutterings. 'The little boys from the truck were crying when they were taken into the tiled room' – flicker of talon on the mattress – 'They were scared, but didn't know why they were going to be hurt. They didn't understand' – stretching of a single bony leg under the sheets – 'What did they look like on your plate?' – final kick of twisted foot, and yellow nail snags on silk – 'There was laughter in the boardroom during dinner. I heard you. I was outside and I heard you all' – all the thin bones relax and go soft under me – 'Then you made me bring the left-overs up here in white bags. They banged against my legs on the stairs. They felt heavy. The bags were wet inside.'

Now she's still. Nothing under me but bird bones, fossils wrapped in silk and some hair, but not much else.

I stay on top of her for a while. Now it's done I feel warm inside. Milky sweat cools on the skin under my night gown. I take the pillow off Mrs Van den Broeck's face and step back from the bed. I pad out the part that was over her beak. Leaning across her I put the pillow back behind her warm body.

Underneath my body one of her chicken-bone arms suddenly moves, quicker than I thought something old and skinny could move. Yellow claws curl around my elbow. I look down. An egg-shell brow wrinkles. Pink eyes open and make me gasp. I try to pull away.

Bird snarl.

Pinched mouth opens wide. Two rows of tiny yellow teeth sink into my wrist.

Now I'm drowning. Pain and panic fills my balloon skull like hot water. I pull and tug and yanky-shake at her biting beak that wants to saw off my dolly hand. Grunting, she holds on. How can an old thing like Mrs Van den Broeck, made from such tiny bones and paper skin, make so deep a noise?

Digging my heels into the rug, I push backwards with all my strength, but her body comes forward in a tangle of sheets, pulled across the mattress by her mouth. Snarly and spitting, she shakes her head from side to side and I think my wrist is broken. I should have guessed 170 years of her evil life could not be stopped by a soft pillow in the night.

Mad from the pain, I swat my free hand around in the air and it hits something solid. Now there are stabbing pains in the knuckles of that hand too from where it struck the heavy lamp. Strength leaks out of my feet and into the rug. Black dots float in front of my eyes. I might faint. It feels like her serrated beak has gone through a nerve.

I fall backwards and pull her whole body off the bed. Her stick-body hits the floor but makes no sound. I stand up and try to shake her off like I'm trying to pull off a tight shirt that has gone inside-out over my face. Tears blur my eyes.

I reach for the lamp on the bedside table. My little hand circles the hot smooth neck below the bulb. Pulling it off the table, I watch the thick green marble-base drop to the biting head on the rug. There is a *thock* sound as the sharp stone corner strikes the side of her head by the small ear. She stops biting.

I twist my wrist free of the loose beak and step away. I look down and can't believe so much liquid could spill from the broken head of a very old bird. The liquid is black. It's been going through her thin pipes and tubes for 170 years, and now it is soaking into a rug.

Working fast I wrap the white cord of the lamp around her claw and make it go tight. Maybe they will think she fell from her pillows and pulled the lamp down on top of her bird head. With the tail of my night shirt I then wipe at all the things my dollish fingers have touched around the bed.

I flit from her room like a ghost. Go down the long hall and close the front door behind me. In the light of the landing I inspect the circle of bruises and cuts her beak has made on my stiff wrist. Not as bad as it felt.

I find it hard to believe Gemima is not screaming and that doors are not opening and that phones are not ringing and that residents are not shuffling down the stairs in dressing gowns. But there is only silence in the west wing.

Then the shaking starts.

Down the stairs I go on my hands and knees like a spider with four legs torn off. Back to my bunk.

Curled up in the warm place I have made in the middle of my bed, with the thin sheet and itchy grey blanket pulled over my head, I try and stop the shakes and try and wipe away all the pictures that swirl around my pumpkin skull. There is so much room inside the big space, so I guess it can hold more memories than a smaller head. Over and over I see the chewing bird that was Mrs Van den Broeck, her beak fastened on my wrist, and then I see the heavy lamp land with a *thock . . . thock . . . thock . . .* It's all I can hear: the sharp marble corner breaking the wafer of her veiny temple.

What have I done in this giant house? What will become of me? They will know that my dolly hands got busy with a pillow and bedside-lamp to crush that flightless vulture in its own nest. I wonder if turning back the hands on my little brass clock will take me back to the time before I went sneaking and creeping into her room.

An impulse makes my face scrunch up to cry and my body

shivers under the blankets. Then I stand up beside the bunk and peer into the top bed where Vinegar Irish snores. I wish I was him. With no killing pictures inside his head, only thoughts of clear liquid to sup from plastic containers, flowing through his twitchy sleep.

The cold in the porter's dormitory makes my shaking worse. My wrist throbs. I want to get back into my bed and curl into a ball. Like the baby in the tummy before I was cut out and made my momma die.

I leave the dormitory and look down to the washroom door.

No one is shouting, there are no alarms or lights being turned on. All is quiet in the building. No one knows Mrs Van den Broeck is dead. No one knows it was me, yet.

Inside I feel better. No one saw me. No one heard me. Gemima was asleep the whole time, dreaming of the hot green place across the oceans where she was born. I just have to stay calm. Maybe no one will suspect me, the big-headed boy with the doll hands. What can he do with those puppet legs and pencil arms? That big bulb head with the baby face stuck on the front is not capable of thinking of such things, maybe that's what they will think. That's what they thought at the orphanage too. That's how I got away with it before. They never even thought of me at the same time as they thought about the nasty smacking carers all found dead in their beds. I did three of them carers with these small china hands.

I grin with joy. My little grey heart slows down its pumping. All the pebbles of sweat dry across my skin. Warmth spreads through every teeny toe and twig finger, up through my see-through body to my roundish head, until I am glowing with the happiness of escaping and of tricking them. All of them who don't know about the power in my tiny hands.

And in my head now, I see the little boy who came in the white truck. The one they ate yesterday. He is dancing in heaven. Up there, the sky is totally blue. He likes the long grass that is soft between his toes and he likes the way the yellow sun warms his jumping running body. It was for him and his brother that I dropped the heavy lamp. *Thock*. What happened to him must always be remembered. I see it again now. I see it all behind my squeezed shut, black button eyes.

But what of the other one?

And then I go down to the washroom and I unlock the door. Behind the wood of the door before it is even open, I hear the skitter of dry feet retreat into a corner. A whimper.

No, they shall not have you too.

I open the door and walk past the dark wet bench beside the white wall. And I go to the huddled yellowish boy in the corner. I smile. He takes my small outstretched hand. Blinks wet eyes.

I think of the Cathedral of Our Lady and of the mist. We'll need a blanket.

'Your brother's waiting for us,' I say, and he stands up.

THANA NIVEAU

GUINEA PIG GIRL

SHE WAS BEAUTIFUL. Quite the most beautiful woman Alex had ever seen. But it wasn't just her beauty. What he loved most about her was the way she suffered.

He had been horrified the first time. He'd felt the stirring in his loins and then the growing hardness in his trousers. A sidelong glance at his mate Josh, whose film it was, then some uncomfortable shifting.

'Holy shit,' Josh said with a laugh as the freak in the lab coat cut off one of Yuki's fingers.

She screamed, her beautiful mouth stretched open, her slanted eyes as wide as they would go. She screamed. Josh laughed. Alex got hard.

'Yeah,' he said, to say something. Then he squirmed as Yuki's torture continued and his erection grew.

Oh, how she suffered.

That night he'd wanked himself silly over the image of her terrified, pleading face. He didn't dare go as far as imagining himself pinning her down on the filthy mattress in the basement room, fisting a hand in her long black hair and telling her how he would take her to bits, piece by piece. No, he didn't dare. The image flickered in the background of his thoughts but he shied away from it. Pictured himself instead as the guy who came to tend her wounds, give her water and a bit of food, hold her and reassure her that he would help her escape if he could, honest, but they were watching him too . . .

It was sick.

He felt ashamed and disgusted once the last throbs of pleasure had faded and he'd cleaned himself up and thrown the handful of tissues in the bin, wishing he could incinerate them. He felt as filthy as the room she'd been imprisoned in throughout the film. He'd let himself go this time but that was it. He didn't get off on stuff like that, no way. In junior school some bullies had once tried to make him join in with torturing old Mrs Webber's cat and he hadn't been able to do it. He'd suffered then, suffered their ridicule and taunting and calling him a pussy. But he wasn't like them, couldn't bring himself to hurt something else, something helpless.

So why did Yuki make him feel like this?

Days later he still couldn't get some of the imagery out of his head. It was just some dodgy Japanese torture porn film he couldn't even remember the name of but he remembered every moment of every scene Yuki was in. She was tiny and fragile, the way so many Japanese girls were. Sexy and girlish, slutty and innocent all at the same time. An intoxicating package in any context but seeing her so helpless and vulnerable had done something to Alex. That wounded expression, her eyes streaming with tears, her hands clasped as she pleaded in words he couldn't understand . . . It got under his skin.

He'd wanted to dive into the film and save her, protect her, and yet that wasn't where his fantasies steered him afterwards. On the way to work his hands had clenched on the steering wheel as he sat in traffic and he imagined them wrapped around Yuki's slender throat. If he closed his eyes he could hear her gasping for breath. He could smell her urine as she pissed herself in terror.

Sick.

And yet every night his hand slipped down between his legs and all it took was the thought of her wide eyes and high-pitched cries to make him unbearably hard. He couldn't banish the images. All he could do was let them wash over him as he came so hard his ears rang. Again and again.

Yuki Hayashi. Actress. Born 13 April 1989 in Hokkaido, Japan. Filmography: *Victim Factory 1 & 2*, *Love Hotel of the Damned* and *Aesthetic Paranoia* (filming).

Alex clicked on each film and read the synopses. They were all low-budget rip-offs of the notorious 'guinea pig' films from the 80s. Girls got kidnapped and tortured and that was basically it. Sometimes they also got raped.

The fourth one in the filmography wasn't finished yet and *Love Hotel of the Damned* didn't seem to be available anywhere, not even on Josh's pirate site. But Alex ordered the others.

Like all rip-offs, Victim Factory aspired to take things a step further than its inspiration. The gore was over the top, even by Alex's standards, and it was made worse by the homemade feel of the production. They looked like snuff films shot on someone's home video camera.

Yuki's debut was as '2nd victim' in an unpleasant scene where she was grabbed off the street and taken to an abandoned asylum. There she was stripped naked and thrown into a room stained with the blood and of previous victims. To wait. After listening in terror to the screams and cries of another girl, Yuki was dragged off to the torture chamber next door for her turn. The killer bound her wrists tightly with rope and looped them over a large hook. He turned a crank that noisily hoisted her off the ground while she screamed and wept and kicked her pretty legs. Even her slight weight looked as though it was dislocating her shoulders and Alex winced. How could you fake that?

Finally, in a bizarre moment of artistry, the killer carved a series of Japanese characters into Yuki's skin with the jagged edge of a broken samurai sword. The subtitles only translated the spoken dialogue so Alex had no idea what the words inscribed on her flesh meant.

It drove him mad.

The exotic swashes and flourishes streamed with blood that looked disturbingly real, a striking contrast to Yuki's pale skin. Alex could almost believe that the mutilation had actually happened but for the fact that in the second film, the one Josh had shown him, she was unmarked. Pristine and ready for more. Ready to have her fingers and toes snipped off one by one, her mouth forced open with a metal dentist's gag and her tongue cut out.

He searched the Net for more information but the films didn't appear to be widely known. There was the occasional mention on a message board but Alex couldn't find any translation for the characters in the carving scene. Nor was there much information about Yuki. He found one screen grab from the first film, which he immediately stored on his phone. Her eyes pleaded with him through the image and he felt obscurely guilty, as though he'd imprisoned her in a tiny digital cage. But he didn't delete the picture.

The films made him feel uncomfortable, almost sick at times. And truthfully, he didn't enjoy the violence. When he played the DVDs again he only watched the scenes with Yuki and even then he felt funny afterwards. But he couldn't get her out of his head. The very thought of her was enough to make him hard and even though he tried to picture her whole and undamaged, the images of torture would quickly take over. He tried to imagine her voice, cheerful and sweet as she chattered on her phone before being abducted in each film, but the musical sounds always devolved into screams of pain and madness.

Her anguish was so excruciatingly real. He couldn't tune it out, couldn't un-see it. And he couldn't help the effect it had on him.

She was there behind his eyes every night, pleading with him to stop, her tiny body struggling helplessly against ropes and rusty chains. And no matter how much he tried to transform the images in his head, he always saw himself wielding the blades, the needles, the bolt cutters. Her blood ran like wine over his hands and he was drunk on the taste of her.

'Hey, mate, you know that DVD you were after?'

Alex froze, staring at his phone with apprehension. Then he took a deep breath before forcing himself to ask calmly, 'Which one?'

'*Love Hotel of the Damned*. I found it.'

'Oh, cool,' he replied, as nonchalantly as he could manage.

'Yeah, some guy up in Leeds has it and he said he'd burn me a copy for a tenner.'

'Thanks, mate. I'll pay you back.'

'No problem!' Josh sounded pleased, no doubt proud of himself for tracking down the obscure film. If he had any suspicions about Alex's obsession it wasn't obvious. 'I'll drop it by your place next week.'

Next week. Alex felt his insides churn hungrily at the thought of seeing Yuki again, seeing her suffer and die in new and terrible ways.

The synopsis of *Love Hotel* made it sound like the worst of the lot. Same 'guinea pig' concept but this time set in one of those weird Japanese hotels he'd read about online. The kind where you could fuck a manga character on a spaceship or grope a schoolgirl in a room designed like a train carriage. He'd found the trailer for the film on a J-horror fan site and it looked seriously reprehensible. Even some of the hardcore gorehounds said the level of sexual violence was too much for them.

Alex slid down in his chair as his cock began to stir.

The film was even worse than he'd anticipated. Murky and grainy, as though someone had simply held up a cheap camera and filmed it playing on a TV. The poor quality actually made the gore seem more real.

Yuki didn't appear until halfway through and Alex almost didn't recognise her. She was thinner and paler and she seemed even more fragile. But she was still beautiful. She wore an elaborate gothic Lolita dress with frilly petticoats and a lacy apron and mop cap. But not for long. Her 'customer' cut the flimsy costume away with a pair of shears. From the way Yuki yelped and twisted, it was clear he was cutting her too. Blood trickled down one arm and over her belly and she stared straight into the camera for one heart-stopping moment. Alex had the uncomfortable sense that he was watching a genuine victim this time and not an actress.

His thumb hovered over the STOP button for a few seconds before he reminded himself that there was a fourth film on the list, *Aesthetic Paranoia*, which she was apparently still shooting. If this was real, surely she wouldn't have made another such film. Surely she'd be shouting 'Police!' or 'Help!' He was sure he'd recognise that level of distress even in a language he couldn't speak. No, it was just that weird sense of authenticity you sometimes got with ultra low-budget films.

Yuki cried and begged in plaintive Japanese while the man stripped the mattress off the bed and threw her onto the bare springs. He bound her, spread-eagled, with wire that Alex could see biting into her delicate wrists and ankles. Then he threw a bucket of water over her and she screamed again and again, writhing on the springs.

The man lifted the head of the bed and propped it against the wall so that it rested at an angle. The camera zoomed in and around Yuki's naked, shivering body, shooting from underneath the bed to show the mesh pressing painfully into her back, the wires cutting into her skin. In close-up the springs looked rusty and Yuki was bleeding in several places. The detail was too subtle not to be real and Alex began to feel light-headed again. But he couldn't tear his eyes away.

The man held up a series of huge fishhooks with what looked like electrodes attached and Yuki screamed herself hoarse as the hooks were threaded through her skin one by one in a scene that went on for nearly ten minutes. When he was done the man connected the trailing wires to a machine at his feet. He pressed a button and there was a terrible buzzing sound, followed by another piercing scream. Yuki leapt and bucked against the springs for what felt like an eternity before the current stopped. Wisps of smoke began to rise from the contact points and Alex thought he could smell something burning. Blood ran from Yuki's eyes like tears as she gasped and panted, too breathless to scream. The camera zoomed in on her face and she stared directly out of the screen again, as though she were looking through a window right at Alex.

When the buzzing sound began again Yuki tensed and began to plead frantically, this time with whoever was behind the camera. Alex closed his eyes against her screams and the metallic rattle of the springs and the zap of electricity. He held his breath as it went on and on, wishing it would end.

At last there was silence. Silence and the smell of scorched meat. He shut the film off and ran for the bathroom. He almost made it.

It was several days before Yuki came back.

Alex had put the three DVDs in a carrier bag, knotted it and pushed it to the back of the bathroom cupboard. When Josh had asked how he liked the film he'd forced a laugh and said it was rubbish, with crappy effects. And if his voice had trembled when he'd said it, Josh didn't seem to notice. Yuki's picture was gone from his phone and the J-horror sites he'd bookmarked were erased from his browsing history.

As disturbing as it had been, he knew it was fake. That was part of the point of films like that – to trick the viewer into thinking it was real. Actual snuff films were an urban legend. None had ever been found and they certainly wouldn't be readily available online in any case. People had been fooled by special effects before. And while it was a compliment to the makers of Yuki's films, Alex had seen enough.

He was in bed, almost asleep, when he first heard the sound. A soft rustle, as though someone were reading a newspaper in the next room. He froze. He had the mad urge to call out 'Who's there?' even though there was no one else in the flat. Unless someone had broken in. It was that kind of neighbourhood but the flat was too small for a burglar to hide in without Alex knowing. A rat, then? It would have to be an awfully big one.

His heart hammered in his chest, drowning out any sounds that might be coming from the other room. Seconds passed like hours as he sat staring towards the open doorway, feeling like a child who'd woken from a nightmare. He should get up and switch on all the lights but the thought of putting his feet on the floor, exposing them to the empty space under the bed, was too frightening.

'Get a grip,' he mouthed, trying to spur himself into action. But still he didn't move.

There was another sound. A soft slap, like a bare foot on the hard floor. Then another. And another.

His blood turned to ice water as the footsteps came closer and closer. A thin shape was emerging from the darkness of the corridor. Then he heard the dripping. He could almost believe it was some girl he'd brought home from a club and forgotten about. She'd just got out of the shower without drying off and now –

Except it wasn't. It was Yuki.

When she reached the bedroom Alex bit back a scream. She stood in the doorway, naked and dripping with blood. Her arms hung loose at her sides and Alex's stomach clenched as he saw the symbols carved into her body. The calligraphy was more extensive than he remembered from the scene in the film. The cuts ran from the base of her throat, across her small breasts and down her torso.

A strangled sound escaped his throat and Yuki's head turned towards him. It was a careful, deliberate movement, as though she had only located him by the sound and was trying to fix his exact position. She turned and took a step into the room. Alex stared at her in horror, desperate to run but unable to move.

It wasn't real. It couldn't be real. It was a dream or a hallucination, just like the images in his head he hadn't been able to get rid of. But worst of all, he felt himself responding as he always had. Hot desire pulsed in his groin even as bile rose in his throat.

Each step she took opened the cuts further. Blood flowed over her body like water, pooling on the floor. What was almost worse was the residual grace in her movements. She didn't shuffle or sway drunkenly. Rather, she moved with the precision of a dancer, each movement full of purpose. Blood gleamed in the light from the window, shining on her mutilated skin like a wet carapace, and Alex shuddered as he felt himself growing hard.

'No,' he managed to whisper. 'No, please.'

Yuki responded to his voice, reaching out for him. Her eyes were empty pools of black but her lips seemed to be forming a smile.

It took all his courage to shut his eyes and wish the sight away.

He counted to three before his eyes flew open again in fright. Yuki was gone.

It was some time before he was able to get up off the bed and even then his legs threatened to buckle with each step he took towards the doorway. There was no blood on the floor, no evidence that anything had ever been there.

It was the middle of the night but Alex got dressed and drove all the way to work to throw the DVDs away. He snapped the disks in half and scattered them, along with the packaging, into the three large industrial bins behind the office building. He wondered if he ought to say something, but what? A prayer? He wasn't religious so he didn't imagine it would do any good. But surely it couldn't do any harm.

'Goodbye, Yuki,' he whispered, and her name felt like an obscenity on his lips. 'Please don't come back.'

But she did.

It was four nights later and Alex was asleep. He was deep inside a pleasant childhood dream when his eyes fluttered open with a start and there she was, standing over him.

He screamed and scrambled away until he was cowering on the floor against the wall. Yuki cocked her head as if in confusion, her eyes streaming with black, bloody tears, her temples scorched and pierced by fishhooks. She looked thinner, more wasted.

Yuki raised one pale arm and reached for him. He could see the gleam of bone through the cuts on her chest. The wounds gaped like tiny mouths with each movement, as though trying to speak the words they represented. Alex shuddered with revulsion as Yuki drew her hand down over his torso. Her touch was gentle as she took hold of his cock. He stiffened in her grasp, unable to move, unable to resist as she stroked him like a lover. She pressed her blackened lips to his and he closed his eyes with a sickened moan as he came.

Then he crumpled to his knees on the floor, crying.

'Mate, you look like hell.'

Alex had been tempted not to answer the door but Josh had kept pounding, shouting that he knew Alex was home.

'Yeah,' he mumbled. 'Got some bloody bug.'

'I've been ringing you for days. The guys at work thought you'd died or something. You didn't even call in sick.'

Alex managed a rueful smile. 'Too sick to.'

'Well, is there anything I can do for you? You need food? Booze? Drugs?'

'No, I'm fine.'

But his assurances didn't get rid of Josh. His friend muttered about how stuffy it was in the flat before planting himself on the battered sofa where they'd watched so many DVDs together. He shrugged out of his leather jacket, revealing a black *Faces of Death* T-shirt. Alex stared at the grinning skull and spiky red lettering for several seconds before looking away. Josh didn't seem to notice his uneasiness.

An awkward silence stretched between them but Alex couldn't think of anything to say. He couldn't tell Josh he was seeing ghosts, much less the specifics of the encounters. But Yuki's presence hung in the air in spite of his silence. He could still smell her blood and burnt flesh, still feel the slick touch of her fingers on his skin.

He'd scrubbed himself raw in the shower after the first time but it hadn't changed anything. She'd returned the next night, and the next. She looked worse with each visit but each time Alex's own body had betrayed him, succumbing to her touch even as he choked back the sickness welling in his throat. He couldn't resist or escape and each violation only seemed to excite him more.

He was pretty sure he understood what the symbols were now. Hours of online searching had led him to a website about curses. He didn't need to read Japanese to know that one of the characters represented 'desire' and another 'obsession'. He hadn't dared to search further to see if 'love' was also among them.

Josh was talking, telling him about some new film he'd just seen, one his girlfriend hadn't been able to stomach.

Alex felt his own stomach churn queasily.

'Anyway,' Josh continued, oblivious to his friend's discomfort, 'pretty weird about that actress, huh?'

Alex blinked. 'What are you talking about?'

'Didn't you get my email?'

'What email?'

'The one I sent you last week. About that Japanese girl. The one in the film you had me track down?'

Alex felt a crawling sensation in his guts. So his fixation on Yuki hadn't been lost on Josh after all. 'What about her?'

'She's dead.'

The words seemed to come from a long way away, like a transmission he'd already heard. He couldn't speak. The skull on Josh's shirt seemed to be laughing now.

'Alex? You OK?'

He nodded weakly. 'Yeah, I think so.' Some part of him had already known, of course.

Josh went on. 'I figured you liked her since you wanted all her films and I was trying to find a copy of that last one for you – *Aesthetic Paranoia*. She died on the set. Some kind of freak accident.'

'When?' Alex managed to ask.

'That's what's so weird, mate. It was only a few weeks ago, before I even showed you *Victim Factory 2*. She was dead the whole time we've been watching her films. Hey, are you sure you're OK? You're white as a fucking sheet.'

~

That night Alex lay in bed listening for the familiar sticky wet slap of her feet. There was no point in trying to resist. Yuki would come for him, would keep coming for him, until there was nothing left of either of them. He'd met her eyes through the screen and she had chosen him. He was special.

He hadn't liked the way Josh had said *we*. *We've* been watching her films. He didn't like the thought of Josh seeing Yuki the way he did.

She was no longer able to stand upright but she could crawl. Her hair hung in matted clumps around her face as she pushed herself towards him on rotting hands and knees. Her skin was peeling away from the bone in places, hanging like strips of charred, wet paper.

'I'm here,' Alex said softly, tapping the floor to guide her.

When she reached the source of the sound she stopped. A heavy obstacle was in the way. She reached out a tentative bony hand to touch it. Her fingers moved over the grinning skull and the red letters that were smeared with blood, then found the tear in the material. She prodded the gaping wound in Josh's chest, gingerly touching the bloody edge of the kitchen knife while Josh stared vacantly up at the ceiling.

Yuki frowned, looking lost for a moment before recoiling from the unfamiliar body. Hurt by the deception, she raised her head and a feeble sound emerged from what remained of her throat. Alex could see the glistening strings of muscle trying to work to form words. His heart twisted.

'I'm sorry,' he said. 'But I had to know I was the only one.'

She responded to his voice, turning her head towards him and then making her way to the bed with painful care. Too weak to climb up, she raised her thin arms like a child. Alex ignored the crunch of disintegrating bone as he lifted her up and sat her in his lap, his cock already swelling hungrily. Her lips hung in bloody tatters and he smoothed them into the semblance of a pout as he kissed her.

'I love you too,' he whispered. Then he slid his hand between her ruined legs.

ELIZABETH STOTT

TOUCH ME WITH YOUR COLD, HARD FINGERS

FRIDAY IS ALWAYS lads' night for Tony, but Saturday is their night. It's sacrosanct. Maureen had to work today, or she'd have been there at lunchtime and they'd have spent the afternoon shopping. To make up for it, she buys pizzas on the way to Tony's flat – they'll have a cosy night-in together.

The pizzas smell inviting from the boxes on the back seat of her car. Maureen parks in the usual place opposite his flat, under the streetlight. Tony said it was safer to park the car there where it can be seen. And she has come to think of it as her personal parking space; that she has a stake on his territory now. He's given her the key to his flat, putting the key ring over her ring finger. Tony had been something of a womaniser, but Maureen has changed him. Now, she is his one and only. Now, she has the key to his flat. No woman has ever been given the key to his flat. It's only a matter of time before she moves in.

Tony's flat is on the ground floor of a small modern block in a good area. It's not big – two-bedroomed – but nicely finished and newly fitted out with a stylish kitchen and bathroom. Maureen thinks she could be content to move in here – make it do for two.

She knocks gently, to warn him, although he should expect her. She'd left a message on his phone. He should welcome her with a kiss, a snuggle in the doorway . . . But the hall is in darkness. There is no music, no television, no sound of a shower or any sign that anyone is home.

The ticking of the kitchen clock pushes through the dark as Maureen makes her way through the hall, calling Tony's name. She turns on the kitchen light. All looks normal, tidy. Tony is fussy like that, but it looks like he hasn't prepared any food today. She places the pizzas on the kitchen table. The blind is open and the window looks blackly back at her. She closes it and notices that the plant she put on the windowsill is drooping; she waters it from the tap, flushing away loose bits of potting compost. The water makes a cold rushing sound in the sink, loud in the quiet flat. Surely he would have heard her? But there is nothing.

The lounge door is closed. Maureen stands outside, hesitantly touching the door handle.

'Tony?'

No answer.

She pushes open the door. The room is lit by a single table lamp – one that Maureen bought to make the room more homely. The television is off. The curtains are drawn shut.

Tony is in his usual spot on the sofa, facing away from the door, looking towards someone sitting in the place where she usually sits, but Maureen cannot see who she is – her body is obscured by Tony's. Yes, it is a *her*; a halo of feminine blonde hair catches the light. Maureen stands in the doorway and looks, feeling like a voyeur. Tony does not turn to acknowledge her, even though she speaks his name several times. Her voice shakes. There's no sign that he has even noticed her. The room is fusty, as if it has been closed up all day. Maureen wants to open a window and let in some fresh air, but she is rooted to the spot. It is as if the blood has congealed in her veins.

No matter how hard she tries to see the woman, the figure eludes her. She calls Tony's name again; it comes out as a crow-like squawk. Maureen thinks she sees his head twitch, and glimpses the side of a woman's face. A bare shoulder. The curve of a naked breast. Anger rises within her and she slides her foot over the door plate. As Maureen steps into the room, the naked figure slips towards Tony, landing in his lap. But it is soon clear that Tony's 'guest' is an extraordinarily realistic mannequin. Its face looks towards her, over Tony's hip. It has an expression that seems like insolence.

The mannequin is a detailed model of a woman, manufactured with complex joints so that it can be posed naturalistically. Its face is life-like, with real-looking eyes. Its – *her* – hair is long, remarkably like Maureen's, and moves in a disturbingly realistic way. Maureen almost expects the mannequin to sit up and toss its head to lift the hair from its face.

Tony looks at her confused and afraid, as if she is a spook.

'What the fuck is going on, Tony?'

With difficulty, Tony stands, the mannequin tangled around his legs. It twists sideways and falls over the opposite arm of the sofa, its pale backside flouted like an insult.

'It's you,' he says confusedly, attempting to re-seat the mannequin in Maureen's place.

'If this is another of your games, Tony . . .'

Tony seems to gather his thoughts, and moves towards her, looking over his shoulder at the mannequin. Stiffly, he holds out his arms to her. Maureen backs away.

'Get *that* out of here. It gives me the creeps.'

He puts his arm around the mannequin's waist, picking it up with his other arm under its knees as if it is a real woman. It seems to look at Maureen with a hostile expression. He takes it to his bedroom door.

'Surely you're not going to put it in there?'

'Of course not,' he says dreamily, turning around, fumbling

at the handle of the spare room as if he isn't sure what he is doing. From the lounge doorway, Maureen can hear him placing it on the bed, adjusting its legs, talking to himself.

She doesn't want to sit on the sofa where the mannequin has been. She stands in the middle of the room waiting. Tony seems to take a long time. When he returns, Maureen has her car keys in her hand, ready to leave.

'What is that thing doing here?'

Tony shrugs. He looks rumpled, as if he is wearing his clothes from the night before. His hair hasn't been brushed.

'I really missed you last night,' he says.

It sounds as if he has just made it up.

'You must have been off your head last night.'

Tony manages a smile, a flicker of the apparently ingenuous smile that always works to bring her round.

'Yeah, I suppose that's it. We sank a few . . . But I told them – enough was enough.'

'It never is, Tony. That's the trouble. *I've* had enough this time.'

'Please stay, Maureen. I'll call for a take-away.'

'I brought pizzas. They'll be cold.'

She heats the pizzas in Tony's oven whilst he freshens up. The pizza boxes look untidy on the table. They will annoy Tony. She leaves them there anyway.

Maureen turns the cushion over where the mannequin had been, and they sit on the sofa in front of the television eating, but without speaking. It feels like a picnic in a graveyard. Maureen eats all of her pizza and starts on Tony's, which is barely touched.

'You shouldn't eat that,' he says.

'Why? You don't seem to want it.'

Tony looks puzzled. 'You'll put on weight . . .' It sounds more like a question.

'At least I *can* eat. I'm a real living woman.'

Tony stuffs a slice into in his mouth. Then another.

'You haven't eaten today, have you?' she asks.

'I don't remember much after last night.'

'What possessed you to bring that thing home?'

'I don't remember. We were in this club.'

'Not another of your *I'm so sorry, Maureen it won't happen again . . .*'

'Nothing happened. They wanted to go to a lap-dancing place. I said I didn't want to. I told the lads we were getting serious. That I considered myself spoken for . . .'

He pauses for another bite of pizza.

'They started teasing me about practising for a stag night. They must've brought me home.'

'And the mannequin?'

'She was in my bed when I woke up.'

'In your bed? That's vile.'

'It must've been one of their pranks.'

'A sick prank. A rotten sick prank.' She begins to cry.

Tony's face is helpless, like a little boy's.

'Please stay. I can't live without you.'

He starts to cry too. They cry like two lost children.

She stays. They talk of the future. 'But not here,' says Tony. 'This is a bachelor pad. We'd have to get our own house.'

It sounds like a child's game. They talk of the possible house together, and getting married. Maureen feels it like fantasy confetti around her – melting as she touches it. But she stays.

In Tony's bed, Maureen lies awake. She had made Tony turn the mattress and change the sheets. She clings to his naked back, feeling the slow beat of his heart. She wants to seal him to her, convince herself that there is a real future for them. The mannequin is just on the other side of the wall. She thinks of its face, its doll-like perfection. She has seen similar mannequins in the bridal shop in town. Although none is as perfect as this.

He once told her that she was the most beautiful woman he'd seen, that she was perfect. Although they lay naked together he made no move to touch her; he'd fallen asleep almost as soon as they went to bed. Maureen's stomach cramps miserably. The pizza has given her indigestion. But Tony sleeps so deeply, breathing so softly, she can hardly hear him.

The pain in her guts means she has to get up. Putting on Tony's dressing gown she tiptoes to the bathroom. All is dark, bar the faint light from the street. The sounds of the traffic seem comfortingly normal. She could leave now and spare herself the uncertainty. The thought of leaving spears her with an unexpected sense of hope, but she has invested a lot in Tony, she can't run away now. She stands in the bathroom doorway and thinks of her car parked safely under the streetlight, how easy it would be to get her keys and drive away.

In the passage, Maureen sees that the door to the spare room is framed in light. She hadn't noticed before. Gathering Tony's dressing gown around her, she listens outside. Perhaps she hears a scuffling sound . . . Cautiously, she peeps around the door. It's a small room, just big enough for a single bed and a table. The mannequin is sitting bolt upright on the bed, looking towards her. Its arms are positioned as if it is about to get up, one stiff hand on the mattress, the other on the bed cover. For a long moment, she and the mannequin seemingly regard each other. Maureen's fear becomes anger.

'Oh no you don't!'

She shoves the mannequin backwards onto the bed. Its legs stick up, pushing the covers off. Maureen hears a faint exhalation, but it could just be Tony on the other side of the thin wall. Shaking, she turns off the light and shuts the door firmly. She could go, right now, but she can't leave Tony alone with this – *thing*.

She slips back in beside him. Her place is cold. He has

moved to the far side of the bed, holding on to the edge of the mattress. Maureen can't stop thinking of the mannequin's face. Every time she closes her eyes she can see that spiteful expression, imagine the cold hardness of its hands. She shudders that the thing has been in this bed, in the place where she now lies. From the spare bedroom she hears the sound of something moving against the wall. A distinct scraping, sliding sound.

'Tony, wake up . . .'

She prods him. Tony jolts half awake and sinks back to sleep, but she kicks him on the ankle. There is a loud thump that even Tony cannot ignore. He swears and almost falls out of bed. Maureen can see the silhouette of his back as he stumbles, naked, from the room. Maureen follows him. She is aware of the bizarre scene they make, both naked and shivering, listening at the door of the spare bedroom.

'Be careful, Tony. *She's* awake.'

'Don't be silly.' But his voice is not confident. All is now quiet.

'Don't go in . . .'

'Something must have fallen, that's all.'

He puts his hand on the door handle, but it is stuck, and he forces the door with his shoulder. The room is dark, but Maureen can make out a hunched shape on the floor in the light from the landing. The door narrowly missed it. Rubbing his shoulder, Tony switches on the light, and they see the mannequin on the floor, on all-fours like a dog. Its immaculately painted face looks towards them, hair hanging down in front, alive-looking.

Maureen snatches the cover off the spare bed and throws it over the mannequin. She is convinced she hears it laugh.

'You must get rid of it, Tony. First thing in the morning. Promise?'

'First thing tomorrow,' he says, his voice heavy.

~

It is almost ten on the Sunday morning before she wakes. The bed beside her is empty. She listens out for telltale noises, but all is quiet. Perhaps he has already taken the mannequin away.

Tony's dressing gown is still on the hook on the back of the door; she puts it on. It smells, comfortingly, of him.

'Tony?'

No answer. She goes out into the passage. The door of the small bedroom is closed. She doesn't look inside. From the kitchen she can smell toast and croissants – her favourites. She smiles to think he's prepared them for her.

But in the kitchen Tony is sitting silently at the little round table, stock still and naked. The mannequin sits immediately opposite, in a bizarre domestic tableau. There are glasses of orange juice in front of them, untouched. The toast has popped up and gone cold.

The kitchen clock ticks and the oven whirrs; the aroma of croissants fills the room. Maureen can tell that they are ready, but Tony makes no move to get up. He sits, motionless, ignoring her, saying nothing. Maureen stands in the kitchen, watching, uncertain what to do. Dullness settles over her; her breathing slows. Dimly, she senses her awareness shrinking. It is something like fainting, but this is happening so slowly, she feels the infinite path to oblivion stretch out before her. The ticking of the clock slows until she is stuck between ticks, suspended in forever, as if her consciousness has been stretched out to a thread so thin she can no longer grasp it. A fragment of her mind tells her to pull back, but the desire, with her awareness, has all but vanished.

A brilliant flare ignites inside her head. She falls, as if she has been placed back into the scene, but off kilter. Lying on the floor, she hears the smoke detector shrieking – it must have been set off by the croissants in the oven that are now burning. Tony is rubbing his eyes, bewildered. The mannequin sags onto the kitchen table.

Maureen looks up from the floor at Tony whilst the detector shrills its painfully loud alarm. She wants to tell him how crazy it is, but Tony gently lifts the mannequin's head, pulling back the hair from its face. He does not ask Maureen if she is all right. It's as if she isn't here. She manages to get to her feet, and turns on the extractor fan before pressing the alarm's cancel button with the end of a mop handle. A sob rises in her throat. Tony looks up, but with a dazed expression. Maureen slips out of Tony's dressing gown and flings it at him.

'I, at least, am getting dressed.'

On her return, Tony has made coffee. The ruined croissants are on the hob, the crusts blackened. He has taken the mannequin away and sits at the table in his dressing gown, cradling a mug.

'Stay . . .' he says. It comes out croakily. He holds out a mug for Maureen.

'I'm not sure that I want to. That I can.'

'I can't remember how she – *it* – got there. I made breakfast for you. I thought of you sharing it with me. Then I don't know what happened.'

'That thing is creepy. You're creeping me out with it.'

'We'll get rid of it.'

'How?'

'I'll take her – *it* – to the tip.'

They sit over the little table drinking coffee. Maureen reaches out to touch Tony's hand, but it is icy cold. She pulls away. Tears glaze his eyes.

'Maureen, I do love you. More than anyone I have ever loved. But I can't see myself settling down. Doing the Mr and Mrs routine. It scares the life out of me . . .'

Tony does not stop her from leaving.

They make no attempt to call each other. Two weeks later, Maureen still has his key and thinks she should return it. She will simply post the key and go; she won't speak to him. After work, she drives to the flat, and, as she turns the corner, she spots Tony's car parked in its usual place in the residents' car park.

There is a free spot just along from Tony's car on the opposite side. She will only be here for a couple of minutes. It won't hurt if she uses a resident's space. But as she turns, she sees a female passenger in the front seat of Tony's car. The driver's seat is empty.

She parks her car crookedly, and looks in her rear-view mirror. The woman is waiting – waiting for Tony. Anger seizes her, and Maureen jumps out of her car, leaving the door open. Tony is nowhere to be seen.

His car is dirty, and small leaves have accumulated on the wiper blades and grille. Tony is proud of his flashy car, and cleans it regularly, but the rain has washed dusty streaks down the windscreen. Maureen quickly realises that the 'passenger' is the mannequin, sitting neatly in the front passenger seat, looking like it belongs there, dressed in a T-shirt that she recognises as one of her own. She yanks open the passenger door and, with a growl, drags the mannequin by its hair from the car. It falls in a tangle of limbs onto the tarmac, and seems to quiver, like a waiting spider. It is much heavier than she expects, but, in her anger, she drags it to her car, scraping it along the ground. It makes a loud squealing sound as if in pain. Maureen bundles the mannequin awkwardly onto the back seat of her car and drives off in a fury, directing her car to the waste depot. But as reason returns, she realises it will be closed so late in the day. She is stuck with the mannequin until tomorrow. It's getting dark. Erratically, she drives the streets where she and Tony had talked of looking for houses. The mannequin rattles and squeaks in the back of her car, its noise a parody of speech. In her rear-view mirror, Maureen sees its arms jerk and twitch as if trying to push itself up.

Dread fills her. She must get rid of it.

There is no one around. She could just abandon it on the street. But just along the road, is a skip. Someone is doing out a house, and broken light fittings, kitchen units and a sink are piled into it. It's like the ruin of a home. Maureen stops the car alongside. She doesn't want to leave the mannequin with her T-shirt on it, so she wrestles off the garment in the back of the car. The mannequin's body twists, resisting her. Maureen drags the mannequin out. It takes all her strength, but she grabs it around its waist and lifts it up, moving her hands down its body as she raises it, feeling its arms fall over her back, its torso slide over her shoulder. It scrapes the side of the skip until Maureen feels its legs pivot towards her. With one arm she shoves it in the belly and it lifts off her shoulders, its arms flinging upwards, one hand slashing her face with its cold, hard fingers. For a long moment, it perches, as if seated, upon the edge, its back uncannily straight. She is sure she hears it laugh as it falls backwards into the skip.

A dog barks from the house nearby. Maureen ducks back into her car before she is seen. Blood runs down her neck, and she wraps the T-shirt around it. She starts the engine and pulls away as quickly as she can manage, jerking the clutch like a learner. She drives back to Tony's flat.

At first, her face stings. Then numbness radiates over her cheek and down her neck, like a dentist's anaesthetic. The car feels heavy, as if the steering isn't working properly. She drives it clumsily, like it is a much bigger car and the roads are too small. The street lights seem not to be working – everything is dim. Her parking space is taken by another car, and she turns towards the back of the building, forgetting to change gear, causing the gearbox to squeal. Her headlights flicker weakly on the wire fence of the residents' car park. What is behind the fence is hidden in the gloom. Maureen turns the car into the parking area; her hands rigid on the steering wheel. The pedals make no sense to her stiff feet. But somehow she is parked.

The windscreen is dirty. Leaves have accumulated on the wiper blades. She is wearing a T-shirt with a blood stain. She is waiting for Tony.

KATE FARRELL

DAD DANCING

Aren't parents embarrassing when they dance? Especially dads. It's that sideways shuffle they do, with elbows at the sides and feet slithering. Sometimes they click their fingers too. It's not really dancing; with heads flung back, they move to a private rhythm that has nothing to do with the music, the sounds from their youth: The Beatles, (not bad); Boney M, (don't go there); The Bee Gees, (unbefuckinlievable). The slither thing is bad enough, but worse is the disco dance, which is beyond gross. For that one they sort of twist on the balls of the feet, one arm up, one down, or spin slowly pointing at whoever gets into their eye line. Look at me; I am s-o-o-o-o-o dangerous. There's really nothing dangerous about a middle-aged man wearing new jeans with a crease ironed in, and a fancy shirt revealing a gold chain nestling in damp, matted chest hair. However otherwise jovial, generous or charming the parent, it is something no child should ever have to witness.

Twins Nic and Anton were cursed with such a parent. For the first ten years of their lives it was less of an issue though even from a relatively tender age, they felt there was something just not right about such displays. They had been christened respectively Nicholas and Anthony by their mother, and were called Nicky and Tony by their father. The sobriquets Nic and Anton were of their own choosing. Now well into their seventeenth year, they were armed with the vocabulary to give voice to their discomfort. Of an age when poise and style were paramount, their millionaire father from Peckham let them down in so many ways. It wasn't just the dancing; it wasn't just the gold chains and the sovereign rings and the glittering diamond in one ear. This last was a six-month anniversary present from wife number two, Staci. It wasn't just the accent, which marked him out as the son of a South London costermonger. No, also to be taken into consideration was his height. And his weight. Even his name: Ron. Not Ronald, not even Ronnie, but Ron. One syllable, three letters, no embellishment, nothing. Ron. But mainly it was the dancing.

The boys were not effete, not by a long stretch; they played rugby and cricket for their overpriced school in Berkshire, climbed and skied in Scotland, and with their fellows chased the pretty village maidens who they gamely referred to as 'tarts.' They were growing into perfect specimens of manhood. For the past two years they had enjoyed the hospitality of their peers during Easter and summers vacs. While dad went to his whitewashed villa with wrap-around sun terraces on a golf course in Mar-bay-ah, the boys headed to the Highlands or the Vendee. There they would dress in faded shorts and old-fashioned rugby jerseys with the collars turned up, lingering in the company of fragrant virgins called India and Kitty, Flora and Hermione. When they returned from the first such excursion, nothing back at home was ever quite the same again. Their father, who had amassed his not inconsiderable pile through plumbing supplies, was frankly appalled when they told him how the hot water packed up at the Hon. Angus's parent's place, as it so often did. And then there were the high flush toilet cisterns, with bits of old rope attached to the pulling mechanism!

'Bit of a hoot, really,' they said, echoing Angus.

'Nah. You should bring some of yer mates here, let them see some decent plumbing, proper karseys,' he had offered.

He was justifiably proud of the five-bed-five-bath house, a symbol of his upward mobility from Peckham to the leafy acres of Wimbledon Common. Each *en suite* was a different colour: peach, champagne, sea mist, eau de nil, sun blush. All very tasteful, very classy, and chosen by Staci after consultation with the developer.

'Mmm,' said Anton.

'Yah, right,' said Nic.

Christmas was looming. Before the twins were able to go and frolic on the ski slopes with India, Angus, and the gang, there was the small matter of the festivities to be endured. The Christmas period itself was bad enough with relatives descending on them, but at least there was some perverse fun to be picked from the carnage, and Dad's legendary generosity also helped. The real problem was New Year, more specifically, New Year's Eve. A big party. Catering. Live music. Karaoke. And dancing. Lots and lots of it.

Anton said, 'The thought of it, Nic . . .'

'Simply chills the blood,' finished his brother, the older by six minutes.

Some weeks previously they had tried to negotiate a peaceful withdrawal from the end of year revelries.

'Thing is, Dad, some of the gang will be heading up to Aviemore after Christmas. Ruairidh's people have a place. They'd love us to join them.'

The reality was that an invitation was yet to be forthcoming, but the twins would worry about that at a later date. The priority was to avoid another ghastly New Year's Eve with Ron.

'I daresay they would, Nicky. I don't doubt it. However I want my boys here for New Year. We'll have everyone round, just like we've always done. They all talk about it for weeks afterwards, and it wouldn't be the same without my boys.'

Here the proud paterfamilias stretched up and clapped an arm round each of them, the fruit of his loins. He slapped their backs with an enthusiasm which neither son felt the occasion merited.

'Tell yer what, get yer mates to come here, Roar-ree and Anus and all the rest of 'em.'

His sons chose to ignore the charmless pun on their friend's name.

'Plenty of room for everyone. Whaddaya say?'

He beamed up at them, turning his head from one boy to the other, his small brown eyes twinkling with the excitement of it all.

Nic paled. Some time ago he and Anton had made an unofficial pact that none of their friends could ever cross the threshold of the family home. Not one. Never. It would be a slow and painful social death.

'Don't think so, Dad,' he said.

'No,' added Anton. 'They've made their plans. It's a . . .'

'Family tradition thing. They go straight up there . . .'

'Right after Christmas every year,' finished the younger boy, honing the lie.

They hoped Dad would empathise with the notion of family + tradition as it was close to his heart. They were to be disappointed.

'Well, never mind, eh. You can go and join 'em after New Year's Day.'

Nic made a last effort, a reckless bid for freedom.

'Yah, but we sort of told them we'd join them before Hogmanay . . .'

'Hogmanay schmogmanay, you stay here.'

'But it'd be rude not to keep our word,' said Anton.

Ron's currant sized eyes glittered and turned as black as coals. He removed his hands from the boys' backs and walked around them, rubbing a hand over his cropped bullet head.

'They're rather expecting us,' continued Anton.

Their father rounded on them, faster than a bull turning into the matador's cape.

'Fuckin 'ell,' he said. 'What have I spent on your education? What part of 'no' don't you get? N – O equals *no*. No. Got that?'

A stubby forefinger waggled under each nose, as Ron spun from Anton to Nic, then back again.

Nic towered over his father by some six inches and opened his mouth for one final attempt.

'But we told them . . .'

He got no further. Ron drew back his hand with the be-ringed fingers and slapped the face of his first-born. A pistol crack, a stinging, then it was over. Nic stood his ground and did not even touch the smarting cheek nor staunch the trickle of blood. As his face reddened with the blow, his father's was wreathed in smiles once more.

'Right, now we got that sorted. Good boys, good boys. We'll have a laugh, few bevvies, bit of a dance. Just like we always do,' he said, treating them to a twirl in the manner of an overweight middle-aged Greek gigolo. He clapped his hands together, rubbing them with unbridled joy.

'Yeah, just like we always do.'

The incident was not referred to again, and Nic and Anton chose not to speak of it when alone together. There was no need. Ruairidh's people eventually issued an invitation, and so with Ron's benediction, the brothers made plans to join their friends in Scotland early in the New Year for some skiing once the public transport system was accessible again. Next year there was the promise of seventeenth birthdays and driving tests and cars, which assuaged the disappointment somewhat. But only somewhat.

Christmas Day came and with it some spinster aunts and Staci's aged parents, who bought a giant jigsaw puzzle for the boys. Nic and Anton managed to smile and permit furry kisses from the old girls and bore it all with a stoicism that is only found in teenagers who have been given very large cheques to spend at will.

December 30th saw the house a hive of activity as a small army of party planners took up occupation in preparation for the event the following evening. Staci didn't want to wear herself out as she said it might bring on 'one of my 'eads,' but anyway Ron was happy to hand over management to a team of well drilled and highly paid professionals.

His theme, according to the printed invitations, was 'Saturday Nite (sic) Feeva (sic)' and guests were expected to arrive suitably attired. He had opted for a white suit with waistcoat, and a black satin shirt. In anticipation of the night to come, his mood brightened while that of his sons' darkened. The vast array of cheques, Christmas socks and jigsaw puzzles gathered dust in their respective bedrooms, overlooked and ignored, as their loathing for the forthcoming event grew and grew. With every chair that was moved, every glass that was polished, they flinched anew. The ceremonial installation of the glitter ball in the conservatory was the final straw.

'It's like being crucified,' moaned Anton.

'Yah, like the nails going in,' agreed Nic.

'It's horrible, too horrible . . .'

'. . . to contemplate. He and Barbi are having a dress rehearsal.'

That was their private name for Staci. Her similarity to the plastic toy with the pneumatic body and overly large blonde hair was not lost on them.

'Trying on their disco king and queen outfits? Oh God no. I don't think . . .'

'. . . I can stand much more.'

'No, me neither.'

'If only . . .' said Nic.

'Yes, if only . . .' said Anton.

They sighed in tandem.

Anton looked at Nic. Nic looked at Anton. They had inherited their mother's very pale blue eyes and dark brown hair, plus her slender build and height.

As each boy gazed deep into his twin's pair of icy orbs, words were no longer necessary for empathy was total. Their mother had died when they were eight and it was a capacity they discovered within themselves from that time onwards. Their father found their silent communication unnerving to say the least, that and the tendency to finish each other's sentences. Staci agreed with her husband, it was downright creepy. In fact, she privately thought they were a pair of insufferable little snots, with their posh airs and their rugby matches, smelly, cracked old Barbour jackets, and skiing trips, and friends who spelled their names all wrong. I mean, Rory was spelled R-O-R-Y for God's sake, not Ruairidh.

Anton went to his father's room, the room with the super-king-sized bed, where Staci would join him on occasion. Birthdays, anniversaries, good wins for Chelsea, that sort of thing. The arrangement between husband and wife worked well enough, though she preferred to wait for the bruises to heal between visits.

Ron was standing in front of a full-length mirror in his dressing room, posing in the white suit and black shirt. The jacket was hooked over one finger and slung carelessly over his shoulder. He seemed strangely unembarrassed at being discovered thus, and unless he had lost weight in the week since Christmas, the only other possible explanation was that he was wearing a corset.

His second born was almost lost for words.

'Wow,' he managed.

'Waddya think? Yer old man still got it then? Eh?'

His father came at him, aimed a jocular punch at his son's upper torso in the way so beloved of men of a certain age. He exuded bonhomie from every pore.

'Goodness,' said Anton. He smiled.

'What you two rascals up to then? Getting yerselves something fancy sorted for tomorrow night? Something to get the girls goin' then, eh?'

This was accompanied by a nifty bit of footwork and a swift one-two jab-jab at Anton's body.

If he touches me once more I might just break his back, thought the boy. He was capable.

'Well yes, we're working on something. Something a bit special.'

He only avoided the two playful taps his father was about to place on both his cheeks by sidestepping a little and pretending to arrange his fringe in the mirror.

'Brilliant! Bleedin' marvellous!'

'Pleased?'

''Course I am. My two boys! Who wouldn't be?'

Anton took the plunge.

'So well, all that unpleasantness before, when we said we wanted to go to Scotland straight after Christmas . . . ?'

He let the question hang. He knew his father would pounce on it.

'Nah. All forgotten. Me and my boys, that what counts.'

Ron looked ready to split in two; he was beaming harder than seemed possible. And was that a glint of something moist in his eyes? His lovely boys were planning something special for New Year's Eve, and it was all for *him*! Blessed, that's what he was. Blessed.

Anton sighed, suddenly downcast despite this tender rapprochement.

'Thing is, Dad . . .'

'Woss up, son? Woss wrong?'

'Thing is, Nic's a bit, well, he's still a bit hurt by um, what happened then. The slap thing? I know we had a great Christmas and all that, but you know how he takes things to heart, and well . . .'

He trailed off, leaving his father to ponder a while.

Having given him time to consider, he then applied his masterstroke.

'Dad, could you, would you tell him you're sorry? You don't even need to say it to his face. You could write it. Just let him know you're sorry. Then we can all start afresh. New year, new start, all that?'

Ron looked up at his younger son, in some ways so much the wiser than his sibling.

'Nicky put you up to this, 'as he?'

'Oh Lord, no. He'd be really hacked off if he knew . . .'

Anton smiled, a picture of innocence, and tossed his fringe out of his eyes to gauge his father's response.

Ron went to his bureau, took a blank piece of paper, wrote just one word on it and signed it. He folded it over, handed it to the boy and said,

'Garn, now get outta here.'

As Anton left his father's room and walked the length of the upper landing towards his brother's, he heard the dreaded opening bars of 'Stayin' Alive' and his father joining in with the lyrics.

Some hours later the house, decked in all its seasonal finery, was in darkness. Staci slept in her own room, as she didn't feel strong enough for a visit with her husband just yet. She couldn't leave it too long though. Due gratitude must be shown for the Lexus. Ron slumbered in the master suite while frost twinkled on the stone lions at the gateposts.

The house held its breath for the excitement that was to come.

A figure crept into Ron's room; a shadow stole across the carpet and leaned over the hillock in the bed that was his body. Somewhere a clock struck three and the only other sounds were his own measured breathing, and the slightly shorter breaths of the intruder.

A hand reached out, touched the sleeping man on the shoulder, then shook him. Struggling with the duvet, he fought his way to consciousness, angered at the invasion of his domain.

'Whatthefucksgoinon?'

Anton revealed himself.

'Shhh, Dad. It's only me.'

'Tony?'

'Dad, you need to come downstairs. I think there's someone in the garage. I couldn't sleep and I thought I heard something. I went into Nic's room, and he's gone down already.'

Ron shot out of bed, and for a big man could move with some speed when stirred. Without even bothering to get slippers or robe – no need as there was under-floor heating, and the house was kept at a constant temperature throughout the night – he hurried past his son, out onto the landing and down the curved staircase. He didn't stop to consider how his younger boy might have heard noises travel all the way from the downstairs garage area to the bedrooms on the upper floor, but logic did not dictate his reactions. Concern for his Aston Martin and for Staci's Lexus did.

'Those fuckin caterers, they've been sniffing round all day. I bet one of them's behind it. Cunts. Woss Nicky gone down there for? Fuckin idiot. He could get his head stove in.'

With Anton hard on his heels he went through a connecting door from the hallway to the garage, which was in darkness. Ron slapped the switch, once, twice, nothing happened. Unbeknown to him, the overhead light bulbs had been loosened some moments before. He heard a movement and saw a figure beside his Aston Martin, bending over the windscreen.

'Oi you, just fucking stop right there. Tony, go and phone the rozzers.' He couldn't help himself, he often spoke like a character from a second-rate television drama. Anton stayed put.

In the murkiness of the garage, the only faint light was from the buffed bodywork of a quarter of a million pounds worth of motorcars. As his eyes grew accustomed to the gloom the figure propped against his prize car began to take on a more familiar aspect.

'Nicky? That you?'

'Yah. 'S'me.'

Ron stumbled over to him. 'Where'd the fuckers go?'

He slept in brown silk pyjamas with his initials on the pocket and presented no immediate threat. How the 'burglars' would have laughed!

'Panic over, there was nobody here after all,' said Nic, lounging on the car's bonnet. 'Must have . . .'

'Imagined it,' added Anton, joining him at the car.

Ron leaned over, his hands on his knees, as if he had been running and needed to catch his breath.

'Thank Christ for that. Fuck me. Coulda been nasty.'

'Could have,' agreed Nic.

'Very,' said Anton.

'Still could,' said Nic, for his brother's ears only.

'Mmmm,' said Anton.

Their father rose to his full five feet and five inches.

'Right. Well then, get away from the car, and let's go back to bed.'

Neither son moved.

'I said, get away . . .'

'From the car. Yah, heard you,' said Nic.

Until the night's act of assumed, if thwarted, heroism, the boys had been banned from the garage for the past three years since one of them – he never knew which – had scratched that season's Ferrari with careless parking of a bike. Their bicycles from that day forth were left in a specially constructed shed.

Suddenly and swiftly, working as one and with no prompting, Nic and Anton, graceful as black cats, moved towards Ron. They pounced. His feet left the ground as he was lifted onto a footstool, barely thirty centimetres high. Anton wrapped him in an embrace that was designed purely to pinion his arms at his sides and confound his struggles.

'Whoa,' he said.

'Shut up,' Nic said.

Before he was able to make another comment, he found something slipped over his head and tightened round his neck; it felt coarse and constricted his breathing immediately. It was jerked sharply by Nic who had moved behind him and as he struggled, he looked up and saw that it was in fact a length of rope that had been coiled over a roof beam. His head was inside a noose. The rope dug deep into his neck, and his face began to swell, though due to lack of light it was not possible to fully appreciate the colour it was turning. In rapid succession it went from carmine to burgundy to the yellowish purple of an old bruise. Anton released his arms and he stood precariously on the stool, wobbling, thrashing and turning, fully awake at last. Speech was not possible, only wheezing, and a bubble of blood trickled down from his nose to be absorbed by the silk pyjama top. His chubby fingers went to the rope, though there was no slackening of it, no loosening, no give, as the strong young man behind him applied all his own weight to the job in hand. Turning once too often, Ron lost his footing and the stool slipped from beneath him. He was gurgling and choking, spitting and sighing, dying at the end of a piece of rope. Never a pretty man in life, in death he was an obscene caricature of the hanged man: deep plum face, bug eyes ready to pop from their sockets, and a bloated fat grey worm of a tongue protruding from liver coloured lips. His arms fell to his sides, fingers spasmed like sausages on a griddle; his legs kicked, while his feet continued to describe invisible steps in the air. A pool of urine formed just ten centimetres beneath his feet and steamed lightly on the cool floor.

Anton recorded the whole thing on his iPhone 7, newly purchased with a Christmas cheque.

'Oh look, Nic. Dad dancing!'

The older twin came round to inspect his handiwork and watched the instant replay on the phone.

'Bloody good show.'

Content with their night's work, they tightened the light bulbs in the sockets, removed their latex surgical gloves, and retired to their respective bedrooms.

On the windscreen of the Aston Martin was a folded piece of paper. On it, written unmistakably in Ron's own hand were just two words: Sorry, Dad.

STEPHEN VOLK

THE ARSE-LICKER

I HAVE TO say I'm not really temperamentally suited to business, as such. It's never been a particular interest of mine. To succeed, to really succeed, you have to have a ruthless streak and a selfish, ambitious bent. I have neither of those attributes. I don't think of them as being particularly desirable attributes to have, to be honest with you. But you have to fit in, obviously. You have to pretend you're one of them. It's a dog-eat-dog world out there. So I've learnt to look like a dog and bark like a dog, but I'm not really a dog at all. I'm probably a worm.

Not that it worries me unduly. You have to come to terms with who you are in life and I realised fairly early on I wasn't exactly a go-getter. I wasn't somebody who others looked up to or were impressed by in any way. I was physically unprepossessing and intellectually average. My parents never deluded themselves I was special, because I wasn't. In school I always envied the children in class whose arms always shot in the air when they had answers to the teacher's questions. The ones who got gold stars. The ones who got the school prizes or won cups on sports days. I never acquired any of those noble achievements for effort, probably because I never really applied any effort to anything. Though I did pick plums from the tree in our garden once and leave them in a paper bag for our English teacher, and I'm sure that was instrumental in getting me get a B+ at the end of term. After that she definitely looked over at me with a smile on her face, Miss Hexham, so that had to mean something, I thought. She had a nice smile, Miss Hexham.

This is the crucial thing, you see. From an early age I learnt how to get what I wanted by ingratiating myself.

I found that if my mum said she loved me as she tucked me up in bed, it was politic to say 'I love you too' back. Experience showed things worked in your favour that way. If you said to your grandparents 'I miss you' when they visited, as often as not it meant they'd buy you more Lego. Basically, if you show people you like them they'll find it very difficult not to like you back. All the more so in the workplace. If you treat the right people – always the big cheese, never the breadsticks – with innate reverence and pander enthusiastically to their every whim, however ill-founded or undeserved, there's a good chance you might prosper, while others who have been less conspicuous in their admiration go to the wall.

My behaviour was simply a strategy for survival in life. I didn't plan it. It just fell into a pattern that way. I didn't know I was doing it, half the time. It was just – well – *me*.

Telling X that they'd saved the company. Telling Y that the way they dealt with a situation was impeccable. Telling Z that I envied their resolve and business acumen beyond measure. That I thought their wife was great fun and their children were gorgeous enough to be photographic models – though neither was even remotely the case.

Frankly, it was my default position. It was also, frankly, the one thing I was good at.

For instance, I would offer to cast my eye over one of Innox's internal reports in my spare time, saying the next morning I thought it was brilliant. Sometimes, as a way of nuancing my effluent praise, I'd offer spurious notes – '. . . not that one can really improve on *perfection* . . .'

I'd get him a tea or coffee. 'Milk, no sugar, isn't it?' (I'd long since made it my business to know it was.)

Staying late. Making sure not only was I last in the office but that he *saw* I was the last in the office.

'Don't work too hard!'

'I won't, Brian! Love to Margaret and the boys!'

Careful to leave a spare jacket on the back of my chair, so it looked like I was first in the next day.

Opening doors before he got to them.

Calling the lift.

Calling a cab. Paying the taxi driver before he could delve into his pocket for change.

Getting flowers for his wife on their anniversary. 'No worries. There's a florist right next to where I get my baguette at lunchtime. No trouble at all. What does she like? Roses, d'you think? How much do you want to spend? No, don't give it me now. We can worry about that later.'

Brushing crumbs from a seat before he sat down. Wiping the table under his coffee cup with a paper napkin. Offering him my expensive retractable ball-point pen across the board room table when his had run out.

'Keep it.'

'No . . .'

'Don't be silly. Really.'

'Are you sure? Well, that's . . .'

Bingo.

More brownie points.

'Nice tie. Beautiful colour. Brian, I'm not being rude, but do you mind me asking where you get your male grooming products? Do you use moisturizer? Because lately you look ten years younger. No, you really do.'

Birthday cards. Naturally.

Christmas cards. Vital. Quality ones. None of your cheap charity rubbish. The message written inside carefully composed for the occasion. Not too long. Not too obsequious. Not too crawling or obvious. Just striking the right balance between formal and friendly. Just implying, slightly, that his friendship as a colleague and mentor was so important that without it you might take your own life. That kind of thing.

It was an art.

An art I'd perfected over years of diligent application. It put me in a special position. Close to the throne. It gave me the ear of the King. It made me secure and unassailable.

Or so I thought.

His name was Terry Kotwika, and the moment he said 'Hi' I decided I didn't like him. I don't like 'Hi' at the best of times. I don't see what's so wrong with a good, old-fashioned, Anglo-Saxon 'Hello'. But mainly I disliked him because he wore his suit like a best man at a wedding who wanted to sneak out at the earliest opportunity for a Silk Cut. He also had a haircut like Paul Weller. Never a good idea. Not even if you're Paul Weller.

We were all called into the board room and change was announced. I don't like change. Innox was rubbing his hands with glee – never a pretty sight – and we were introduced to two thrusting new executives joining the company with the specific brief of bringing in new clients. Oh, goodie.

There was another chap, Rashid Barker, who seemed pudgy and ineffectual, incessantly hoisting his belt up over his draught-excluder of a midriff bulge. Even his moss-like beard was apologetic. I could handle him. He was invisible even as you looked at him. This other one – this *Kotwika* – that was another story.

As soon as the meeting dispersed, I hurried up and shook him enthusiastically by the hand – old habits die hard –

impressing on him how eager I was to work together. He didn't reply, simply staring me out with a fixed, oily grin and crow's feet entrenched at the sides of his face in an expression somewhere between indifference and contempt.

I was the one who should have been contemptuous, if anything. I was the Financial Director and this was the first I knew about us taking on new blood. The other board members wandered off, silently peeved at being cut out of the loop. I merely knocked on Innox's door, poked my head round, gave him a staunch thumb-up and whispered that I thought his decision had been 'really exciting'.

I lied.

The duo were good at their job, no doubt about it, but they looked down their nose at us in accounts. We were the bean-counters, while they were the alpha males of the pack. They even sat in their chairs differently. They *lolled*.

Even so, it didn't bother me at first. Live and let live is my motto. I never rock the boat. Then something did rock it. My boat, anyway.

We were in a meeting. Kotwika had his little take-out cardboard cup of latte from Starbucks because it was just after lunch, but I didn't have a coffee and, as I was going to the kitchen, I asked Innox if he'd like me to get him one too. 'Milk, no sugar?'

'Three bags full, sir,' muttered Kotwika. And *sniggered*.

I pretended not to notice, but there was a definite smirk on his face. And when I came back from the coffee machine, the smirk was still there.

I think it was the smirk that did it.

After that, whenever I opened a door for Innox, or pushed the lift call button, or brushed his chair with my hand before he sat down – I knew Kotwika was watching. I knew Kotwika was at his desk, yards away, *lolling*. Not saying anything. He didn't need to *say* anything. It was enough just to *loll*.

Pretty soon I didn't need to look at him to get a cold chill on the back of my neck. And when we'd go to The Cittie of Yorke in High Holborn after work, that's where it would happen again. I was always first to the bar, ordering the first bottle of red wine. Knowing the Shiraz Innox liked best. And when the others drifted off after the first bottle to catch their little trains home to suburbia from Farrington or Waterloo East, I'd habitually keep my beloved M.D. company over the second bottle, and third. Listen to his tiresome tales of woe, however boring. Laugh at his long-winded jokes and stories I'd heard a hundred times before. Endure yet again why his wife didn't understand him and his spoilt children made his life a nightmare. And if he got too paralytic, I'd make sure he got a cab to the station. Sometimes be there to mop the dribble from his tie and make sure he got on the right train to Dorking.

'Colin. What a surprise, mate.' It was Kotwika, already with a bottle of Shiraz and three glasses. 'Are you going to hang up Brian's coat? There's the rack over there. Go on, old son. Chop, chop.'

When I turned back from the coat hooks, there he was, laughing. Innox sitting beside him, laughing too.

Which was the moment I knew it could all be taken away from me in an instant. Everything I'd worked for. Everything I'd put my heart and soul into all those years.

I felt inadequate. I felt pathetic. Most of all, I felt threatened. But I didn't know what to do about it. I suppose I waited for an opportunity to land in my lap. And land in my lap, eventually, it did.

I was presenting the annual figures for the company and they weren't good. They weren't optimistic at all. I couldn't sugar-coat it. Budget restraints had to be made. The question of redundancies came up, as I knew it would. The directors had gathered in the conference room – we all knew the writing was on the wall, quite frankly – and I'd been up all night working on the only rescue strategy I had to offer, but really it was a strategy to do what I wanted and had waited for patiently for the previous three months.

'Last in, first out.' I lifted my eyes nervously. 'Sorry, but it's the only practical solution. The blunt fact is it's far too expensive to get rid of people who've been with the company for years – twenty, thirty years, some of them. The pay-offs, pensions. Look at the bottom line . . .' I could see Innox's normally florid complexion turn the colour of Milk of Magnesia. 'Horrid, I know – but we can't think with our heart, we have to think with our heads, if we want this company to survive. It's rotten, but . . .' A pall of gloom descended like a slab of concrete as they silently perused my single, brutally concise, final page of A4. 'I like Barker and Kotwika as much as anybody, I really do, but . . .'

For a long while nobody spoke, and neither did I.

Innox said, 'Bugger.' He leaned back and exhaled air at the ceiling, looking like a *putto* misplaced from the ceiling of the Sistine Chapel. 'Hell.' He threw down my spreadsheet, which skidded across the surface of the board room table and ended up, almost magically, in front of me. 'Fuck.'

'I wouldn't like to be in your shoes, telling them,' murmured the ash-blonde stick insect from Human Resources. 'Do you want me to do it?'

'Fuck off, Christine,' said Innox.

'Brian's fantastically good at giving people bad news,' I said. 'I've seen him in action first-hand. He really is exceptional. Even inspirational.'

Innox didn't look at me. Maybe he didn't even hear me, and for a short, unpleasant frisson of time I thought I might have overstepped the mark.

'Fuck off, the lot of you,' he said. 'And Chubb, tell the two of them to step in here and let's get it over with. Bollocks,' he added, like punctuation.

Most of the staff had gone home. They tended to drift away early on a Friday. I never did, of course. I think I was arranging a BACS payment to a freelancer who'd chased me twice by e-mail and three times with a phone call, virtually claiming he was living a hand-to-mouth existence and his house was about to be repossessed and his children sold into slavery, no doubt. The usual sob story. Water off a duck's back to me. I always tried to avoid payments in the month they're invoiced, delaying them into the next quarter by subterfuge or obfuscation, preferably. That was my job.

Innox was working late too. Seeing a tweak of an opportunity, I rapped the glass separating our two offices and mimed the drinking of a hot beverage. He nodded as if I'd read his mind.

'Coffee or tea?' I mimed.

He lip-read, calling back: 'Coffee. Thanks. You're a life saver!'

I smiled, at the time absolutely convinced we were the last ones in the office. Most of the overhead lighting panels over the desks were off and the black lady was circumnavigating with her ridiculously large vacuum cleaner, a machine roughly contemporaneous with Stevenson's Rocket. So when I saw Terry Kotwika standing at the coffee machine, it stopped me in my tracks.

I hadn't spoken to him since the fateful day. Not surprisingly, I had kept my distance. This was the first time I had seen him close to, and it shocked me to see that he was a shadow of his former self, monochromatic under the fluorescent tube.

'Hi. What did you want? Coffee?'

'Yes,' I said. The wind taken out of his sails, he seemed almost human.

'I'll make you one.'

'No, it's all right. Actually I'm getting one for Brian.'

'That's OK. I'll get one for him, too.'

'Sure?'

'How does he like it?'

'Milk, no sugar. I'm the same. Are you sure about this?

'Yeah. Why not?'

'OK. Well. That's really kind of you. Thanks. Thanks a lot.'

If it was a parting gesture, it was a nice one. I felt my cheeks reddening, so turned away and returned to my monk's cell.

On the way I passed his desk and could see now that it was starkly denuded of personal possessions. Everything – the robot pencil-sharpener, crayon drawing to 'Daddy', pictures of his wife and kids making faces on a rollercoaster ride – all had been piled into a cardboard box.

I sat at my own, dumbly staring at my screen saver until he brought me my mug. As he turned to go I said: 'There are cuts across the board these days everywhere. You can't be certain of anything these days. It's terrible.'

He shrugged philosophically.

'Terry, you know it was pure logistics. Nothing Personal.'

'No. Of course not.'

'You know what they say. One door closes another one opens. Got to stay positive, eh?'

'Sure.'

'Everyone's suffering in the current economic climate.'

'Absolutely.'

Then, to my astonishment, he turned around, came back in and, smiling, took my hand in both of his, smiling as he shook it, but he didn't meet my eyes and I thought he looked – *diminished*. After he shut the office door gently after him, I sat there drinking my coffee, draining it to the dregs.

When I woke up on the floor of the conference room, the first thing I realised was that the cleaner's contraption was no longer thrumming in my head. The panic question of how I'd got there kicked me fully awake and I jolted involuntarily, eyes popping open, legs flailing in all directions as I discovered a gag in my mouth and wire or some kind of plastic flex tying my wrists together behind my back.

I crabbed, spidered, Catherine-wheeled with my left buttock as a pivot until my shoulder blades hit the wall.

Kotwika sat opposite me, semi-slumped, legs out straight on the carpet tiles, the tread of his shoes facing me. As I squirmed wildly and fought for breath he merely picked up a greasy bundle of paper smeared with chilli sauce and devoured what remained of a half-eaten doner kebab, remaining non-plussed as I writhed, wiggling as best as I could towards the door, struggling to hoist myself to my knees and attempting whilst keeping my balance to head-butt the door handle and effect my escape.

The most he did was to lick the chilli sauce from his fingertips and squint slightly in irritation at my gyrations. He knew of course – as I was soon to discover – that escape was impossible. It only took a few bangs with my chin and nudges with my cheek-bone to deduce the door was locked. I could see through feverishly blinking and de-focused eyes that the open-plan office beyond was swathed in darkness, and I was trapped with – for want of a better word – a fucking madman.

Needless to say my futile attempts at screams for help and miserably stifled howls of anguish fell on deaf ears. Kotwika let them pass like a wind through the trees, with a degree of patience under different circumstances, I might have found laudable. Not that my exertions got me anywhere, geographically or psychologically. They resulted only in a drastic lack of breath within minutes and I concluded the very minimum I needed to stay alive was to keep breathing. Easier said than done, when you're trussed up like a Christmas turkey in the company of an insane person. Then I saw the legs.

As my shoulder slid down the door, the sound of a moan that wasn't mine made me twist awkwardly. From this position I could see a man's lower limbs under the boardroom table on the far side. He was standing up but leaning over, the upper part of his body – which I couldn't see from that angle – outstretched on top of it. Flanked by an avenue of chairs, the legs were bare and pale and sparsely hairy, pin-striped trousers and white boxer shorts bunched at the ankles over lime-green spotted Happy Socks and slip-ons. Even without the moan, which was distinctively bovine behind its gag, the Happy Socks were a clear identifier that the person was Brian Innox.

I yelped in a voice shrill as a woman's, straightened my spine in a snap, scuttling away from the sight, bringing my knees up sharply when I reached the corner to stop myself from keeling over on my side.

'I'll open the door for you, sir. I'll carry your lunch, sir. Warm your seat sir? Third floor, sir? Like the taste of your Kiwi, sir. Open your zip sir? Shake it for you now, sir?' Kotwika crouched to look me in the face. 'Do you know how *irritating* that was? How *sick* it made me feel – *Every, Single, Day*?' I felt the cold O of the barrel of the pistol – later identified by the police as a Glock 9mm – against the centre of my forehead: from my eye-view it looked like a silver Boeing 757 had embedded itself into my pineal gland '"But don't worry, *everyone's suffering in this economic climate*."' The pupils of his eyes shone like nail heads. 'No. *You're* going to suffer, arse-licker!'

I felt my scalp give a little as he dragged me on all fours to the far end of the conference table, the gun to my skull the whole time. Then he hoisted me by the hair so that I was forced to a kneeling position and slapped me lightly on the cheeks as if to ensure my fullest attention. Only when he moved aside, clearing my line of sight did I truly understand what was happening. Only then did I grasp the full extent of his lunacy.

What faced me was Innox's naked arse, in all its pallid glory, its flesh textured with gooseflesh now it was exposed to the elements, albeit warmed by the hot breath of the fan heaters overhead. I was facing two dunes separated by a tight-lipped crack, each puckered and dimpled by the herniation of subcutaneous fat and age-old blackhead craters as well as fresher eruptions, a few in the constellation turning acid yellow at their tips. Below and between, where his underwear must have gathered too tightly, I could detect a blush of chaffing not unlike nappy rash.

I felt sick. I heard the fridge open and close behind me and a bottle top hush as it unscrewed and Kotwika emptied a bottle of orange juice over my boss's exposed behind with the panache of a chef adding olive oil liberally to a salad.

I had to fight to stop my gorge rising in my throat because I didn't want to suffocate, but I emitted strange strangulated sounds of protest.

The liquid ran into the V-shaped cleft at the coccyx and followed the down-guttering to stripe the legs, dripping onto the floor, chased by a generous squirt of the soda siphon that was always on the drinks table, delivered with a painterly flourish. Innox's buttocks clenched and shuddered as the force of air and water hit them. After the tsunami the skin shone like Michelangelo marble. I half expected the next phase to be a swift buffing by Polish windscreen-cleaners with chamois leathers. But no . . .

Kotwika yanked the gag off me and presented to the tip of my nose a thin slice of lemon held in small metal pincers kept beside the ice bucket.

'No . . .'

'Yes. Oh yes . . .'

Turning away from me, he slid it into the crack of Innox's behind, where it hung precariously, half-in, half-out.

'Do it, *Arse-Licker*. Do what you're best at. Go on! *Do it* and I might just let you *live!*'

He stood behind me and shoved the gun barrel against the back of my head.

For a second I wondered if having my brains blown out might be preferable to the obscene act he was asking me to perform – and perhaps others would have made a different decision – but I realised instantly, or pretty instantly, I had no choice. My mind was racing but I couldn't afford it to be racing. Racing wasn't going to help me. I had to concentrate. No, I had to *stop* concentrating, stop thinking, and just do it. *Just do it*, I thought. *Just stop becoming dead*. That was my priority. Anything else can wait. What you feel about it can wait. What you feel afterwards can wait. Don't even go there. Make my mind blank. Blank.

For Christ's sake – just do it!

I shuffled forward on my knees, level with Innox's arse. It grew closer. It loomed. I could see his back buckling, the tails of his shirt and jacket rolled back. I saw the back of his bald head and the fact that his arms were tied down by rope from the blinds, but as I hobbled closer I lost sight of that and his rear end became my sole focus as it had to be. The arse with the soda water dripping off it was all. All I dared think about. All I dared consume in my brain. I couldn't allow in anything else. Any sliver of guilt, regret, reluctance, repugnance, revulsion . . .

My stomach heaved. I made noises like a crow. Like I'd swallowed a crow. I couldn't help it.

My nose inches away, its contours hypnotised me. Then became uncannily sharp and vivid. My mouth and lips became desert-dry. My eyes fixed and dilated. I felt I they were exploring the foul landscape like an ant on the face of God. Or God roaming the cold, shivering flesh of a plucked chicken at Tesco's. I was almost touching it . . .

I tried to empty my mind as my face approached the white, hairy, pimply, surface. I licked it, tentatively at first. My tongue retracted involuntarily. My body buckled and spew shot out.

I regained my composure, telling myself it was just water, water and orange juice, water. Nothing, nothing at all.

My insides were having none of it. Coiled like a cobra, my cheeks filled up and I vomited a second time, spraying my knees and forming a puddle on the carpet before me. It came out like a stop-valve had been released. I felt light-headed as colourful spittle hung from the chair-backs.

I forced my tongue out a second time, extending it fully. It was unbearable. The very idea was repulsive. Appalling. Obscene. But what could I do? I was at the mercy of a total maniac. How did I know what he might do if I refused? People got abducted, tortured, kept prisoner, for weeks sometimes. Awful things happened to them. Unspeakable things. How did I know what he would do if I didn't do this?

This was the least of evils, the very least of all possible evils. I knew that. I definitely knew that. And I had to embrace it.

And so, I went in. Feverishly now, to get it over with. Like a dog at its bowl. I ignored the grunts and whimpers coming from the figure bent over the table, quivering as he was, shuddering with impotent rage. I simply stuck to the task in hand, went over every inch of that arse with my tongue extended, rasping against the whiskery flesh like sandpaper. Ignoring the vile stabs that spiked at my taste buds. Ignoring the fact that everything in my biology was telling my stomach to retch yet again – but I couldn't let that stop me. I had to go on. And soon it would be over. The stink of fear expelling from his bowels would be over. The stale nitrogenous urea on my tongue would be over. The heady intoxication of terror as I rubbed the tongue against the full, mythic power of the *glutei maximi* to lick the last droplets of liquid would be over . . .

And finally – it was.

'Arse-Licker!'

I fell back on my knees, gasping, my chest lurching. I think I may also have been sobbing like a baby when he pulled me up by the hair again.

'You think you're done, Arse-Licker? We're not done. We're not even *started* yet. That was just an aperitif, an *amuse bouche*. Now we have the main course.'

Which was when he opened the tin of baked beans.

I whimpered.

'Go on. Go for it, Arse-Licker. You know you want to. You know you love it. Licking the old arse . . .'

The sweet sugar of the tomato sauce hit the air and I refused to even think about it this time. I went right in, with a certain sort of defiance. I didn't even look at him. I got my nose right in, starting at the top of the left leg where the beans were running down as if chasing each other, and flicked my tongue at them individually, chameleon-like, working it in long, lingering diagonals, then figures of eight, finally diverting in the latter strokes into short dinky lapping like a cat. All the while thinking of the beauty, because if you thought of the ugliness you were lost. Ugliness would destroy you. Only the beauty would help. Only the beauty would keep you strong.

Gradually the artificial sweetness from the can was displaced by the all too human odour of putridity, sweat and stale urine of my colleague's nether regions. Gradually my roaming pink protrusion delved down to the wrinkles behind his testicles, wiggling at the tufts and warts and dangleberries ensconced there, his gelatinous backside pushing against the orbit of my eyes.

When it was done I keeled back then buckled, hunching forward, exhausted, mentally and physically drained. And wept.

'No, please. No more. Please.'

'What do you mean, Arse-Licker?' He was grinning. 'You don't want to miss out on *dessert*.'

I swayed on my knees and heard the hiss of the aerosol, and tilted my body forward to lick the squirty cream off Innox where the baked beans had been. Truth is, I never liked spray cream. But it wasn't a question of liking, it was a question of surviving.

And I realised then, as my retching subsided, that nothing was too far for me any more. I could do anything. Be anyone. Do anything. And that, as I closed my eyes and licked my lips, frightened me.

I had no idea what time it was now. It might have been midnight. It might have been the early hours of the morning.

'Can I go home now, please?'

'You *are* home, Arse-Licker. Don't you know it yet?'

I think I did. I really think I did.

Then I heard the ping of the microwave, and the smell hit me as its door opened.

Over the next half-hour he spoon-fed Innox a hefty supply of instant curry mixed with laxative, leaving the Vesta and Ex-Lax packaging in my eye-line as an act of sadism. I didn't give him the satisfaction of being horrified. In fact, perhaps surprisingly, a pleasing numbness descended on me as I contemplated the inevitable.

Trying to keep it in, Innox contorted, belly-down, in agony, his suffering made all the more poignant by the fact that the gag stopped any full expression of his feeling being vented as his digestive system protested against the onslaught. What *was* vented in the fullness of time was his unrestrained bowels, in a stuttering explosion of loose, khaki-coloured shit.

The 'hung for a sheep/lamb' analogy sprang to mind. When you had licked baked beans and squirty cream from a grown man's arse, it was but a small step to lick shit from it too. It was an extreme to which I'd never dreamt I'd go, an action to which I never in a million year imagined I'd descend. But such is life. Full of little surprises. And sometimes we have no real idea of our true potential, but we find it.

I waddled forward and stuck out my tongue once more.

A line was crossed. I crossed it.

I subsumed myself in the task. The awfulness overwhelmed me. I was sickened, yes, but I went beyond the sickening. Beyond the foul and the fetid and forbidden. Beyond what society and civilisation labels with words like *obscene* and *repellent* – reaching, in that heightened moment at the bum-hole of my managing director, a kind of epiphany.

As I visited and revisited it, like a shrine, like an icon, I began to see the arse – that arse and any arse – as something not to be loathed and rejected, just as Christ himself was loathed and rejected by those who misunderstood him, but as the holiest thing in creation. It was *complete* in its arse-holiness. It was the lowest thing in creation, the very mechanism of poison and detritus, not to mention sinfulness and sodomy – but could it not be *exalted*? Like the sinner who is embraced in Heaven?

After all, as I often now say, does not the word 'anus' contain 'us'?

It began there in that conference room with a gun at my head. That's when I saw the light. The light of that dark, dark passage that is part of every one of us.

There were no rules. There was just the doing, the doing of the unknowable. And what came next didn't even matter. All that mattered was the moment. Savouring the moment. Because you knew, you really did know, it meant freedom.

I licked it off. Taking my time now. What time was it? There was no time.

Kotwika placed an After Eight between the bum-cheeks. I teased it from side to side with the tip of my tongue and snaffled it up, rewarding Innox with two large, parenthesis-shaped licks either side of his rectum.

I was saying it along with Kotwika now:

'Arse-Licker! Arse-Licker! Arse-Licker!'

'Almost done.'

He put down the Glock and picked up a drill, which looked like a gun, but bigger and chunkier. It was in the rucksack he brought to work every day. He fitted it with the largest in a set of drill bits and tested it in the air. It whirred noisily as it spun. Standing with his legs apart with his back to me he inserted it into Innox's exposed rectum and switched it on. The sound muffled Innox's death rattle as his back passage split and blood splattered out as if from a plumbing leak on all sides of the figure blocking my view.

'Arse licker.' Kotwika said it like an invitation, turning to me, scarlet from the waist down.

'Arse licker,' I replied. It was like a language now. We didn't need any more words. We were beyond that. We understood each other. Perfectly.

This time I didn't just lick, I immersed myself.

The arse closed on me, like a communion. The blood from a hundred abrasions filled my mouth. The cup of my tongue did runneth over. The ravaged anus was a cavity. I buried myself in it gladly, bloody-buttocked-blind and at one with the universe.

Which was how they found me, twelve hours later.

My face pressed to the rear end of my dead boss.

The police, that is. They had to prise me out. Literally. I didn't want to leave. When the gun had gone off, I metaphorically buried myself in the dark. In the shit. In the blood. It was a safe place to hide.

When I came out I hardly noticed the body on the floor with not much of its head left, Kotwika's suicidal brains splashed over the wall. Not in a neat pattern but as if someone had thrown a pizza at it and some of the bits of peperoni still clung there. I was almost sad when the paramedics wiped the shit from my cheeks and nose with their antibacterial wipes, but I could hardly protest.

At the hospital I was given a clean bill of health. The police officer in charge asked me what had happened in some detail. I think he expected me to break down in tears but I was quite good at describing the events fairly dispassionately. He and his sidekick, who wrote down everything, became increasingly pale as I gave them chapter and verse on what I'd been through. They said it must have been hell. I wasn't about to tell them it was quite the reverse.

In time a young counsellor asked if I thought about my ordeal much. I said I didn't, but I lied. I thought about it all the time. He said I must be relieved that the judge imposed reporting restrictions regarding details of the crime. In fact, as he talked to me, I could think only of the arse secreted in his black slacks and what his buttocks might feel like under my tongue.

I've moved on to a bigger and better company now. I have a bigger salary, a more commensurate pension plan, a hefty bonus structure and a far larger house, but the truth is, I've moved on from such petty concerns.

My mission in life now is much more basic, and much more difficult.

To find the ultimate experience of the kind that excites me.

Luckily, my job takes me many places. Amsterdam. Copenhagen. New York. Hong Kong. Shanghai. Sydney. I go to high-powered meetings and trade conferences. Stay in four-star hotels.

Fortunately, all over the world there are places that you go to do what I do, well known to the *cognoscenti*. I sniff them out, if that isn't too vulgar a metaphor. Sometimes I don't have to. Sometimes your eyes just meet across a crowded bar in Bangkok or Bolton, and you know without exchanging a word. You just read the signals. It's pretty obvious, really.

By day, I sit in meetings about corporate finances, fantasising about enormous rumps pressed to the plate-glass windows of the skyscraper, their glorious, bulbous musculature offering itself to my tongue, and I give thanks to the undiagnosed sociopath Terry Kotwika for imparting his wisdom, for introducing me to a new world of kaleidoscopic sensation previously merely black and white.

My search is a personal one, and, dare I venture, a profound one, for all its apparent simplicity.

It is, you see – for all the impossibility of the quest – to find, and lick, the absolute apogee of bare buttocks. To explore the A-list of A-holes and discern the perfect pair, the *Anus Mirabilis* – 'rump of wonders'. The Premier Cru of arses. End of all ends. Absolute perfection.

I've become something of a connoisseur. The German butt tends to be either athletically taut, or overly flabby. Americans are ill-defined. The English, loath to reveal themselves. Antipodeans, surprisingly eager. The Chinese invariably giggle at the roughness of my tongue. Scandinavians grunt. Welshmen grip the floor covering. The Spanish buck like bulls. The Japanese treat the whole thing with the decorum of a tea ceremony. Some behinds are suffocating Montgolfiers. Some are like two peaches in a bag. Some have slack or over-used tunnels. Others, bruised anuses the colour spectrum of a baboon's face. Some bum-flesh is cold as Arctic Roll, others hot as molten lava. But I love them all. I want to have them all. Lick them all. Every sun-bed orange or Miami-tanned inch of them. And every pale, pimpled pouch that seems never to have seen the light of day.

And there you have it . . .

There's little more to say except, here. Here's the two

hundred dollars. Can I have a glass of water? My throat gets rather dry after all that talking.

Thank you. It's important for my tongue to be moist. It's important to have enough saliva.

Is here all right? Are you warm enough? I'll kneel on the carpet. You face that way. That's right. Legs slightly apart. That's perfect.

Thank you for listening. You've been a good listener.

Now, please bend over.

TANITH LEE

DOLL RE MI

FOLSCYVIO SAW THE Thing in a small cramped shop off the Via Silvia. In fact, he almost passed it by. He had just come from the Laguna, climbed the forty mildewy, green-velveted steps to the Ponte Louro, and crossed over to the elevated arcades of the Nuova. Then he glanced down, and spotted Giavetti, who owed him money, creeping by below through the ancient alleys. Having called and not been heard – or been ignored – Folscyvio descended quickly. But on entering the alley he saw Giavetti was gone (or had hidden). Irritated, Folscyvio walked the alley, clicking his teeth together. And something with a rich wild colour slid by his right eye. At first his attention was not captured. But then, having walked a few more steps, Folscyvio's mind, as he would have put it, tapped him on the shoulder: *Look back, Maestro.* And there behind the flawed and watery window-glass, hung about by old, plum-coloured bannerets and thick cobwebs, was the peculiar Thing. He stood and stared at it for quite five minutes before going into the shop.

He was, Folscyvio, of medium height, but seemed taller due to his extreme leanness. His was a handsome face, aquiline, and reminiscent, as was more genuinely much of the city, of The

Past. His hair was very long, very dark and thick and heavily if naturally curled. His eyes, long-lashed and bright, were narrow and of an alluring, or curious – or repellent – greyish-mauve.

No one was immediately attendant in the shop. Folscyvio poised for some while inside the open window-space, staring at the Thing. In the end he stepped near and examined a paper which had been pinned directly beneath.

Not many words were on the paper, these written old-fashionedly by hand, and in black ink: *Vio-Sera. A vio-siren-alino. From the Century Seventeen. A rare example. Attributable, perhaps, to the Messers Stradivari.*

Folscyvio scowled. He did not for an instant credit this. Yet the Thing did indeed seem antique. Certainly, it was a *sort* of violin. But – but . . .

The form was that of a woman, from the crown of the head to her hips, the area just between the naval and the feminine pudenda. After which, rather than legs, she possessed the tail of a fish. She was made of glowing auburn wood – he was unsure of its type. All told, the figure, including the tail, was not much more than half a metre in length.

It had a face, quite beautiful in a stark and static kind of way, and huge eyes, each of which had been set with white enamel, and then, at the iris, with a definitely fake emerald, having a black enamel pupil. Its mouth was also enameled, pomegranate red. The image had breasts too, full and proud of themselves, with small strawberry enamel nipples. In the layers of the carved tail had been placed tiny discs of greenish, semi-opaque crystal. Some were missing, inevitably. Even if not a product of the Stradivari, nor quite so mature as the 1600s, this piece had been around for some time. The two oddest features were firstly, of course, the strings that ran from the finger board of the Piscean tail, across the gilded bridge to the string-clasper, which lay behind a gilded shell at the doll's throat; while the nut and tuning pegs made up part of the tail's finishing fan. Secondly what was odd was the *hair*, this not carved nor enameled, but a fluid lank heavy mass, like dead brown silk, that flowed from the wooden scalp and meandered down, ending level, since the doll was currently upright, where, had the tail constituted legs, its knees might have been.

A grotesque and rather awful object. A fright, and a sham too, as it must be incapable of making music. For the third freakish aspect was, obviously, at the moment the doll was upright, but when the instrument – if such were even possible – was *played*, what then? Aside from the impediment of its slightness yet encumberedness, the welter of hair – perhaps once that of a living woman, now a hundred years at least dead? – would slide, when the doll was upside-down, into everything, tangling with the strings and their tuning, the player's hands and fingers – his *throat* even, the bow itself.

Thinking this, Folscyvio abruptly noted there were also *omissions* from the creature, for she, this unplayable mermaid-violin, this circus-puppet, this *con-trick*, had herself neither arms nor hands. A mythic cripple. Just as he had thought she might render her player. *Another* man, he thought, would already loathe her, and be on his way out of the shop.

But it went without saying Folscyvio was of a different sort. Folscyvio was unique.

Just then, a thin stooped fellow came crouching out of some lair at the back of the premises.

'Ah, Signore. How may I help you?'

'That Thing,' said Folscyvio, in a flat and slightly sneering tone.

'Thing . . . Ah. The vio-sera, Signore?'

'That.' Folscyvio paused, frowning, yet fastidiously amused. 'It's a joke, yes?'

'No, Signore.'

'No? What else can it be but a joke? Ugly. Malformed. And such a claim! My God. The *Stradivari*. How is it ever to be played?'

The stooped man, who had seemed very old and perhaps was not, necessarily, gazed gently at this handsome un-customer. 'At dusk, Signore.'

Even Folscyvio was arrested.

'What? At dusk – what do you mean?'

'As the fanciful abbreviation has it – *vio-sera* – a violin for evening, to be played when shadows fall. The Silver Hour between the reality of day and the mysterious mask of night. The hour when ghosts are seen.'

Folscyvio laughed harshly, mockingly, but his brain was already working the idea over. A concert, one of so many he had given, displaying his genius before the multitude of adoring fanatics – sunset, dusk – the tension honeyed and palpable – *chewable* as rose-petal lakoum – 'Oh then,' he said. Generously contemptuous: 'Very well. We'll let that go. But surely, whoever botched this rubbish up, it was never the Famiglia Stradivarius.'

'I don't know, Signore. The legend has it, it was a son of that family.'

'Insanity.'

'She was, allegedly, one of three such models, our vio-sirenalino. But there is no proof of this, or the maker, you will understand, Signore. Save for one or two secret marks still visible about her, which I might show you. They are in any case, Masonic. You might not recognize them.'

'Oh, you think not?'

'Then, perhaps you might.'

'Why anyway,' said Folscyvio, 'would you think me at all seriously interested?'

The stooped old-young man waited mildly. He had whitish, longish hair. His eyes were dark and unreadable.

'Well,' said Folscyvio, grinning, 'just to entertain me, tell me what price you ask for the Thing? If you do ask one. A curiosity, not an instrument – perhaps it's only some adornment of your shop.' And for the very first he glanced about. Something rather bizarre then. Dusty cobwebs or lack of light seemed to close off much of the emporium from his gaze. He could not be certain of what he now squinted at (with his gelid, gray-mauve eyes). Was it a collection of mere oddities – or of other instruments? Over there, for example, a piano . . . or was it a street-organ? Or *there*, a peculiar vari-coloured railing – or a line of flutes . . . Folscyvio took half a step forward to investigate. Then stopped. Did this white-haired imbecile know who the caller was? Very likely. Folscyvio was not unfamous, nor his face unknown. A redoubtable musician, a talent far beyond the usual. *Fireworks and falling stars*, as a prestigious publication had, not ten weeks before, described his performance both in concert halls and via Teleterra.

Suddenly Folscyvio could not recall what he had said last to the old-young mental deficient. Had he asked a price?

Or – what was it?

When confused or thrown out of his depth, Folscyvio could become unreasonable, unpleasant. Several persons had found this out, over the past eighteen years. His prowess as a virtuoso was such that, generally, excuses were made for him and police bribed, or else clever and well-paid lawyers would subtly usher things away.

He stared at the ridiculous auburn wood and green glass of the fish-tail, at the pegs of brass and ivory adhering to the glaucous tail-fan.

He said, with a slow and velvety emphasis, 'I'm not saying I want to buy this piece of crap off you. But I'd better warn you, if I did want, I'd get it. And for a – shall I say – very *reasonable* price. Sometimes people even *give* me things, as a present.

You see? A diamond the size of my thumb-nail – quite recently, that. Or some genuine gold Roman coins, Circa Tiberio. Just *given*, as I said. A *gift.* I have to add, my dear old gentleman, that when people upset me, I myself know certain. . . *other* people, who really dislike the notion that I'm unhappy. They then, I'm afraid, do these unfortunate things – a broken window – oh, steelglass doesn't stop them – a little fire somewhere. The occasional, *very* occasional, broken . . . bone. Just from care of me, you'll understand. Such kind sympathy. *Do you know who I am?*'

The slightest pause.

'No, Signore.'

'Folscyvio.'

'Yes, Signore?'

'Yes.' Oh, the old dolt was acting, affecting ignorance.

Or maybe he was blind and half-deaf as well as stooped. 'So. How fucking much?'

'For the vio-sirenalino?'

'For what fucking else, in this hell-hall of junk?'

Folscyvio was shouting now. It surprised him slightly. Why did he care? Some itch to try, and to conquer, this stupid toy eyesore – Besides, he could afford millions of libra-eura. (Folscyvio did not know he was a miser of sorts; he did not know he was potentially criminally violent, an abusive and trustless, perhaps an evil man. Talent he had, great talent, but it was the flare and flame of a cunning stage magician. He could play instruments both stringed and keyed, with incredible virtuosity – but also utter emotional dryness. His greatest performances lacked all soul – they were fire and lightning, glamour and glitter, sound and fury. Signifying nothing? No, Folscyvio did not know any of that either. Or . . . he thought he did not, for from where, otherwise, the groundless meanness, the lashing out, the rage?)

Unusually, the stooping man did not seem unduly alarmed.

'Since the need is so urgent,' he said, 'naturally, the vio-sera is yours. At least,' a gentle hesitation, 'for now.'

'Forget "for now",' shouted Folscyvio. 'You won't get the Thing back. How much?'

'Uno lib'euro.'

Everything settled to a titanic silence.

In the silence Folscyvio took the single and insignificant note from his wallet, and let it flutter down, like a pink-green leaf, into the dust of the floor.

The enormous lamp blazing stadium, fretted by goldleafery and marble pillars, with a roof seemingly hundreds of metres high, and rock-caved with acoustic-enhancing spoons and ridges, roared and rang like a golden bell.

It had been a vast success, the concert. But they always were. The cheapest ticket would have cost two thousand. Probably half a million people, crushed luxuriously onto their velvet perches like bejeweled starlings, during the performance rapt or sometimes crying out in near orgasmic joy, were now exploding in a final release that had less to do with music than . . . frankly, *with* release. One could not sit for three hours in such a temple and before such a god as Folscyvio, and not require, ultimately, some personal eruption. They were of all ages. The young mingled freely with those of middle years, and those who were quite old. All, of course, were rich, or incredibly rich. One did not afford a Folscyviana unless one was. Otherwise, there were the disks, sound-only as a rule, each of which would play for three hours, disgorging the genius pyrotechnics of Folscyvio's hands, all those singing and swirling strings of notes, pearl drops of piano keys. Sometimes, even included on a disk, since a feature, often, of the show, the closing auction, and the sacrifice. The notes of that, (though they were not notes) faultlessly reproduced: the stream-like ripple, the flicker of a holy awakening, the *other* music, and then the *other* roar, the dissimilar applause, very unlike, if analysed, the bravos and excelsiors that were rendered earlier.

Oddly though, these perfect disk recordings did not ever, completely, (for anyone) capture the thrill of being present, of *watching* Folscyvio, as he played. Even the very rare, and authorized, visuals did not. If anything, such records seemed rather – flat. Rather – soulless. Indeed, only the bargaining and sacrifice that occasionally concluded the proceedings truly came across as fully exciting. Strange. Other artists were capturable. Why not the magnificent Folscyvio? But naturally, his powers were elusive, unique. There was none like him.

For those in the stadium, they were not considering disks, or anything at all. They knew, as the concert was over, there was every likelihood of that *second* show.

Look, *see* now, Folscyvio was raising his hand to hush them. And in his arm still he held the little vioncello, the very last instrument he had performed upon . . . tonight.

Colossal quiet fell like a curtain.

Beyond the golden stadium and its environs, hidden by its windowlessness, the edges of the metropolis lay, and the Laguna staring silver at the moonlit sea. But in here, another world. Religious, yet sadistic. Sacred, yet – as some critic had coined it – savage as the most ancient rites of prehistory.

Then the words, so well known. Folscyvio: 'Shall we have the auction, my friends?'

And a roiling cheer, unmatched to any noise before, shot high into the acoustic caves.

The *Bidding For* began at two thousand – the cheapest Seat-price. The *Bidding Against* sprang immediately to four thousand. After this the bids flew swift and fierce, carried by the tiny microphones that attended each plushy perch.

For almost half an hour the factions warred. The Yes vote rose to a million scuta-euri. The No vote flagged. And then the Maestro stilled them all again. He told them, with what the journals would describe as his 'wicked lilt' of a smile, that after all, he had decided perhaps it should not be tonight.

No, no, my friends, my children, (as the vociferous and more affluent *Yeses* trumpeted disappointment) not *this* time, not now.

This time – is out of joint. Perhaps, *next* time. This night we will have a stay of execution.

And then, in a further tempest of frustrated disagreement and adoring hosannas, Folscyvio, still carrying the vioncello, left the stage.

'But what are you doing there, Folscy-mio?'

Uccello the agent's voice was laden with only the softest reproach. He knew well to be careful of his prime client; so many of Folscyvio's best agents had been fired, and one or two – one heard – received coincidental injuries.

Yet Folscyvio seemed in a calm and good-humoured mood. 'I came to the coast, dear Ucci, to learn to play.'

'To – to *learn?* You? The *Maestro* – but you know everything there is to – '

'Yes, *yes.*' One found Folscyvio could become impatient with compliments, too. One must be careful even there. 'I mean the new Thing.'

'Ah,' said Uccello, racking his brains. Which new thing? Was it a piano? No – some sort of violin, was it not. 'The – mermaid,' he said cautiously.

'Well done, Ucci. Just so. The ugly nasty wrongly-sized little upside-down mermaid doll. She is quite difficult, but I find ways to handle her.'

Uccello beamed through the communicating connection. Folscyvio, he knew, found ways often to cope with females. (Uccello could not help a fleeting sidelong memory of buying off two young women that Folscyvio had 'slapped around,' in fact rather severely. Not to mention the brunette who claimed he had raped her, and who meant to sue him, before – quite astonishingly – she disappeared.)

'Anyway, Ucci, I must go now. Ciao alia parte.'

And the connection was no more.

Well, Uccello told himself, pouring another ultra-strong coffee, whatever Folscyvio did with the weird violin, it would make them all lots of money. Sometimes he wished Folscyvio did not make so much money. Then it would be easier to let go of him, to escape from him. Forever.

He had found the way to deal with her infuriating hair. Of course he could have cut it off or pulled it out. But it was so indigenous to her flamboyant grotesquerie he had decided to retain it if at all possible. In the end the coping strategy came clear. He drew all the hair up to the top of the wooden scalp, and there secured it firmly with a narrow titanium ring. This kept every fibre away from his hands, and the bow, once he had upended her and tossed the full cascade back over his left shoulder, well out of his way. Soon others, at his terse instruction, had covered the titanium in thick fake gold, smooth and non-irritant. Only then did he have made for her a bow. It was choice. What else, being for his use.

As for the contact-point, it had been established thus: her right shoulder rested between his neck and jaw. Now he could control her, he might begin.

By then she had been carefully checked, the strings found to be new and suitable and well-tended, resilient. He himself tuned them. To his momentary interest they had a sheer and dulcet sound, a little higher than expected, while from the inner body a feral resonance might be coaxed. She was so much better than Folscyvio had anticipated.

After all this, he adapted to his normal routine when breaking in a novel piece.

He rose early and took a swim in the villa pool, breakfasted on local delicacies, then set to work alone in the quartet of rooms maintained solely for the purpose. Here he worked until lunch, and after siesta resumed working in the evening.

The house lay close to the sea, shut off from the town, an outpost of the city. In the dusk, as in the past, he would have gone down to the shore and taken a second swim in the water, blue as syrup of cobalt. But now he did not. However pleased with, or aggravated by the mermaid he might have become, at twilight he would always play her. He had not, it seemed, been entirely immune to the magical idea that she was a vio-sera, a violin of the Silver Hour.

It was true. She did have a fascination for him. He had known this, he thought, from the moment he glimpsed her in the sordid little shop off the Via Silvia. He had become fascinated by instruments before in this manner, as, very occasionally, by girls. It happened less now, but was exciting, both in rediscovery, and its power. For as with all such affairs of his, involving music, or the romantic lusts of the body, he would be the only Master. And at the finish of the flirtation, the destroyer also.

By night, after a light dinner, he slept consistently soundly.

The Maestro dreamed.

He was walking on the pale shore beside the sea, the waves black now and edged only by a thin sickle moon. At spaces along the beach, tall, gas-fired cressets burned, ostensibly to mimic Ancient Roma. Folscyvio was indifferently aware that, due to these things, he moved between the four elements: earth and water, fire and air.

Then he grew conscious of a figure loitering at the sea's border, not far from him.

In waking life, Folscyvio would have kept clear of others on a solitary walk – which anyway, despite its wished-for aloneness, always saw, in a spot like this, one of his bodyguards trailing about twenty metres behind him. Now, however, no guard paced in tow. And an immediate interest in the loiterer made Folscyvio alter course. He idled down to the unraveling fringes of the tideless waves, and when the figure turned to him, it was as if this meeting had been planned for weeks.

No greeting, even so, was exchanged.

Aside from which, Folscyvio could not quite make out who – even, really, *what* – the figure was. Not very tall, either bowed or bundled down into a sort of dark hooded coat, the face hidden, perhaps even by some kind of webby veil. Most preposterously, none of this unnerved Folscyvio. Rather, it seemed all correct, exactly right, like recognizing, say, a building or tract of land never before visited, though often regarded in a book of pictures.

Then the figure spoke. 'Giavetti is dead.'

'Ah, good. Yes, I was expecting that. Has the debt been recovered?'

'No,' said the figure.

It was a gentle, ashy voice. Neither male nor female, just as the form of it seemed quite asexual.

'Well, it hardly matters,' said Folscyvio who, in the waking world, would have been extremely put out.

'But the death,' said the figure, 'all deaths that have been deliberately caused, they do matter.'

'Yes, yes, of course,' Folscyvio agreed, unconcerned yet amenable to the logic of it.

'Even,' said the figure, 'the death of *things*.'

Folscyvio was intrigued. 'Truly? How diverting. Why?'

'All things are constructed,' the figure calmly said, and now, just for a second, there showed the most lucent and mellifluous gleam of eyes, 'constructed, that is, from the same universal, partly psychic material. A tree, a man, a lion, a wall – we are all the same, in that way.'

'I see,' said Folscyvio, nodding. They were walking on together, over the shore, the waves melting in about their feet, and every so often a fiery cresset passing, as if it walked in the other direction, casting out splinters of volcanic tangerine glass on the wrinkles of the water.

'You are an animist,' said the figure. 'You do not understand this in yourself, but you sense a life-force in every instrument on which you set your hands. And being sufficiently clever to recognize the superior life in them, you are jealous, envious and vengeful.' There was no disapproval, no anger in the voice, despite what it had said, or now said. 'To a human who is not a murderer, the destruction of life is crucially terrible, whether the life of a man, a woman, or a beast. To an animist these events are also terrible, but, too, the slaughter of so-called *objects* is equally a horror, an abomination – a tree, a wall – and especially those objects which can speak or sing. And worse still, which have spoken and sung – for the one who kills them. A piano. A violin.'

'A violin,' repeated Folscyvio, and a warm and stimulating pleasure surged up in him, reminiscent, though physically unlike, the sparkle of erotic arousal. 'A *violin.*'

Then he noticed they had reached the end of the shoreline. How strange: nothing lay beyond, only the gigantic sky, scattered with stars, and open as the sea had seemed to be moments before. Although the sea, evidently, had been contained by a horizon. As this was not.

Folscyvio worked with the doll-mermaid-violin, mostly sticking to his routine, where departing from it then compensating with a fuller labour in the day or night which followed. (During this time he discovered no secret marks, Masonic or otherwise, on its surface. But of course, the shop-keeper had lied.)

Three, then four months passed. The weather-control that operated along the coast maintained blissful weather, only permitting some rain now, at the evening hour of the Aperitivo.

He ordered Uccello to cancel a single concert he had been due to give in the city. Uccello was appalled. 'Oh never fear, they'll forgive me. Change the venue of my next one, to make room for those worshipers who missed out.' Folscyvio knew he *would* be forgiven. He was a genius. One must allow him room to act as he wished. Only those who hated and despised him ever muttered anything to the contrary. And they – and Folscyvio knew this also well – would be careful what they said, and where. It was well known, Folscyvio's fanatics did not take kindly to his defamation.

Without a doubt, beyond all question, he had mastered her. It was the beginning of the fifth month. He stood in front of a wide mirror (his habitual act prior to a performance) and put himself, in slow-motion, through his various flourishes, emotives, intensities, particularly those that were intrinsic to the new and extraordinary instrument. Already he had formulated the plan for her deployment and display before he should – finally – and after prevarication – take hold of her. She was to preside, to start with, at the off-centre front stage. She would then be upright, that way the doll appearance of her would be the most obvious. Her hair would pour from the gold tiara, carefully arranged about and over her breasts, her face smooth and glowing from preparatory days of polishing, her emerald eyes, (also polished) shining and her pomegranate lips inviting. She would be standing on her aquatic tail, in which all the missing scales by now were replaced. The fantail base of it would balance on a velvet cushion of the darkest green. Magnetic beams would hold her infallibly in position. (The insurance paid for this, not to mention the threats issued, both legal and otherwise, would make certain all was well.)

After posing and scrutinizing all his moves and

postures, Folscyvio played to the mirror the selected pieces on the vio-sera, as he proposed to at the forthcoming concert now only two weeks away. Everything went faultlessly, of course.

Sometimes he would be assisted, during a concert, by an accompanying band, comprising percussion, certain stringed instruments, a small horn section, and so on. All these accoutrements were robotic; he never employed human musicians. The Maestro himself always checked the ensemble over, tuned and – as a favourable critic had expressed it – '*exalted*' them for a show. However, on this occasion, when he reached the moment that he accessed the vio-sirenalino, (the Mermaid, as she had been billed) the exquisite little robot band would fall quite silent. At which, being non-human, no flicker of envy would disturb any morsel of it.

Then, and only then, at a signal from the Maestro, ultra protective rays would spin the mermaid violin, whirling her to her true position, upside down.

Folscyvio, amid the crowd's predicted applause and uproar, would lift her free. Like a heroine in some swooning novel of the nineteenth, twentieth, or early twenty-first Century, she would lie back upon his shoulder, her hair drifting in a single silken, burnt-sienna wing down his back (the hair had been refurbished, too). In this fainting and acquiescent subjection of hers he would hold her, and bring the slender bow to bear upon her uptilted, supine body, stroking, spangling, *making love* to her, breasts to tail.

In the wide mirror he could see now, even if he had already known, the eroticism of this act. How gorgeously perverse. How sublime. How *they* would love it. And oh, the music she could make –

For her tones *were* beautiful. They were – *unique.* And only he, master of his art, had brought her to this. Even that dolt Uccello, hearing a brief example, a shred of

Couperin, a skein of Vivaldi, and of Strarobini, played, recorded and audioed through the speaker, had exclaimed, 'But – Folscy-mio – never did I hear you play anything – with quite this *vividity*. What enchantment. Folscyvio, you have found your true voice at last!' And at this, unseen since the viewer was not switched on, the Maestro had scornfully smiled.

The concert was quite sold out. Beyond even the capacity of the concert stadium. Herds had paid, therefore, also to *stand* and listen in the gardens outside, where huge screens and vocalian were to be rigged. It was to be a night of nights, the Night of the Mermaid. And after that night? Well.

She was a doll. A toy. An aberration and a game – which he had played and won.

One night for her, then, the best night of her little wooden life. That would be enough. Live her dream. Who should aim at more?

The venue for the concert was two miles inland of the city and the Laguna, up in the hills. This stadium was modern, a curious sounding-board of glazing, its supporting masonry embedded with acoustic speakers. The half-rings of seats hung gazing down to the hollow stage. They would be packed. Every place taken, the billionaire front rows to the craning upper roosts equipped with magnifying glasses. Amid the pines and cypresses outside, the huge screens clustered. Throughout the city too others would be peering at the Teleterra, watching, listening. And beyond the Laguna, the city, in many other regions all across the teeming and disassembled self-absorption of the planet, they too, whoever was able and had a mind to, they too glued to the relay of this performance.

Unusually the concert was to begin rather early, the nineteenth hour of that light-enduring mechanically-extended summer night. Sunset would commence just before twenty-one. And the dusk, prolonged by aerial gadgets, would last nearly until the twenty-second hour.

Almost everyone had learned about the new and special instrument – though not its nature. A *mermaid?* They could barely wait. Speculation had been rife in the media for weeks.

So they entered the stadium. And when first they saw – *it* – during that vast in-gathering, startled curses and bouts of laughter ran round the hall. What was it? Was it hideous or divine, barbaric or obscene? Unplayable, how not. Some joke.

Eventually the illumination sank and the general noise changed to that wild ovation always given the Maestro Folscyvio. And out he came, impeccably clad, his lush dark hair and handsome face, his slender, strong hands, looking at least a third of a metre taller than he was due to his lean elegance, and the lifts in his shoes.

Hushing them benignly, he said only this, 'Yes. As you see. But you must *wait* to *hear*. And now, we begin.'

From the nineteenth almost to the twentieth hour, just as, muted and channeled through the venue's glassy top, the sun westered, Folscyvio performed at his full pitch of stunningly brilliant (and heartless) mastery.

As ever, the audience were stirred, shaken, opened out like fans – actual fans, not fanatics gasping, weeping, tranced slaves caught in the blinding blitzkrieg of his glare; they slumped or sat rigid until the interval. And after it, fueled by drink, legal drugs, and chat, they slunk back nearly bonelessly for another heavenly beating.

And Folscyvio played on, assisted by his little robot orchestra. He took to him a piano, a mandolino. But all the while, the mermaid doll stood upright on her green cushion, with her green tail, her green eyes, her *smallness* – dumb. Obscure and . . . waiting.

Some twenty minutes before twenty-one, the sunset swelled, then faded. The ghostly dusk ashed down. It was the

Silver Hour, when the shadows fell. And tonight, here, it would last an hour.

The penultimate acts of the show were done. The orchestra stopped like a clock. Folscyvio put aside the mandolin. Then, stepping forward quite briskly, he gave the signal, and the mermaid was whirled upside-down – whereupon he seized her. And as the crowd faintly mooed in suspense he settled her, in a few well-practiced moves, her head upon his shoulder, the hair flowing down his back like a wing. He lifted the bow out of its sword-like sheath, which until then had been hidden in a cleverly-spun chiascuro.

Silences had occurred in history. The city knew silences. This silence however was thicker than amalgamating concrete. In a solid silver block it cased the concert hall.

Folscyvio played to them, within this case, the mermaid violin.

High and burningly sweet, the tone of the strings. Pelt-deep and throbbing with contralto darkness, the tone of the strings. A vibrato like lava under the earth, a supreme up-draught like a flying nightingale. A bitter pulsing, amber.

A platinum upper register that pierced – a needle to conjure an inner note, some sound known only at the dawn of time, or at its ending. Consoling sorrow, aching agony of joy.

Never, never had they heard, nor anyone ever conceivably, such music. Even they could not miss it. Even he – even Folscyvio – could not.

He had not mastered the instrument. It had mastered him. It played him. And somehow, far within the clotted blindness and deafness of his costive ego – he knew. The Maestro, mastered.

Perhaps he had dubiously guessed when practising, when planning out this ultimate scene upon his rostrum of pride. Or perhaps even, at that watershed, he had managed to conceal the facts from himself. For truth did not always set men free. Truth could imprison, too. Truth could kill.

On and on. Passing from one perfect piece to the next, seamless as cloth-of-Paradise, Folscyvio the faultless instrument, and the violin played him. All through that Silver Hour. Until the shadows had closed together and not a mote of light was left, except where he still poised, the violin gleaming in his grip, the bow fluttering and swooping, a bird of prey, a descending angel.

But all-light melted away and all-quiet came back. The recital was over.

How empty, that place. – As though the world had sunk below the horizon as already the sun's orb had done.

The artificial lights returned like fireflies.

There he stood, straight and motionless, frowning as if he did not, for a second or so, grasp where he was, let alone where he had been during the previous hour.

But the audience, trained and dutiful, stumbled to its feet. And then, as if recollecting what *must* come next, began to screech and bellow applause, stamping, hurling jewels down on to the stage. (It had happened before. Folscyvio had even, in the past, graciously kept some of them; the more valuable ones.)

After the bliss of the music, this acclaiming sound was quite disgusting. A stampede of trampling, trumpeting things – that had glimpsed the Infinite, and could neither make head nor tail of it, nor see what should be done to honour it.

Seemingly unceasing, this crescendo. Until it wore itself out upon itself. The hands scalded from clapping, the voices cracked with over-use. Back into their seats they crumbled, abruptly old, even the youngest among them. Drained. Mistaken. Baffled.

Inevitably, afterwards, there would be talk of a drug –

illegal and pernicious – infiltrated into the stadium, affecting everyone there. But that rumour was for later, blown in like a dead leaf on the dying sigh of a hurricane.

Probably Folscyvio did suspect he was not quite himself. Some minor ailment, perhaps. A virus, flimsy and unimportant. Nevertheless he felt irritated, dissatisfied, although realizing he had played superbly. But then, – he always did. Nothing had changed.

Now he would swiftly draw this spectacle to a close. And in the favourite way: theirs. *His*.

He said, very coldly, (was he aware how cold?) 'We will finish.'

No one any more made a noise. Sobered and puzzled, they hung there before him, all their ridiculous tiers of plush seats, like bits of rubbish, he thought, piled up in rows along gilded and curving shelves, in the Godforsaken fucking cupboard of this mindless arena.

He must have hesitated a fraction too long.

Then, only then, a scatter of feeble voices called out for the auction.

Folscyvio smiled, 'wintry and fastidious' as it was later described by a hysterical critic. 'No. We will not bother with the *auction*. Not tonight. Fate is already decided. We will go directly to the sacrifice.' For once some of them – a handful among the masses there – set up loud howls for mercy. But he was adamantine, not even looking towards them. When the wailing left off, he said, 'She has had her night. That is enough. Who should aim for more.'

And after this, knowing the cue, the stadium operatives crushed the lights down to a repulsive redness. And on to the stage ran the automatic trolley which, when all this had begun those years ago, had been designed for the Maestro by his subordinates.

Again, afterwards, so much would be recalled, accurately or incorrectly, of what came next. All was examined minutely. But it did no good, of course.

They had, the bulk of this audience, witnessed 'The Sacrifice' before. The sacrifice, if unfailingly previously coming after an auction, when invariably the majority of the crowd bayed for death, and put in bids for it, (the cash from which Folscyvio would later accommodate) was well known. It had been detailed endlessly in journals, on electronic sites, in poems, paintings and recreated photo-imagery. Even those who had never attended a Folscyvio concert, let alone a sacrifice, *knew* the method, its execution and inevitable result. The Maestro burned his instruments. Sometimes after years of service. Now and then, as on this night, following a single performance.

Pianos and chitarras, such larger pieces, would tend to sing, to shriek, to call out in apparent voices, and to *drum* like exploding hearts in the torment of the fires. But the vio-sirenalino – what sound could she make, that miniature Thing, that doll-mermaid of glass, enamel and burnished wood and hair?

Despite everything, many of them were on the seats' edges to find out.

She leaned now, again upright in the supporting rays of the magnetic beams. When he poured the gasoline, like a rare and treacly wine, in a broad circle all about her, saturating the green cushion, but not splashing her once, a sort of rumbling rose in the auditorium. Then died away.

Folscyvio moved back to a prudent distance. He looked steadily at the mermaid violin, and offered to her a solitary mockery of a salute. And struck the tinder-trigger on the elongate metal match.

Without a doubt there was a flaw in the apparatus. Either that, or some jealous villain had rigged the heavily security-provided podium. Or else – could it be – too fast somehow for any of them to work out what he did – did he, Folscyvio, somehow reverse the action? As if, maybe, perceiving that never in his life after that hour would he play again in that way, like a god, he wished to vacate the stage forever.

The flame burst out like a crimson ribbon from the end of the mechanical match. But the mermaid violin did not catch fire. No, no. It was Folscyvio who did that. Up in a tower of gold and scarlet, blue and black, taller even than he had been – or seemed – when alive, the Maestro flared, and was lost at once to view. He gave no sound either, as perhaps the violin would not have done. Was there just no space for him to scream?

Or was it that, being himself very small, and cramped and hollow and empty, there was no proper crying possible to him?

In a litter of streaming and luminous instants he was obliterated, to dust, a shatter of black bones, a column of stinking smoke. And yet – had any been able to see it? – last of all to be incinerated were his eyes. Narrow, long-lashed, gray-mauve, and – for the final and first time in Folscyvio's existence – *full of fire.*

D.P. WATT

LAUDATE DOMINUM

(for many voices)

'How things are in the world is a matter of complete indifference for what is higher.

God does not reveal himself *in* the world.'

LUDWIG WITTGENSTEIN, *Tractatus Logico-Philosophicus*

SITTING ON A bench, on the outer harbour wall, wrapped in a wintery coat – despite the encouraging sun of a late March afternoon – we find Stephen Walker. He is eating an egg mayonnaise sandwich and drinking from a flask of tea, both prepared that morning in his holiday cottage in the seaside village of Polperro. He has just returned from today's walk, this time along the nine miles of coastal path to Fowey, and back again. Holidaying, for Stephen Walker, was less a relaxation than a demonstration of vitality.

His demeanour might once have been termed – some years ago now – curmudgeonly. Today he might, more straightforwardly, be described as a 'grumpy old man', now that such nomenclature is popular, and always assigned with mocking affection. Of course the fault for this miserable attitude lay not with him, but rather with everyone else. As he was fond of telling anyone who would listen, the problem with today's youth was the lack of military service. Despite having served only three months in the Ordnance corps, before being invalided out (a detail always omitted in the retelling), it had, apparently, been 'the making of him'. Young people today had no *stamina*, no *will*, and no *backbone*.

It was no surprise then to find him holidaying alone in Cornwall, a place that had been dear to him for many years, mostly for its seclusion (if you chose the right places) and beautiful coastal walks. He would visit most years in late March, to take advantage of the last few weeks before the place hummed with tourists and their children, dogs and ice creams.

Whenever visiting Polperro, and when the place was available, he liked to hire a small cottage at the end of The Warren that Oscar Kokoschka had spent time in during the war, painting the outer harbour repeatedly. As an amateur oil painter himself Stephen Walker liked to feel that a little genius might rub off on him by inhabiting the dwelling of one of his favourite artists.

Painting and walking; two wonderful pursuits, balancing the equal requirements of every human being: quiet, contemplative creativity and vigorous, outdoor exercise.

Whilst he was naturally frugal he was certainly not mean. He was, *how do they say it*, careful. His savings from lunch would then contribute towards that evening's treats; real ale, crab salad, and sticky toffee pudding and custard, at The Blue Peter. This was a small inn only a few feet away from him, and a place he always enjoyed spending a couple of evenings at during his holiday.

You can imagine him though, there at one of the larger window seats, begrudging sharing his table with a young family that have nowhere else to sit; the children staring up at the curious man uneasily, their dog occasionally nuzzling at his crotch.

To avoid unwanted small talk he takes a leaflet from one of those racks advertising local attractions and unfolds it across the table so that he should not be interrupted during his meal.

'The Looe Valley line.'

His eyes are drawn to a picture on the inside flap, of a small well, rather mossy and overgrown – 'St Keyne wishing well', read the caption, with an arrow pointing to one of the stops on the railway line. There were a couple of stanzas of poetry beneath that, by Robert Southey, the second mentioned that the well was surrounded by an oak, an ash, an elm and a willow tree. Apparently, the leaflet went on, 'Whichever of a married couple drinks first from the well, they will "wear the trousers." So, hurry, lest your spouse beats you to it!' Despite this folklore nonsense it sounded intriguing. Also, the leaflet proclaimed, 'On your way back from the well why not visit The Mechanical Music Museum, where you will find all manner of music playing devices from yesteryear!'

It was rare that Stephen Walker was interested in anything of the kind, believing that most of them were aimed at extorting money from gullible parents through the relentless, imploring nagging of their children. Such as those sat opposite him now, slurping their cheap cola through bendy straws, and squabbling over their crisps. But, he was certain, there would be few children desperate to go to this museum; they were not interested in the magic of yesteryear's innovations, the spirit of the craftsman and the skill of the mechanic.

He would visit the museum the very next morning, he resolved. He drained the rest of his beer and headed back to the cottage planning his day.

First, a brisk walk along the coastal path to Looe – he would have completed the five miles of it before most of the nation's adolescents were awake, he chuckled. And he would then be on the train to visit the St Keyne wishing well, then take in the museum on his way back, before continuing to Liskeard to round the day off.

The walk went to plan, although the steep paths and cliffs to Looe, especially around Talland Bay, seemed to take their toll on him more this time than when he had last walked them a few years previously. He had over an hour to kill before the train at 10:32. He browsed around some shops, but didn't buy anything.

The train was on time, and he enjoyed the restful juddering of the carriage as it made its gentle way through some splendid scenery. The ticket inspector had informed him that St Keyne was a 'request' stop and he would let the driver know. If only all train services these days had such courteous and helpful staff, Stephen Walker mused.

He alighted on a deserted platform, with newly-painted white picket fencing, with a quaint passenger shelter. He could almost be back in the 1950s he thought, even though for the most part, he already was.

He checked his watch. 10:50. He had over two hours before the next train at 12:59 that would take him on for the afternoon to Liskeard. This should be plenty of time to find the well and then return to explore the museum.

He headed off up the steep lane into the village of St Keyne, eager to find this beautiful little wishing well. Who knows, he thought, even this late in life I might find a wife, and if so I'll have one up on her by having drunk at it first. He laughed quietly, at the improbability of either event.

The well proved elusive though. The little map on his leaflet did not appear to scale and he found himself trekking across some muddy fields, looking this way and that, without any idea of where he was. He headed back to the main road and back down the steep, narrow lane, towards the railway station.

Then he spotted – just where the steep lane joined the larger road at the top of the village – a signpost, mostly covered by low hanging branches. In his eagerness to rush on he must have missed it.

It did not prove particularly informative though. One side pointed north, saying 'St Keyne Wishing Well', and the other, pointing south, read exactly the same. Some local was clearly having a joke on the tourists. Stephen Walker did not really consider himself a tourist and was not amused.

He consulted his watch. 12:30. That damned wishing well really had taken some time up. He needed to get to the museum before the train arrived at 12:59.

Then the thought struck him, he could catch a later one. Why waste the opportunity to enjoy the musical machines when he could catch the *next* train to Liskeard. He filled a pipe – a little luxury he allowed himself only when out walking – and consulted the timetable again. It would have to be the 14:30. Oh well, why not take things easy, and with a little shrug of the shoulders he ambled down the lane to visit the museum.

Had he looked a little further behind the signpost he would have seen a set of greenish crumbling steps leading down to the wishing well. There were no longer any trees beside it, if ever there had been. And whether it was a magical well, or not, would have to remain a mystery. All that was forgotten now; Stephen Walker had set a new itinerary.

As he took slow puffs on the pipe he found himself humming a little tune, as the museum came into view. This was most unusual as he did not approve of humming. Still, it didn't hurt did it, out here where there was nobody to hear him. It showed that he was taking full advantage of his leisure time.

The sign for the 'Mechanical Music Museum' pointed to a large industrial building with corrugated roof that lay behind a cottage. Some steep steps led down to them both and Stephen surmised the owner of the museum must also live in the cottage. As he tapped his pipe out on the wall at the top of the steps he heard a wonderful chorus of song coming from the museum. It sounded like a choir rehearsing. He listened a while. He was not sure what the hymn was, but it was delightful, and he spent a minute or two enjoying it.

The choir finished the hymn as he got to the bottom of the steps. Stephen was relieved as he hadn't wanted to interrupt their practice; perhaps they shared the building with the museum.

He poked his head through the door, even though the sign read 'closed'. The building might even have been a warehouse once, so vast was the space inside. At the far end there were great red curtains that gave the place the feel of a village hall, sometimes used for local am-dram performances, no doubt. All about the perimeter of the building were varying musical devices, maybe a dozen or so, ranging in size from small gramophones to larger organs.

There was a tall man, maybe in his early sixties, standing some distance away. He was dressed in scruffy work clothes and seemed quite busy. But there was certainly no choir. It must have been a recording, Stephen thought, even though it had been quite loud.

The tall man spotted him and shook his head apologetically.

'Oh, I'm sorry, sir,' the man said, depositing a handful of wooden blocks onto a workbench. 'We don't open to visitors until April. It takes so much to maintain all of these machines that I have to use all of the winter months to keep them in pristine condition.'

'Ah, I see . . .' Stephen began.

'I'm working flat out on these dampers as it is,' he interrupted, gesturing to the blocks and a scattering of felt and leather patches strewn across the bench.

'Oh dear,' Stephen said, 'how disappointing. I had hoped so much to see the place before I leave for home in a few days. I recall my grandfather had a music machine in the living room; it played great metal disks, and even had a clock in it too.'

'An old upright, eh!' the man said, his eyes bright and his face suddenly interested, as though a little switch had been flicked somewhere inside him. 'It will have been a Polyphon, no doubt, or maybe even a rare Symphonion.'

'That was *it*!' Stephen said, the name suddenly bringing back his grandfather's pronunciation of it. 'Sym-*phon*-ion! He'd always say, after we'd had some lunch, "Shall we have a few tunes from *Mr Sym*phon*ion*." And my sister and I would be delighted. The *Symphionion* – well I never . . .'

'Might I ask, sir, do you sing?' the man said, rather incongruously.

Stephen Walker was perplexed. 'Do I *sing*?'

'Yes,' the man said, as though his sudden change of topic were entirely appropriate. 'Do you belong to a choir? Do you *sing*?'

'Er, no, well, I mean, not for many years now, not since I was a child,' Stephen replied, feeling rather badgered by a certain school-masterly tone the man had adopted.

'I was particularly struck by the quality of your voice, you see,' the man continued, heading over to him. 'It has depth, and richness. But is that tobacco I smell? It would be a shame to spoil such a wonderful voice with the *evil weed* now, wouldn't it.'

'I've just had a pipe, as a matter of fact, on my way down from the wishing well – a wishing well that I couldn't damned well find,' Stephen said, defensively. 'But I don't really see what business my smoking habits are . . .'

'No doubt the Connor boys have been playing with the well signposts again,' the man interrupted, offering his hand in greeting. 'I'm Philip Morin, owner, restorer and guide here at the Mechanical Music Museum.'

'I'm Mr Walker, Stephen Walker,' he replied, shaking

Philip's hand timidly, without having shaken the sense of being rather admonished.

'Let me show you around then, Mr Walker,' Philip said (the issue of being closed for the season apparently having been entirely forgotten).

'My own grandfather was an actor, I come from a long line of performers,' he said, going over to a small, dark wooden box. 'This is one of the earliest machines I have, and one of great sentimental value.' Philip seemed a connoisseur of the non-sequitur.

He cranked a handle a few times and opened the lid. What looked like a black wax cylinder was spinning inside. From underneath the table he produced a large metal horn, fluted and almost shell-like. He attached the horn to a pivot arm and rested the base of it, housing a large needle, on the thick cylinder.

An eerie noise came out, mostly a great cloud of static and white noise, but in the background one could just make out a voice, but not the words.

'This is my grandfather,' he said, proudly, 'reading Dickens' *Christmas Carol* in 1896.'

Stephen was still unable to make out the words. All he could discern was a strange echoing of the sentences going on within the machine.

'It takes a while to warm up,' Philip said, 'like any voice really.'

He angled a lamp down close to the cylinder, to warm it. 'Perhaps we can try that one again later when the old man's back in tune.'

Then, the sound seemed to clarify and there was a great laugh from the reader, Philip's grandfather, followed by a peal of bells – Scrooge on Christmas morning, without a doubt!

'Marvellous,' Stephen exclaimed.

'Yes, it is rather, isn't it,' Philip said. 'This voice, my ancestor's, brought to life here for us, one hundred years later. For all of its terrible crimes there are also some miraculous things achieved through technology.'

'Yes, it really must have been magical to hear the human voice reproduced through a machine in that fashion, for the first time,' Stephen said.

'Indeed,' Philip replied. 'But what of the instruments that *played themselves*, they would have been no less incredible.'

He led Stephen over to a fairly ordinary-looking upright black piano. In the centre of it, where the music stand would have been, there were two horizontal bars, onto which Philip locked a long roll of thick punched paper. It looked a bit like the paper cards he had used many years before in the computer room at the post office, where he had worked briefly as an apprentice.

Having threaded the roll, Philip then set about dismantling the front of the machine so that they could get a good look at the mechanism.

'Now this one was made by an incredible craftsman,' Philip began. 'Ernst Steget of Berlin. He engineered the pianos, but he couldn't produce the musical rolls. This had to be done by another craftsman, Giovanni Galuppo, down the road from him. However, Steget was fond of a schnapps, or two, in the local bar of an evening.'

They both laughed, in the conspiratorial fashion that late middle-aged men do when issues of alcohol surface – such false bonhomie; beneath the forced laughter only half-remembered conquests that were never really conquered, opportunities squandered by a loose tongue, loved ones slighted and friends abused.

'Sadly, his love of the schnapps resulted in the gradual dwindling of his business and eventually he became so indebted to Galuppo that he had to go and work for him to pay it all off,' Philip continued. 'Such is the way of the world I'm afraid, when one's bounty and talents are squandered on *vice*.'

Stephen didn't like the tone of that last remark, aimed – as it clearly was – at his own indulgence in a pipe or two. But he did not have time to dwell upon the slight, if such it was, as the piano suddenly erupted into sound and motion. The keys danced beneath invisible fingers and the inside of the machine was feverish with the work of pulleys and wheels, valves, bellows and levers, all animated by the little blank squares on the paper roll as it slid through the instrument like a great white tongue.

'What use the pianist, eh?' Stephen joked.

'Oh, we still have our uses, Mr Walker, with the right instrument,' Philip retorted, rather viciously, Stephen felt.

Then a shrill electronic ring called out from the workbench, crashing the world back into the present. Philip went over to answer a cordless telephone and then called out. 'It's my wife, there's a delivery for me. I'll be back in a moment. I'll bring some tea too, enjoy the rest of the tune!'

Stephen smiled and nodded. The piano was playing away and he felt rather nostalgic for the music his parents would entertain him with on the record player when he was a boy. His father loved the old music hall ones, and the spoken word records. The hours they would spend together on a Sunday listening to Flanders and Swann, or old Henry Hall and the BBC orchestra on scratchy 78s.

The paper was still rolling around as Philip returned with a tray laden with cups, saucers, milk jug and a great steaming pot of tea. There was also a plate of biscuits, enough to service an AGM of the Women's Institute, Stephen thought.

'Doris thought you might be a bit peckish, so she put out some biscuits,' Philip said, carefully balancing the crammed tray on a little stool beside a low chair with rather grubby paisley upholstery. 'It's Earl Grey, I hope that's okay.'

Stephen smiled and nodded.

'I thought you were an Earl Grey chap,' Philip said. 'I didn't know if you took it with milk or lemon, so there's both.'

'Oh, milk for me, please,' Stephen said, his knees bending a little to the tune still tinkling from the piano.

'I thought so, milk it is, do help yourself,' Philip said. 'I hope you don't mind, I must help this driver with some items I've had shipped over. I shan't be a moment. You carry on, there's a good few minutes left on that reel, I'm sure you won't be bored.'

'Oh, most certainly not,' Stephen replied. For the first time in many years – despite Philip's frosty undercurrents – he felt he had discovered a kindred spirit.

He must have listened to the piano for too long, carried back to hedonistic Weimar, for when he poured himself a cup of tea it tasted a little odd, rather sour. Stewed probably. That, or the milk was off. He gave the little jug a sniff. Yes, it was the milk. Never mind, he needed a little refreshment now, as it might be some time before he got to Liskeard and found a tearoom. What was it mother used to say – a few germs won't kill you! He poured himself another cup and as the last few notes on the piano tinkled out, and the scroll of paper unravelled its last coded dots, he looked about the expansive building.

As he had noted on his arrival the place was by no means full of instruments. Each had its own particular space. Some were small, like the little wax cylinder player he had heard Philip's grandfather reading Dickens upon; some larger, such as the piano from Berlin in the 20s. There were some larger organs on the other side of the room, one near the large curtain across the back wall. This seemed much like the kind of grand Wurlitzer organs he'd seen as a child, both in the theatre and at the fairs. It would be wonderful to hear Philip play that when he returned. Behind that though, and rather oddly positioned, was something more individual. It looked like quite a small organ, and Stephen thought it may have been uniquely crafted, so unusual was its construction. There seemed to be no ornate element to it, all was pure function. The panelling had obviously been crafted from a variety of different woods, each giving their particular rich colour to the overall piecemeal effect. And, from where he was standing, he could see no discernible maker's plate.

Finishing his second tea in a swift gulp, Stephen walked over and inspected it cautiously. As he had first thought, there seemed to be no maker's mark (emblazoned proudly upon all the other machines) and none of the keys, or mechanical dials and knobs had any lettering, or numbers upon them, as was common on the other models. Perhaps this was in the first stages of restoration, he thought, running a hand along its well-polished, although awkwardly constructed, wooden frame.

He thought he heard a noise then, from within it; a sort of escape of air. Perhaps a valve or piston decompressing.

It quite startled him, and he jumped a little.

Shh. Shh. It came again, twice, but sounded so like someone shushing a crowd to be quiet before a performance began that he didn't know what to make of it.

He looked around to check that Philip hadn't come back yet from unloading the delivery van. He didn't want to look a fool, and didn't want to be noticed touching something that was probably delicate and very expensive.

But, he just couldn't help himself.

He pressed one of the keys.

From the back of the instrument there came a voice – *lah*!

There could be no mistaking it; this was the sound of a *human voice*, singing a note. Stephen was intrigued, and a little disturbed. This latter sentiment did not prevent him from trying again though. He pressed the same key, and another one from nearer the other end of the board. A soprano voice sang out, at the same time as an alto joined in. But they did not sound recorded, it seemed as though the singers stood right beside him.

He shivered a little, but determined that it must be due to the cold of the airy industrial building. It was not particularly cold that day, and besides Philip had turned the storage heaters on only the week before and they were pumping dry, warm air around the building to fend off any chill.

Despite his fear, Stephen shuffled cautiously around the back of the machine to find where the 'voices' were coming from. There was a wooden grill at the back, rather like an old speaker. A faint draught was coming from it, and upon that delicate air there wafted an odd, meaty scent, as of cured European sausages.

He noticed that above the speaker there was a panel of some sort, made of long timbers of what could only be olive wood; their swirling grains and strange knots had been lovingly jointed together and finished with a little latch of leather and a bone toggle. This gave a strangely archaic feel to the instrument. Yet, all of this did not dissuade Stephen Walker from loosening the cord and carefully easing the panel down.

At first he thought they were the chicks of large birds, all arrayed on wooden plinths, calling, silently, for food. So bizarre was the thing before him that it took a moment for his mind to fully comprehend what he was witnessing.

These were the organ pipes, and each an *organ* of sorts.

There were about twenty large wooden tubes, rather like inverted didgeridoos, in three rows of varying height. Each was crafted from a different wood and atop many of them there was stretched a thin, pulsating blob of organic tissue, with an oval opening across the top of the tube. There were five blank pipes.

Each fleshy aperture slowly opened and closed, like a gaping raw mouth, and dripped a clear fluid down the pipe which collected in metal trays below, in which there rested a number of short sticks, each wrapped with swabs of cloth soaked in this thick liquid.

The smell was foul, but in the face of such horror that was the least arresting detail.

Stephen Walker was appalled. Yet he could not shake off a perverse desire to touch one of these things, to run his finger across it – there was something sadly familiar about their monstrosity. Almost against his will his hand reached slowly forward.

Then a voice echoed across the cavernous space.

It was Philip, returned from his delivery.

'How you getting on in here?' he called, merrily, wiping his oily hands with a rag.

As surreptitiously as he could, and with a terror welling within him, Stephen Walker slid the wooden panel back into place and carefully fastened the toggle, as Philip approached him, smiling his cheery smile.

'I was just, erm, admiring the woodwork on this one,' Stephen said, shakily. He felt rather dizzy all of a sudden, hot and flustered. 'It's very . . . beautiful . . .'

'Oh, that's a little pet project of mine,' Philip said, making his way over to the larger Wurlitzer organ. 'I'm afraid it isn't in full working order at the moment so I can't play you a tune on it yet; maybe one day, when I get the time to finish it.'

Stephen felt sick, claustrophobic and terrified. He was nervous that if he even made an attempt to move he would faint.

'This little beauty is my pride and joy,' Philip began, seating himself at the controls of the vast organ; controls that looked more like a spacecraft than a musical instrument.

Philip flicked a switch and the huge red curtains at the back of the building rolled back to reveal an array of shiny metal pipes, row upon row of them.

Stephen Walker could think of nothing but the fleshy, gaping wounds calling out silently in the contraption behind him.

'Now, Mr Walker,' Philip shouted out. 'Give it your best voice. I'll keep it simple, don't you worry.'

A great flare of sound assailed Stephen from the rows of pipes.

Roll out the barrel! What a ridiculous song to hear only moments after having made his horrifying discovery. Stephen just managed to stop himself vomiting.

'Come on,' shouted Philip, his upper body rocking about like some demented toy. 'Join in! *We'll have a barrel of fun . . .*'

Stephen mumbled a few words in an attempt to show willing, '*We've got the blues on the run.*'

'Oh, *Mr Walker*, give it some *oomph*!' Philip cried, clearly getting irritated.

Stephen Walker gave in. His head was spinning and the whole place began to look blurry and distorted. He tried to turn the insanity of the situation to his advantage – to get a bit of courage up.

'*Ring out a song of good cheer*,' Stephen belted out. Quite where the spirit came from to sing in such an absurd situation he didn't know. '*Now's the time to roll the barrel, for the gang's all here . . .*'

'Now *that's* what I'm talking about, *Stephen*,' Philip said, ceasing his playing.

It was the first time he had addressed Stephen Walker by his Christian name and something in the intonation was sinister and threatening. 'What a beautiful baritone you have there, *Stephen*; real quality, and something we're sorely lacking here in our little choir.'

It may have been the blast of noise, or his own singing, or even Philip's ominous tone, that had disoriented him, but Stephen Walker felt most peculiar.

He staggered a little and slumped in the paisley chair to get his strength back, strength he would need if he were to get away from this crazy man. The seat was weak though and the bottom gave way. He crumpled into it like a rag doll, arms and legs at ridiculous angles. He hadn't the energy left to correct his posture; his arms felt numb, his legs useless. His eyelids were heavy, and his mouth dry. He just sat there as everything around him became hazier, and darker, imploring Philip to help him with lips that merely twitched rather than pronouncing words.

Philip sat down opposite him, getting blurrier by the moment. He poured himself a cup of Earl Grey, dropping a slice of lemon into it with a sad chuckle.

'I always take it with lemon, and *plenty* of sugar,' he said, sniffing at the milk jug, 'besides the milk is always a bit funny at this time of year, I find.'

Stephen made one last effort to get up. He succeeded only in knocking the chair into the little stool sending the tray crashing to the concrete floor.

The teapot, jug, cup and saucer all shattered.

'Oh, never mind,' Philip said, 'Doris has plenty of spares. It's worth it anyway; you don't know how hard it is to get people to join the choir out here. Trust me, I'll be able to take much better care of that voice than you have.

'I hope you understand, *Stephen*.

'What is it the good book says, *I will sing with the spirit, and I will sing with the understanding also*. It is best this way; your gifts will be most *cherished* – dutifully *maintained*.'

Stephen couldn't speak.

He couldn't move.

As the lights dimmed in Stephen Walker's eyes Philip Morin took up his seat at the other, primitive, grotesque organ, looking every bit the maestro. And as he played the building filled with strange, lonely voices; exultant in mechanical agony, rapturous in automatic praise. Their beautiful, tortured song carried across the fields to fall upon the ears of the grazing cattle and sheep, and was drowned only momentarily by the 15:41 from Liskeard to Looe, filled with schoolchildren returning home, eager to forget their last class of the day. It did not stop at St Keyne, for nobody was waiting on the platform, and few ever alighted there.

MARIE O'REGAN

SOMEONE TO WATCH OVER YOU

EMILY GLANCED OVER her shoulder again, hoping to find nothing – but her shadow was still there, keeping pace. She sped up, annoyed to find that the increased tempo of the tap-tap of her heels was making her feel worse, not better – the fact that they'd picked up a gruffer echo was something she tried to ignore. She was only a few feet from the stairs leading down to the exit now; and she cursed her penchant for sitting at the front of the train – all it had done was leave her with further to go to get to safety.

The lights in the waiting room went out, and she moaned – thank God she was at the stairs now. What on earth had possessed her to wait till the last train home when she knew damn well how dark it got on the platform at this time of night? East Finchley was a beautiful station, but it was also the first station going northwards that wasn't underground – and when the staff switched the waiting room lights off, it got dark quickly.

She heard her pursuer's breathing quicken and grow ragged as he started to run, and she launched herself at the stairs with little thought of how hard it would be to keep her balance at that speed. She clattered downwards, praying someone would hear her and come to investigate – but no one did. Towards the bottom she tripped, and felt herself grasped by strong arms – her rescuer stood her up and moved on before she had a chance to register who it was; her only impression was of strength and the cloying smell of tobacco smoke.

Then he was gone. She stood in the corridor and stared upward, scared her pursuer would still follow – there was a scuffle up there, then a cry, and finally the sound of squealing brakes as the last southbound train was brought to a sudden halt. An alarm sounded and she blanched, knowing what had happened. She just didn't know to whom. A shadow moved at the top of the stairs, and she saw a man's silhouette against the lights of the incoming train – a tall figure in a long, dark coat; a hat obscuring his features. He seemed to look down at her, just for a moment, and then he was gone.

Now staff arrived. She found herself shouldered to one side as guards ran up the stairs, and a very nervous young man tapped her arm, tried to shepherd her back towards the ticket offices, and the way out. 'If you'd come this way, Miss . . .'

She nodded, and allowed herself to be led. From behind her came the unmistakable sound of someone throwing up.

As she walked into the office next morning, chatter stilled – she saw heads turn as she passed by, eyes drop as she sought to engage them and find out what was so interesting. Then she saw her boss, George Burrows, appear at his door and beckon her into his office, and her heart sank.

'If I could have a word, Miss Lane,' he said, and stood back to allow her entrance.

She nodded and swept past him, trying to ignore the nervous muttering that swelled behind her.

He followed her in and indicated the chair opposite his, and waited 'til they were both seated before he continued. 'I'm surprised to see you in this morning,' he said, his tone kind.

'You are?'

'You've been up most of the night, after all,' he went on. He registered the incomprehension on her face and smiled. 'This is a newspaper, Emily, surely you realised we'd hear of a death on the line?'

Realisation dawned, and Emily was embarrassed. 'I didn't think. I mean, I knew you'd hear about the body on the line, I just didn't connect the fact you'd find out I was on scene, as it were.'

'You're tired, of course,' George said. 'There's no reason for you to be up to speed with the office at this hour.' He pressed a button on his intercom and spoke to his secretary. 'Can you bring those files in, please, Carole?'

The door opened almost immediately, and Carole swept in with a manila folder clutched to her frail chest, tattered pieces of paper creeping from its edges. She smiled at Emily, before a 'humph' from George dissolved her grin and sent her scuttling back to her desk.

George opened the file, and took out various clippings – placing them side by side on the desk before her. 'You're not the first one, you see.'

'I'm not the first one . . . ? I'm not following you.'

He tapped the clippings, impatient now. 'Look! It's right there, see?' He sighed at her confused expression, and sat back. 'I wouldn't be a million miles from the truth if I said you were about to be attacked before this happened, am I right?'

Emily stared. 'How . . . ?'

'Look at the clippings,' he said. 'There have been a number of instances of 'phantom rescues' over the years; yours is just the latest.'

'Phantom what?' Emily laughed. 'I'm sorry, but just because I got the willies late at night on a train platform doesn't mean I was attacked.'

'What were you scared of? Last night, on the platform?'

Emily laughed. 'It sounds stupid now, but I thought someone was following me.'

'And you felt threatened, yes?' George was bending forward now, his hands clasped in front of him, a finger on his lips.

Emily nodded. 'Of course. A woman on her own, late at night, no one around . . . and someone's walking behind you, at the same pace as you, speeding up when you do . . .' She stopped, spooked all over again, her mind back with the events of the previous night, the man's heavy footsteps catching up with her own, each heel tap accompanied by a deeper echo . . .

'Of course.' George sat back, satisfied he was right. 'And then someone appeared, out of the night, and saved you.'

'He saved me from falling, I suppose,' she conceded, 'but I hadn't actually been attacked, had I. I just got scared.'

George shook his head. 'I believe you were about to be attacked, and if you're honest,' here he stared at her over his half-rim glasses, his expression serious, 'so do you.'

Emily attempted a smile, but failed miserably. 'Because it's happened before, right?'

'That's right,' he nodded. 'Read the clippings.'

The clippings were of varying age, she saw, from issues of the paper as far back as the 1970s. All told similar tales – a young girl leaving the station late at night, complaining of a sense of being followed – a man attempting to catch up with them. All the girls had been grabbed at the head of the stairs (she'd been lucky, she realised, to get down them without being caught) and pulled towards the darkened waiting room. So far, so unsurprising. The odd fact was that, in each case, the girl concerned spoke of the smell of pipe smoke, and strong arms wrestling them away from their attackers . . . and a brief glimpse of a manly shape in a long dark overcoat with square shoulders and a hat, brim down over the eyes, as it descended upon their assailant; a style that had been old-fashioned enough to stand out, even then.

Stapled behind each of these clippings was a shorter article from the following day – a tale of a body on the tracks, no sign of a struggle. One girl had seen her rescuer fall onto the line alongside her attacker, and screamed until help came – but the railway workers thus summoned only found the body of her attacker; there was no trace of anyone else having been at the scene.

She placed the clippings back in the folder, congratulating herself on the fact that the shaking in her fingers was almost imperceptible, and let out a breath. 'They can't all be the same.'

'And yet the similarities just keep stacking up.'

'Someone's exaggerating, making things up.'

George sat forward, frowning. 'That doesn't track though, Emily, does it. Different people, different times . . . yet all tell of a man in a coat and hat.'

'Doesn't have to be the same man,' Emily pointed out.

'I'll grant you that in the forties a lot of men wore dark coats and hats,' he said. 'But what about since then? And all of them smelled of pipe tobacco?'

'Lots of people smoke,' she tried . . . but she could see George already shaking his head.

'Not pipes,' he said, sighing. 'It's a very different smell, as you know. And besides, not that many people smoke anymore, compared to then. I mean, look at films – in the seventies everyone was doing it. Not these days, though; these days if a character in a movie smokes, he's usually a baddie.'

Emily had no answers. 'I didn't really see anyone,' she said. 'Just felt his arms, and smelled the tobacco.'

'So you do admit it was tobacco and not a fag you smelled?'

'I have to, don't I,' she said. 'It was Dad's brand, Old Holborn.'

'And the man was wearing a long coat, and a hat, just like the other times?'

Emily nodded. 'I don't know what kind of hat, though . . . the name, I mean. It was like those old films – with that actor Dad loved. James Mason.'

George laughed. 'God, that's right – he did, didn't he?'

Emily stared out at her colleagues; all staring in, amazed he was laughing. 'George, they're looking.'

He frowned again, but the corners of his mouth were twitching, and Emily knew he'd be laughing again before long. He and Dad had been two of a kind that way, and she felt his loss all the more keenly when she was with her uncle.

'All right, lass,' he said. 'Best get out there and investigate this, eh? We wouldn't want everyone knowing the cub reporter's my favourite niece.'

She smiled, then scraped her chair back and stood up. Leaning forward to pick up the files she whispered, 'Can I come and see you and Auntie Ann on Sunday?'

'Course you can,' he said. 'Can't see you doing a roast, somehow.'

She grinned and held the files tight as she turned, forcing herself to look serious. 'See you then, then.'

Two hours later, poring over the files she'd found in the paper's archives, Emily was forced to admit George had been right. East Finchley station had, over the years, been prey to a number of these incidents – the earliest one she'd found had happened in October of 1972 when a seventeen year old girl had been coming home from a day visiting family in Camden Town. She'd been followed as she got off the train, and grabbed before she reached the stairs leading down to the exit. The only witness had been a middle-aged man in a black overcoat and a grey hat, who'd shouted for help and run to her aid. The two men had scuffled, and in the melée the girl had been thrown to the floor. She'd struggled to her knees just in time to see the older man grab her attacker as he made for her once more, knife in hand. In the struggle, both men had apparently overbalanced and fallen on to the tracks, into the path of an oncoming train. Both had died almost instantly.

No one had listened to the victim's protestations that her saviour hadn't fallen; he'd *pulled* her attacker down onto the tracks, and held him there as the train bore down on both of them. Emily didn't believe it either; who would willingly go to their own death, when all they'd had to do, really, was knock the attacker down and pin him there until help arrived – which in a staffed underground station shouldn't have taken more than a minute or two?

She spent another hour going through various other reports from over the years, but none seemed to quite fit the facts of what she'd been told by her uncle. There was a long and dispiriting list of the usual muggings, fights and accidents – some resulting in death, others in injury – none of these mentioned the man in the hat and overcoat.

Looking at the clock, Emily was surprised to see it was almost four o'clock; she hadn't even taken a lunch break, or had a coffee. No wonder she felt sick.

A shadow appeared at her left side and, looking up, she saw her uncle there, frowning again. 'Any progress?'

She shook her head. 'Not much; the usual list of violence – brawls, attacks, not much else.' She reached into the hanging drawer on her right and drew out her handbag. 'Do you mind if I go home a bit early? I've got a thumping headache.'

'I'm not surprised,' he answered. 'You haven't left your desk all day, and you can't have got much sleep last night.' He started to walk back to his office. 'Go home, get some rest, but clear your desk first.'

She nodded. 'I will. Thank you.'

'Bright and early tomorrow, mind,' he called. 'And I'll expect some progress tomorrow, alright?'

She groaned. She knew she'd better have something he

could run by the end of the next day, but had no idea what to write. She trudged towards the exit, shoulders bowed. She'd worry about that later.

Twenty minutes later she was sitting on a train, heading back towards East Finchley. She glanced at her watch, and was comforted to find it was only four thirty. There should be plenty of people about when she reached her destination.

Sure enough, she hit the beginning of the rush hour, and East Finchley was teeming with people as she got off the tube and headed for the stairs. She couldn't help being over-cautious, jumping when anyone got too close – which earned her more than a few dodgy looks from people who couldn't decide if she was on drugs, drunk or just plain crazy. She was starting to think they might have a point – perhaps she was mad, after all. As she turned left at the bottom of the stairs, heading towards the ticket barrier and the High Road, she caught a glimpse of a hat. A very old-fashioned hat that looked uncomfortably familiar. The crowds parted and she saw that the hat belonged to an elderly gentleman, being buffeted towards her by the evening tide of commuters.

She stood back to let him pass, earning herself a few choice comments in the process, but she didn't care – he looked worried enough without being accosted by a loon of a woman demanding to know where he'd got his hat.

Keeping her head down so she didn't find herself getting into even more trouble, she made her way out to the High Road and hopped on a bus heading towards North Finchley. Twenty minutes later, she was letting herself into her flat above a shop just off Tally Ho Corner, trying not to fall over the cat winding its way between her feet and purring. 'Come on, puss,' she said, nudging the animal gently with her toe. The cat jumped and started off towards the kitchen. Emily laughed as she followed, shedding her jacket onto the bannisters as she followed. 'You've got me right where you want me, don't you?'

Later, dinner cooked and eaten, cat fed and watered, Emily found herself channel-hopping as she thought over the events of the previous twenty-four hours. She felt such a fraud – it wasn't as if the man at the station the previous night had actually attacked her, after all. She'd been scared, yes, and he might well have tried to drag her off if the man in the hat hadn't . . .

Hadn't what, exactly?

She'd felt someone. She had. The feel of his body as he pulled her upright and the smell of pipe smoke that rose from his damp wool coat; she couldn't have imagined that. She examined her arms, and was a little surprised to find no trace of his clasp. He'd *hauled* her to her feet; surely there should be a mark? Something to show the strength of his grip? Whoever had been following her had definitely felt his strength – her rescuer had swept him off the platform to his death. Hadn't he?

She tried to focus on the TV screen before her, aware she'd just missed something important. Offering up a silent prayer of thanks to the great god Sky Plus, she picked up the remote and rewound. The local news was on, and a reporter was standing outside East Finchley station, microphone in hand, with a suitably solemn expression on his face. He was reporting the apparent suicide of a young man the previous night – a Warren Lytton, nineteen years old, a history of minor problems with the police; a couple of mugging convictions that seemed to consist more of aggravated shoving than outright violence, no one had been hurt, shoplifting . . . nothing too sinister.

Someone just off camera was shouting, and Emily strained to hear what was being said. No use; whoever it was had been pushed out of range of the microphone, and all she could make out was raised voices. A female voice, shouting, and more voices speaking in a conciliatory tone. The reporter stopped speaking, and in the silence that followed Emily heard quite clearly: 'My boy wouldn't kill himself! He wouldn't do that!' The report cut back to the studio, and the newscaster shaking his head in disapproval.

Emily turned the TV off, her stomach churning. She ran for the bathroom and just made it in time before she doubled over and lost her supper. She sank to the floor, shaking, and wiped the sweat from her face. So it was being labelled a suicide. Perhaps it even had been, who was she to say? She couldn't help feeling a sense of relief that it was over – she'd been dreading more questions by the police. They'd been lovely to her, calming her down and taking her home – but no one had taken her story of the man in the hat seriously, that was obvious. She supposed in the absence of any sign of someone else at the scene they'd had no choice – no one else had even seen him.

She found herself crying, and rubbed her face clean of tears. She would not let this get to her. It was done, and she could move on now. She'd file a piece in the morning about the suicide, and that would be the end of it.

She smelled pipe smoke, and flashed back to the tunnel – she *had* seen him, she knew. So why had no one else?

The next morning found her at her desk bright and early, typing up the report of Warren Lytton's apparent suicide – she felt someone standing beside her and looked up to see George, reading the copy as she typed it.

'What about the attack?' he asked.

Emily shrugged. 'What can I say? There's no record of anyone else being seen at the station at that time, just this guy. Who knows? Maybe he slipped off the platform running away.'

'You don't believe that.'

'No,' she answered. 'I don't. But I don't want to look like an idiot, or crazy.'

He said nothing.

'Would you?' she pushed.

George stared at her for a long moment before nodding. 'Fair enough.' Then he was gone.

Emily sat, nonplussed, not entirely sure from their exchange whether she should go ahead and file the piece or not. Gradually the office started to fill up, chatter replacing the peace of a few moments before; not making things any easier to focus on. Someone laughed and she whirled round, the voice familiar, but no one seemed to be responsible – most of her colleagues were by now seated at their desks, concentrating on the monitors in front of them.

She tried to work out why the laugh was familiar, but to no avail – it had been a man's voice, of that she was sure; probably an older man, but no one in her immediate area fitted that description.

Her nostrils filled with the scent of Old Holborn and tears welled up as she thought of her father; she'd loved to sit on his lap as a child, and this smell brought her back to those days in an instant. Yet no one around her was smoking.

She gave up, and sent her article to her editor, then closed the screen down. She needed some air.

As she left the building, someone jostled her, and as she automatically apologised she realised this was no accident. Her attacker's mother stood before her, her expression furious. Emily glanced back over her shoulder to see if anyone was on hand to help should it be necessary, but she was on her own.

'Excuse me,' she said, and moved to side-step the woman.

Mrs Lytton, however, was having none of this. She stepped in front of Emily once more, her eyes narrowed.

Emily wondered if she thought this made her appear more

intimidating, and bit down on the smile that threatened to bloom. Perhaps she'd have found it more frightening if she hadn't found herself looking down at the older woman.

Mrs Lytton took a step forward, not content 'til she was close enough to share Emily's breath, something Emily found vaguely distasteful, but not particularly scary.

'My boy didn't kill himself,' she spat.

'Emily nodded. 'You might be right,' she said before adding with uncharacteristic cruelty: 'But he's dead, so we can't ask him, can we?'

The woman gasped, and now she didn't look threatening – she looked heartbroken, and Emily felt heat blossom in her chest before spreading to her face. How could she have said that?

'I'm sorry,' she said. 'I didn't mean it to sound so . . .'

'Fucking cruel?' Mrs Lytton interrupted, and Emily had the grace to look sorry.

She nodded. 'I'm sorry he's dead, I really am. But it's not my fault.'

'Then whose is it?' the woman wailed. 'Who killed my boy?'

Emma sighed, and steeled herself for the inevitable response to what came next. 'I didn't see anyone,' she said. 'I just heard a cry, and then the alarm. I was running away.'

'From what?'

'From Warren.' The woman hissed as if scalded, and Emma hurried to apologise. 'I'm really sorry, but he was chasing me . . . and then he was gone, and I heard him yell . . . and then there were brakes, and . . .'

'Stop it!' Mrs Lytton screamed, raising her arms as if to fend Emily off. 'Bloody stop it, you lying bitch!' Her hand was up and planted firmly against Emily's cheek before either of them knew it was going to happen, and then she was gone, leaving Emily alone and sobbing, hand raised to the livid imprint on her shocked face.

Emily caught a whiff of that tobacco again, and shook her head. 'No,' she said. 'Please don't.' The smell faded, and she breathed out a juddering sigh of relief. 'I'm going home,' she said, to no one. 'Alone.'

No one followed.

Emily's piece came out the following day, and her phone started to ring as people realised she'd been involved.

The article made no mention of the attack she'd been sure was about to follow, but did mention her presence at the station; she found herself to be a celebrity, and decided – with her uncle's permission – to stay indoors for a few days, until something else of interest happened and she was no longer 'interesting' to the gawkers and on-lookers that had crawled out of the woodwork.

A few days later Emily found herself making her way home alone once more, having spent the evening at a local theatre for a review of a play being put on by the local amateur dramatics society. *Blithe Spirit*. The joke wasn't lost, but Emily didn't think she'd ever find that funny again.

As she left East Finchley station, she saw a man leaning against the wall, hat pulled down low over his face, shoulders hunched against the cold. She slowed, then drew herself up and hurried forward – she'd be safe inside.

The man stood up as she approached, and as he lifted his head she saw she'd been scared of nothing.

'Uncle George,' she said. 'I wasn't expecting to see you here.'

He smiled. 'I thought you might want some company. Seeing as it's late.'

'I'm glad you came. It's a bit quiet tonight, isn't it?'

George nodded, and took her arm. 'Come on, we'll take the bus.'

Emily found herself propelled down the hill, towards the bridge. 'I normally get the bus at the next stop up,' she said, trying to pull away. 'It's a bit dark this way.'

The bus stop they were heading to was closer, she knew, but she didn't like going under the bridge where it was dark. And there was a stretch of road just beyond the adjacent pub that was bordered by gardens with overhanging bushes – she preferred to be more visible, especially after . . .

George sighed, impatient. 'It's all right, I'm with you.' And kept pulling her on, past the bus stop they should have waited at.

As they reached the corner of Bishops Avenue, George pushed her to the side, and she found herself by a house with a low fence – and a lot of foliage.

'What are you doing?'

George laughed. 'I thought we could take a bit of a walk.'

'Why down here?'

George's grip on her arm grew painful, and she got ready to scream.

'Uncle George, what's going on? You're scaring me!'

'I'm sorry, love,' he said. 'I didn't want to do that. I just wanted you to see. I want you to make everyone see.'

'You're not making any sense,' she said. 'See what?'

George nodded at the house, but had the grace to loosen his grip. 'He lived here.'

'Who did?'

'Your saviour. You were right; he's done this before – and it's time people knew.'

Emily turned to stare at the house – unprepossessing in the gloom, she could see, nevertheless, that it was neglected. An air of loneliness pervaded its surrounds, making it stand out from the expensive, well-tended houses that adjoined it. 'Who lived here?' she asked.

'A man called Arthur Fuller. I went to school with him, or rather your dad did. They were a couple of years below me.'

'He knew Dad?'

'Very well. They were mates.'

'What happened to him?'

George's eyes glittered as he started to talk. 'He was killed. Walking home one night, late, he saw a girl being attacked by some thug at East Finchley station. Decided he had to have a go, save the girl.' He laughed, the sound bitter in his throat. 'Bloody idiot.'

Emily didn't quite understand. 'Why was he an idiot, if all he did was try to help someone?'

'The girl was your mother, and Arthur knew her, of course.'

Emily stared.

'You look like her, you know,' he said; and tried to touch her hair.

She flinched.

George grinned, his teeth bared white in the dark. 'You see? You're just like her.'

She took a step back, and he gripped her arm tighter.

'It's not like she was going out with your dad at the time,' he said. 'She was fair game.'

'Oh, George,' Emily moaned. 'You were the thug?'

'So the papers called me. I just wanted a kiss, that's all. But she wouldn't be quiet.'

'And Arthur heard her? Came to help?'

George nodded. 'I always felt bad that he got hurt. I just pushed him off. I didn't see the car coming.'

The smell of Old Holborn surrounded her now, and she felt herself relax. They weren't on their own any more.

George took a step towards her, and Emily stiffened. 'I want you to tell his story,' he said. 'I want people to know he's still saving people.'

'Why?' she asked. 'Because you feel guilty?'

George nodded. 'That, yes, and because people should know it wasn't just an accident. He was a good bloke, and he tried to help your mum. Just like he's still trying to help people.'

Emily took George's hand, and peeled his fingers away from her arm, one by one. 'I can't do that,' she said. 'It wouldn't be right.'

'Why not?' he demanded. 'Why shouldn't he get some recognition for what he did?'

'Because then they'd know what you did,' she said, and saw the realisation dawn in his eyes. 'And, even worse, what you nearly did to Mum.'

George launched himself forward and pushed her towards the busy road.

She felt herself falling, but was overwhelmed by the scent of pipe tobacco, even as she felt herself being set back on her feet. She stood, gasping, as she saw the cloud darken around her uncle, a smoky figure reaching out for him and drawing him towards the main road. A bus was hurtling up the hill towards them, but she couldn't make a sound – and it was too dark for them to be seen, just yet.

George was trying hard to break free, but to no avail. As the bus drew close, the cloud solidified, and Emily saw her saviour, hat pulled low over his face, dark coat pulled tight around him. He pushed George down, and both men fell under the oncoming vehicle – brakes squealed, someone screamed, and Emily found herself witnessing everything this time, at close range, as Arthur held him there.

She saw George's hand, protruding from underneath the front of the bus – blood trickling towards the kerb. There was no sign of the rest of him. The hand twitched, just once, then was still. A woman who'd been walking up the main road was screaming: scream after scream pealing out, with barely time to breathe between. The bus driver was sitting in his cab, head buried in his hands – the few passengers were staring forward, shock etched on their faces. She could already hear the sirens.

Emily staggered to the kerb and threw up, and when she looked up, he was there. He smiled at her, and touched his fingers to his hat – an old-world gesture. The smell of Old Holborn caused her stomach to clench, and she vomited again. When she looked up again, he was gone.

She couldn't tell the story, she realised. And not because it would ruin her aunt's life, and her parents' memory. She couldn't tell the story because then everyone would know about Arthur – and much as she hated the idea of him continuing his vendetta, she hated even more the idea that he wouldn't be able to help any more girls daft enough to wander home on their own in dangerous places.

V.H. LESLIE

NAMESAKE

HER NAME WAS Burden. Cecelia J Burden. Her parents had at least tried to compensate by giving her a pretty first name, hoping no doubt to disguise the surname behind flowery sibilance. Yet neither name was really quite right. The J stood for Joan or Jan or Jane, a legacy of some distant aunt. Whichever name, it had been forgotten and mislaid long ago with her birth certificate in a loft full of paper. J was happy just to have retained the initial, whatever it stood for. Jane, most probably, on account of how plain she was. Its mystery appealed to her, so that's what she went by. J.

J had liked her surname once. Before she really understood what the word meant. She liked the sound of it and would break it into syllables and imagine her name was a place where birds lived. *Bird-den*. Burden. She even decorated her textbooks with scribbles of robins and owls, and dotted her i's with curved silhouettes of birds in flight. It would have been the perfect name for a life a crime, she often thought, or a serial killer. She read a lot about serial killers; they often had hard childhoods, unrealistic responsibilities forced upon them at a young age, a huge emotional chip on their shoulders weighing them down until they finally reacted with violence.

She'd thought about changing her name – she even had

the forms at home, ready and signed – but she worried about how her parents would react. Did they like being Burdens? She'd never asked her mother how she felt about taking on her father's name. A test of love, perhaps, a declaration of her devotion, taking on such a heavy toll. But her mother was attracted to suffering – she'd prolong a cold, or walk instead of taking the bus. She probably should have married a Martyr instead.

No, J was resigned to waiting it out. She looked forward to her wedding day for reasons different to most young women; it wasn't the fairytale castle or the princess dress that she fantasised about, it was about finally being shot of her name.

But finding a husband was no easy feat. It wasn't like you were going to run into Mr Rochester or Mr Darcy at your local greeting card shop, where J worked stacking shelves. To make matters worse, J wasn't exactly brimming with self-confidence. The weight of her surname accompanied her through her adolescence and into her twenties and had lived up to its meaning, a constant pressure on her neck and shoulders that made her feel like she was hunched.

At least Internet dating allowed you to disguise your projected defects as well as your name. J's mother said only freaks and perverts used the Internet. J thought a hunchback like herself would fit right in. She described herself as busty and bubbly, avoiding the obvious B word on her mind, and issued herself instead a nice humdrum surname – Bentley. She avoided all the potential matches the computer spat at her. She had her own method of selection. When she saw the name, she knew he was the one.

Blithe.

The bar had changed. It hadn't been much to look at back when J knew it, but there'd been something reassuring about the shabby décor, the sticky floor. It had character. You knew what to expect. It was called Frank's or Ed's then, something suitably proprietary and ordinary. Now it was Bar None and J wondered how many drunken men had appealed to the bar's signage as they were manhandled out the door by bouncers. Inside was modern, the tables high, surrounded by bar stools which gave you a strange feeling of vertigo when you managed to get up there. Red lights shone from behind the bar in regimented unison, the glow refracted in the chrome and glass surfaces like the beams of sniper rifles. Sitting by the bar felt like an ambush.

She sat near a large spiral staircase, an artistic showpiece of metal and wire that allowed the men gaping at the bottom to look up women's skirts as they descended. With mock confidence the women negotiated the chrome stairs in their three-inch heels, gripping the banister desperately to prevent themselves falling into the pit of testosterone below.

J scanned the men lining the bar, trying to remember the picture of Andrew on his profile. She hadn't really cared what he looked like, it was the name she was interested in. The bar's clientele had changed as well, which made it harder to spot him. All the men wore suits as if they'd just come from work and the women were as groomed and as glossy as their surroundings, sipping expensive cocktails from martini glasses. *Bar None* seemed pretty apt; there was no individuality here, everyone looked the same. J felt adrift on her bar stool, she glanced at the cocktail menu: *Adonis, Tom Collins, Harvey Wallbanger, Scarlett O'Hara*. Good names. She ordered herself a *Bloody Mary* and waited.

'J?' a man in a red jumper asked.

'Yes. Hello.' She held out her hand and he shook it.

'Andrew,' he said. 'I'm sorry I'm late. Parking was a nightmare.'

'You won't be drinking, then?' J regretted the two glasses she'd had at home and the cocktail in front of her.

'I might. I can leave my car here, pick it up in the morning if . . .' he trailed off, hoping not to have sounded presumptuous.

Andrew sat down on the barstool opposite. J had already learnt it wasn't easy to do elegantly and a puff of air dispersed as he made contact with the upholstery. His face reddened.

'The stool . . .' he began,

J laughed. 'Mine's the same. But there is one cool thing about them.'

She pressed the lever on her chair and suddenly disappeared under the table. She reappeared with a hydraulic hiss.

'That *does* look cool.' Andrew found the lever and began to disappear from view.

Behind them the barman shook his head at the newcomers bobbing up and down like fish caught in a net.

The chrome spiral staircase must have been an architect's joke or a test of sobriety. How many people had fallen down, J wondered, trying her best to concentrate on each step. It didn't help that her vision was blurred.

Andrew was waiting at the bottom, holding her coat. She hoped he was gentlemanly enough not to glance up through the rails. She'd allowed herself to get ridiculously drunk on the first date; there would be no coming back from this, she thought. She'd be ruined in his eyes forever as wife material.

'I'll walk you home,' Andrew said, helping her with her coat.

'I'm a Burden,' she spluttered in reply.

'It's no hassle.'

'No, that's my name. Burden. Not Bentley.'

Andrew looked at her for a moment, weighing up whether to make a joke or not, wondering whether she'd be able to make light of it.

'It's not funny. *You* try being a Burden?'

'It could be worse.'

'Could it?'

'I went to school with a girl called Paige Turner. Seriously.'

J smiled.

'Anything else I should know?' he asked. 'What does the J stand for?'

Plain Jane. But buoyed up with alcohol, on Andrew's arm, she didn't feel plain at all. She felt blithe.

'Nothing at all,' she replied.

'What's in a name anyway?' Andrew asked later as they lay in bed.

J shrugged, content and satisfied, sleep weighing heavier on her than her name ever had. Andrew's flat was small and comfortable, surprisingly decorative for a bachelor. Not that she'd seen a great deal, led almost straight away to the bedroom. It was a small room but felt bigger because of the high ceiling, with mezzanine at the far end, which Andrew said led to the attic, though J couldn't see a ladder. From where she lay, she could watch the shadows gathering up there, black shapes converging behind the rails. She blinked and the shadows dispersed.

'It's a hard name to live up to,' Andrew continued, 'Blithe. People expect you to be constantly happy.'

J hadn't intended to be so easy on the first date, but he'd been so understanding about her name, her initial deceit. If he'd noticed the way she hunched over he hadn't mentioned it, he made her feel beautiful and he was so much more attractive than she'd hoped. Naked in his arms, she thought of other names for herself, taunting herself with the insults her mother threw at the TV when celebrities wore too few clothes. *Whore, Slut, Slag*. She didn't want to think about that right now, but the words repeated themselves over and over in her mind until they became a litany. Blithe's voice in her ear couldn't compete.

'People don't imagine that you'd have troubles and strife with a name like mine. J? J?'

But J was fast asleep, dreaming of any name but her own.

Burden and Blithe went well together. J hadn't expected Andrew to call after such a drunken first date but he did, the very next day. And he'd surprised her further by asking to see her that night. Three weeks later, they'd spent every available minute in each other's company. J had even acquired a drawer and a cabinet in the bathroom and her stuff was slowly creeping in, cluttering up Andrew's small flat.

'Maybe I could store some stuff up there,' J asked one day, pointing at the mezzanine. 'You don't seem to use it.'

It was the only area in the flat that gave the impression of space. Andrew hadn't said as much, but without a ladder it was clearly off limits.

He shook his head. 'I'm in the process of decorating. I'll clear out the cupboard in the hallway instead, how about that?'

J smiled, happy that he was making space for her in his life. She looked up at the mezzanine all the same and for a brief moment had the curious feeling of being watched.

To change the name but not the letter is to marry for worse and not for better. Such was her mother's response to the news that they'd set a date. It was typical of her mother to kill her enthusiasm, to lace her mood with a little bit of the misery that she enjoyed so much. J didn't care about old wives' tales; changing her name was her priority and she wanted to be blithe more than anything.

Yet it wasn't just her mother cautioning her whirlwind romance. J had moved in entirely now with Andrew, yet she was far from settled. *Cold feet* she told herself, though she knew that wasn't true. The negativity wasn't of an emotional kind, it was more tangible and it stemmed, she was certain, from the mezzanine.

'Maybe we could move,' J asked one night in bed. Andrew had always regaled her with his stories of foreign travel yet he looked uncomfortable at the suggestion.

'I can't, J, I'm tied here.'

'Why?' she asked. He wasn't particularly enthused about his job, though it allowed him to work from home. He'd never introduced her to friends or family, in fact he was frustratingly vague about all family ties. What was keeping him here?

'I'd never get out of this mortgage,' he said, taking her hand. 'I'm up to the hilt in debt, I'm afraid.'

Marry for worse and not for better sprang to mind, but she swept it away with *for better or worse*.

J woke in the middle of the night, conscious that someone was watching her. Andrew was asleep at her side, his snoring obscuring the sound of something above. She wanted to reach for the bedside lamp but she couldn't move. She stared back in the blackness and listened hard.

She heard footsteps on the mezzanine.

She lay still, willing the noise to repeat itself, wondering if she had heard it at all. She waited, gripping Andrew in readiness.

A creeping movement this time. Unmistakable now. Something was up on the mezzanine. Her mind conjured the image of a person walking up there, sneaking about in the dark.

She shook Andrew awake.

'There's someone up there,' she whispered, pointing in the darkness.

Andrew looked about, barely comprehending. He switched on the bedside lamp, flooding the room with light. 'What?'

'I heard a noise,' she repeated, 'up there,'

Andrew sighed. 'Oh. That. Sometimes birds get into the

attic. It's happened before. They're protected, would you believe. Allowed to nest up there.'

'It didn't sound like birds,' J said.

'Listen, J, there's nothing to worry about.'

'But Andrew –'

'I'll check it out in the morning if you like.' And with that he turned off the light.

Burden.

Bird-den.

She imagined a room full of birds in flight. She watched them orbiting an attic space, circling it again and again and again, until she drifted back to sleep.

J was in the wedding aisle again, stacking the shelves with images of happy couples, garters, and wedding cakes. Since her engagement she spent longer in this part of the shop than any other, arranging the cellophane-wrapped cards in order of preference instead of price codes. The manager, Sharon, a girl barely out of college, was more interested in her mobile phone than what J did. She barely noticed that J had neglected the birthday and bereavement aisles, along with the balloons and silly string display.

J looked around the shop. It expressed every sentiment but the one she felt. She couldn't stop thinking about the birds in the attic. Andrew's conviction that there was nothing to worry about had been enough for her to go to sleep. But the birds had swooped into her dreams instead and flown around and around her mind like an inky whirlwind. It wasn't just the birds; J hadn't liked the way Andrew had cut her off, refusing to listen to her as if she hadn't said anything at all. Was that what she was expected to do? To accept Andrew's word on the subject despite her misgivings, to honour and obey him?

Yet he'd been so considerate before she left for work that day. He'd made her breakfast in bed and promised to check the attic when she left. He said that maybe the wedding stress was getting to her. He'd help more with organising the venue and the caterers. He added that he didn't expect her to take his name if she didn't want to. They were a modern couple after all. He'd happily be a Burden.

J knocked the cards from their stand and they fell like confetti. What were a few birds in the attic compared to the albatross about her neck?

J stooped to pick up the cards from the floor. *Warm Wedding Wishes, To the Happy Couple, May Your Nest Be Filled With Joy*. J slipped the last card into her apron pocket.

J went home sick that afternoon but sat in the café opposite Andrew's flat instead, watching for him to leave. She felt like a criminal casing the joint. She sipped her second tea and considered what she really knew about the man she was marrying. Freaks and perverts, her mother's voice chimed.

Andrew emerged an hour later, his Bag For Life folded neatly under his arm, presumably on his way to the supermarket. J would have adequate time; she could be in and out without him ever knowing. It was only when she stood in the bedroom, staring up at the mezzanine, that she wondered whether she was breaking some moral law, committing some breach of trust. He hadn't exactly forbidden her to go up there, but then why the need for such secrecy? Maybe she should just leave it be.

Just a peek.

So she hauled the bedside drawers across the room, stacked a table on top and a chair from the living room. She stood back, assessing her crude ladder, then began her ascent.

The mezzanine was more spacious than she imagined, unfurnished and bare, with no signs of decorating. It had a perfect view of the room below and the bed in the centre. J imagined something monstrous watching them sleep, like a gargoyle on a Gothic façade, looking down while they made love.

She turned her attention back to the mezzanine and saw a small door in the wall that presumably led into the loft, though something closer drew her eye. Coiled up at the edge of the platform was a rope ladder. But what was the point of it being up here, J thought? Unless someone could throw it down?

J moved towards the door, trying not to think of the fairytale she'd been told as a child, of the princess with the extraordinarily long hair. The princess who was locked away from the world with her unusual name: Rapunzel.

The door opened onto a dark and musty space. J moved through the darkness, through a rank and pungent smell. She followed it while her eyes adjusted and began to discern shapes.

A stained mattress lay in the middle of a room, amid a scattering of black feathers. It *was* a nest, but not for birds. Someone lived up here.

J looked around in alarm. A squatter? But the ladder implied that Andrew knew.

J stepped backwards, the smell suddenly stronger. Something was close. Something was watching her. She scanned the room and saw the whites of wild eyes staring back at her from a blackened face in the dark.

The figure was filthy, hunched over in the gloom. J could make out a tangle of hair, a ripped and tattered nightdress, a strong abhorrent feminine smell. And at her feet, a coil of rope tied at her ankle.

Why would she be tied here? Why wouldn't she scream? And then she saw. She nearly screamed herself.

The woman had no mouth.

J moved closer – it was a trick of the light, surely, but the woman's face was oddly smooth where her mouth should have been and her face was expressionless and vacant, except for her eyes which blazed with rage at J's intrusion.

The wild woman moved so fast that J barely had time to react. She managed to stumble back, through the impossibly small door, back onto the mezzanine. Crouching, she tried desperately to unroll the ladder but her hands were shaking and the figure was at the door, rushing towards her, hands clawing at the air.

J remembered the night she met Andrew. The ridiculous chrome staircase in the trendy bar. *Bar None*. How she had to concentrate on each step.

And J was falling, landing on the tower she'd made, scattering the furniture like a house of cards. She landed hard against the floor, knocking the breath from her chest so she had nothing with which to scream.

Burden-Blithe did have a ring to it. Double barrels were the trend nowadays, but she'd always thought it cruel forcing someone else to share her Burden. Tempting as it was to let someone else carry it with her, she'd rather simply be rid of the whole thing.

Just Blithe, she thought. How did the song go? *Be you blithe and bonnie*. Bonnie and Clyde. *Blithe and Bonnie, Bonnie and Clyde, Jekyll and Hyde*. Some partnerships were destined for infamy.

J shook her head clear and she looked up at the mezzanine, remembering what she'd seen. She put her hand to her temple and was surprised to find she was bleeding.

Some couples amalgamated their surnames. A stab at gender equality, no doubt, merging parts of their names to make something wholly original. Smith and Jones became Smones or Jith. J smiled but felt a stabbing sensation behind her eyes. Burden-Blithe would be Burthe or Blurden. *Bludgeon*, she thought, looking up at the mezzanine.

~

Andrew deposited the groceries in the kitchen and walked through to the bedroom. The rope ladder was down and he smiled, undoing his shirt and pulling off his trousers. In just his underpants, he climbed up.

'Honey, I'm home,' he called.

He moved through the darkness with familiarity. 'Where are you, Mary?' he said.

He smiled more broadly when he saw Mary lying face down on the mattress, her nightdress pulled up, waiting for him.

'So you want your turn do you?' he said. 'Happy to see me?'

'Ecstatic,' said a voice behind him.

Andrew turned and saw J hunched in the dark, a bloodied gash on her brow.

'What are *you* doing here?'

'I could ask the same of you. Checking for birds?'

He looked at his feet.

'I found your little secret.'

Andrew made to object but J merely glanced toward the figure on the mattress. Andrew could see that J had tied her down with the rope.

'There shouldn't be any secrets between a husband and wife.'

Andrew sighed. 'I tried to tell you that very first night. I tried to tell you about my trouble and strife. My –'

'Wife.'

J had seen the gold band on the wild woman's finger as she'd lunged at her, pushing her back down to earth.

'I was too young,' Andrew said. 'She was so different. I didn't notice that she wasn't quite right.'

'You didn't notice? You would have *married me,*' J said. There was a name for what he was. Her mind struggled over the syllables – a polygamist. There was a name for what she was, too, though she wasn't ready to say it.

Andrew wiped the tears from his eyes. 'I *still* want to marry you. I'd do anything for you, J. Just name it.'

For a moment J saw the Blithe she'd met on the first night. But he'd lured her with false promises and a name that was already taken.

'I should have divorced her,' he said, 'but I'm all she has. She needs me.'

More likely the other way around, J thought. 'You're still making the most of your conjugal rights, I see.'

Andrew covered himself with his hands. 'I know it's hard to understand, but I'm bound here. I'm tied.'

Mrs Blithe – the name was already occupied. That made her the other woman. She wasn't wife material at all.

She'd wanted so much to be blithe. *Blithe and Bonnie. Bonnie and Clyde. Jekyll and Hyde.* A life a crime. She would have done anything for him. She had. She'd done it for his name's sake. Names ache.

'You need to untie her, J,' Andrew said, walking towards the mattress. J thought it was a bit rich considering that he was the one who'd tied Mary up in the first place. The old ball and chain. J didn't like his tone but she let it go because of what she had done.

As Andrew edged closer he saw it too.

'J?' he whispered.

'I finished the decorating,' she said evenly, pointing at the blood on the walls.

There had been a lot of it, more than J had expected. So much that it had drenched the wild woman's face, obscuring her features. J wondered whether she had imagined the absence of lips, the pink slip of a tongue. Either way, Mary was his silent partner now.

Andrew collapsed onto the mattress, taking Mary's limp hand in his. He sobbed into the bloodied sheets.

There couldn't be any lawful impediment in the way of their happiness, but J saw now that Andrew would always be tethered. A memory was stronger than a name.

Blithe and Bonnie, Bonnie and Clyde, Jekyll and Hyde.

The names soared around and around in her mind like birds in flight. J flew with them, barely noticing that she'd forced the rope around Andrew's neck. That she'd pushed him down onto the marital bed, that she'd made him stare into what was left of the face he'd made his vows to.

Afterward, J climbed back down the rope ladder. The pressure on her neck and shoulders had eased and she walked into the world standing tall, ready to make a name for herself.

REGGIE OLIVER

COME INTO MY PARLOUR

Will you walk into my parlour?' said the Spider to the Fly,
'Tis the prettiest little parlour that ever you did spy;
The way into my parlour is up a winding stair,
And I've a many curious things to shew when you are there.'
from *The Spider and the Fly* by Mary Howitt (1799–1888)

Somehow I always knew that there was a problem with Aunt Harriet.

She was my father's only sister – step-sister, as it happens – and older than he was by eleven years. She was unmarried and her work was something to do with libraries: that much was clear, but the rest was rather a mystery. She lived in a small flat near Victoria Station in London which we heard about but never saw, but she often used to come to stay with us – rather *too* often for my mother's taste. In fact, the only time I ever remember my parents 'having words', as we used to say, was over Aunt Harriet yet again coming down for the weekend.

'Yes, I know, I know, dear,' I heard my father say. 'But I can't exactly refuse her. She is my sister.'

'Exactly,' said my mother. 'She's only your sister. You *can* say no to her occasionally.'

But apparently my father couldn't. Fortunately she did only

stay for weekends, that is, apart from Christmas, but I'll come to that later.

At that time we lived in Kent and my father commuted into London by train every weekday morning. Where we lived was semi-rural; there were places to walk and wander: there were woods and fields nearby. I like to think that my younger sister and I had a rather wonderful childhood; if it were not for Aunt Harriet.

Am I exaggerating her importance? It is a long time ago now, but I rather think I'm not. I suspect that she loomed even larger then than she does in my memory.

She was a big, shapeless woman who always seemed to be wearing several layers of clothing whatever the weather. She dyed her hair a sort of reddish colour and rattled a little from the various bits of jewellery she had about her. (She was particularly fond of amber.) Her nose was beaky and she carried with her everywhere an enormous handbag, the contents of which remained unknown.

When she came she brought with her an atmosphere of unease and discontent. She never allowed herself to fit in with us. If we wanted to go for a walk, she would stay behind. If we decided to stay indoors, she would feel like going out. She rarely took part in any game or expedition we had planned, and when she did there was always a fault to find with the arrangements. On the other hand, almost invariably she wanted, often at the most inconvenient times, to 'have a talk' as she put it, with my father. He never refused her demands and so they would go into his study, often for several hours, to have their talk.

I once asked my mother what it was all about.

'They're probably discussing the Trust,' she said.

I never really understood this Trust. I once asked my father about it but he refused to reveal anything. Many years later, after my father's death, I searched among his papers for evidence of it and could find nothing. The little I knew came at second hand from my mother. She said that some distant relation had left a sum of money jointly to my father and Aunt Harriet, and Aunt Harriet was always trying to get more income from it, or do something mysterious called 'breaking the Trust' so that she could extract a lump sum for her personal use.

I don't think my aunt ever really cared about my sister and me as people, but she would ask us the kind of questions that grown-ups tend to ask: questions that are almost impossible to answer. 'How are you getting on at school?' 'Have you made any nice friends there?' I don't think she would have been interested in our answers even if they had been less boring and evasive than the ones we gave her.

Mealtimes were especially grim. In the first place Aunt Harriet was a vegetarian and my mother, out of courtesy I suppose, insisted that we were also vegetarian during her stays. That meant doing without a Sunday Roast which we resented. My mother was not a great cook at the best of times, but she was particularly uninspired in her meatless dishes. Then, during the meal, Aunt Harriet would either be silent in such a way as to discourage conversation from us, or indulge in long monologues about office politics in the library service. This always struck us – that is, my sister and me, and probably my parents too – as horribly boring. We gathered from her talk that work colleagues were always trying, as she said, 'to put one over' on her, and she was always defeating them.

In spite of this, you may be surprised to know, I came to be fascinated by her. I suppose it was because she was, at the same time, such a big part of our lives, and yet so remote. Her life in London, apart from those dreary office politics, was a closed book. She never talked about going to theatres or concerts or exhibitions or watching sport. She didn't even really talk about books. She never mentioned any friends. It was this mystery about her that started all the trouble.

It began, I suppose, one Sunday in September when I was nine, and Aunt Harriet was then approaching sixty. We had just finished lunch and the meal had not pleased Aunt Harriet. It had been, if I remember rightly, Cauliflower Cheese, not one of my mother's cooking triumphs admittedly, but perfectly edible. My aunt's complaint had been that my mother should have made an effort to supply something more original from the vegetarian repertoire.

She began: 'I'm not complaining, but –' a disclaimer which, paradoxically, often prefaced her complaints '– I'm just saying. You might occasionally like to take a look in a vegetarian cook book for your own benefit. Of course *I* don't mind; *I'm* just your sister-in-law, but if you were to have guests here, important guests – of course I know *I'm* not important – and *they* happened to be vegetarian –'

At this point my father, usually the most patient of men, exploded. He could put up with a lot of things but this was not to be borne, especially as it involved my mother whom he adored. Even so, it was a brief explosion, and fairly reasonably expressed.

'Oh, for heaven's sake, stop talking nonsense, Harriet!' he said, not in his usual quiet voice.

My aunt sniffed, rose from the table and announced that she had never been so insulted in her life and was going for a walk. She then quitted the dining room and a few seconds later we heard the door bang. We ate the rest of the meal in virtual silence.

After lunch my curiosity got the better of me. It was a damp dull sort of day, so the prospect of going out was not inviting, even without the possibility of meeting Aunt Harriet, sullen faced, tramping about the countryside. I decided that this was my moment for exploring her room and seeing if I could find any clues to her bizarre behaviour.

There was one spare bedroom in the house for guests, and because few occupied it but she, it was known as Harriet's Room. She stayed there most weekends in the year and, though the furnishings of the room were very impersonal, she had somehow made the place her own.

First of all, there was the smell. It wasn't an unpleasant smell in itself, but it because it was from the perfume she wore it had dark associations. It was musky, spicy, not exactly unclean but somehow not fresh. The atmosphere was heavy with it because, with typical disregard for my parents' heating bills, she had left the bar of an electric fire on in her room.

The dressing table was crowded with an assortment of bottles of unguents and medicines. Aunt Harriet was, in her quiet way, a hypochondriac, always suffering from some kind of affliction, from heart palpitations to boils.

On the dressing table were also a number of black lacquer boxes, some rather beautiful, either painted or decorated with inlaid mother-of-pearl. Tentatively, and knowing that now I was somehow crossing a line, I opened one box, then another, then another.

They all contained jewellery or trinkets, the stones semiprecious and mostly made out of her beloved amber. Many were in the shape of animals or strange beasts of mythical origin. One in particular intrigued me. It sat on a bed of cotton wool in a small box of its own. The box was black like the others with a scene painted in gold on the top in the Japanese style of cranes flying over a lake bordered by waving reeds. The thing inside this box was carved out of amber, a dark, translucent reddish brown, smooth and polished to perfection. It appeared to be an insect of some kind, perhaps a beetle or spider with a bloated body and eight strange little stumpy legs of the kind you see on caterpillars. The workmanship was extremely fine and, as I now think, Japanese, like the box. Its head was round and dome-like, with two protruding eyes; almost complete spheres emerging from the middle of the head. Into these amber eyes the carver had managed to insert two tiny black dots which gave them a kind of life and, somehow, malignity. He (or she?) had carved the mouth parts to give an impression of sharp, predatory teeth – or whatever it is that insects have instead of teeth. It was beautifully made, and horrible, I shut the box quickly.

I turned my attention to the bedside table. It was piled high with books, mostly old and somewhat battered, but some finely bound. I noticed that many of the bindings had little square discolourations as if a label had been removed from their surfaces. I wondered if my aunt had brought them here to read because they were an odd selection. There was an early nineteenth-century treatise on metallurgy, a volume on alpine plants by a Victorian clergyman with some fine colour plates, a few modern novels in their original dust jackets, and several children's books. Besides these books I noticed a small plain wooden box, this time not containing trinkets but a neat set of small brushes, a needle-sharp scalpel knife, two pairs of tweezers and small square glass bottles containing fluids such as ink eradicator. I was puzzling over this mysterious collection when I heard someone behind me.

'What are you doing in my room, little man?'

I think I jumped several feet into the air in my fright. I had been sitting on the bed facing away from the door and Aunt Harriet had crept in unnoticed. The next moment she had me by the ear.

'I asked you what you were doing. Well . . . ?'

It was some moments before I was sufficiently in control to reply.

'Just looking.'

'Looking? Looking for what?'

'I don't know.'

'Do you make a habit of snooping around the rooms of your parents' guests?'

'No!'

'Oh, so you think it's all right to snoop around in *my* room. Is that it?'

'No! Let me go!' She had not released my ear.

'What do you think your father would say if I said I found you in my room trying to steal my things? Mmm?'

'I wasn't stealing anything! You won't tell him, will you?' I was not afraid of my father as such – he was not a fierce man – but I was afraid of disappointing him. At last Aunt Harriet began to relax her grip on my ear, but she had left it throbbing and painful, full of the blood of embarrassment.

'We shall have to see about that. I *may* not have to tell him,' said Aunt Harriet in a softer, almost caressing voice which was, however, no more reassuring. 'It all depends on whether you're going to be a helpful boy to me. Are you going to be a helpful boy, or a nasty, spiteful, sneaking boy?'

'Helpful,' I said, instantly dreading the menial task she would almost certainly set me.

'So I should think. All I'm going to ask is something really quite simple –' Suddenly she looked alarmed and turned round. My six-year-old sister Louise had wandered in and was standing in the doorway, her wide blue eyes staring at us in amazement. She had pale golden curls in those days and looked the picture of innocence, but evidently not to my aunt.

'Run away, little munchkin,' she said. 'Can't you see I'm talking to your grown-up brother?' Louise had never been called a 'munchkin' before. She probably didn't know what it meant – neither did I, for that matter – but it sounded cruel from my aunt's lips, so she burst into tears. Aunt Harriet stared at her in astonishment. She obviously had no idea why she had provoked such a reaction. After Louise had run off, still wailing, to find my mother, my aunt said: 'That child has been dreadfully spoilt.'

I felt that it was my turn to leave, so I started to shuffle towards the door. Aunt Harriet hauled me back by the ear again.

'Hold hard, young Lochinvar. Where do you think you're going? I haven't told you what I want you to do, yet, have I?'

'You can do it later, Aunt Harriet.'

'Later won't do. Later will never do.' Then she told me what she wanted. At some time during the week I was to go into my father's study and from the second drawer down on the left hand side of my father's kneehole desk I was to extract a blue folder labelled FAMILY TRUST. I was then to place it under the mattress in my aunt's room so that when she came the following weekend she might study it at her leisure.

It was a simple task, but it terrified me. I didn't know which was worse: to defy my aunt or to betray the trust of my father. I was going back to school shortly so I decided to postpone any decision and hope that Aunt Harriet would have forgotten all about it by the time she came next. That, of course, was a vain hope.

When she came the following weekend I avoided her as much as I could until finally she caught me early on Sunday morning as I was passing her door on the way to the bathroom. She dragged me inside and closed the door. She was strong for her age and build.

'Where is it?' she hissed into my face. She wore a Chinese silk dressing gown covered in dragons over a red flannel nightdress.

'Where's what?'

'Don't you play games with me, little man. You know perfectly well what I wanted. Why didn't you get it for me?'

'I couldn't,' I extemporised. 'The drawer was locked.'

'Little liar!' she said. 'I've seen your father open that drawer a thousand times and never once has he used a key. Dear God, can't you do just one simple little thing for me?'

'Why can't you get it yourself?'

'Because I can't. Never you mind. Because I need you to prove to me that you're not a nasty sneaking little boy, but someone who is loyal and will do his aunt a small favour. I am very disappointed with you. As a matter of fact, I was planning a little treat for you if you had succeeded. I was going to invite you up to London like a proper grown-up guest, and I would have given you tea in the Victoria Hotel with toasted tea cakes covered in butter and taken you to see a pantomime, and the Victoria and Albert Museum, and shown you the beautiful and valuable things in my home. You'd have liked that. You like nosing into other people's property, don't you? But now you'll never have any of that because you won't do a simple thing for your poor old aunt.' She paused for breath and studied me closely. She could see I was unimpressed.

'Do you know what is going to happen to you if you don't do as I say?' she said, putting her face so close to mine our noses almost touched.

'No,' I said. Then, suddenly feeling that she was engaged in a game of bluff, I added: 'And I don't care.'

'Don't care, eh?' she said, withdrawing her face and studying me intently. 'Don't care was made to care. I want to see that file by Christmas, or else . . .'

'Or else what?'

Aunt Harriet once again put her huge old face very close to mine. I was almost overwhelmed by her musky perfume. In a loud croaking whisper, she said: '"I can show you fear in a handful of dust." Do you know who said that?'

I shook my head.

'A very famous poet called Tom Eliot. I knew him once: rather well, actually. He was very much in love with me at one time. A great many famous men were in love with me in those days, you know.'

I found this impossible to believe then, but years later, when I was going through my late father's things, I found a single photograph of Aunt Harriet as a young woman in the mid 1930s. It was a studio portrait and she was posed, rather artificially, elbow on knee, face cupped in her palm, staring at the camera. She wore a long double rope of pearls knotted in the middle as was the fashion, and a loose rather 'arty' dress. Her dark shiny hair was cut in a page-boy bob which framed a perfectly oval face, like one of Modigliani's women. Below the fringe of hair her big dark eyes had allure. You might well have described her as attractive; you might also have said that the hungry look in her eyes and the sulky, sensual mouth signalled danger.

'"I can show you fear in a spider's web",' she said. 'Do you know who said that?'

Again I shook my head.

'I did. And I can too. So beware, my young friend. Beware!'

With that I was dismissed. I was inclined to regard her threats as empty, or rather, that is what I wanted to believe. In the months running up to Christmas she came, much to our relief, less frequently at weekends, but when she did she always found an opportunity to get me on my own. Then she would ask one question: 'Have you got it yet?' I would shake my head and that would be that, or so I thought. She seemed strangely untroubled by my refusal to co-operate. Then came Christmas.

She always spent several days with us over Christmas, arriving on Christmas Eve and occasionally lingering until New Year's Day. Her presence was not so annoying as it might have been because my parents were hospitable during the season. In the company of people other than family, Aunt Harriet would occasionally make an effort to be pleasant, provided that she felt that the guests were not beneath her notice socially. It was the one time too when my mother would not make any concessions to my aunt's vegetarian diet, simply feeding her with the vegetables that dressed the turkey.

Aunt Harriet came that Christmas Eve, as usual, with great fuss and circumstance. She did not drive, so my father had to fetch her from the station in the car. It was dark when she arrived at our house and a light snow was falling, the little specks of white dancing in the wind. I remember looking out of the window of our house as her vast black bulk squeezed itself out of our car and onto the drive. She seemed to regard the snow as a personal annoyance, and flapped her hand in front of her face to brush away the flakes, as if they were stinging insects. As she lumbered towards the front door my father was busy getting her suitcases and parcels out of the boot.

I knew about these parcels from previous Christmases. They were all very grandly wrapped and decked out with tinsel and fancy ribbons, but they never contained anything anyone really wanted. To my father she gave cigars, which he very rarely smoked; and to my mother, almost invariably, a Poinsettia plant with its piercingly red and green foliage.

I once heard my mother say to my father: 'Doesn't she know I hate Poinsettias? Nasty gaudy plants. They look like cheap Christmas decorations. Ugh!'

'Why don't you tell her?' said my father smiling.

'Good grief, no! Can you imagine the scene she'd make?' And they both laughed.

Louise and I always got books, but they were hardly ever new ones, and never what we actually wanted. Some of them, I now think, were probably quite valuable, but even that was a cheat, as I'll explain later.

My mother, Louise and I were lined up in the hall, as usual, to greet her. When she got to me she murmured: 'have you got it?' I shook my head. She sort of smiled and pinched my cheek in a would-be friendly manner, but she pinched so hard that my face was red and sore for quite some time afterwards. I had a feeling that there was worse to come.

Christmas passed off much as usual. Aunt Harriet refused to come to church, saying that she worshipped God in her own way, whatever that meant, and that anyway the whole business of Christmas was just a debased and commercialised pagan ceremony. When the Turkey was being carved, she insisted on referring to it loudly as 'the bird corpse.' It was no better and no worse than usual. Then, after the dinner, came the present-giving.

My father got his usual cigars and my mother her hated Poinsettia. I forget what Louise received, but I certainly remember my present. It felt heavy inside its red and gold Christmas paper.

When I unwrapped it I found, not much to my surprise, that it was a book. Of its kind it was rather a sumptuous volume, bound in green artificial leather, heavily embossed with gold. It was in astonishingly good condition considering that the date on its title page was 1866. The pages were thick and creamy, their edges gilded. I noted that the book was illustrated throughout: 'drawn,' as the title page announced 'by eminent artists and engraved by the brothers Dalziel.' All this might have attracted me, but for the title of the book itself:

A CHILD'S TREASURY OF INSTRUCTIVE
AND IMPROVING VERSE

I did not like that at all. Now, I was nine at the time, but I already considered myself a young adult, not a child. Louise, at six, was still a child, not me. I read quite grown-up books like Sherlock Holmes, and *Treasure Island*, and *The Lord of the Rings*. Moreover, I did not want to be instructed and improved: I got quite enough of that at school, thank you. I felt the first sting of Aunt Harriet's revenge for my failure to do as she had told me. Then I looked at the fly leaf.

It was not quite as smooth as the other pages. It was slightly buckled and looked as if it had been treated with some kind of bleach. On it Aunt Harriet had written in purple ink: 'to Robert. Happy Christmas from Aunt Harriet.' Then, in smaller writing a little further down the page she had written: 'p256'.

When I thanked Aunt Harriet for her present with a rather obvious lack of enthusiasm, she merely smiled and tried to pinch my cheek again, but I avoided her. 'It's a very precious book,' she said, 'I think you'll find it interesting.'

'Oh, it's beautiful,' said my mother, for once backing up my aunt. 'Those wonderful Dalziel engravings. They were the best, weren't they? And such perfect condition! Where did you find it, Harriet?'

Aunt Harriet gave my mother a dark look, as if she suspected some kind of insinuation in her question. Then, seeing that my mother was, as always, being innocently straightforward, she smiled. 'I have my methods,' she said.

Later that night when I was in bed I began to ponder over Aunt Harriet's present and that cryptic little note, so I got the book and turned to page 256. It was a poem entitled 'The Spider and the Fly' by someone called Mary Howitt.

Will you walk into my parlour?' said the Spider to the Fly,
'Tis the prettiest little parlour that ever you did spy;
The way into my parlour is up a winding stair,
And I've a many curious things to shew when you are there.'
'Oh no, no,' said the little Fly, 'to ask me is in vain,
For who goes up your winding stair can ne'er come down again.'

At the time I wasn't much into poetry and this was really not my thing at all, but the verse had an oddly compelling quality. I somehow had to read on. There was this ridiculous conversation going on between a spider and a fly – as if two insects could talk! – and the spider was enticing the fly into her den and the fly was, so far, refusing. It was so strange, this weird blend of insect and human life, like a dream, that I was held. I turned the page.

It was then that I got a shock. I was confronted with a black and white engraving. It showed a creature standing in front of a cleft in a rock with the winding stair within going up into the darkness. I say 'a creature' because it was half-human half-spider, and it appeared to me to be a 'she', mainly because the head bore a quite shocking resemblance to Aunt Harriet. There was the same longish nose and wide shapeless mouth; above all, the bulging eyes had the same predatory stare. The head was fixed, without a neck, onto a great bloated, bulbous body, again rather like Aunt Harriet's. From the base of this sprang two long, thin legs that sagged at the knee joints as if the great body was too heavy to be held upright. From the body – or thorax, I suppose – came four almost equally thin arms, two from each side. The muscles on the arms were as tight and wiry as whipcord, and what passed for hands at their extremities were more like crabs' pincers and looked as if they could inflict terrible pain.

Standing in front of this monstrous creature, its back to the viewer, was what I assumed was the fly, though it barely resembled one. It looked more like a very tall, thin, young Victorian dandy. Its wings were folded to form a swallow-tailed coat, one thin arm rested on a tasselled cane and a top hat was set at a jaunty angle on top of its small head. It looked a feeble, doomed creature.

The picture and the poem seemed to me all of a piece, at once surreal and yet frighteningly vivid, inhabiting a world of its own, full of savage, predatory monsters and enfeebled victims. I read on until the inevitable ending.

With buzzing wings he hung aloft, then near and nearer drew,
Thinking only of his brilliant eyes, and green and purple hue –

Thinking only of his crested head – poor foolish thing! At last,
Up jumped the cunning Spider, and fiercely held him fast.
She dragged him up her winding stair, into her dismal den,
Within her little parlour – but he ne'er came out again!

There were some moralising lines after that, something about 'to idle, silly flattering words, I pray you ne'er give heed.' But that was just a piece of nonsense put in to give the poem respectability. It was the image that remained, and the torturing fear of being seized and carried up a winding stair into the darkness.

I barely slept that night, and when I did it was worse than being awake. Waking or sleeping there was the sense that something was in one corner of my room. I saw it – if I saw it at all – only on the edge of my vision, and not when I looked at it directly: a bloated thing with a head but no neck, and with several arms or legs that waved at me in a slow way, like a creature at the bottom of the sea. This torment lasted until the frosty dawn when light began to filter through my thin window curtains. At last I managed some untroubled sleep until, hardly two hours later, I was summoned down to breakfast.

On Boxing Day afternoon my parents had a party for neighbours and their children. Aunt Harriet was less than enthusiastic about the affair and went out for a walk immediately after lunch so as not to involve herself in the preparations. On her return, just as a cold sallow sun was setting, the party had begun. She sat among the guests in the sitting room sipping tea and smiling on the proceedings as if she were a specially honoured guests. Occasionally she would condescend to talk to some of our older friends. Various games were organised for the children who came, including Hide and Seek. When this was proposed Aunt Harriet beckoned me over and said:

'I give you permission to hide in my room. They'll never find you there.'

The idea did not appeal to me at all, but it stayed in my head. Those of us who were to hide began to disperse about the house and I remember finding myself in the passage outside my aunt's room. It was a moment when the temptation to enter her room seemed unconquerable as I heard the numbers being counted inexorably down to one in the hallway below. I entered her room.

I did not turn the light on. The room was warm and had that familiar musky smell. In the dim light I felt my way across to a walk-in cupboard which I entered and then shut behind me. I was now in utter darkness and silence. The noise and bustle of the house had vanished and the only sensation to which I was alive was that of touch. As I sat down on the floor of the cupboard, my face was brushed by the soft cool tickle of my Aunt Harriet's fur coat. How did she reconcile the possession of this article with her vegetarianism? That was a question that only occurred to me long years later.

At first I felt a curious exhilaration. I was alone, unseen and quiet. I had myself to myself and no one would break in on my solitude for a long while. I was free of the importunings of my little sister or the more serious demands of my parents. Moreover, the house, heated generously for once by central heating, Christmas candles and company, had become a little stuffy. In here it was exquisitely cool. I allowed my undistracted thoughts to slow to a standstill; I may even have fallen asleep.

Darkness is a strange thing: it is both infinite and confining; it holds you tight in its grasp, but it holds you suspended in a void. Silence operates in a similar way. Slowly the two combine to become a threat. I had no idea how much time had passed before I began to feel that it was time that someone found me, but how could they? I was so well hidden. It was then that I decided to open the cupboard door and let myself out. But it would not open.

My heart's thumping was suddenly the loudest noise in the universe. I was trapped forever in darkness and silence. I banged and kicked at the cupboard door, but to no effect. It seemed to have the strange unyielding hardness of a wall rather than a piece of wood. I shouted as loud as I could, but my voice was curiously close and dead as if I had entered a soundproof studio at midnight.

It was then that I became aware that the space I was in was not entirely dark. Yet, I was confused because, though I knew the cupboard I was in to be about three feet by six feet square, the light that I saw seemed to be coming from a great distance. It was an indeterminate blue-green in colour, a rather drab hue, I thought. I stretched out my hand towards it in the hope of touching the back of the cupboard, but I felt nothing but the faintest brush of cold air, as if someone were blowing on my hand from beyond my reach.

By this time I had no sense of where the front, or the back, or the sides of the cupboard were. All appeared to be beyond my reach, and when I felt upwards I could not even sense the cold softness of my aunt's fur coat. Moreover, the floor began to feel icy and damp. I stood up. Nothing now existed but the distant blue-green light.

The next thing that happened was that the light began to grow. The difficulty was that I could not be sure whether I was moving towards it or it towards me. All I knew was that with each move, the atmosphere became more icy, as if I had been transported out of doors into an Arctic void.

The light began to assume shape, and I started to sense that it was a luminous object that was moving towards me. It came not steadily but in little fits or scuttlings. The thing had six legs or arms and a bulbous body that glowed. The head, smaller but equally round, was darker, though the eyes shone. Their colour was reddish, like amber. It came on and my own body became paralysed with fear, so that I could not retreat from it.

The eyes fixed themselves on me. I tried to raise my hands and found them confined by some fibrous substance, heavy and sticky. In an imitation of my movement the creature stopped and raised two of its forelimbs in the air and began to wave them in front of its face. It appeared to be in the act of communicating with someone or something, but not with me. Then with a sudden leap it was on me and its sinewy, fibrous legs were pawing at my face. I cried out and fell, and when I opened my eyes again I found that I had fallen out of the cupboard into my aunt's room. I was covered in cobwebs.

When I emerged from her room the house was quiet and for a moment I thought it was deserted, but a faint sound from below reassured me. When I came downstairs, I found that my parents, Aunt Harriet and Louise were there, but all our guests had gone. I was chided for having fallen asleep in my hiding place. My Aunt Harriet smiled, but my mother was looking anxiously at me.

'You're shivering,' she said. 'You must be sickening for something. Come along. Off to bed with you.'

I was told later that it was flu of some sort and quite serious, but I remember virtually nothing about the next few days. Fortunately, none of the others in the house caught my influenza and Aunt Harriet went home early to avoid infection. When I had recovered some sort of consciousness and was beginning to convalesce, I asked for some books to read. I noticed that the ones provided did not include *A Child's Treasury of Instructive and Improving Verse*. I asked after it but was told by my mother that she had burned it in the garden. In the delirium of my fever I had talked about it endlessly, and with apparent terror. 'And when I looked in it, I could see why. There were the most beastly illustrations in it. Beautifully done, but beastly.'

'What sort of things?'

'I don't know . . . Hobgoblins and demons, and . . . All sorts of horrid things.'

'But why did you have to burn it?'

'Oh, I had a book like that when I was a girl. It caused no end of trouble,' she said, and that was all she would say.

Some weeks later news reached us that Aunt Harriet had died. She had been crossing a busy road near her flat in Victoria late at night and a car had hit her and she had had some sort of heart seizure from which she never recovered. The details are vague in my mind and I have never sought clarity by looking at her death certificate. It is enough to say that in death she was as much trouble as she was in life. It transpired that shortly before that Christmas when she last came to us she had been dismissed from her job in the library service. There were allegations about missing books which were never fully resolved and my parents had to satisfy the authorities that we did not have any stolen books in our possession, nor had we profited from their illegal sale.

With the exception of a small bequest to an obscure animal charity, Aunt Harriet had left everything she possessed to my father. There came a time when both my parents had to go up for a few days to deal with the sale of my aunt's flat and its contents. I begged to be allowed to come with them and help, but they firmly refused, so Louise and I were left at home in the care of a neighbour. On their return, my parents looked exhausted and somehow haunted. It was only a few months later that my father began to show signs of the illness that later took his life.

Deprived of a sight of it myself I begged my father and mother for details of what they had found in Aunt Harriet's flat, but they were not forthcoming. My father simply would not discuss it, and all my mother said was:

'You wouldn't have liked it. It's a horrible place. There were cobwebs everywhere.'

MARK MORRIS

THE RED DOOR

'Let us pray.'

Although Chloe closed her eyes and clasped her hands together, she barely heard the words that her brother Luke was intoning. She had never had a panic attack, but as she stood among her family and her parents' friends she felt light-headed and jittery; felt her heart-rate increase and sweat break out on her body.

'Amen,' Luke said finally, and although Chloe murmured the word along with everyone else, it seemed like a husk in her throat, hollow and dry and hard to expel.

Her problem – if such a cataclysmic life-shift could be termed so mildly – had started even before her mother had been diagnosed with the liver cancer, which had taken most of the last year to kill her. Although her mother's unbearable suffering had made it even more difficult for Chloe to re-discover the path from which she had strayed, she firmly believed that her London life had been the true catalyst – or, more precisely, the fact that she had finally moved away from home two years ago, thus distancing herself, both geographically and ideologically, from her devout parents.

Not that her mother and father had been fire and brimstone types, intent on indoctrinating Chloe and her siblings with the notion of a vengeful and belligerent God. On the contrary, the God that Chloe had grown up with had been a merciful and loving one; a God that gave comfort and succour. As a small child she had thought of Him as a seventh member of the family – a kindly grandfather figure, whose influence was overwhelmingly benign. He was someone to whom she felt she could pour out her problems, someone who could always be relied upon to make things better.

It distressed her greatly, therefore, that she had recently begun to have doubts, not simply about the nature of God, but about His very existence. Back home in Buckinghamshire for her mother's funeral, she decided to confide in Joanna, her older sister.

On the night following the funeral, the two girls found themselves sleeping in the bedroom which they had shared as children, the bedroom in which they had swapped secrets and gossip, and in which they had done so much of their growing up. Chloe found it nostalgic and yet at the same time, now that their mother was gone, desperately sad to be sleeping in her old bed, with Joanna in *her* old bed, just a few metres away. When the two girls had been small, their mother had tucked them in every night after listening to their prayers. She had kissed them on the forehead and whispered, 'Sleep well, sleep tight, may God protect you through the night.'

The only thing whispering to Chloe now was the harsh wind in the branches of the denuded apple trees in the back garden. She listened to them scraping and rustling as she worked up the courage to speak, and then finally she whispered, 'Jo? Are you awake?'

'Yes,' Jo said immediately, as if she had been expecting the question.

'Can I ask you something?'

'If you like.'

She was only two years older than Chloe, but Jo, who had

always been considered the practical, pragmatic one, often acted as if the gap between them was much wider.

'Have your views changed at all since you left home?' Chloe asked.

'About what?'

'Well . . . about anything? God, for instance.'

'No. Have yours?'

The response was blunt, and threw Chloe for a moment. Finally she admitted, 'I think they have.'

'In what way?'

'I don't know. I suppose I'm not as . . . certain as I used to be.'

'You mean you don't believe any more?'

'It's not that, it's . . . well, I'm not sure.'

Jo paused for less than a second, and then she said almost crossly, 'Well, either you do believe or you don't. Which is it?'

Chloe felt dismay seize her, felt herself shrivelling inside. *I'm not going to cry*, she told herself. But when she again said, 'I don't know,' her voice cracked on the last word, and all at once she was sobbing.

Lying in the dark, she half-expected Jo to move across to her bed, to offer comfort, but the older girl remained so still that Chloe might have believed she was suddenly alone in the room. Eventually Jo asked, 'Have you spoken to Dad about this?'

With an effort Chloe swallowed her tears. 'No. I don't want to worry him. Especially not now, when he's got so much to contend with.'

'Probably wise,' said Jo. Silence settled between them again, albeit one filled with the frenzied scraping of the tree branches outside. Then Jo asked, 'What's made you have doubts?'

Chloe struggled to put it into words. 'It's not one thing. It's an accumulation. I suppose when I was at home I saw evil as . . . I don't know . . . the Devil's work. Something separate from humanity. I knew it existed, I knew people did terrible things to one another, but it was as if it was this separate thing that bubbled up every now and again like . . . like lava from a volcano.'

'And now?' said Jo.

'Now I realise that it isn't like that. Living in the city I suppose it's made me realise that evil isn't always big and grand and uncontrollable. It's petty and vicious and banal. It's there in everybody. Every day, in one way or another, I come up against cruelty or cynicism or selfishness or envy or indifference. I was sitting on the tube the other day, and the day before there'd been delays on the District Line because a girl had thrown herself under a train, and this couple were griping about her, saying what a selfish bitch she was because she'd made them late for the pub.'

'Welcome to the real world,' Jo murmured.

'But why is the world *like* that?' protested Chloe. 'Why, if God exists, has he let things get in such a state? A girl where I work was mugged the other week by two guys outside Ladbroke Grove tube station. People just walked past while one of the guys held a knife to her throat. And I read in the paper that a fifteen-year-old girl at the local school had been beaten up, and that even while she was lying on the pavement unconscious her attackers had carried on punching and kicking and stamping on her while other children laughed and filmed it on their phones.'

She subsided into silence, aware that her voice had become stretched and almost whiny. Jo's response was as cool and considered as ever.

'God gave us free will,' she said. 'How we choose to live in this life will determine our role in the next one.'

'But why?' Chloe asked. 'Why give us free will if so many innocent people suffer for it?'

'We all need to be tested,' said Jo.

'But *why*? That's what I don't understand. If God is all-good and all-powerful, why does he *need* to make us suffer? Why put us through this at all?'

'To test our faith, of course. If we can suffer the hardships of life and still have faith in God, then we will prove ourselves worthy of sitting at His right hand. We have to *earn* our place in the Kingdom of Heaven, Chloe. If we didn't suffer the hardship and misery of our earthly lives we wouldn't appreciate the ultimate glory of life everlasting. We would be complacent, selfish beings, with no concept of good and evil, no perspective.'

'But what about good people who *don't* have faith in God?' Chloe said. 'What about people who don't believe in Him, but who are still kind and generous and loving to their fellow men? Don't *they* deserve their place in the Kingdom of Heaven?'

'Without God, there is no Kingdom of Heaven,' said Jo firmly.

Chloe spent the train journey back to London the next day gazing bleakly out of the window. How easy it would be to abandon her career and return home. She imagined herself withdrawing from the stress and responsibility of city life, of giving up her independence and becoming an unofficial housekeeper to her father. She could grow stout and spinsterish in the bucolic tranquillity of the village where she had grown up. And once there, surrounded by God's love, perhaps she would rediscover her faith, even if only by default.

These thoughts dismayed her, even while they comforted her. Was her faith *really* so fragile that the merest test was enough to rattle it to its foundations? Jo had told Chloe that the *real* test of faith was to remain steadfast in the face of challenge and adversity, but it was easier said than done. Jo was tough, inflexible. Was it Chloe's fault that she was less robust than her sister? Was it a sin to be sensitive, to be lacking in confidence?

As the train drew closer to London, and the surrounding fields and villages were gradually superseded by urban sprawl, Chloe felt her spirits sinking still further. In recent weeks she had become obsessed with the notion that the very fabric of the city had become imbued with the decades of wickedness perpetrated within its confines, that the stones and bricks and timber of its buildings had soaked up every bad deed, every foul thought.

The walls and roofs of houses and factories and apartment blocks flashed by the grimy window, many of them old and crumbling and dirty, their facades stacked and angled haphazardly, as if the buildings they supported had been crammed in wherever there was space. Lost in her thoughts, Chloe barely registered them, and yet all at once something snagged her eye – something so fleeting that it was nothing but an impression, gone before she could focus upon it.

Nevertheless, whatever she had seen was unusual enough to lodge in her mind, as irritating as a sharp morsel of food stuck between her back teeth. As she disembarked at Euston, her mind was probing at it, trying to bring it into the light, but it wasn't until she had sat on the rattling Northern Line tube to Tufnell Park, and had trudged the maze of streets back to the Victorian house containing her third-floor flat, and was fitting her key into the lock of the front door as the daylight faded into smoky dusk, that it suddenly popped into her mind.

It was a door. That was what she had seen. A door in a wall. The door had been painted a deep, shimmering red, though what had been odd about it – what had snagged her attention – was that it had been not at ground level but half-way *up* the wall. And furthermore, it had been *upside-down*.

That, at least, was how she remembered it. That was the image that had lodged in her mind. A bright red, upside-down door, half-way up a wall.

It was ridiculous, of course. That *can't* have been what she'd seen. And even if it was, there must have been some reason for it. It must have been a contrivance, an architectural gimmick, perhaps even part of some obscure advertising campaign. London was full of oddities, of things that didn't make sense. Some people loved that about the city – its quirkiness, its hidden corners, the fact that it was crammed with bizarre sights and bizarre stories.

By the time Nick called, Chloe had put the red door to the back of her mind. She ate some pasta and was washing up her plate, pan and cutlery in her tiny kitchen when her mobile rang. Thinking it might be her dad calling to make sure she'd got home okay, she went through to the main room, drying her hands on a tea towel, and retrieved her burring phone from her jacket pocket. Seeing Nick's name she almost didn't answer. But then she reluctantly pressed the 'Accept' button and said, 'Hi.'

'Chloe?'

'Yeah.'

'Oh, it *is* you. I wasn't sure. You sounded weird.'

'I'm just tired.'

His voice grew soft, concerned. 'Are you okay? How was it?'

'It was fine. As far as these things go.'

There was a silence, as though he expected her to elaborate. When she didn't, he said, 'You're not all right, are you? Do you want me to come over?'

The thought wearied her. 'Not tonight, Nick. I really *am* tired. I'm going to have an early night.'

'Tomorrow then. Let's do something tomorrow. Take your mind off things.'

She knew he was only trying to be kind, but she wanted to snap at him, 'Do you think I can just forget as easily as that? Do you think I'm *that* shallow.' But instead she said, 'Yeah, okay, I'll see you tomorrow.'

'This used to be a power station,' Nick said, the wind whipping at his wispy blond hair and twitching the scarf at his throat. 'It's pretty impressive, don't you think?'

Chloe gazed at the imposing edifice of the Tate Modern, the chimney stack high above her stabbing at the grim sky as if mockingly pointing the way to Heaven. Troubled, she turned her attention to the wide slope leading down to the entrance doors.

'I think it's ugly,' she said.

'Really?' Nick looked half-surprised, half-offended, as if he was personally responsible for the building's design and construction. 'Well, just wait till you see inside. It's amazing. Like a cathedral.'

It had been Nick's idea to come here. He had wanted Chloe to see an installation in what he called, with a sense of ominous grandeur, 'The Tanks'. Since they had met two months ago, after Chloe's friend and work colleague Christine had all but bullied her into trying online dating, he had made it his mission to take her to all the places in London where she hadn't been that he thought were worth visiting. In recent weeks he had introduced her to the South Bank, to Highgate Cemetery, to Camden Market, and to several of his favourite restaurants. Chloe had tried to match his enthusiasm as he unveiled each new treasure, but she had thought the South Bank hideous, Highgate Cemetery depressing, Camden Market gaudily pretentious and most of the restaurants too expensive.

Nick was a nice guy, and had been nothing but supportive throughout the last days of her mother's illness, but Chloe had begun to wonder whether their relationship was really going anywhere. They had little in common – he loved London, she didn't – and she had so much to contend with right now that she couldn't help thinking the timing was all wrong. A year hence things might have been different, but currently Nick was less a pleasant distraction than simply one more thing to worry about.

'Isn't this amazing?' he said as they passed through the entrance doors and entered the vast, echoing space inside. Shivering, she tugged her coat tighter around her. In truth she felt nothing but dwarfed and daunted, and further away from God than ever.

'It's certainly big,' she admitted.

'Come on,' Nick said, taking her hand. 'What I want to show you is this way.'

The Tanks, located on level 0, had originally been a trio of huge underground oil tanks, and were accessed via a series of side doors arranged either side of a wide, dank, low-ceilinged corridor. The sign outside the door that Nick led her to bore the name of a Japanese artist – all spiky, sharp syllables, like jags of broken glass – and a long explanation about dreams and shifting states of consciousness which Chloe's eyes skimmed over without taking in.

The interior was dark, though not pitch black. However the lighting, such as it was, had been angled in such a way that it played with Chloe's perceptions, disorientating her, making her unable to tell where the floor met the walls, and the walls the ceiling. As a result she felt unsteady and uncertain, even a little sick.

'I'm not sure I like this,' she whispered.

'It *does* take a bit of getting used to,' Nick murmured. 'But it's worth it. There's nothing here that can hurt you.'

Ahead of her, Chloe could see shadows blundering about – other visitors tentatively picking their way forward. The room was full of ambient noise – slow, soft booms and the continuous echo of wordless whispers – and undercutting that, as though coming from a nearby but as-yet-unseen room, she could hear the drone of a voice speaking in a foreign language, its tinny quality suggesting that it was a radio or TV broadcast of some kind.

Edging forward, she was distracted by movement to her left, and turning she saw a number of figures, blacker than the darkness around them, standing in silhouette, their arms upraised. They looked to be pleading for their lives, or begging for help, but drifting closer Chloe realised that they were simply visitors like herself, standing on the other side of a thick glass wall which, she had assumed, until she was close enough to touch it, was a continuous dark space. These people had their faces pressed to the glass and were peering through; Chloe could see the glint of their eyes in the gloom. From their blank expressions she guessed that the glass was one-way, that she could see them, but that they couldn't see her. The thought unsettled her, and she shivered and moved away.

It was only now, with a jolt of surprise, that she realised Nick was no longer holding her hand. When had the two of them disengaged? It must have been when she had stepped to her left, but she couldn't for the life of her consciously remember tugging her hand free of his grip. She peered into the gloom, but could not distinguish him from any of the other shadows bobbing ahead of her.

'Nick?' she said softly, but her voice was instantly swallowed up, incorporated into the ambient soundscape. She tried again, raising her voice a little, though oddly reluctant to draw attention to herself. 'Nick?'

None of the shadows responded.

For a moment Chloe considered retracing her steps, waiting for him outside, but then she moved forward. He couldn't be more than a few metres ahead. He was probably waiting for her to catch up. She held her hands out like a blind woman as she tentatively placed one foot in front of the other. Remembering how the glass wall had been invisible until she was standing right next to it, she felt vulnerable, certain she was about to walk into or trip over something.

The shadows ahead seemed to be bearing left, like fish following the course of a stream, and so she moved with them, going with the flow. She realised she must have rounded a corner, for all at once the space in front of her opened up, and she could see the source of the droning voice, which had abruptly become louder. It was a television, icy blue in the gloom. It seemed to be suspended in mid-air, hovering like a ghost. On the screen a bespectacled Japanese man – possibly the artist – was giving what appeared to be a lecture direct to camera. However, as he spoke, white circular scribbles jittered constantly around his eyes and mouth, giving him a monstrous, corpse-like appearance. Chloe knew that the effect had been achieved simply by scratching circles around the man's features on each individual frame of film, yet in this environment the sight was unsettlingly nightmarish. A huddle of dark shapes was clustered around the TV, motionless as mannequins; they seemed to be hanging on the man's every word. Did they really understand what he was saying? Or could they see something in the overall work that she couldn't – something fascinating, even profound?

Feeling isolated, she peered into the shadows beyond the droning man on the screen, and her eyes were instantly tantalised by a shimmer of red in the distance. Drifting away from the throng around the TV, she moved deeper into the darkness. She wondered if what she was seeing was an illusion, whether it was even possible to pick out colour when there was no discernible light source. Certainly at first the redness seemed to shift both in and out of her vision, and in and out of the darkness, causing her to constantly adjust her eyesight. Then as she moved closer it seemed to rise from the gloom around it, to become more solid, and she realised that it was a door.

She halted in astonishment. Not only was it *a* door, but it was *the* door she had glimpsed yesterday from the train – or at least, like that door, it was upside-down, and positioned not at ground level but a metre or so above it. All at once Chloe felt frightened, as if she had stumbled across something very wrong, possibly even dangerous. Instead of backing away, however, she instinctively stepped forward, overwhelmed by a compulsion to touch the door, to check whether it was real. But before she could raise a hand, something hard slammed into her forehead, rocking her backwards and filling her head with sudden, unexpected pain.

Almost abstractedly, as if the shock had jerked her consciousness from her body, she became aware of her legs giving way, of her surroundings dissolving into black static. The only thing that prevented her from passing out was the sensation of surprisingly strong arms curling around her body, holding her upright. A particularly strident burst of static close to her right ear gradually resolved itself into a voice.

'Chloe? Chloe, can you hear me?'

Ten minutes later she was sitting in the café with a handkerchief which Nick had soaked in cold water pressed to her forehead. She could feel a lump forming there, the blood pulsing in thick, soupy waves just above her right eye. There was a clatter of crockery and Nick was back with tea and cake. She looked up to see his concerned face, and then turned her attention to the cup and saucer which he was pushing across the table towards her.

'Here you go,' he said. 'How are you feeling now?'

'Like an idiot,' she admitted.

'How's the head?'

'Throbs a bit, but I'll be fine.'

'Oh God, I feel so responsible,' he said. 'They ought to warn people about those glass walls. They're dangerous.'

Chloe sipped her tea and said nothing.

'Maybe we should complain,' he continued.

Chloe squinted at him. The electric light hurt her eyes. 'Did you see anything through the wall?'

'Like what?'

She took a deep breath. 'A red door.'

'No. But then I was more worried about you.' He looked at her curiously. 'Maybe we ought to get you checked out. You might have concussion or something.'

'I'm fine,' she said firmly. 'I just need a couple of paracetomols and a lie down.' She finished her tea and replaced the cup in the saucer with a clatter. 'Sorry to be a party pooper,' she said, 'but I think I'd like to go home now.'

'Hi, Dad, it's me.'

'Chloe, my darling. How are you?'

'Oh . . . fine. A bit sad.'

'Well, that's understandable. How was your journey back yesterday? I'm sorry I didn't ring. I felt exhausted once everyone had gone. These last few weeks have taken it out of me rather.'

Chloe felt tears prick her eyes. She pictured her stout, bespectacled father, the wispy white hair receding from the pink dome of his head. Trying to keep the waver from her voice, she said, 'Will you be all right in that big house on your own?'

'Oh, I'll be fine,' he said, with a confidence she suspected was entirely for her benefit. 'My parishioners are spoiling me rotten. You should see how many fruit pies and lasagnes and goodness knows what else I've got in the freezer. And of course none of us are ever truly alone, are we? Not with God to see us through.'

At first Chloe was unsure whether she could respond, but finally whispered, 'No.'

Her father's voice was suddenly full of concern. 'Chloe, my love? Are *you* all right?'

She sniffed and swallowed. The tears which had been threatening to come brimmed up and out of her eyes, forming dark coins on the leg of her jeans as she leaned forward. Forcing out the words, she said, 'It's just . . . Mum. I miss her, Dad.'

'I know,' he said softly. 'We all miss her, my love. But isn't it a great comfort to know that her suffering is finally over, and that she's now at one with God?'

'That boyfriend of yours been knocking you about?' said Christine cheerfully.

Chloe blinked at her. 'What?'

Christine gestured at her forehead. 'That lovely bruise on your bonce. Get a bit carried away in the bedroom, did we?'

Chloe hoped she wasn't blushing, though she rather suspected she was. Chris was the best of only a handful of friends Chloe had made since moving to London, but that didn't prevent her fellow copy editor from taking a perverse delight in poking fun at what she regarded as Chloe's naiveté.

'Believe it or not, I bumped it on a glass wall,' Chloe said.

Chris's false eyelashes gave her widening eyes the appearance of Venus fly traps sensing prey. 'I'm intrigued. Tell me more.'

Ironically, for a magazine with a ceaselessly relentless publishing schedule and a strict remit to keep its finger firmly on the rapidly beating pulse of city life, the atmosphere in the *London Listings* editorial office was mostly relaxed and easygoing. Chloe would have preferred to have worked slowly and steadily through the week, but so much of what she did was reliant on the output of her colleagues that she had little choice but to adapt herself to the long-established regime and culture of the workplace. What this effectively meant was that for eighty per cent of the time she was either making or drinking coffee, exchanging gossip and twiddling her thumbs, and for the other twenty per cent she was engaged in a grim, feverish, to-the-wire race to meet her weekly deadlines.

Chloe told Chris about her and Nick's less than successful visit to Tate Modern, though felt oddly reluctant to mention the red door. Already it was adopting the texture of a dream-memory in her mind, of something that, paradoxically, was both vivid and unreal. It disturbed her to think that the door might be a figment of her imagination, though the alternative was more disturbing still. She tried to console herself with the assertion that she had been under stress, that grief could play funny tricks with the mind, and that this was subsequently only a temporary aberration. She had even been trying to convince herself that 'seeing' a door was a sign of hope and optimism, that it was a symbol of new beginnings.

'I take it you still haven't shagged him then?' said Christine.

Chloe grimaced. 'No, and I'm not planning to.'

'You want to watch it, girl,' Christine warned. 'Even the nicest bloke in the world won't stick around for ever if you don't give him a bit of what he needs.'

Chloe looked away, trying to appear casual, though in truth she felt uncomfortable, out of her depth. If Christine ever found out that she was still a virgin, Chloe thought she might shrivel up and die with humiliation.

'I'm not sure if I'm really that into him,' she said. 'I don't think he's the man for me.'

Christine rolled her eyes. 'I'm not saying you should *marry* him, for God's sake. Just have a bit of fun while you can.'

'But I don't think I even fancy him that much,' Chloe said, trying not to sound defensive.

Now Christine looked pained. She shook her head slowly. 'You know what your problem is?'

'I'm sure you're going to tell me.'

'You're too picky. Ten years from now you'll be desperate

to get a man into bed. And you won't be so fussy then, believe me.'

Chloe shrugged, a dismissive gesture to hide the tightening in her stomach, and wandered over to the window. From up here on the third floor she could look down on the bustle of Tottenham Court Road, the continuous flow of people and traffic, and kid herself that she was removed from it all, that for the moment, at least, her world was an oasis of calm amid the chaos.

Directly across from the *London Listings* office was a row of unprepossessing retail outlets – a printer's, an office equipment suppliers, shops selling mobile phones, white goods, music and electronics equipment. Gazing out at the familiar view, Chloe suddenly gasped, as if someone had placed a cold hand on the back of her neck. On an anonymous patch of wall, between a sandwich shop and a display window packed with second-hand TVs, was the red door.

As before, it was upside-down, and was situated not at ground level, but about half-way up the wall. People were walking to and fro past it, partially obscuring it at times, but despite its unusual aspect, no one appeared to be giving it so much as a second glance. Chloe stared at it unblinkingly for several seconds, her heart beating hard. Then she closed her eyes, and kept them closed for a count of five, before opening them again.

The door was still there. Immediately a thrill went through her, though whether it was a thrill of fear or excitement she wasn't sure. She shuddered, her arms bristling with goose bumps, but in her head she was thinking, *It* is *there. It* is *real.*

'Chris,' she said, hoping her voice didn't sound odd.

'Yeah?'

'Come over here a sec.'

'What for?'

'I want to show you something.'

'What?'

'Just come here. It's easier to show you than to explain.'

Behind her she heard Christine sigh in exasperation, but she didn't turn round. Now that she had established that the door was there, Chloe didn't want to take her eyes off it, even for a second. After a moment she was rewarded with the sound of Christine's chair scraping back and her footsteps crossing the wooden floor.

'Okay. So what's so amazing?'

'Look across the road at that wall between the sandwich place and the TV shop and tell me what you see.'

Christine was almost shoulder to shoulder with Chloe now, which brought her into Chloe's peripheral vision. Just as she was tilting her head to look where Chloe had indicated, a high-sided delivery van drove past on the opposite side of the road, temporarily obscuring their view of the red door.

When the van had passed, Christine shrugged. 'I see a wall. What am I *supposed* to see?'

Chloe felt sick. 'No,' she moaned.

'What's the matter?'

'It's gone.'

'What has?'

'What I wanted you to see.'

Christine looked at her in exasperation. 'Well, what was it?'

Chloe shook her head. 'It doesn't matter now.'

Christine's expression became an angry scowl. 'Are you taking the piss?'

Miserably Chloe shook her head. 'No, I'm not. I swear, I'm not.'

'So what *was* it then?'

Chloe took a deep breath. 'A door.'

'A door?'

'Yes. A door in the wall.' She groped for an explanation. 'It must have been an optical illusion.'

Christine's eyes bored into her. She looked as though she wasn't sure whether to respond with pity, anger or contempt. Finally she shook her head and turned away. 'You're fucking weird,' she said.

'Thanks for taking this so well,' said Chloe.

Nick gave her a wry look and rubbed absently at the chipped veneer of the circular table. The pub was so cavernous that it seemed relatively empty, though they still had to raise their voices above the buzz of chatter which echoed off the high ceiling.

'I've never been one for screaming and shouting,' Nick said, 'though that doesn't mean I don't care. To be honest with you, I'm crying inside.'

Chloe wasn't sure how to respond. Was he joking? 'Really?'

'Well, maybe not crying, but . . . I can't pretend I'm not disappointed. I thought we had something. I thought we were getting on pretty well.'

'We *do* get on well,' Chloe said. She was briefly tempted to reach out and take his hand, but in the end she kept them folded in her lap. 'And you're a nice guy, Nick, a *really* nice guy. You're good-looking, funny, interesting, kind . . .'

'Please don't tell me you're about to say "it's not you, it's me"?'

The remark could have been cutting, sarcastic, but he said it gently, with a faint, sad smile. Chloe matched his smile with her own. 'I suppose I am in a way. I'm just . . . not ready for a relationship. I'm cut up about Mum, I'm confused . . . to be honest, I don't know *what* I want right now. I've lived in London for two years, but I don't actually like it that much. I might even go home . . . or does that sound too much like giving up, admitting defeat?'

He shrugged. 'It's entirely up to you. Ultimately, you have to do what *you* think is best.'

'I know.' She sighed. 'But the trouble is, I don't know what that is.'

He smiled, a warmer smile this time, and leaned forward. 'You're a sweet girl, Chloe, and I understand about you not wanting a relationship right now, what with your mum and everything – but that doesn't mean we can't still be friends, does it? We can meet for drinks, days out; perhaps we can go to the cinema or the theatre now and again. What say we jettison the romantic baggage and just be mates?'

She looked at him sceptically. 'And you'd be happy with that?'

'Yeah, why not? I *do* have girls who are just friends, you know. I'm not so desperate that I see every woman as a potential partner.'

He looked sincere. 'I'd like that,' she said. 'But what about the whole online dating thing?'

'I'll try again. If nothing else, it's a way to make friends – and you can never have enough of those. What about you?'

She wrinkled her nose. 'I think I'll give it a miss. Not that this hasn't been nice, but it's not really my thing. My friend Chris kind of bullied me into it in the first place.'

He gestured at her empty wine glass. 'Well, now that we've got that sorted, fancy another?'

She hesitated. 'Why don't we go back to mine for a cup of tea instead? It's on the way to the tube station.'

He raised his eyebrows slightly. 'Well, I don't know. Are you sure you'll be able to contain yourself once we're alone together?'

She laughed. 'It'll be tough, but I have a will of iron.'

It was a cold night, windy enough to propel leaves and litter along the street in loops and spirals. They walked briskly up Tufnell Park Road, turning left by the theatre on the corner. The illumination from the street lamps was splintered by a row of wind-blasted trees lining the edge of the pavement, casting a jittering kaleidoscope of vivid orange light and deep black shadow upon the ground. As they walked up Carleton Road, Chloe leaned in to Nick and surprised him by taking his arm. Ironically, now that there was no longer the pressure to become romantically linked with him, she felt more affectionate towards him, more at ease in his company. They were about half-way between the pub and Chloe's flat when a series of elongated shadows detached themselves from the darkness ahead.

Chloe tensed, unconsciously tugging on Nick's arm, but he said, 'It's all right, come on.'

'Let's cross the road,' she whispered.

'There's no need. We'll be fine.'

His confidence was reassuring, but Chloe still felt nervous. As she and Nick approached the hovering shadows, they began to move, sliding forward out of the darkness with a series of soft, snake-like rustles.

There were four of them, boys in bulky jackets and baggy jeans, hoods pulled up around their faces. One of them spoke, his voice both conversational and threatening.

'What you doin', man?'

Nick's reply was friendly. 'We're just walking home.'

Another voice came out of the darkness: 'Oh yeah? Where you live?'

'Not far from here.'

'Where *exactly*?'

Nick barely missed a beat. 'I'd rather not say if you don't mind.'

'Why not? What you think we gonna do?'

'I don't think you're going to do anything.'

'You got a phone?' said the first boy.

'Yes.'

'Can I borrow it?'

'What for?'

'Wanna make a call.'

'Haven't *you* got a phone?' Nick asked.

The boy made a clicking sound with his teeth. 'All out o' charge, innit?'

'What about your friends?'

The boys moved forward en masse. The one who had first spoken, the tallest of them, suddenly had a knife in his hand. 'Never mind about them. Give me your fucking phone, man,' he said.

'No,' said Nick.

'Fucking give it, or I stab your fucking eyes out.'

Chloe's throat was dry with terror, but she managed to croak, 'Just give it to him, Nick. It's only a phone, for goodness sake.'

Nick glanced at her, as if about to say something. As he did so, like a weaving snake sensing a chance to attack, the tall boy sprang forward.

Chloe screamed as Nick and the boy came together. There was a clash of bodies, a grunt, and then Chloe became aware of a dragging weight on her arm and realised that Nick was sliding slowly and silently to the pavement, his legs folding beneath him. She clutched him for a moment, trying to hold him upright, but eventually had to let him go to prevent herself being dragged down with him. As Nick fell, the tall boy stepped forward and shoved Chloe in the chest hard. She staggered back, certain for a moment that she'd been stabbed and that the shock and the pain would kick in later. As she put a hand to her chest, expecting to feel the wetness of blood, the tall boy crouched over Nick like a hawk over a rabbit, picking at his coat and the pockets of his trousers, pulling out a phone, a wallet, keys. Then the boys were slipping away into the night, not hurrying, crowing over their booty, their victims forgotten.

Chloe scrambled forward, legs like water, heart and head

pounding, lips gummed together with saliva that had dried to glue in her mouth. She reached out, touched Nick's body.

'Nick,' she croaked, 'Nick.'

She touched something wet. She lifted her hand. It was black under the street light.

Nick's parents were Jean and Brian. His sister, who was in the second year of her A levels, was called Liz. They arrived around 4a.m., having driven down from Durham. When they walked into the intensive care unit, Chloe rose from the chair beside Nick's bed and said, 'Hello, I'm Chloe. I'm a friend of Nick's. I was with him when it happened.'

Nick's sister looked down at her brother, white-faced; his mum burst into tears. Only Brian acknowledged her.

'How is he?'

'They think he's going to be fine,' Chloe told them. 'The knife punctured his lung, but he's had an operation, and they've patched him up. As you can see he's breathing on a respirator at the moment, but they . . . they think he's going to be fine.'

Her voice petered out. She was exhausted, emotionally and physically. She swayed on her feet, had to sit down again. Then Jean was stepping forward, grasping her hands.

'Look at you, pet,' she said. 'You're just about done in. Thank God you were with him. You saved his life.'

Her eyes were wet with tears, but she was smiling shakily now, beaming with gratitude. Like Brian, she was portly, her hair chestnut brown and worn in a way that made Chloe think of Shirley Bassey.

'I don't know about that,' she said. 'I just called for an ambulance. Anyone would've.'

'He'd have bled to death without you,' Jean insisted. 'Little life-saver, you are.'

Chloe didn't have the courage to tell her the truth – couldn't bring herself to say that if she hadn't arranged to meet Nick in the pub to tell him their relationship wasn't working out, and if she hadn't refused that final drink, and if she hadn't suggested he walk her home, then her son would never have been stabbed in the first place. Sitting beside Nick's unconscious form, staring at the transparent plastic mask covering his nose and mouth, and listening to the machines that were monitoring his life signs, Chloe couldn't help but think that this was all her fault, that if she hadn't been so selfish this would never have happened.

Suddenly, surrounded by Nick's family, she felt stifled, and pushed herself to her feet.

'I'll leave you to it,' she said. 'I'm sure you'd like to spend some time with Nick on your own.'

Ignoring their protests she stumbled from the room. By the time she had pushed through the swinging double doors and was out in the corridor she was all but hyperventilating. She staggered to a chair with a pale blue vinyl seat and dropped heavily into it. The corridor outside the ICU was quiet, the only sound a faint buzz from the fluorescent strip lights overhead. Chloe slumped forward, closed her eyes, clasped her hands together. She didn't realise she was readying herself to pray until she actually started to speak.

'Lord, if you're there, and if you're listening, please help me. Give me the strength to overcome my doubts and believe in you again. I can't tell you how much the thought of losing my faith terrifies and upsets me. Without it I feel . . . cast adrift. But I can't pretend that I believe if I don't, I can't say I have faith if I don't feel it on the inside. Help me, Lord, please. If this is a test, or even a punishment, then believe me when I tell you that I want to overcome it, that I want my faith in you to be restored more than anything else in the world. But I can't live a lie, Lord. I need your strength, I need you to help set me back on the right path. Perhaps that's selfish of me, or weak, but that's how it is. I'm only human, after all.'

Her voice trailed off. She didn't know what she expected to happen, but she felt just the same inside. Empty, lost. It was like a kind of darkness gnawing at her, devouring the light. Groggily she raised her head, her eyelids peeling apart.

The red door was on the other side of the corridor, directly opposite her, no more than half a dozen metres away.

Something rushed through her then – not faith, but a kind of tingling heat that was part awe, part wonder, and part raw, primal terror. For a split-second she wondered if this was it, the sign she had been praying for, but the notion had barely formed in her head before she was dismissing it.

No. This door was something different. Something wrong. Something unholy. She could sense it. She could feel it in her blood, in her nerve endings, in her very essence.

And yet she felt ensnared by the door too. Tempted. Tantalised. Repelled though she was, she had to know what was on the other side. *Had* to.

Almost unwillingly, she rose to her feet. Took a step forward. The door seemed to throb like a heart, to call to her. As before, it was half-way up the wall, upside-down. And now, up close, she could see that its paint was peeling and scabrous, that its wooden panels were cracked, its brass knob scratched and tarnished.

She took another step. She felt stuffed with heat, her eyes and throat pulsing, her heart like a drum whose vibrations shuddered through her body. Slowly she raised a hand, readying herself to knock.

'Our Nick's awake, if you want to see him.'

The voice was like a slap, snapping her head round. Chloe gasped, blinking and swaying. For a moment her vision swam, and she thought she was about to pass out. Then the blur of colours and shapes tightened into focus, and she was looking at Jean, whose cheeks were flushed, and whose eyes were alive with excitement and curiosity.

Before Chloe could respond, Jean said, 'Sorry, pet, did I startle you? What were you doing?'

'Nothing, I . . .' Chloe stammered, and turned her head back towards the red door. It was gone.

She sighed. She felt partly relieved, partly bereft.

'Nothing,' she repeated.

When she woke it was dark. For ten or fifteen seconds she lay in bed, her mind almost comfortingly blank, trying to remember where she was, what had happened. Was it night-time? The early hours? For some reason that didn't feel right. Massaging her hot forehead with a cool hand, she sat up, groping with her other hand for her phone on the bedside table. She brought it up to her face, peered at the time: 7:13. Time to get up, time to go to work – but that didn't feel right either. It was only when she looked again and realised that it was p.m. and not a.m. that the memories came flooding back.

She had got back from the hospital around twelve hours ago, with barely enough strength left to stagger into her bedroom and collapse into bed, peeling off clothes and leaving them in her wake as she went. The adrenaline crash after the trauma of the previous evening had caused her to sleep solidly and dreamlessly for the past twelve hours. Checking her phone again Chloe saw that she had a couple of missed calls and several texts, mostly from work, wanting to know where the hell she was. There was also a message from Nick, who sounded tired but okay, asking her if she was all right, and a text from Jo which said: HOW ARE YOU? FEELING BETTER AFTER OUR TALK?

Still sitting in the dark, Chloe scrolled through her address book until she came to 'Home'. She selected 'Dial' from the Options menu and snuggled down into bed as the cricket-like burr at the other end of the line broke the silence.

'Hello?' Her father's voice was like honey. Emotionally raw

after waking up, Chloe was shocked to feel tears springing instantly to her eyes.

'Dad, it's me. Can I come home?'

A moment of surprised silence. Then her father said, 'Chloe, my love? Are you all right?'

'Not really,' she said. 'I'm not doing so well at the moment. *Can* I come home?'

'Well . . . of course. At the weekend, do you mean?'

'No, I was thinking now. Well, tomorrow. I thought I'd catch an early train.'

'I see.'

'Is that all right?'

'Well, yes. But what about your work?'

'They'll be fine about it,' she said, not caring whether it was true or not. 'They know about Mum. They said if I needed any time off . . .'

There was another moment's silence, and then her father said. 'Right, well, I shall expect you tomorrow. I'll look forward to it.'

'Me too, Dad. And . . . Dad?'

'Yes.'

'I need to talk to you about something. Something important.'

'Right. Well, I shall look forward to that too.'

Chloe rang off, feeling as though she had taken a step in the right direction, as though she had achieved something. Perhaps it was naïve to think her dad would solve all her problems, but talking to him would help, she felt sure of it. His was the voice of reason and compassion. He would untangle her muddled thoughts and put everything into perspective.

'I'm trying, Lord,' she whispered. She threw back the duvet, crossed the room and switched on the light.

The door was back.

Chloe almost dropped her mug when she saw it. As it was, she jerked back from the window, slopping hot coffee over the back of her hand. 'Ow!' she yelled, gritting her teeth as she ran through to the kitchen to douse the reddening skin in cold water. Once she'd patted her stinging hand dry with a tea towel, she returned to the main room, sidling round the edge of the kitchen doorframe and keeping low, like someone targeted by a sniper. It was ridiculous to think she was being stalked by a door, and yet she couldn't help but feel that she was under scrutiny. She crept along the wall on bended knees until she was underneath the light switch, then reached up and snapped it off. With the flat in darkness, illuminated only by the glow of the street lamp outside, she felt marginally less exposed, though her heart was still thumping hard as she scrambled across to the window and jerked the curtains across, shutting out the night.

She rose, parted the curtains a chink with her finger and peered through the gap. She half-expected the door to have vanished, but it was still there, the peeling red gloss that coated it shimmering in the lamplight. It was on a section of wall that was part of the frontage of a second-hand furniture warehouse directly across the road from her apartment block. It was several metres to the left of the rolling metal shutter that was both wide enough and high enough to admit a sizeable truck, and that served as the warehouse's main entrance. As ever, the door was half-way up the wall and upside-down, and to Chloe it seemed to be flaunting its wrongness.

'You're not there,' she muttered, and then, when that was not enough to dispel the image, 'Go away, go *away*.'

She let the curtain drop back into place, telling herself that if she ignored it, it would disappear, that next time she looked it would be gone.

She turned on the TV, checked her emails, made herself another cup of coffee, flicked through yesterday's *Metro*, even though she'd already read it. Try as she might, however, she couldn't put the door out of her mind; it was like an itch she was desperate to scratch. Her flat was full of clocks – there was one on her kitchen wall, one on her computer, one on her phone, one on her DVD player tucked neatly beneath the TV – and every few moments she found her eyes straying to one or another, whereupon she would catch herself mentally calculating how many minutes had passed since she had last looked out of the window. She moved restlessly from room to room, sitting down for no more than two or three minutes at a time before feeling compelled to jump up and prowl again. Finally she tried to lie on her bed and close her eyes, but her mind was buzzing with anxiety, her stomach churning, and in the end she jumped to her feet, marched into the main room and twitched the curtains aside again.

The door was still there. Chloe gasped, feeling something between despair and fear curl inside her. She wondered whether, ultimately, she would be able to outrun the door, whether it was confined to London, and whether if she left the city and returned home it would somehow be unable to follow her.

She tried to glean comfort from that thought, though couldn't help but be aware that she was only speculating, and that sometimes the only way to overcome a fear was to confront it. Allowing the curtain to drop she made herself a promise: if the door was still there in an hour she would attempt to discover what lay behind it.

For the next hour she forced herself to sit in front of the TV, to stare at the screen, even though her mind was elsewhere and she had no idea what she was watching. For the last ten minutes her eyes kept flicking to the digital clock on the DVD player, and with a minute to go, she shuffled to the edge of the settee, hands braced either side of her. As soon as the green numerals changed, completing the hour, she shoved herself to her feet and rushed across to the window. Jerking aside the curtain she cried out, as though at a sharp stabbing pain, and felt her legs begin to shake.

The door was still there.

'Oh God,' she breathed, unsure whether her words were an oath or an appeal for strength, 'oh God.' As she pulled on a jacket and gloves, the shaking spread from her legs, into her hands and belly.

'Come on, Chloe,' she told herself, 'you can do this.'

She walked out of her flat and down the stairs, gripping the banister as though it was her only connection with reality, as though without it she would drift away and become lost. At the bottom of the stairs she hesitated a moment, then plunged towards the front door. As she twisted the Yale lock and pulled the door open, her heart was pounding so much it hurt.

Please be gone, she thought, *please be gone*.

She stepped outside.

And there was the red door, across the road, waiting for her.

Chloe descended the steps at the front of the house and moved down the path towards the gate. There were several seconds when the red door was hidden from view by the high hedge bordering the front of the property. *When I step through the gate, it will be gone*, she thought.

But it wasn't. She crossed the road towards it as though in a dream. She wanted it to flicker and vanish, wanted something to distract her so that when she looked back she would see only a blank wall. She reached the opposite pavement and the door was metres away. It looked as real and as solid as everything around it.

'One more chance,' she whispered, and closed her eyes. She kept them closed for a count of ten, breathing hard and fast. When she opened them again there was the door, its surface red and peeling like burnt skin.

'Okay,' she said, crossing the pavement in four strides. The door was directly above her now, its lowest point level with her chin. She reached out, forming her hand into a tight fist. When she knocked what would she feel beneath her knuckles? Wood or solid brick? If brick, perhaps it would break the illusion, snap her out of whatever was causing this.

She knocked. Knuckles on wood. The sound echoed away from her, as though carried along some unseen, impossible corridor.

Three, four seconds slipped by. Then she heard something beyond the door. Slow, approaching footsteps. She wanted to turn and run, forced herself to stand still. The footsteps stopped. The door opened.

Light spilled out. Chloe took a step back, screwing up her eyes. Through the door she saw a corridor, almost as narrow as the door itself. A cylinder on a thin pole jutted from a white floor about half-way along; much closer to her, just beyond the door, something large hung from what appeared to be a carpeted ceiling. She couldn't make sense of it at first, and then she realised that what she was seeing was upside-down. The cylinder on the pole was a lamp hanging from a ceiling flex. And the large, dark shape drooping from what appeared to be a carpeted ceiling like an over-sized bat was a figure, its feet planted firmly on a carpeted floor, to which upside-down furniture clung as if glued or nailed into place.

With the light behind it the figure was mostly in silhouette, though Chloe got the impression that it was a woman – small and hunched and wizened.

'Mum?' she said before she was even consciously aware that she had made the connection. 'Mum, is that you?'

The figure remained silent. Chloe could not even hear her – if it *was* a her – breathing.

'What's happening?' Chloe whispered. 'What do you want from me? Why are you upside-down? How can you defy gravity like that?'

The figure leaned forward. It creaked and rustled, as though made of parchment, as though it was nothing but a dried-up husk.

Its voice, too, was papery. 'Gravity is an act of faith,' it whispered.

'What do you . . . ?' Chloe began, and then her eyes widened in horror. 'No!' she cried. '*No!*'

And all at once her feet were leaving the ground, she was kicking at the air, she was falling. As she plummeted helplessly towards the infinite blackness of space, the night sky rushed up to engulf her.

MICHAEL MARSHALL SMITH

AUTHOR OF THE DEATH

FINALLY I DECIDED I'd had enough and I wasn't going to put up with it any more and it was high time something was done the hell about it. My father was a vague character at best but there's one way in which I evidently do take after him. Once he'd decided to do something, apparently, that was it. That thing was going to happen, and it was going to happen *now*. As soon as I realized I was clinically fed up with the situation, compelling verbs were required – and there was only one immediate course of action I could think of. I grabbed my coat and looked for my gun, but I couldn't find it. Sometimes it's here, sometimes it's not, and probably it wasn't such a great idea to take it anyhow. I had a mission, a simple goal. I didn't need a weapon.

I needed focus.

I knew tracking down a writer wasn't going to be an easy task. They're everywhere but yet nowhere, too – a state of affairs I'm sure reminds some of them of one conception of deity. (Is it called 'Pantheism'? I can't remember. I probably shouldn't know anyway). I have only ever been in New York, except for a couple of short chapters in a small town nearby called Westerford. It was never clear to me how I even got to Westerford, however – as I was just cut there and back on chapter breaks – so that idea was a non-starter and to be absolutely honest I suspect he just made the place up anyhow.

Bottom line was that I was stuck with looking for him in the city. If I'd believed he knew the place very well then this would have been a very daunting prospect – NYC is a hell of a big patch of ground even if you stick to the island and don't start on the other boroughs. I had reason to suspect that his knowledge was limited to Manhattan, however, and far from comprehensive even there.

I made a list of locations, the places I knew well, and got out into the streets.

Six hours later my feet hurt and I was getting irritable. I'd looked everywhere. Everywhere I could remember having been, or where scenes with other characters had taken place, or that I'd heard described by other people – finally washing up at the Campbell Apartment in Grand Central Station, a bar surprisingly few people know about. I'd been there once for a meeting about a job that got derailed. The meeting had always felt to me like filler, but I'd liked the venue. Dark, subterranean-feeling, dirty light filtered through a big stained glass window. It looked and felt exactly as described, and so I thought it likely the guy had actually been there, rather of merely having read about it. He wasn't there now, though.

I had a drink anyway and left and started to walk wearily back down 5th Avenue, cigarette in hand. It was mid-afternoon and starting to get colder. I'd had plenty of time to consider whether what I was doing was a good idea (and if it even made any kind of ontological sense), but something I evidently inherited from my mother (much better fleshed out as a character than my father, featuring in two long, bucolic memory sequences and a series of late-climax flash-backs) is that once I've embarked on a project, it does tend to get done.

So I walked, and I walked some more. Instead of cutting over to 3rd and down into the East Village – which is where I live, for better or worse – I went the other way, switching back and forth between 6th, 7th and 8th, down through Chelsea, back over to Union Square, then over and down into Meatpacking, though only briefly, because I didn't seem to know it very well.

No sign of him, anywhere. I didn't know what I was expecting, if I was hoping I'd just run into him on a street corner or something, but it didn't happen.

He evidently didn't know what was going to happen next, how to get me onto the next series of events.

The short paragraphs were a giveaway.

He was treading water.

It was a hiatus.

So I made my own choice.

I was down on the fringes of Soho when I spotted another Starbucks. I'd already been in about ten. He is forever dropping a Starbucks into the run of play – situating events there, revisiting recollections, or having people pick up a take-out to engineer a beat of 'real life' texture. Each was well-described, as though he'd actually been there, and so I'd taken the trouble to seek them out. This one was new to me, however.

The interior was big enough to have three separate seating areas, and looked comfortable and welcoming. It smelled like they always do. There was the harsh cough of steam being pumped through yet another portion of espresso. Quiet chatter. Anodyne music. People reading Letham and Frantzen or Derrida and Barthes.

Weird thing was, it felt familiar.

Not familiar to *me*, but still . . . familiar. I know that sounds strange. I knew that I didn't know the place personally, but it felt like I *could* have done. I decided I might as well have yet another Americano, and was wandering over toward the line when I realised some guy was looking at me.

I turned and looked back at him. He was in an armchair by a table close to the window. Late twenties, with sharply defined and well-described facial features. Something about him said he was no stranger to criminal behaviour, but that's not what struck me most about him.

He looked how I felt. He looked weary.

He looked stuck.

I took a pace in his direction. 'Do I know you?'

'Don't see how.'

'That's what I thought. So why are you staring at me?'

'You look familiar,' he said. 'Like . . . I dunno.'

'Can't be. I've never been in here before.'

'You sure?'

'Yes. I've done stuff in the Starbucks on the corner of 42nd and 6th, the one on 6th between 46th and Times Square, and another at an unspecified street address up near Columbus Circle. Also I've stuck my head in a bunch more today, uptown, and on the way down here, just in case. But I've never been in this particular one. I'm sure.'

He shook his head, sat back in his chair, ready to disengage. 'Sorry to have bothered you.'

I was struck by a crazy thought.

'Who's your writer?'

'Michael Marshall Smith,' he said, diffidently, fully expecting the name not to mean anything to me.

I stared at him. 'No way.'

'What,' he said. He sat forward again in his chair, looking wary. 'You're . . . you're one of his too?'

'Well yes, and no. Actually I'm in a Michael Marshall novel – different name, different genre, but the same guy.'

'Holy shit.' He looked at me, dumbfounded. 'That's outside the *box*. I never met someone else before. I mean, the people in this place, obviously, but not someone from a whole other *story*.'

'Me neither,' I said. I pulled a chair over to the table. 'You mind?'

'Go ahead,' he said, and I sat.

We looked at each other for a full minute. It felt very weird. I've met other characters before, of course – but only ones from my own story, like the guy said. They had their place and were all situated in relation to the star at the centre of their firmament: which would be me.

This guy wasn't like that. He was totally other. I had no idea what he was about.

'How come you're here?' he asked, eventually. 'I mean, suddenly, like this. You've never been in this place before. But now here you are.'

'I got tired of waiting,' I said. 'Bored of being in that scummy apartment in the East Village. He barely even knows the area. Spent half a morning walking around it, like, five years ago. That's all. There's a couple of streets that are pretty convincing and he nailed a few local shops – including a deli and a liquor store, thank God – but after that it's basically atmosphere and a few well-chosen adjectives.'

'How long do you have?'

'About a hundred and fifteen thousand words.'

He stared at me. 'You're in a *novel*?'

'I'm the protagonist, dude.'

'Shit.'

I shrugged. He sat back in his chair, caught between envy and resentment. 'Jesus, then you don't know you're born. I'm only in a short story, and even by the standards of the form, it's pretty fucking brief. Three thousand words. Whole thing takes place right here in this Starbucks. I don't even get to go *out the door*. I don't know shit about the city. I can *see* it, through that the window, but that's all I get.'

'Hell,' I said. 'That's tough.'

'Tough is right. And look at what I'm wearing.'

I'd already noticed his clothes were nondescript. Jeans. A shirt in some indeterminate colour. Shoes that I couldn't even see. 'Pretty vague.'

'Exactly,' he said. 'I don't have a coat because I don't do anything but be in here and so he didn't bother to describe one, not even a thin jacket hanging over the back of my chair, for Christ's sake.'

'That's understandable,' I said. 'He can't be bogging down with extraneous details, not at your kind of word length. Plus if he did mention a coat, people might assume it was going to become relevant at some point and get pissed off when it wasn't. Any good editor would pick him up on it, blue line it out.'

'Yeah, maybe so. But it gets *cold* in here, come the middle of the night.'

I thought about that, and about the idea of being trapped in one location forever, pinned to one small location for eternity. It made me feel cold too.

'I'm going to find the guy,' I said. 'Tell him I'm grateful for being – though some pretty harsh things happen to me, especially in back story – but I'd like some broader horizons now.'

'*Find* him? How the hell do you hope to do that?'

I shrugged. Again. I shrug a lot. 'By searching the city – the parts of it he knows, at least. That's what I'm doing now. It's how I ran into you. Which is something that's never happened to me before, and that makes me think that I'm achieving *something*, at least.'

'But what are the odds of banging into him?'

'Not good. I know that. But weren't there any co-incidences in your story?'

'Like what?'

'I don't know. Things that were kind of convenient, that helped drive the plot forward without too much hard work?'

He thought about it. 'Not really.'

'There were in mine. Small things, he didn't take the piss with it, but –'

'"Take the piss"? What's that supposed to mean?'

'See, that's interesting. We don't say that here, do we? It's a British expression, I think. I'm supposed to be American born and bred, yet once in a while I'll say something that's a little bit off.'

'Maybe the guy *is* British, but sets his stuff here in the US. Blame the copyeditor for not picking up on it.'

'Could be. But my point is that while he didn't fall back on any whopper co-incidences, he was happy to ease the way every now and then with a combination of circumstances that was a little convenient.'

'I guess in a novel you have to, maybe. My thing, it happens in real time, so he didn't need to resort to that kind of kludge.'

'Right. But given that I'm driving *this* story, I'm hoping that my rules apply. And so it's possible, if I keep walking, there's a small co-incidence out there waiting to happen. Like meeting you.'

I waited for him to think about this. It was strange, but also exciting, to be dealing with someone new, *completely* new, who wasn't subservient to my protagonist status. It felt as though doors might be opening. I didn't know where they'd lead, but I was starting to think I could find them. If I *believed* enough. Maybe I could make it back to Westerford after all, that leafy town upstate where I'd been for those brief chapters. I could start a new life, do new things. Perhaps I could even get to the beach down in Florida featured in a small flashback. That would be great, but actually *anywhere* would do. Somewhere new. A place I could stretch my wings and find some other way to be.

The guy was frowning at me. 'Are you okay?'

'What do you mean?'

'You stopped talking. Just sat there looking intense.'

'Sorry. I had a stretch of interior monologue. Slightly lyrical. Takes a while to get through.'

'I guess you first-person guys get a lot of that. Me, I'm in third. I just *do* stuff, pretty much.'

'So let's *do* stuff,' I said. 'Let's get out of this generic coffee house and go looking for him.'

'I can't.'

'Why?'

He looked sheepish. 'I don't think I can leave here. I've never been through that door. My whole life, I've been in here. I think that's it for me.'

'Have you ever tried? Gone up to the door and pulled on the handle and seen what happens?'

He looked down at his feet. 'Well, no. I'm just supposed to do what I do, right?'

'Not necessarily,' I said. 'I've spent longer with the guy than you, remember. I think he kind of likes it when one of us does something off our own bat. There was a minor character in my book, he dies in the end, but he sometimes got the chance to go do his own thing, and the writer would work around it. Maybe you're the same way.'

'I don't want to die in the end.'

'No, of course. Not saying that's going to happen. Just . . . if you're like me, if you're the narrator, the audience *knows* you're going to live – unless the guy's prepared to do something tricksy or flip into unreliable narrator at the end. So there's a set arc for me, and I kind of have to stick to it, because I manifest the story and vice versa and he can't screw with that. But with the more minor characters – no offense – he can let them roam free a little more, see where they end up.'

''Unreliable narrator'? What the hell is that?'

'It's a literary term. Not sure how I know it, given that I used to be a cop, but . . .'

The guy looked nervous. 'You're a *cop*?'

'No. *Ex*-cop. That way he could short-hand me as a tough guy with certain skill sets and a troubled past, without having to do much actual research, or getting stuck with writing a police procedural.'

'That's a relief. My character's not a very nice guy, I don't think. There's a pervading sense of guilt throughout, though it's never clear what for.'

'Doesn't matter. I'm not going to arrest you, even if I still could. Come on. Let's go.'

I stood, and waited for him to follow suit.

'I just don't think I can, dude,' he muttered, looking wretched. 'I look out that window and all I see is two-dimensional.'

We turned and looked together. The light outside was beginning to fade. 'Barely even that,' he said. 'It's just two sentences, to me. "It was cold and grey and flat outside". And "A couple of leaves zigzagged slowly down from the tree along the sidewalk, falling brown and gold and dead". That's it.'

'Look,' I said, pointing. Two leaves were doing just what he'd said, and it *did* look cold out there, and the light was grey and flat.

'Every day,' he said. 'Every day they do that.'

'So evidently what happens out there *is* your domain, at least to a degree. You could –'

He shook his head. 'I can't do it. I'm sorry.'

I felt bad for him, and realized how lucky I was. 'I'll come back,' I said. 'I have to keep looking, but I will come back.'

'Really?'

'Sure. I know where you live, right? And you're in this new story now, too. That's something, at least. You branched out. You're recurring.'

'Yeah, I guess. Though I'm still stuck in the same place.'

'I'll come back tomorrow.'

'Okay,' he said, shyly. 'That . . . that would be cool.'

We shook hands. 'The name's John.'

'Oh,' he said. 'So's mine.'

I laughed. 'Guess we were never supposed to wind up on the same pages. Never mind. We'll cope. I'm going to find the guy, and when I do, we'll talk.'

'Good luck,' he smiled.

I felt jealous. I'd never been allowed to do that. I have to *say* things, or *ask* them. Shout them, once in a while. I can't 'smile' them. There's tougher editing on the novels than with the short stories, I guess, or a more restrictive house style. Though . . . right now I was *in* a short, wasn't I?

'Thanks,' I smiled, and took off my coat. 'Here.'

'Don't you need it?'

'I've got an apartment. There are closets. I've never looked inside, but there must be something. Worst case I can put on a sweater or another shirt.'

'Thanks, man.'

When I got to the door I heard him wish me luck again. I turned back and winked.

'Thanks. And keep the faith, my friend.'

When I stepped outside onto the sidewalk, however, everything changed. I knew right away that a decision had been made. It's happened to me before. I stroll aimlessly through a chapter, with lots of thinking and not much doing, and then suddenly there's a blank line break and the next event arrives.

I noticed a man on the other side of the street. He was wandering along, slowly, aimlessly, smoking a cigarette. He glanced across at the Starbucks I'd just left and I could see him wondering if he could face yet another coffee. There wasn't so much traffic, but what there was, was moving fast enough that he'd have to go back to the corner to cross. It was enough to make him decide it wasn't worth it.

I'd never seen the man before, but I knew who he was. I knew I'd found him.

I thought it again, for emphasis.

I knew.

He looked a little like me and also a little like the guy I'd just left in the Starbucks, the other John. A bit shorter, and a little older, with a touch of grey in the temples. Less distinctive overall. He looked tired, too. Jet-lagged, was my guess. Come over from London for a meeting with his publisher and some research, doggedly using his first day in the city to walk the streets. Not for him, I knew, the hours of reading or scanning the Internet or using Google Streetview. He liked to do his research with his feet, wanted to get to know the city through the miles he moved through it.

Suddenly I realized what this could mean.

The writer *could* merely be reminding himself of these streets for the sake of it, because that's what he always did and it was better than lurking in his hotel room. Or it could merely wind up as background in another short story.

But . . . it *could* also be that there was a sequel in the works. A sequel to my book.

He could be *considering* doing it, at least. He didn't normally. He usually came up with a new bunch of characters for each book, which was why we ended up in such fixed and limited worlds, without a future. But maybe he was clueing in to the fact that many readers don't *want* to sit through the wheel being reinvented each time, but would prefer to settle back into a recurring set of characters like a comfortable old chair.

The more I thought about it, the more plausible it seemed. I'd always felt that there were elements in my story that hadn't been tied up as satisfyingly as they could have. I'd been left on a cautiously upbeat note, but there was a lot more to be said.

Maybe he was going to do it.

Maybe there was going to be more.

I felt myself smiling. Meanwhile the writer ground to a halt, looking up and down the street. I saw his eyes lighting on this and that – store fronts, fire escapes, passers-by – absorbing everything without noticing, passing it down to the part of his mind that stored these snippets of local color for later use.

I turned away, not wanting him to see my face. When I'd left the apartment that morning, a meeting had been exactly what I wanted. Now I didn't. I didn't want to run the risk of derailing him. I wanted whatever was going through his head to run its course, just in case there was a chance that I was right.

I heard a noise behind me.

I turned to see the guy from the Starbucks, the other John. He was standing in the doorway of the coffee shop, and the sound he'd made was a grunt of disbelief.

He'd done it. He'd tried the door, and opened it.

He stepped cautiously out onto the sidewalk. 'Holy crap, John,' he said, seeing me. 'Look!'

'You *did* it, man.'

The joy I felt was partly for him, but mainly for myself. He'd come out because of me, after all. I'd met him and I'd *changed* things. If that much was possible, then maybe everything else was too. Perhaps the writer was considering a sequel precisely because I'd started to prove myself capable of independent movement, worthy of further development.

Maybe I was even going to be a series.

The other John was staring around in wonder. He took a couple of steps up the sidewalk. He turned and looked back the other way. Another pair of leaves came zigzagging gently down from the tree, falling brown and golden.

He reached out and grabbed one, crumpling it in his hands. 'I did that,' he shouted. 'I *did* that!'

'Way to go,' I said.

He waved his hands in the air triumphantly, still shouting. He was making a lot of noise now. Enough that it reached across the street, evidently . . .

. . . because at that moment, the writer looked up.

He saw John, of course. John was the guy making all the noise, dancing around on the sidewalk, brandishing a crushed leaf in his hand.

The writer frowned, cigarette halfway to his mouth, as though something about John struck him, but he wasn't sure what. It could be that he was merely wondering if he could use the guy in something, not realizing that he already had.

But then his eyes skated past John, and landed on me. And he froze.

He knew who I was.

He was bound to, I guess. I'd recognized *him* immediately, after all, and he'd spent nearly a year with me inside his head, every day, every working hour. Could be that he'd already been thinking about me, too, moments before, if he genuinely was considering pulling me out of the backlist for another turn in the light, as I hoped.

He kept on looking at me. He blinked.

'Hey,' I said. 'You're Michael, right?'

He started to back away up the street.

I was confused – this was the last thing I'd expected – but then I realized. He was scared. I'd assumed he'd understand how things work, but maybe not. I guess these guys just put down the words and chase their deadlines, not realizing what comes to life between the sentences that come out of their heads in torrents or fits and starts.

He thought he was losing his mind.

'No, it's okay,' I said, hurrying up my side of the street,

trying to catch up with him. There were too many people and so I darted across the road instead.

'Go away,' he said, between clenched teeth, hurrying backwards as I got closer. His eyes were wide. 'Go *away*.'

'It's *okay*,' I said, trying to sound soothing. 'I got no problem with you. Not any more. I . . . I think I know why you're here. And that's cool. It's *great*, in fact. I don't want to freak you out. I just wanted to say "hi", and, you know, wish you good luck.'

'You are *not* real,' he hissed, and kept backing away – but he realized he was right up against a crossroads, and had to stop. 'I am *very* tired, that's all.'

'Absolutely,' I said. 'That's all it is. And I just happen to look a little like a guy you wrote. Look, we'll go our separate ways. It's the way it should be. But let's at least shake hands, okay? No hard feelings. And, you know, obviously I love your work.'

I raised my right hand. His eyes got wider still.

I realized my hand felt cold and heavy, and when I glanced down at it I remembered that actually, I *had* found my gun before I left the apartment. It seemed like he was prepared to go down the unreliable narrator route after all. I tried to throw it away, to prove I was harmless, but it wouldn't leave my hand.

'Michael,' I said, trying to sound reassuring. 'It's okay. You know me – I'm not a killer. I'm basically a good person. More sinned against than sinning, like all your protagonists. Just ignore the gun, okay?'

But he'd started to back away again, so scared now that he'd forgotten where he was standing, and he stepped back into the road and lost his balance and a cab came around the corner and smacked straight into him.

I haven't been back to the Starbucks in Soho. I said I would, and I will, but I haven't yet. I don't know what to say to John. I don't know how to explain what happened. I don't want to have to describe how it felt to look down at the writer's head on the street, with all the blood leaking out of it, or to watch his eyes as they went from clear to glassy to frosted. I don't want to admit to the fact that I was the author of that event.

I also don't want to see John yet because afterwards I tracked down one of the writer's story collections. I found it in the discount section in a Borders. Borders may be history in the real world – more's the pity – but my novel was set back in 2006, so for me they're still around. I found the short story John's in, and I read it. It's pretty good, but it's kind of spooky and heads toward a dark, bad conclusion. I don't want to have to explain to John that he dies in the end after all, or why that may be better than being me.

Because . . . I do not.

I do not die. I walk these streets and these pages forever, and there will never be a sequel now.

I should have just stuck to my arc, to my own story, been satisfied with what I had. Now I'm trapped in this dead end.

Down at the bottom of this chunk of words.

It doesn't even end properly. It fades to white.

It just stops.

STEPHEN VOLK

THE MAGICIAN KELSO DENNETT

ALL TRICKS, ALL illusions, funnel down to a few basic misdirections, at the end of the day. The majority of it is the patter, the *spiel*, the storytelling. The gift of the gab. Taking someone on a journey, but a journey that goes somewhere they don't expect, in a way they didn't expect it.

I was born in Seagate and I've lived here all my life. It's strange that people flock here for holidays, or used to, and used to have smiles on their faces and happiness in their hearts at the thought of going somewhere different. To me Seagate was never different, never fun-loving or exotic in any way, never a place to get away from it all and have a good time. It was simply my home. I suppose at times I've envied the little families I saw inside the ice-cream parlour on the sea front, or sitting with their fish and chips in newspaper on the benches facing the sea. But to be honest, most of the time I thought they were stupid for thinking this place was in any way special just because there were sticks of rock with its name going down the middle. It certainly wasn't special to me. It was a dump.

The fun fair I remember being seedy ever since my childhood is derelict now, segregated by a massive chain-link fence and guard dogs, its name – *Wonderland* – nothing but a sick joke. The only people who have 'fun' there are the pill-heads and drug dealers whose scooters whine around the Esplanade from mini-roundabout to mini-roundabout touting their wares. Up on Cliffe Road, a whole run of grand Victorian-era hotels lie abandoned, semi-restored by property developers who inevitably ran out of cash.

Sometimes you see a light on inside one at night time and wonder if it's a solitary owner living under a bare light bulb eating beans on toast, or a bunch of junkie squatters shoving needles in their veins. This is the image of the resort now, not candy floss and deck chairs, but inflatable li-los flapping in a bitter wind outside beach-side shops that get more money from selling lottery tickets.

When they announced a big, new, posh art gallery was going to be built at the old fish market near the harbour, a lot of London people argued it would bring much-needed prosperity to the town. Predictably, the locals didn't want it. In fact they gathered hundreds of signatures on a petition about the loss of a car park where old ladies came in coaches to buy cups of tea and go home again. But that was typical. Seagaters have no interest in the outside world. They just want to keep all the things that made a crappy 1950s seaside resort crappy, even though it's dying on its feet.

Anyway, the art gallery happened, with a bistro-style café offering Mediterranean stuffed peppers and risottos of the day. Meanwhile the most artistic thing you were likely to see two streets away on the High Street was a wino coughing his guts up outside an amusement arcade or pound shop.

Sorry for not having a rose-tinted view of the great British seaside town, but I'm not the Tourist Information Centre. I live here. And I've spent all my life listening to people telling me I'm lucky – I'm not.

I guess when I heard that Kelso Dennett was coming, I thought that might change.

And it did.

I work in a hotel, though don't have any professional qualifications. When my grandmother died, my dad had enough money to give up teaching, which he hated, and invest in a hotel, the White Hill – two AA stars, fuck knows how – on one of the narrow streets off Quayne Square leading steeply down to the sea. That's where I was born and that's my day job, setting the tables for breakfast and dinner. Serving hard, crusty rolls with watery, microwaved soup so hot it gives you mouth blisters. My father's made a profession of being pleased with himself. What he has to be smug about I have no idea.

What is he? The owner of a shitty hotel in a shitty little town, and there he is, sounding the gong to call people down for dinner like it's the Ritz? What a loser. Still, he's happy running his little empire, and I've seen that gleam in his eye when he tells people he's fully booked. It's power, that's all that is. It's pathetic, but in the present economic meltdown, in this armpit of the universe, there's precious little to give you any feeling of power over anything.

The power to change. To make things better. It's always seemed almost impossible. Yet there was one person in the world who was regularly telling us that *anything* was possible. That 'the impossible' was just a mindset to be overcome.

And suddenly, according to *The Advertiser*, he was coming to Seagate – to perform his most outrageous stunt ever.

Everyone knew that Kelso Dennett was a Seagate boy. Or, more accurately, from The Links – which, I remember from my childhood was the 'rough part' of town, which was synonymous with the poor part. You didn't want to mix with boys from the Links, my mum used to say. They were always kids who used to smoke in the street, and that said it all. To her mind, anyway.

It was also well known that the TV star's return to his home town was being touted as something of a gesture of thanks to the residents. Though the fact he said he was looking forward to it either meant he had lived in blissful ignorance of how much the place had gone tits-up (to put it mildly), or that the sentiment was complete PR bullshit to get the locals on side. After all, he had a reputation as a master manipulator. He was hardly going to rubbish the place. He was too much of a canny operator for that. He wouldn't have done it in Seagate if there wasn't something in it for him. As everyone who watched his television shows knew, there was always more than meets the eye. That was the attraction. That, and the prospect of real physical or mental harm.

Within days of the official announcement, the production company took out ads looking for runners. No prior experience necessary, but good local knowledge a bonus. I reckoned I was in with a chance, and my dad could find a temporary replacement or get stuffed, so I applied and got an interview. The form I had to fill in was about thirty pages long.

'Nick Ambler.' My name.

'28.' My age.

'Single.' My status.

The girl with the razor-sharp marmalade fringe asked if I had a relationship.

'Sort of. A girlfriend. But only sort of.' She asked her name and I said Cyd, spelt that way. 'After Cyd Charisse. The dancer? *Singing in the Rain* and shit?'

She nodded in a vacant, prosperous kind of way and seesawed her expensive roll-point pen as she asked the all-important question about local knowledge.

'I have that.' I shrugged. 'I've lived here all my life.'

'Then you're perfect.' She brightened, nodding again. 'Nice town.'

I thought, 'You haven't lived here.'

She showed a lot of teeth but was pleasant enough, though the guy next to her, black guy – I mean *really* black, like ink – didn't say a word. But they must've liked me, because later, in The Bear, I got a text saying I'd got it.

The teaser ads were already going out between programmes, so it was no secret this was going to be a *Kelso Dennett Special*, as they called them now. This one, leaving very little to the imagination, and full of succinct, if dubious, promise, was called *Buried Alive*. (No prizes for guessing its central premise.)

The magician was planning to be buried in a wooden coffin six feet under on the beach at Seagate – his most daring stunt to date – with no means of escape or communication, and no access to food or drink for the entire period. He would be sealed in the casket and that would be it, until they dug him up forty days and forty nights later.

As soon as they'd heard about it, certain corners of the media were, predictably, incendiary with outrage. It was shocking, yes. Audacious, yes. Mad, yes. But, frankly, you'd hardly expect anything less. Pushing boundaries – not only physical boundaries, but boundaries of what was acceptable as popular entertainment – was his stock-in-trade. 'Going too far' had rapidly become his business model.

Previous 'specials', which had involved apparent decapitation, invisibility, and even a poltergeist haunting, always caused controversy. It was almost part of the Kelso Dennett 'brand' – but now there was a new element, the element not just of jeopardy, or of harm, but of death.

From the moment it was announced there was a great deal of conjecture as to whether what he was attempting to do, and survive, was even medically possible. Was consummate showman Kelso Dennett really simply tarting up weary old illusions in new clothes (always the accusation), or genuinely (as he claimed in this case) forcing his physiological and psychological endurance to the absolute limit? It was, of course, impossible to tell.

Certainly, as a TV-viewer, it was always hard to know exactly what methods he was using to achieve his mindboggling effects. You definitely couldn't trust what he *said* he was doing. His sometimes wild, irrelevant gestures or pseudoscientific preambles may be just that – irrelevant. And just because he said he wasn't using stooges, did that really mean he wasn't? His previous compulsive extravaganzas had relied on not just trickery but the use of techniques such as hypnosis and suggestibility – or did they? The paranormal waffle might just be window dressing for a gag no more complex than Chase the Lady or Tommy Cooper's bottle/glass routine.

Was the poor guy who thought he'd been in a time machine, or the couple who were convinced a serial killer was hunting them down, actually in on the joke all along? You always sensed that your eyes, and ears, were on the wrong thing – which was exactly where Kelso Dennett wanted them.

My job was to keep an eye on the assembled crowds standing at the rail on the Promenade – to keep them at bay. 'At bay' is probably too strong a phrase. But I had a Hi-Viz vest and a walkie-talkie which kept me in direct contact with the Third Assistant Director in case some of the locals wanted to get a closer look at the set before the team wanted them to. I watched them setting up a white tent on the beach above the high-tide mark. The crew were busy in their various capacities, but I had little idea what most of them did. There seemed to be a lot of quilted windbreakers, a lot of pointing, a lot of coffee in polystyrene cups, and a lot of talk.

The production company, for their own convenience, were putting me up in the hotel where they were based. I told my dad my shifts would be weird so wouldn't be back to lay breakfast or wait at tables for dinner, and I squared it with Cyd I might not be around much too. In view of what happened, that was just as well, on my part. You might even think it was forward planning. It wasn't. I wasn't planning anything. All I was planning was earning some money.

I watched them digging the grave with a JCB. It wasn't like digging into soil, and the sand was dry, but eventually they managed to get a fairly good, rectangular hole without the walls crumbling or it filling with water. For some reason the police were in attendance, and so were the fire brigade. Possibly to do with Health and Safety. Probably to do with just seeing themselves on TV. We were going live at 10pm and everything was stressed to the hilt.

On the far side of the beach I saw somebody talking to the man who did the donkey rides. Whether they were asking him to get into shot or get out of shot I couldn't tell. In the end he just stood there.

The crane shot went up beside me so that the crowd, which had now increased to several hundreds if not thousands on the Promenade and down the length of the pier, could see a high angle view of themselves on the big screens erected on the beach.

A second camera panned along the route of a hearse down the High Street. Security men parted the throng to allow it to drive down a slipway to a flat bed of concrete normally kept clear for use by the lifeboat crew and ambulances. Five undertakers got out and I was surprised to see that they weren't actors but the family firm that had operated in town for as long as I could remember – adding a macabre dimension of authenticity. Four acted as pallbearers, sliding a pale teak coffin from the back, hoisting it to their shoulders and following the fifth with complete solemnity towards the grave.

The dignity of the enactment seemed to make people forget they were watching an entertainment programme, and the strangely reverential silence that fell continued as the undertakers lowered the coffin onto a rustling purple tarpaulin laid flat beside the grave, then stood aside with their heads bowed. The sense of anticipation was electric.

Similarly followed by street cameras, a black Mercedes with tinted windows glided through town and descended the slipway. A chauffeur opened the back door and Kelso Dennett stepped out – fashionably mixed-race, distinctive shaved head. Small. Tiny. I hadn't seen him in the flesh before, but it was weird. I've heard people famous from TV have a presence when you meet them in real life, a kind of vivid familiarity because we feel we know them, we're intimate with them, I don't know, or maybe it was the make-up or the lighting – but he seemed to *glow*. His skin seemed literally *golden* against the black zippered tracksuit one of the tabloids later said gave the proceedings a 'dark Olympics' vibe. Anyway, the crowd went mental. If I didn't have a job to do, I think I might've gone mental too.

Calmly taking a microphone from a production assistant, he thanked everyone for coming and said in a high, surprisingly boyish voice he'd do his utmost to reward them for their faith and their patience. He faltered a little, very slightly giving away his nerves (unless that was part of the act), finishing by saying he got 'succour and strength from their love and their prayers.' He almost made it sound like a prayer itself.

Then, according to the voice-over, he was off into the graveside Winnebago 'to mentally prepare for the greatest challenge of his magical career.'

While he did, and while forensic experts from the Navy and RAF examined the coffin inside and out, a pre-prepared VT about the Victorian fear of premature burial played to the gathered fans, with an obligatory nod to Edgar Allan Poe. It quoted from a hundred-year-old article in the *British Medical Journal* about human hibernation, in which it was said Russian peasants in the Pskov Governance survived famine 'since time immemorial' by sleeping for half the year in a condition they called *lotska*, while James Braid (father of hypnotherapy) wrote in his 1850 book *Observations of Trance* that he had seen, in the presence of the English Governor Sir Claude Wade, an Indian fakir buried alive for several months before being exhumed in full health and consciousness. More recent findings came from a 1998 paper in *Physiology* which described a yogi going into a state of 'deep bodily rest and lowered metabolism' with 'no ill effects of tachycardia or hyperpnea' for ten hours. Another study, on a sixty-year-old adept named Satyamurti, recorded that he emerged from confinement in a sealed underground pit after eight days in a state of 'Samadhi' or deep meditation, during which time electrocardiogram results showed his heart rate fell below the 'measurably sensitivity of the recording instruments.'

Kelso Dennett, in ten-foot-high close-up, then gave chapter and verse on the techniques perfected by such mystics and gurus to cut down their bodily activity to the frighteningly bare minimum. The essence of hatha yoga, he said, is the maximization of physical health as the necessary basis for self-realisation – the purification and strengthening of the body as the means to effectively channel powerful but subtle forces (*prana*) – in this case, to slow the processes down to an extremely low rate, and so achieve a state of physiological suspension. 'But this terminology and classification is multi-layered and elusive – not easily open to standard observation and measurement. The concepts are far from being embraced into mainstream biology and science. Some might say that makes them *primitive* or *superstitious*, but turning it the other way round, maybe science has got a lot to learn.' A tiny light reflected in his dark irises. 'My hope is to replicate these physical states – to hover on the very brink between life and death – and test them to the ultimate limit of what is humanly possible. I have prepared for this event, not just for months, but for years. Perhaps even my whole life. Now I believe I am ready to successfully attempt it. But do the experts?'

As we were about to be told, clearly not.

The medical professionals interviewed were unanimous that the enterprise was foolhardy to the point of insane recklessness. As if to confirm this, we saw footage of Kelso Dennett training for long periods in a sensory deprivation tank – but only for as long as *eleven* days, after which he sounded the alarm and was lifted out, gasping, dripping, shielding his eyes from the camera light. This time there would be no alarm button. No microphone. Nothing. For *forty* days.

The coffin having been pronounced tamper-free, a disembodied voice asked the crowd to remain absolutely quiet when the star emerged from the trailer so as not to disturb his intense level of concentration. The murmuring drained to a complete hush. He emerged barefoot and stripped to the waist, distinctive sleeve of tattoos up his left arm, pentagram on his right shoulder, astrological symbols inked all over his back, pure muscle, but wiry, a runner's physique, wearing only a pair of black lycra shorts.

A woman wearing a fur coat, tight jeans, thigh-length boots and shades threw her arms round him, and he kissed her. I saw she didn't want to let go of his hand. It looked as though she genuinely didn't want him to go through with it. She seemed upset but trying to control it. He hugged her and held her by the shoulders for a moment and looked into her eyes and she obediently backed away, tucking lariats of blonde hair behind her ears.

Everyone knew who she was. His wife, Annabelle Fox – most famous from a fish fingers commercial when she was five years old. Not done much since, other than date famous boyfriends, rock stars or actors, from what I could tell.

We waited patiently in the freezing wind as the supervising

medical team fitted him up to their biofeedback machines, attaching electrodes wired to their contraptions, the EEG and ECG. Immediately flickering wavy lines appeared on the big screens and we could hear the magician's amplified heartbeat coming from the gigantic speakers. We were told it was forty beats per minute. A normal basal heart rate is between sixty and a hundred. Under sixty is called bradycardia and can be dangerous, but it's not unusual for an athlete to show a normal rate as low as forty – and Kelso Dennett was certainly as fit as an athlete.

He put his hands together over his chest in an attitude of prayer and gave a miniscule nod to the crowd, Hindu fashion. He climbed into the coffin and lay flat as the undertakers screwed the lid back into place.

The crowd remained silent and still as the pallbearers lowered it into the bespoke grave. Sand was first piled in by a bulldozer, then flattened by spades – an irrationally or perhaps rationally disturbing experience for those of us watching, resembling as it did some laboriously drawn-out execution in some far-off barbaric fundamentalist dictatorship. Later on some bright spark had the theory that there was an escape hatch to a fully-fitted underground apartment kitted with plentiful food and drink, though how a 'fully fitted apartment' could have been constructed under the beach of a popular English holiday resort without anybody noticing is anybody's guess.

Barely seconds after the spot was marked by a wooden cross, the magician's face appeared back on the massive screens, showing us in a pre-recorded message that he had written something down and put it in a sealed envelope, handed to the Mayor of Seagate to place in a safe deposit box in a bank of his choice.

Close-up. 'This envelope contains something vitally important – but it must only be revealed when the coffin has been removed from the grave after forty days and forty nights. Not before.' Finally, and movingly, he said he believed he could perform the superhuman task he has set for himself, but Fate might have other plans – and that if he failed, he wanted his family to know that he loved them very much. 'And Annabelle, what can I say? You are my rock, my sun, my moon. I will see you in forty days and forty nights, my darling, or I will see you in the afterlife. God bless you all.'

The end credits rolled – no music – as the camera tracked back from the grave, cross-fading to the ECG.

The woman with wind-tossed hair watched. Eyes behind sunglasses. Cheeks white. Lipstick red.

That night, when the crowds had dispersed and the production crew had drinks and canapés on the beach to celebrate, she left early. It must've been quite an ordeal for her, so I wasn't that surprised. It must've been a strange sort of thing to celebrate, if you were her. I watched her cross the beach alone, leaving the penumbra of the television lights, her husband's heart still pulsing with an even monotony in the air. When I went back to the hotel, there was no sign of her.

The next morning the cross was at an angle. Messages had been left there. Flowers, predictably. I guess security let them through the cordon. A trail of thin wires led from the grave to the trailer where the scientists had their equipment. The bass throb of the magician's heart was still beating loud from the speakers. It had become slower over the first twenty-four hours, imperceptibly at first, the number in the corner of the screen flashing thirty beats per minute – technically well into bradycardia. Near it I saw Annabelle Fox drinking one of the coffees in polystyrene cups. She was surrounded by members of the production team, but she looked terribly alone.

Eventually I plucked up courage to sit next to her in the hotel bar, because nobody else did. She didn't know my name, but knew I was one of the runners. I'd brought her those coffees enough times. She said she thought she needed coffee right now.

'I love his shows.' I ignored the fact she was tipsy. 'What a great man.'

She laughed. 'Nothing is what it seems.' She could see I didn't know why she said that, so changed the subject. Or did she? 'You know, people talk about *charisma*, but they don't really know what charisma means. Charisma is power. The power to make the other person, the weaker person, to do exactly what you want.'

'Is it?'

'Look at Aleister Crowley. You've heard of Aleister Crowley? Frater Perdurabo. Ipsissimus. Master Therion.' I tried not to look blank. 'Magick with a "k". The Great Beast 666. Crowley wasn't particularly attractive. Pretty fucking far from it. He was a repulsive, pot-bellied old goat – but he was *charismatic* in spades.' Her eyelids were heavy. 'He'd say to a friend, "Watch this." And he'd follow a person down the street, make them faint to the floor by just *willing* them to. Just by staring at the back of their head. That's *real* magic. Through Crowley – through Thelema. Tantric rituals . . . Sex magic . . .' She looked at me lop-sidedly. 'My husband is really, *really* interested in sex.' Then she held me with a steady gaze, rolling ice cubes in her glass. 'You're interested in sex, right?'

'Yes.' I said without thinking.

She rose and swayed and pronounced the need to go to bed. My room was on the same floor as hers and I said I was tired too. By the time we got out of the lift I wasn't sure what I'd heard or why I'd heard it.

'Do you want to come in for a . . .' She paused before the last word. '. . . chat? I was going to say "drink", but I think I've had more than enough of that.'

Immediately I was through the door she started to undress

and so did I. The bedside lights were on and neither of us switched them off. I told her I'd never felt so hard before. She laughed and pressed me down on my back, and knelt beside me and slipped a Durex over me with her fingertips. I came almost immediately but she kept me erect, a smile on her face the whole time. We switched positions and I felt her cold hands stroking my lower back then gripping hard as I drove in. She covered her mouth so that nobody could hear, but I snatched her hand away and held her lips with mine until we ran out of breath.

Afterwards I lay inside her and said I wanted to lie that way all night. She laughed like it was a childish but nice thing to imagine. Her skin burned against mine, but her hands and feet were like ice from a day on the beach. The soft thrum of his heartbeat touched the window panes as we lay in each other's arms.

She said she didn't like hotel rooms. They made her a bit crazy. I grinned, saying you can do crazy things in hotel rooms. She said Kelso liked the anonymity. The fact nobody could tell anything about you because a hotel room contained none of your belongings. None of your history.

'He doesn't like people knowing things about him. He's a bit paranoid like that. He's worried about the *paparazzi*, yes. It's enough to make anyone think they're being watched, bugged, hacked. It's a terrible feeling. But it's more than the Press, to him. They're not the enemy any more. *Everybody's* the enemy. *I'm* the enemy. He likes me to stay indoors as much as possible, or know exactly where I am every second of the day.'

'Why?'

'He thinks I might give away his secrets.'

'What secrets?'

'All kinds.'

She went and crouched at the mini bar, a sprig of damp

pubic hair visible in the gap between her buttocks. She returned with shots of whisky emptied into tea cups from the hospitality tray.

'When we were on honeymoon in Rome we woke up one morning and the bells were chiming in St Peter's Square. We'd asked for breakfast to be delivered to our room, and pastries and coffee arrived piping hot. He got up, stark naked, and put crumbs on the windowsill. I asked him what he was doing. He said he could control which bird would peck it up. I giggled, but he said he meant it. He came back and sat cross-legged on the bed next to me. I waited for seconds, minutes. Then he smiled at me and clicked his fingers and right at that moment – that *exact* moment, a bird landed and started eating up the crumbs.'

'What first attracted you to millionaire Kelso Dennett?' I ran kisses up her arm.

She smiled. 'Maybe his – manual dexterity . . .' She took my hand and placed it over her private parts, guiding my middle finger towards her clitoris.

'Obviously he likes to be in control.'

'That's what magic is. The ultimate control of the external world.'

'Well,' I said. 'He can't control you now.'

I arched over to kiss her on the lips, but she stiffened.

'I think you should go.' She held my face in her hands. 'I'm enjoying this too much.'

'So am I.'

'I mean it.'

She got off the bed and put her dressing gown on, pointlessly, not moving as she watched me dress.

'What's your name again?'

'Nick.'

'Nick, this never happened.'

'Pff. Gone,' I whispered before closing the door.

My own room was significantly colder than hers, so I turned up the thermostat. My mind was racing. I knew I wouldn't sleep so I put on the bedside light to read, but the bulb was dead. I switched it off and on again, mystified, because it hadn't been dead earlier.

I saw Kelso's wife again at breakfast but she didn't acknowledge me with so much as a glance. I also saw her later in the catering wagon – a converted double-decker bus. I wanted to sit with her, in fact I had a fantasy of touching her up under the table, or her touching me up – but that was impossible. There was no way any of these people could find out what had happened between us. What was I thinking? That she would call a meeting? Announce it from the rooftops?

I looked at the rota. I stood at my allotted station, by the coin-operated telescope overlooking the sweep of the bay.

The grave had almost lost any delineation against the rest of the sand. You wouldn't have known where it was, if not for the circle of footsteps around the small cross, the fence of plastic ribbon attached to iron rods, the trailer containing the equipment, and of course the video projection screens and tall, angled spotlights, the kind you often pass on motorways when they have road works at night.

People gathered occasionally in small groups, pointing or taking snapshots or videos with their camcorders. Then they'd move on, or linger, sometimes not moving or speaking. Typical British holidaymakers with their anorak hoods up, peering around like meerkats, not wondering for a second about the metaphysics of life and death, wondering where to go to get a two course lunch for under a tenner.

As well as the channel's news programme, which gave it a minute slot every day, there were teams from most of the terrestrial and cable networks, a few from America – where Kelso was big – and Japan, where he was even bigger. Then there was the locked-off CCTV cam pointed at the grave itself, uploading to the internet on a dedicated website, buriedalive.co.uk, where you could watch 24/7. The fact there was very little to watch was irrelevant. It was already going viral on twitter, with endless comments and retweets – ('OMG loving @buriedalive'; 'KD #completenutterorgenius?'; 'Cant watch 2 spookie'; 'Diggin the Kels') – the numbers exceeding even the broadcasters' high expectations. It was quickly obvious that this wasn't just 'event' television, it was a national event, period.

The tall lights came on as the sunlight faded. The slippery rocks where Dad and I used to catch crabs reflected a shiny glow. The men in Hi-Viz vests protected the twelve-foot cordon around the grave, but they let through a little girl in a sky blue parka and matching wellies who stuck her little windmill in the ground next to the flowers before running back to her mum and dad.

When my shift was over I went to the hotel bar. Kelso's wife wasn't there. I waited. She didn't appear.

I went to my room. Drifting to sleep, I started to hear scratching, like a small animal trapped in the cavity wall behind the head board. A bird but bigger than a bird. Perhaps a squirrel. Wings or paws scurried as if desperate to escape. I was annoyed because I knew it would keep me awake. Obviously something had fallen down the chimney and got trapped – then I heard a sudden bang, like a door slamming, and it stopped completely.

I pulled on my jeans and went out into the corridor. Nobody else was out there. Surely the person in the next room must've heard it too? I raised a fist to knock on the room next to me, but I could hear the TV on. They were listening to the live coverage of *Buried Alive*. I looked down the corridor to the far end. For some reason I expected Kelso's wife to be standing there, but she wasn't.

The next day I saw her overlooking the beach. I went up to her and leaned on the rail beside her. I wondered if she felt guilty and might move away, but she didn't. It was almost as if I wasn't there. Her eyes were fixed on the circus – by which I mean, her husband's grave.

'It's getting to people,' I said. 'Anticipation.'

'That's what it's all about.' She took a deep drag on her cigarette. I wondered if it warmed her. 'Will people lose interest, d'you think?'

'They adore him. Look at the viewing figures.'

'Things can change.'

'Can they?'

'Have you read the newspapers today?'

'They can't get enough of him.'

She exhaled a short, sharp breath. 'You know what the papers are like. They build people up and up, then they like to knock them down. He's a cash cow right now, yes. But they could turn against him without batting a fucking eyelid.' She sucked the cigarette like an addict.

'Are you afraid?'

'For him? Yes, of course. Always. But he knows what he's doing. He *always* knows what he's doing, don't worry. He plans it to the nth degree. You have no idea. He leaves nothing to chance, my husband the magician. He knows everything, absolutely everything that can happen, and will happen.'

'That's what I mean. Does that scare you, ever?'

'What do you think?'

She crushed dead ash on the balustrade and brushed it off into the wind, her hair flickering and lashing like the torn shreds of a flag. I heard a rasping voice in my walkie-talkie and switched it off.

'The woman from *Hello* magazine is waiting to do an interview. She says she waited all day yesterday, with her photographer. The office are hassling me to hassle you, but if you don't want to do it, don't do it. Fuck them. I'll tell them you're not feeling well.'

'Thank you.'

Over the next few days I decided not to intrude into her space. In my spare hours I slept or when I couldn't sleep I watched old DVDs of Kelso Dennett's magic shows: *Bamboozler* and *Scaremongering* and *MindF****. You probably remember them all. I know I do. The man who wakes up to find all the doors and windows of his house have been bricked in. The girl made to think she can bend spoons. Even more astonishingly, the guy who wakes up in what he thinks is the past, thirty years ago, and meets *himself* as a child, having been hypnotised to think a lookalike boy actor was literally him.

This one set the tone for the outrageously ambitious and controversial 'specials' to come, some of the greatest 'did you see?' TV moments of all time. *Abduction* – inducing a UFO abduction experience. *Guillotine* – inviting an audience who believes in the death penalty to witness a beheading. *Invisible* – making a young woman think she is invisible for a day. *Sleepwalkers* – getting a dozen people to sleepwalk at exactly the same time, on the same night – making them climb onto roofs across the London skyline – a stunning image caught by a helicopter camera as the sun came up. In the minds of many it was the culmination of the use of technology and sense of 'event' that had become Kelso Dennett's hallmark.

Then there was the infamous Easter Special, *Crucifixion*. Not hard to see why Christian groups were immediately up in arms. Badgered by the Press, the magician explained he simply wanted to find out whether the experience was as truly transcendental as some claimed. No slight to any religion intended. Nevertheless, lobby groups found a loophole in the broadcasters' charter and the transmission was cancelled. It was rumoured that he went to Philippines anyway, going through with the ritual without the presence of cameras. However there *were* cameras at Heathrow on his return, to film him – as I saw now – getting off the plane, hobbling, and with bandages round his hands.

I paused the picture as the phone rang. It was Annabelle's voice asking me to come to her room. I left the DVD in the player and went. She was already naked and her first kiss as she captured me in it tasted strongly of white wine. She almost gnawed off my lips, tore out my tongue. I wanted to do it the same way as before but she had different ideas and got onto the bed on all fours.

As we lay afterwards in our salty sweat, I asked her how she'd got the long, puckered scar I'd felt across her shoulder blade. She said her mother always told the story that when she was born she shot out so quickly she hit the bed post.

'Unlikely.'

'All right then. My father said I was an angel come down to earth. And that's where they had to cut off my wings so that nobody would notice. You prefer my father's version?'

'What about the other wing?'

She laughed and kissed my bare chest. I thought I could hear my own heart beating, but it wasn't. She didn't need to say anything.

I sat up and pulled on my socks and underpants. The sliding door of the closet was half open. Beyond my bisected reflection I could see a row of Kelso Dennett's suits on hangers, all black, all identical. Black patent leather shoes arranged perfectly on the floor.

'Nick? Stay.'

On sentry duty, I looked down at the grave, a mandala-type geometry incised around it by a myriad of footprints, now.

The print place in Church Street had the enterprising thought of printing *Buried Alive* T-shirts and were doing a roaring trade from a stall next to the fishing boats and cockle vendor. Groupies descended, some booking into B&Bs for the whole forty days. Others, the vultures of the tabloids for instance, seemed to be hovering in morbid expectation, eager for him to fail, to die. I thought about him dying too. I thought about him lying in complete darkness in that coffin under the sand and not coming out. I thought about that a lot.

When I passed a camera crew one day, a female student from Israel was saying, 'People are tweeting he's dead, but he isn't. That's just evil. He's not dead. He wouldn't leave us like that. He'll come back, I know he will.'

On day twelve I asked permission to take Annabelle away from the set. I said I thought she needed it, and they bought that. They gave me petty cash to get a hire car. We drove somewhere, only about twenty miles away, but a nice place with a spa, and stayed overnight. We swam in the heated swimming pool. Booked two rooms but slept in one. Didn't even set foot outside the door one day. Made love ridiculously, non-stop. I called room service and ordered more champagne.

'Are you paying for this? You can't afford this.'

I told her it was all on the production company's dime. Her expression changed completely. I crawled across the bed towards her, said it didn't matter, did it? 'So what?'

She prowled the room for her smokes, then said she'd like to drive back to Seagate after lunch.

I said, 'Fine.'

We didn't converse over the food. Picking at her salad, she was dived on by some spotty lad from the local rag who asked her about the rumours her husband is dead, that the television company knew it and were covering it up. Annabelle seemed to tighten and wither, covering her face with her hands. I told the moron to get out and get lost, following him through to reception to make sure he did. Outside I caught another guy taking photos through the dining room window with a hefty lens. The two of them stood back and stared me out, like cornered rats, afraid of nothing. *Cunts*. That explained it. I'd had a weird feeling all day. I'd sensed somebody watching us at the poolside while we swam. I'd thought I saw somebody, back-lit with the sun behind them, but when I'd wiped the water from my eyes they were gone. Like I say, that explained it.

We drove back in silence. When we were five minutes from the hotel Annabelle placed her hand on my thigh.

That evening I couldn't stand the laughter and music in the bar. I stood overlooking the beach, listening to the sombre toll of his heartbeat coming from the speakers, seeing the iridescent green lines of the projected ECG. Thirty people or more were gathered down there with candles, though whether they were Christians praying for his wellbeing or avid fans I couldn't tell. Were they proper visitors at all, or was it prearranged? You couldn't take anything at face value any more. What was genuine public reaction and what was part of the *schtick*? The channel was after ratings, but they were legally culpable too, weren't they? Wasn't there some kind of professional duty of care? Could they be sued if he *didn't* come out alive? And if something went disastrously wrong, wouldn't they do everything they could to bluff it out, play for time – just like the reporter was saying?

Children played hopscotch on the sand near the giraffe lights and generator. I shivered at the unbidden fantasy that the trucks would move away, the electrics and machinery towed off, and he'd be left down there though lack of interest, a victim of the viewing public's fickle apathy. I shivered because I found myself almost willing it to happen.

'He's strong.' Annabelle's voice, right behind me. 'You have no idea how strong. He'll never let down his public. Never. They made him who he is. He'll never forget that. Never.'

I held out my hand. Pale as paper, she took it. Pressed her lips against mine. When she stepped back she must've seen my eyes flicker.

'Nobody can see us.'

'I know.' I turned up my jacket collar and we walked to somewhere out of the icy wind, the little gift shop by the turnstile to the pier that sold fishing bait and postcards.

My teeth were chattering. 'What are we going to tell him?'

'When?'

'When? When he comes out. What do you think I mean?'

'We tell him nothing, of course. Why would we?' She looked at me like I was the stupidest, most naïve idiot in the world. 'Oh, Nick . . .'

'Don't be a fucking bitch, all right?' I turned my back to her.

'Well, what are *you* going to do? Tell your girlfriend?'

'Yes.'

'No you're not.'

'I *will*. I'm prepared to.'

'To do what? Throw away what you've got?'

I barked a laugh. 'Got? What have I "got"? I've got nothing. You're kidding. This place? This life? In this dump? It means fuck-all to me.'

'You don't mean that.'

'I fucking do. And don't act as though all this is bollocks, what we've been doing together for the last twelve days, because I know –'

'Oh, grow up! You've had good sex. I've had good sex. I'm not saying I haven't enjoyed – '

'Oh, thanks a fucking – '

'I just don't want to take away – '

'You're not taking away *anything*!' I turned on her. I'd had enough. 'For fuck's sake, you're *bringing*. Bringing me everything I've ever wanted! Christ. I've never felt so . . .'

'What?'

I choked back the word, then thought, fuck it. 'So . . . *alive*.'

Her eyes filled up and her lip curled. 'Go. Go.'

I knew I wouldn't be invited to her hotel room that night. I thought I may even have blown it completely. I sat in my room and sobbed. I felt like doing a Keith Moon and tearing the room apart, disgusted with myself that I was so fucking well brought up I'd never do anything that would embarrass my parents. I thought, fuck my parents! I looked down at the ghost-written biography of Kelso Dennett I'd thrown at the wall. It had fallen open at a photograph taken in India. He was fire-walking. Everybody was grinning. He was taking Annabelle by the hand. She was doing it with him, stepping barefoot onto the coals, but she looked frightened to death.

I heard a rap at the door. She took me by the hand and led me down to the beach. She found a secluded spot out of sight of the men in Hi-Viz jackets, under the shadow of the lip of the Promenade, not far from the concrete slipway. She knelt and took me into her mouth. The mixture of hot and cold was explosive. I almost passed out in a shuddering fit. My fingers ran through her hair. It was the colour of seaweed in the spill of artificial lighting. I cried, 'No.' I said, 'No.' I was facing the grave and she wasn't. I turned my cheek to the wall and shut my eyes.

At the twenty-day mark, I thought things would settle into a routine as far as the stunt was concerned, but I couldn't have been more wrong. The tension, far from easing off, was ratcheting up unimaginably. Everyone could feel it, and the callous metronome of those insidiously slow heartbeats – fifteen beats per minute now – did nothing to calm anybody's nerves.

I was getting blinding headaches. Maybe it was because I was existing on Red Bull to pep me up through a whisky hangover most of the time, or maybe the pressure of lying to Cyd was getting to me. I was flying off the handle and giving excuses why I couldn't sleep at her grotty one-bedroom flat, cuddled up on stinking nylon sheets. I blamed it on the job, but the truth was I couldn't stand the sight of her any more with her M&S cardigan and lank, boring hair. I'd say I was going for a walk, but I wasn't going for a walk, I was going to her. To Annabelle Fox from the fish fingers commercial I used to watch when I was seven years old.

'Did he really spend months at a Tibetan monastery?'

'No. Not months. Years.' She was sitting up, twisted in crisp white sheets in the afterglow. 'See, what people don't understand is his body doesn't matter to him. It's just an instrument. The mind is what matters. That's how he got into tattoos and scarification and body modification. Medicine men who put needles through their cheeks and don't feel a thing. It's all about physical extremities, pain, distress, fear – whatever – anything to remove you from your sense of self, your sense of mortality.'

'I'd have thought his mortality would be all too important to him, down there in the dark, alone.'

She looked at her own reflection. 'That's because you're not him.'

'Good.'

She didn't turn to me. 'It *is* good.'

We fucked again, deliciously, freer now, and while I was in the bathroom disposing of my used Durex, I heard the sound of a glass smashing. I shouted but Annabelle didn't answer. When I came back into the bedroom she said it was an accident, she'd dropped it. Although she was in bed and the glass was over on the coffee table. I didn't say anything, but I had a strange feeling that wasn't what had happened at all.

Later that night I woke up in the dark of the room. It must've been four or five in the morning, but really I had no idea. It scared me that my heart was drumming in my chest. It was inside my ears and it made me think of the heartbeat coming from the speakers down on the beach. At the same time I had a definite, overwhelming sense of a presence. Of someone in the room. Luckily my eyes had opened because if I'd had to open them I wouldn't have.

A spill of intense yellow came from the bathroom – one of us must've left the light on. Illuminated by it stood a figure. A man standing there, arms hanging at his side, simply looking at me. Looking down at the bed. It was Kelso Dennett, dressed exactly as he was when he stepped into the coffin. Naked to the waist, lycra pants, sleeve of tattoos, pentagram, shaved head.

I switched on bedside light.

'Wha?' Annabelle rubbed her eyes, contorting against her pillow. 'Nick? Jesus . . .' I was blinking too, inevitably – the sudden brightness flooding my vision, a complete searing white-out. 'What the hell?'

But by the time my eyes had got accustomed to the glare, there was nothing to tell her, because there was nobody there. 'Fuck. Nightmare. Really bad. Shit. Sorry. Sorry.' I kissed her. 'Sorry. It's gone. Gone . . .'

But it didn't go.

It didn't go at all.

The next night I sensed him in the room again. In the exact same place, like a replay. Like the image from the DVD. Except this time I didn't turn and face him, and this time I could feel him walking slowly towards the bed.

I didn't open my eyes.

He stayed there for several minutes, but it seemed like hours. Perhaps it *was* hours. I have no idea.

And I thought: *How long has he been there? How many times before and I haven't noticed?* And I tried to close my eyes even tighter, and shut out the sound of his beating heart, but it only seemed to get louder.

The days come, and the nights, and I haven't told Annabelle what I saw standing by the bathroom door, not that I'm sure what I saw, or even if I saw it. When you think about what you did yesterday, it's like a dream, isn't it? If somebody told you it didn't happen, or it happened differently, you wouldn't be able to contradict them, would you? All you could say is – well, what would you say? I don't know.

I don't know what to say to her. I don't know whether to ask her to come to my room instead of me going to hers, or whether that will even make any difference. Why should it?

Now, I hardly sleep anyway because I can't bear the thought of waking in the middle of that night with that feeling of panic in my chest. I can't bear it because I know who will be there, looking down at me.

Jesus Christ. Jesus Christ.

Twenty-nine days now. Thirty tomorrow.

I count them like a prison sentence. With my unblinking eyes fixed on it, the digital clock at the bedside moves past midnight. I can hear her gentle breathing inches away from my back. I feel the aura of another warm body next to me. I cling to her the way a child clings to its mother, and she strokes my hair. She has no idea what is inside my head. She has no idea what is in the room. Now it's my secret. It's all about *my* secret now.

Day thirty-six.

The headaches are worse than ever. I need to go to the doctor. The doctor has to give me something for this. It's not normal. It just isn't.

And I know the viewing public is getting excited, but I'm starting to spend all my waking hours thinking what they are going to find when they dig down and bring up his coffin. My stomach knots on a regular basis. Is he going to be dead? Is that his last, greatest trick, after all? The great almighty fuck-you? Then, at other times, I become absolutely certain that when they dig him up, the coffin will be empty.

I'm not sure which of the two eventualities terrifies me the most.

Which is why I dare not sleep any more. I can go four nights without sleep, can't I? Just four nights. Of course I can. I'll make sure I can.

Then it will all be over.

I dare not close my eyes. Because shutting them means opening them – and opening them . . . what the *fuck* will I see?

BBC News (UK)

BAFFLING TV 'STUNT' ENDS IN HORROR:
MYSTERY OF MAGICIAN'S 'FINAL TRICK'

Thursday 11 April 2013 12.44 BST

DNA tests are expected to confirm that the body found under Seagate beach yesterday – buried in a coffin as part of a stunt by an acclaimed television illusionist – is that of local man Nick Ambler.

Mr Ambler, 28, was the son of hotel proprietor Stuart Ambler and his wife Corinne, and had been working on the production as a runner.

Detectives have said they want as a priority to interview TV magician Kelso Dennett, whose present whereabouts are unknown. They are also urgently seeking his wife, actress Annabelle Fox, to help them with their inquiries.

Famous for controversial and sometimes blasphemous stunts, the showman had returned to his home town claiming, in typically audacious fashion, that he would survive being buried alive for forty days and forty nights. It was only when the coffin was exhumed yesterday that the body of the dead man was discovered.

A spokesperson for Kent Police said: 'Initial findings indicate that the young man had been in the coffin for the entire forty days. Scratches on the inside of the lid, together with broken fingernails, indicate a desperate and no doubt prolonged and agonising attempt to escape.'

Last night, in the glare of the news cameras, a visibly shaken Mayor of Seagate opened the sealed envelope entrusted to him by Kelso Dennett before he stepped into the coffin forty days earlier. It contained a single sheet of paper, folded once, on which was written just two words in block capitals – the name of the deceased.

ROBERT SHEARMAN

THAT TINY FLUTTER OF THE HEART I USED TO CALL LOVE

Karen thought of them as her daughters, and tried to love them with all her heart. Because, really, wasn't that the point? They came to her, all frilly dresses, and fine hair, and plastic limbs, and eyes so large and blue and innocent. And she would name them, and tell them she was their mother now; she took them to her bed, and would give them tea parties, and spank them when they were naughty; she promised she would never leave them, or, at least, not until the end.

Her father would bring them home. Her father travelled a lot, and she never knew where he'd been, if she asked he'd just laugh and tap his nose and say it was all hush hush – but she could sometimes guess from how exotic the daughters were, sometimes the faces were strange and foreign, one or two were nearly mulatto. Karen didn't care, she loved them all anyway, although she wouldn't let the mulatto ones have quite the same nursery privileges. 'Here you are, my sweetheart, my angel cake, my baby doll,' and from somewhere within Father's great jacket he'd produce a box, and it was usually gift wrapped, and it usually had a ribbon on it – 'This is all for you, my baby doll.' She liked him calling her that, although she suspected she was too old for it now, she was very nearly eight years old.

She knew what the daughters were. They were tributes. That was what Nicholas called them. They were tributes paid to her, to make up for the fact that Father was so often away, just like in the very olden days when the Greek heroes would pay tributes to their gods with sacrifices. Nicholas was very keen on Greek heroes, and would tell his sister stories of great battles and wooden horses and heels. She didn't need tributes from Father; she would much rather he didn't have to leave home in the first place. Nicholas would tell her of the tributes Father had once paid Mother – he'd bring her jewellery, and fur coats, and tickets to the opera. Karen couldn't remember Mother very well, but there was that large portrait of her over the staircase, in a way Karen saw Mother more often than she did Father. Mother was wearing a black ball gown, and such a lot of jewels, and there was a small studied smile on her face. Sometimes when Father paid tribute to Karen, she would try and give that same studied smile, but she wasn't sure she'd ever got it right.

Father didn't call Nicholas 'angel cake' or 'baby doll', he called him 'Nicholas', and Nicholas called him 'sir'. And Father didn't bring Nicholas tributes. Karen felt vaguely guilty about that, that she'd get showered with gifts and her brother would get nothing. Nicholas told her not to be so silly. He wasn't a little girl, he was a man. He was ten years older than Karen, and lean, and strong, and he was attempting to grow a moustache, the hair was a bit too fine for it to be seen in bright light, but it would darken as he got older. Karen knew her brother was a man, and that he wouldn't want toys. But she'd give him a hug sometimes, almost impulsively, when Father came home and seemed to ignore him – and Nicholas never objected when she did.

Eventually Nicholas would say to Karen, 'It's time,' and she knew what that meant. And she'd feel so sad, but again, wasn't that the point? She'd go and give her daughter a special tea party then, and she'd play with her all day; she'd brush her hair, and let her see the big wide world from out of the top window; she wouldn't get cross even if her daughter got naughty. And she wouldn't try to explain. That would all come after. Karen would go to bed at the usual time, Nanny never suspected a thing. But once Nanny had left the room and turned out the light, Karen would get up and put on her clothes again, nice thick woollen ones, sometimes it was cold out there in the dark. And she'd bundle her daughter up warm as well. And once the house was properly still she'd hear a tap at the door, and there Nicholas would be, looking stern and serious and just a little bit excited. She'd follow him down the stairs and out of the house, they'd usually leave by the tradesmen's entrance, the door was quieter. They wouldn't talk until they were far away, and very nearly into the woods themselves.

He'd always give Karen a few days to get to know her daughters before he came for them. He wanted her to love them as hard as she could. He always seemed to know when it was the right time. With one doll, her very favourite, he had given her only until the weekend – it had been love at first sight, the eyelashes were real hair, and she'd blink when picked up, and if she were cuddled tight she'd say 'Mama'. Sometimes Nicholas gave them as long as a couple of months; some of the dolls were a fright, and cold to the touch, and it took Karen a while to find any affection for them at all. But Karen was a girl with a big heart. She could love anything, given time and patience. Nicholas must have been carefully watching his sister, just to see when their heart reached its fullest – and she never saw him do it, he usually seemed to ignore her altogether, as if she were still too young and too silly to be worth his attention. But then, 'It's time,' he would say, and sometimes it wasn't until that very moment that Karen would realise she'd fallen in love at all, and of course he was right, he was always right.

Karen liked playing in the woods by day. By night they seemed strange and unrecognisable, the branches jutted out at peculiar angles as if trying to bar her entrance. But Nicholas wasn't afraid, and he always knew his way. She kept close to him for fear he would rush on ahead and she would be lost. And she knew somehow that if she got lost, she'd be lost forever – and it may turn daylight eventually, but that wouldn't matter, she'd have been trapped by the woods of the night, and the woods of the night would get to keep her.

And at length they came to the clearing. Karen always supposed that the clearing was at the very heart of the woods, she didn't know why. The tight press of trees suddenly lifted, and here there was space – no flowers, nothing, some grass, but even the grass was brown, as if the sunlight couldn't reach it here. And it was as if everything had been cut away to make a perfect circle that was neat and tidy and so empty, and it was as if it had been done especially for them. Karen could never find the clearing in the daytime. But then, she had never tried very hard.

Nicholas would take her daughter, and set her down upon that browning grass. He would ask Karen for her name, and Karen would tell him. Then Nicholas would tell Karen to explain to the daughter what was going to happen here. 'Betsy, you have been sentenced to death.' And Nicholas would ask Karen upon what charge. 'Because I love you too much, and I love my brother more.' And Nicholas would ask if the daughter had any final words to offer before sentence was carried out; they never had.

He would salute the condemned then, nice and honourably. And Karen would by now be nearly in tears; she would pull herself together. 'You mustn't cry,' said Nicholas, 'you can't cry, if you cry the death won't be a clean one.' She would salute her daughter too.

What happened next would always be different.

When he'd been younger Nicholas had merely hanged them. He'd put rope around their little necks and take them to the closest tree and let them drop down from the branches, and there they'd swing for a while, their faces still frozen with trusting smiles. As he'd become a man he'd found more inventive ways to despatch them. He'd twist off their arms, he'd drown them in buckets of water he'd already prepared, he'd stab them with a fork. He'd say to Karen, 'And how much do you love this one?' And if Karen told him she loved him very much, so much the worse for her daughter – he'd torture her a little first, blinding her, cutting off her skin, ripping off her clothes and then toasting with matches the naked stuff beneath. It was always harder to watch these executions because Karen really had loved them, and it was agony to see them suffer so, But she couldn't lie to her brother. He would have seen through her like glass.

That last time had been the most savage, though Karen hadn't known it would be the last time, of course – but Nicholas, Nicholas might have had an inkling.

When they'd reached the clearing he had tied Mary-Lou to the tree with string. Tightly, but not too tight – Karen had said she hadn't loved Mary-Lou especially, and Nicholas didn't want to be cruel. He had even wrapped his own handkerchief around her eyes as a blindfold.

Then he'd produced from his knapsack Father's gun.

'You can't use that!' Karen said. 'Father will find out! Father will be angry!'

'Phooey to that,' said Nicholas. 'I'll be going to war soon, and I'll have a gun all of my own. Had you heard that, Carrie?

That I'm going to war?' She hadn't heard. Nanny had kept it from her, and Nicholas had wanted it to be a surprise. He looked at the gun. 'It's a Webley Mark IV service revolver,' he said. 'Crude and old-fashioned, just like Father. What I'll be getting will be much better.'

He narrowed his eyes, and aimed the gun, fired. There was an explosion, louder than Karen could ever have dreamed – and she thought Nicholas was shocked too, not only by the noise, but by the recoil. Birds scattered. Nicholas laughed. The bullet had gone wild. 'That was just a warm up,' he said.

It was on his fourth try that he hit Mary-Lou. Her leg was blown off.

'Do you want a go?'

'No,' said Karen.

'It's just like at a fairground,' he said. 'Come on.'

She took the gun from him, and it burned in her hand, it smelled like burning. He showed her how to hold it, and she liked the way his hand locked around hers as he corrected her aim. 'It's all right,' he said to his little sister gently, 'we'll do it together. There's nothing to be scared of.' And really he was the one who pulled the trigger, but she'd been holding on too, so she was a bit responsible, and Nicholas gave a whoop of delight and Karen had never heard him so happy before, she wasn't sure she'd ever heard him happy. And when they looked back at the tree Mary-Lou had disappeared.

'I'm going across the seas,' he said. 'I'm going to fight. And every man I kill, listen, I'm killing him for you. Do you understand me? I'll kill them all because of you.'

He kissed her then on the lips. It felt warm and wet and the moustache tickled, and it was hard too, as if he were trying to leave an imprint there, as if when he pulled away he wanted to leave a part of him behind.

'I love you,' he said.

'I love you too.'

'Don't forget me,' he said. Which seemed such an odd thing to say – how was she going to forget her own brother?

They'd normally bury the tribute then, but they couldn't find any trace of Mary-Lou's body. Nicholas put the gun back in the knapsack, he offered Karen his hand. She took it. They went home.

They had never found Nicholas' body either; at the funeral his coffin was empty, and Father told Karen it didn't matter, that good form was the thing. Nicholas had been killed in the Dardanelles, and Karen looked for it upon the map, and it seemed such a long way to go to die. There were lots of funerals in the town that season, and Father made sure that Nicholas' was the most lavish, no expense was spared.

The family was so small now, and they watched together as the coffin was lowered into the grave. Father looking proud, not sad. And Karen refusing to cry – 'Don't cry,' she said to the daughter she'd brought with her, 'you mustn't cry, or it won't be clean,' and yet she dug her fingernails deep into her daughter's body to try to force some tears from it.

Julian hadn't gone to war. He'd been born just too late. And of course he said he was disappointed, felt cheated even, he loved his country and whatever his country might stand for, and he had wanted to demonstrate that love in the very noblest of ways. He said it with proper earnestness, and some days he almost meant it. His two older brothers had gone to fight, and both had returned home, and the younger had brought back some sort of medal with him. The brothers had changed. They had less time for Julian, and Julian felt that was no bad thing. He was no longer worth the effort of bullying. One day he'd asked his eldest brother what it had been like out there on the Front. And the brother turned to him in surprise, and Julian was surprised too, what had he been thinking of? – and he braced himself for the pinch or Chinese burn that was sure to follow. But instead the brother had just turned away; he'd sucked his cigarette down to the very stub, and sighed, and said it was just as well Julian hadn't been called up, the trenches were a place for real men. The whole war really wouldn't have been his bag at all.

When Julian Morris first met Karen Davison, neither was much impressed. Certainly, Julian was well used to girls finding him unimpressive: he was short, his face was too round and homely, his thighs quickly thinned into legs that looked too spindly to support him. There was an effeminacy about his features that his father had thought might have been cured by a spell fighting against Germans, but Julian didn't know whether it would have helped; he tried to take after his brothers, tried to lower his voice and speak more gruffly, he drank beer, he took up smoking. But even there he'd got it all wrong somehow. The voice, however gruff, always rose in inflection no matter how much he tried to stop it. He sipped at his beer. He held his cigarette too languidly, apparently, and when he puffed out smoke it was always from the side of his mouth and never with a good bold manly blast.

But for Julian to be unimpressed by a girl was a new sensation for him. Girls flummoxed Julian. With their lips and their breasts and their flowing contours. With their bright colours, all that perfume. Even now, if some aged friend of his mother's spoke to him, he'd be reduced to a stammering mess. But Karen Davison did something else to Julian entirely. He looked at her across the ballroom and realised that he rather despised her. It wasn't that she was unattractive, at first glance her figure was pretty enough. But she was so much older than the other girls, in three years of attending dances no man had yet snatched her up – and there was already something middle-aged about that face, something jaded. She looked bored. That was it, she looked bored. And didn't care to hide it.

Once in a while a man would approach her, take pity on

her, ask her to dance. She would reject him, and off the suitor would scarper, with barely disguised relief.

Julian had promised his parents that he would at least invite one girl on to the dance floor. It would hardly be his fault if that one girl he chose said no. He could return home, he'd be asked how he had got on, and if he were clever he might even be able to phrase a reply that concealed the fact he'd been rejected. Julian was no good at lying outright, his voice would squeak, and he would turn bright red. But not telling the truth? He'd had to find a way of mastering it.

He approached the old maid. Now that she was close he felt the usual panic rise within him, and he fought it down – look at her, he told himself, look at how hard she looks, like stone; she should be grateful you ask her to dance. He'd reached her. He opened his mouth to speak, realised his first word would be a stutter, put the word aside, found some new word to replace it, cleared his throat. Only then did the girl bother to look up at him. There was nothing welcoming in that expression, but nothing challenging either – she looked at him with utter indifference.

'A dance?' he said. 'Like? Would you?'

And, stupidly, opened out his arms, as if to remind her what a dance was, as if without her he'd simply manage on his own in dumb show.

She looked him up and down. Judging him, blatantly judging him. Not a smile upon her face. He waited for the refusal.

'Very well,' she said then, though without any enthusiasm.

He offered her his hand, and she took it by the fingertips, and rose to her feet. She was an inch or two taller than him. He smelled her perfume, and didn't like it.

He put one hand on her waist, the other was left gently brushing against her glove. They danced. She stared at his face, still quite incuriously, but it was enough to make him blush.

'You dance well,' she said.

'Thank you.'

'I don't enjoy dancing.'

'Then let us, by all means, stop.'

He led her back to her chair. He nodded at her stiffly, and prepared to leave. But she gestured towards the chair beside her, and he found himself bending down to sit in it.

'Are you enjoying the ball?' he asked her.

'I don't enjoy talking either.'

'I see.' And they sat in silence for a few minutes. At one point he felt he should get up and walk away, and he shuffled in his chair to do so – and at that she turned to look at him, and managed a smile, and for that alone he decided to stay a little while longer.

'Can I at least get you a drink?'

She agreed. So he went to fetch her a glass of fizz. Across the room he watched as another man approached and asked her to dance, and he suddenly felt a stab of jealousy that astonished him. She waved the man away, in irritation, and Julian pretended it was for his sake.

He brought her back the fizz.

'There you are,' he said.

She sipped at it. He sipped at his the same way.

'If you don't like dancing,' he said to her, 'and you don't like talking, why do you come?' He already knew the answer, of course, it was the same reason he came, and she didn't bother dignifying him with a reply. He laughed, and hated how girlish it sounded.

At length she said, 'Thank you for coming,' as if this were her ball, as if he were her guest, and he realised he was being dismissed. He got to his feet.

'Do you have a card?' she asked.

Julian did. She took it, put it away without reading it. And Julian waited beside her for any further farewell, and when nothing came, he nodded at her once more, and left her.

The very next day Julian received a telephone call from a Mr Davison, who invited him to have dinner with his daughter at his house that evening. Julian accepted. And because the girl had never bothered to give him her name, it took Julian a fair little time to work out who this Davison fellow might be.

Julian wondered whether the evening would be formal, and so overdressed, just for safety's sake. He took some flowers. He rang the bell, and some hatchet-faced old woman opened the front door. She showed him in. She told him that Mr Davison had been called away on business, and would be unable to dine with him that evening. Mistress Karen would receive him in the drawing room. She disappeared with his flowers, and Julian never saw them again, and had no evidence indeed that Mistress Karen would ever see them either.

At the top of the staircase Julian saw there were two portraits. One was a giantess, a bejewelled matriarch sneering down at him, and Julian could recognise in her features the girl he had danced with the night before, and he was terrified of her, and he fervently hoped that Karen would never grow up to be like her mother. The other portrait, much smaller, was of some boy in army uniform.

Karen was waiting for him. She was wearing the same dress she had worn the previous night. 'I'm so glad you could come,' she intoned.

'I'm glad you invited me.'

'Let us eat.'

So they went into the dining room, and sat either end of a long table. The hatchet-face served them soup. 'Thank you, Nanny,' Karen said. Julian tasted the soup. The soup was good.

'It's a very grand house,' said Julian.

'Please, there's no need to make conversation.'

'All right.'

The soup bowls were cleared away. Chicken was served. And, after that, a trifle.

'I like trifle,' said Karen, and Julian didn't know whether he was supposed to respond to that, and so he smiled at her, and she smiled back, and that all seemed to work well enough.

Afterwards Julian asked whether he could smoke. Karen said he might. He offered Karen a cigarette, and she hesitated, and then said she would like that. So Julian got up, and went around the table, and lit one for her. Julian tried very hard to smoke in the correct way, but it still kept coming out girlishly. But Karen didn't seem to mind; indeed, she positively imitated him, she puffed smoke from the corner of her mouth and made it all look very pretty.

And even now they didn't talk, and Julian realised he didn't mind. There was no awkwardness to it. It was companionable. It was a shared understanding.

Julian was invited to three more dinners. After the fourth, Mr Davison called Mr Morris, and told him that a proposal of marriage to his daughter would not be unacceptable. Mr Morris was very pleased, and Mrs Morris took Julian to her bedroom and had him go through her jewellery box to pick out a ring he could give his fiancée, and Julian marvelled, he had never seen such beautiful things.

Julian didn't meet Mr Davison until the wedding day, whereupon the man clapped him on the back as if they were old friends, and told him he was proud to call him his son. Mr Morris clapped Julian on the back too; even Julian's brothers were at it. And Julian marvelled at how he had been transformed into a man by dint of a simple service and signed certificate. Neither of his brothers had married yet, he had beaten them to the punch, and was there jealousy in that back clapping? They called Julian a lucky dog, that his bride was quite the catch. And so, Julian felt, she was; on her day of glory she did nothing but beam with smiles, and there was no trace of her customary truculence. She was charming, even witty, and Julian wondered why she had chosen to hide these qualities from him – had she recognised that it would have made him scared of her? Had she been shy and hard just to win his heart? Julian thought this might be so, and in that belief discovered that he did love her, he loved her after all – and maybe, in spite of everything, the marriage might just work out.

For a wedding present the families had bought them a house in Chelsea. It was small, but perfectly situated, and they could always upgrade when they had children. As an extra present, Mr Davison had bought his daughter a doll – a bit of a monstrosity, really, about the size of a fat infant, with blonde curly hair and red lips as thick as a darkie's, and wearing its own imitation wedding dress. Karen seemed pleased with it. Julian thought little about it at the time.

They honeymooned in Venice for two weeks, in a comfortable hotel near the Rialto.

Karen didn't show much interest in Venice. No, that wasn't true; she said she was fascinated by Venice. But she preferred to read about it in her guide book. Outside there was noise, and people, and stink; she could better experience the city indoors. Julian offered to stay with her, but she told him he was free to do as he liked. So in the daytime he'd leave her, and he'd go and visit St Mark's Square, climb the basilica, take a gondola ride. In the evening he'd return, and over dinner he'd try to tell her all about it. She'd frown, and say there was no need to explain, she'd already read it all in her Baedeker. Then they would eat in silence.

On the first night he'd been tired from travel. On the second, from sightseeing. On the third night Karen told her husband that there were certain manly duties he was expected to perform. Her father was wanting a grandson; for her part, she wanted lots of daughters. Julian said he would do his very best, and drank half a bottle of claret to give him courage. She stripped off, and he found her body interesting, and even attractive, but not in the least arousing. He stripped off too.

'Oh!' she said. 'But you have hardly any hair! I've got more hair than you!' And it was true, there was a faint buzz of fur over her skin, and over his next to nothing – just the odd clump where Nature had started work, rethought the matter, given up. Karen laughed, but it was not unkind. She ran her fingers over his body. 'It's so smooth, how did you get it so smooth?'

'Wait a moment,' she then said, and hurried to the bathroom. She was excited. Julian had never seen his wife excited. She returned with a razor. 'Let's make you perfect,' she said.

She soaped him down, and shaved his body bald. She only cut him twice, and that wasn't her fault, that was because he'd moved. She left him only the hairs on his head. And even there, she plucked the eyebrows, and trimmed his fine wavy hair into a neat bob.

'There,' she said, and and looked over her handiwork proudly, and ran her hands all over him, and this time there was nothing that got in their way.

And at that he tried to kiss her, and she laughed again, and pushed him away.

'No, no,' she said. 'Your duties can wait until we're in England. We're on holiday.'

So he started going out at night as well, with her blessing. He saw how romantic Venice could be by moonlight. He didn't know Italian well, and so could barely understand what the ragazzi said to him, but it didn't matter, they were very accommodating. And by the time he returned to his wife's side she was always asleep.

The house in Chelsea had been done up for them, ready for

their return. He asked her whether she'd like him to carry her over the threshold. She looked surprised at that, and said he could try. She lay back in his arms, and he was expecting her to be quite heavy, but it went all right really, and he got her through the doorway without doing anything to disgrace himself.

As far as he'd been aware, Karen had never been to the house before. But she knew exactly where to go, walking straight to the study, and to the wooden desk inside, and to the third drawer down. 'I have a present for you,' she said, and from the drawer she took a gun.

'It was my brother's,' she said.

'Oh. Really?'

'It may not have been his. But it's what they gave us anyway.'

She handed it to Julian. Julian weighed it in his hands. Like his wife, it was lighter than he'd expected.

'You're the man of the house now,' Karen said.

There was no nanny to fetch them dinner. Julian said he didn't mind cooking. He fixed them some eggs. He liked eggs.

After they'd eaten, and Julian had rinsed the plates and left them to dry, Karen said that they should inspect the bedroom. And Julian agreed. They'd inspected the rest of the house; that room, quite deliberately, both had left as yet unexplored.

The first impression that Julian got as he pushed open the door was pink, that everything was pink; the bedroom was unapologetically feminine, that blazed out from the soft pink carpet and the wallpaper of pink rose on pink background, And there was a perfume to it too, the perfume of Karen herself, and he still didn't much care for it.

That was before he saw the bed.

He was startled, and gasped, and then laughed at himself for gasping. The bed was covered with dolls. There were at least a dozen of them, all pale plastic skin and curls and lips that were ruby red, and some were wearing pretty little hats, and some carrying pretty little nosegays, all of them in pretty dresses. In the centre of them, in pride of place, was the doll Karen's father had given as a wedding present – resplendent in her wedding dress, still fat, her facial features smoothed away beneath that fat, sitting amongst the others like a queen. And all of them were smiling. And all of them were looking at him, expectantly, as if they'd been waiting to see who it was they'd heard climb the stairs, as if they'd been waiting for him all this time.

Julian said, 'Well! Well. Well, we won't be able to get much sleep with that lot crowding about us!' He chuckled. 'I mean, I won't know which is which! Which one is just a doll, and which one my pretty wife!' He chuckled. 'Well.'

Karen said, 'Gifts from my father. I've had some since I was a little girl. Some of them have been hanging about for years.'

Julian nodded.

Karen said, 'But I'm yours now.'

Julian nodded again. He wondered whether he should put his arms around her. He didn't quite like to, not with all the dolls staring.

'I love you,' said Karen. 'Or rather, I'm trying. I need you to know, I'm trying very hard.' And for a moment Julian thought she was going to cry, but then he saw her blink back the tears, her face was hard again. 'But I can't love you fully, not whilst I'm loving them. You have to get rid of them for me.'

'Well, yes,' said Julian. 'I mean. If you're sure that's what you want.'

Karen nodded grimly. 'It's time. And long overdue.'

She put on her woollen coat then, she said it would be cold out there in the dark. And she bundled up the dolls too, each and every one of them, and began putting them into Julian's arms. 'There's too many,' he said, 'I'll drop them,' but Karen didn't stop, and soon there were arms and legs poking into his chest, he felt the hair of his wife's daughters scratching under his chin. Karen carried just one doll herself, her new doll. She also carried the gun.

It had been a warm summer's evening, not quite yet dark. When they stepped outside it was pitch, only the moonlight providing some small relief, and that grudging. The wind bit. And Chelsea, the city bustle, the pavements, the pedestrians, the traffic – Chelsea had gone, and all that was left was the house. Just the house, and the woods ahead of them.

Julian wanted to run then, but there was nowhere to run to. He tried to drop the dolls. But the dolls refused to let go, they clung on to him, he could feel their little plastic fingers tightening around his coat, his shirt buttons, his skin, his own skin.

'Follow me,' said Karen.

The branches stuck out at weird angles, impossible angles, Julian couldn't see any way to climb through them. But Karen knew where to tread and where to duck, and she didn't hesitate, she moved at speed – and Julian followed her every step, he struggled to catch up, he lost sight of her once or twice and thought he was lost for good, but the dolls, the dolls showed him the way.

The clearing was a perfect circle, and the moon shone down upon it like a spotlight on a stage.

'Put them down,' said Karen.

He did so.

She arranged the dolls on the browning grass, set them in one long neat line. Julian tried to help, he put the new doll in her wedding dress beside them, and Karen rescued her. 'It's not her time yet,' she said. 'But she needs to see what will one day happen to her.'

'And what is going to happen?'

Her reply came as if the daughters themselves had asked. Her voice rang loud, with a confidence Julian had never heard from her before. 'Chloe. Barbara. Mary-Sue. Mary-Jo. Suki.

Delilah. Wendy. Prue. Annabelle. Mary-Ann. Natasha. Jill. You have been sentenced to death.'

'But why?' said Julian. He wanted to grab her, shake her by the shoulders. He wanted to. She was his wife, that's what he was supposed to do. He couldn't even touch her. He couldn't even go near. 'Why? What have they done?'

'Love,' said Karen. She turned to him. 'Oh, yes, they know what they've done.'

She saluted them. 'And you,' she said to Julian, 'you must salute them too. No. Not like that. That's not a salute. Hand steady. Like me. Yes. Yes.'

She gave him the gun. The dolls all had their backs to him, at least he didn't have to see their faces.

He thought of his father. He thought of his brothers. Then, he didn't think of anything.

He fired into the crowd. He'd never fired a gun before, but it was easy, there was nothing to it. He ran out of bullets, so Karen reloaded the gun. He fired into the crowd again. He thought there might be screams. There were no screams. He thought there might be blood. . . . And the brown of the grass seemed fresher and wetter and seemed to pool out lazily towards him.

And Karen reloaded his gun. And he fired into the crowd, just once more, please, God, just one last time. Let them be still. Let them stop twitching. The twitching stopped.

'It's over,' said Karen.

'Yes,' he said. He tried to hand her back the gun, but she wouldn't take it – it's yours now, you're the man of the house – 'Yes,' he said again.

He began to cry. He didn't make a sound.

'Don't,' said Karen. 'If you cry, the deaths won't be clean.'

And he tried to stop, but now the tears found a voice, he bawled like a little girl.

She said, 'I will not have you dishonour them.'

She left him then. She picked up her one surviving doll, and went, and left him all alone in the woods. He didn't try to follow her. He stared at the bodies in the clearing, wondered if he should clear them up, make things tidier. He didn't. He clutched the gun, waited it for to cool, and eventually it did. And when he thought to turn about he didn't know where to go, he didn't know he'd be able to find his way back. But the branches parted for him easily, as if ushering him fast on his way, as if they didn't want him either.

'I'm sorry,' he said.

He hadn't taken a key. He'd had to ring his own doorbell. When his wife answered, he felt an absurd urge to explain who he was. He'd stopped crying, but his face was still red and puffy. He held out his gun to her, and she hesitated, then at last took it from him.

'Sorry,' he said again.

'You did your best,' she said. 'I'm sorry too. But next time it'll be different.'

'Yes,' he said. 'Next time.'

'Won't you come in?' she said politely, and he thanked her, and did.

She took him upstairs. The doll was sitting on the bed, watching. She moved it to the dressing table. She stripped her husband. She ran her fingers over his soft smooth body, she'd kept it neat and shaved.

'I'm sorry,' he said one more time; and then, as if it were the same thing, 'I love you.'

And she said nothing to that, but smiled kindly. And she took him then, and before he knew what he was about he was inside her, and he knew he ought to feel something, and he knew he ought to be doing something to help – he tried to gyrate a little, 'No, no,' she said, 'I'll do it,' – and so he let her be, he let her do all the work, and he looked up at her face and searched for any sign of passion there, or tenderness, but it was so hard – and he turned to the side, and there was the fat doll, and it was smiling, and its eyes were twinkling, and there, there, on that greasy plastic face, there was all the tenderness he could ask for.

Eventually she rolled off. He thought he should hug her. He put his arms around her, felt how strong she was. He felt like crying again. He supposed that would be a bad idea.

'I love you,' she said. 'I am very patient. I have learned to love you.'

She fetched a hairbrush. She played at his hair. 'My sweetheart,' she said, 'my angel cake.' She turned him over, spanked his bottom hard with the brush until the cheeks were red as rouge. 'My big baby doll.'

And this time he did cry, it was as if she'd given him permission. And it felt so good.

He looked across at the doll, still smiling at him, and he hated her, and he wanted to hurt her, he wanted to take his gun and shove the barrel right inside her mouth and blast a hole through the back of her head. He wanted to take his gun and bludgeon with it, blow after blow, and he knew how good that would feel, the skull smashing, the wetness. And this time he wouldn't cry. He would be a real man.

'I love you,' she said again. 'With all my heart.'

She pulled back from him, and looked him in the face, sizing him up, as she had that first time they'd met. She gave him a salute.

He giggled at that, he tried to raise his own arm to salute back, but it wouldn't do it, he was so very silly.

There was a blur of something brown at the foot of the bed; something just out of the corner of his eye, and the blur seemed to still, and the brown looked like a jacket maybe, trousers, a uniform. He tried to cry out – in fear? at least in surprise? – but there was no air left in him. There was the smell of mud, so much mud. Who'd known mud could smell? And a voice to the blur, a voice in spite of all. 'Is it time?'

He didn't see his wife's reaction, nor hear her reply. His head jerked, and he was looking at the doll again, and she was the queen doll, the best doll, so pretty in her wedding dress. She was his queen. And he thought she was smiling even wider, and that she was pleased he was offering her such sweet tribute.

REMEMBERING JOEL LANE (1963–2013)

Joel Lane. Author, editor, stalwart of a maligned genre which he passionately defended. His work was held in the highest of regard by his peers and his lasting influence will be felt by anyone with a keen interest in the weird or supernatural tale.

What follows is a tribute from his friend Simon Bestwick and a reprinting of a story that appeared in his 2013 World Fantasy award-winning collection *Where Furnaces Burn*. I give you Joel at his finest.

JOHNNY MAINS

SIMON BESTWICK

JOEL LANE AND 'WITHOUT A MIND'

2013 WAS A horrible, cruel year for the arts in general: actors, musicians and writers all seemed to fall in their droves. And yet Joel Lane's death, so close to the year's end, seemed the cruellest of all. So, why did his passing stand out from all the rest, so much so that a story of his, first published in 2012, is being included here as a tribute?

There are plenty of good horror writers and a few great ones, but only a few you could legitimately call 'genius.' Even fewer of them are living; there's one less now. Joel wrote two novels and four collections of award-winning poetry, but short fiction was where he excelled most of all; he was, in my view, among the finest short story writers Britain has produced. His work abounds with unsettling imagery, as horror – or 'weird fiction', as he preferred to call it – should, but there was always much, much more to any his tales than that.

There was depth and there was insight, both of individual characters and of the society they lived in, sly humour – he could never resist a pun, and could craft the cleverest knob jokes in creation – and there was, above all, a stunning use of language. Pared-down but intensely poetic, his writing often says more in two thousand words than lesser writers could manage in a full-length novel. And it's full of wonders – dark ones, of course.

On top of that, he was a discerning and incisive critic of horror fiction, and of literature and cinema in general – 'the conscience of horror', as Mark Samuels once called him – and he patiently guided and mentored many other writers, me among them. Every death leaves a hole in the lives of others, but Joel's passing left one of the biggest I've known – in the lives of those who loved him, and in the genre itself.

He was a genuinely great writer, a good and honourable man and a dear friend, and I loved him; if I still feel I haven't grieved properly for him, perhaps it's because on some level I still refuse to accept his death. Living in cities a couple of hundred miles apart, we communicated mostly by email and phone; I still get the urge to ring him, unable to believe he won't answer and tell me it was all a mistake. But he won't.

'Without A Mind' is one of Joel's 'weird detective stories', told by a nameless Birmingham police officer whose cases always take a outré turn. For Joel, as for Robert Aickman, the supernatural wasn't an outside force that crashed in on everyday life, but a part of life itself. It embodies the intangible, but very human forces that shape our lives, inside us and out. In these stories, his anonymous investigator conjures and confronts these demons face to face, in beautiful, wry and understated prose that only makes them more poignant and more chilling.

These stories, which Joel began writing in the early '90s, were finally collected in *Where Furnaces Burn*, which deservedly won the 2013 World Fantasy Award for Best Collection. Its theme of 'the antipeople' harks back to 'And Some Are Missing', a story from Joel's first collection, *The Earth Wire*, but it's an extraordinary story in its own right – taut, spare, imaginative, beautifully written and packing a final emotional punch that will stay with you for a long time.

Joel Lane died, aged fifty, on 26th November 2013, and we still don't know why. I mean that in the sense that it's hard to comprehend a universe that could snuff out such a brilliant writer and such a kind and gentle human being so early, when there was so much he still had to do, and in a far more literal one: Joel just went to sleep that night, and he never woke up again. Knowing that gives 'Without A Mind's opening lines an almost prophetic feel.

His dreams and visions, at least, remain. Turn the page and discover them, if you haven't already. And if you have, welcome once more.

– Simon Bestwick, Swinton, 30th January 2014.

JOEL LANE

WITHOUT A MIND

NONE OF THIS was an investigation. It was personal. Though I first became aware of it when talking with the coroner at the Law Courts about suspicious deaths. He said that people sometimes died for no reason. In the last year, for example, there'd been a cluster of sudden deaths in South Birmingham from previously undiagnosed diseases. 'Sudden organ failure – the heart, the kidney, the liver. No obvious risk factors, no environmental cause. Maybe it's a new trend they'll find a reason for in a few years' time. At the moment, the only medical verdict is that shit happens.'

That wasn't a verdict many people would have disagreed with. It was the early nineties, the nadir of the recession, and emptiness was spreading like an infection through the high streets and trading estates. I was based at the Acocks Green station then, and we were having a bad year. Local crime had jacked up the insurance costs for newsagents and off-licences so high that most of them had gone out of business, robbed or not. The press was blaming negligent policing, while the local authority was slashing our budget.

My own life was a bit jittery at that time. Elaine was trying to combine work with looking after our daughter Julia, and was unhappy about the amount of overtime I was doing. I told her we were busy fighting the crime wave. True enough, but I didn't want to tell her I'd taken out a private loan to compensate for not getting a promotion I'd been relying on. She knew money had disappeared, and hinted that she thought I was salting it away for a mistress or a runner. I'd had no such thoughts – that all came later. There was a phrase from a Springsteen song that wouldn't go out of my head in those days: *debts no honest man could pay.*

One evening I was having an off-duty drink with some friends in the Corvid Arms when an old man staggered in, wearing a faded suit. He paused, leaning on a table, then made his way unsteadily towards the bar. As he tried to make himself heard over the juke-box, the barman picked up his mobile and spoke briefly into it. Two security staff came over from the door and informed the old man that he was leaving. I didn't interfere, though the old man was no worse drunk than half the teenagers around the bar. From the doorway his voice rose in protest, then faded. The bouncers didn't return.

A minute later, prompted by a mild unease, I slipped out the door. It was a crisp October night. Between the doorway and a line of cars, a dark figure lay curled on the pavement. Blood was trickling down his face from a gash over one eye. He was holding onto something that looked like a crumpled plastic bag half-full of soft food. As I came closer, I could see blood was draining into it – but not from his forehead. I couldn't make out what the whitish shape was. Surely I hadn't had that much to drink? I reached out, and it backed away from me. Part of it remained attached to the base of the old man's throat.

As blood drained into the creature, its form became clearer. It was something like a human baby, but twisted up and nearly flat, made of some kind of glassy matter or ectoplasm. Its hands were reaching down to its inert victim; the fingers, which were long and slender, were poking into his neck. Blood was flowing through them into the creature's small body. It made me think of a vacuum bag.

The old man twitched and choked as the attacker pressed in harder. Its tiny face had no eyes or mouth. I reached out to try and stop it, or to prove I wasn't really seeing it – and the thing pulled away, covering itself with the blood-streaked feathery tissue it had pulled out from the old man's chest cavity. And then it was gone, crawling faster than a rat, dragging its spoils with it. I looked down at the silent man. Apart from the gash on his forehead and a few small drops of blood on his neck, there was no sign of injury. But he was dead.

As I knelt there, feeling for a pulse, one of the bouncers came up to me and struck my shoulder with his fist. I looked up. He said quietly: 'Any trouble about this and they'll find your little daughter in the canal.' Then he turned and went back into the bar. I phoned for an ambulance.

The old man, an Irish Brummie aged seventy-two, was found to have died of natural causes. A haemorrhage had ripped through his lungs like a hailstorm through a leafy shrub, killing him in seconds. There was no damage to his skull, or to the flesh of his withered throat. A past history of pneumonia was suspected. Alcohol was assumed to have been a contributory factor.

A few days later, I was called out to make a shoplifting arrest at a shoe shop in Acocks Green. When I got there, the suspect – a woman of thirty or so – was unconscious in the manager's office. The shoes were all defective stock, heavily discounted. That seemed to make the whole thing worse. An ambulance was on its way, the shop manager assured me. 'She just passed out. Unless she's faking it. You never know, do you?'

The woman, who was very thin, was lying diagonally on the carpet of the narrow room. Her long dark hair was tangled below her, as if under water. I knelt to move her onto her side, and my hand passed through something cold above her face. The light was twisting and corrupting into a figure I already recognised. The creature had attached itself to the unconscious woman's ribs, and its pale figures were starting to redden. I swiped at it and felt a terrible chill bite into my fingers, as if they were covered with frost. But I couldn't get any grip on its translucent flesh. I was dimly aware of the shop manager telling me how the thief had been apprehended. Her story continued as, helpless, I watched the visitor drag out a pulsing mass of tissue and scuttle away to a corner, where it and its prize faded.

'... her before. This time she didn't get away with it.' As the manager finished her account, the office door swung open. Two paramedics rushed in, too late. I didn't have to feel for a pulse to know the woman's heart had stopped.

Karen was one of a group of North Birmingham coppers I used to meet occasionally for an off-duty chat in a pub near the Hockley Flyover. We always cleared out sharpish at last orders, before the Friday night lock-in started. One of those nights, Karen told me about the anti-people. It had been a long and stressful week, and despite my financial worries I couldn't resist the lure of their guest ales. I was into my second or third pint when the conversation turned to other people's drinking – always an easy thing to condemn. A senior colleague of ours had recently taken early retirement due to a 'drink problem'.

'It's a way of committing suicide on the instalment plan,' a young officer commented tritely.

'More like bad company – someone hanging on you who won't let you give up your bad habits,' said another.

Karen shook her head. 'Not someone you know. A stranger feeding on you, like a worm. A kind of anti-person.'

'Steady on, wench. You'll be seeing things next. Like Mulder here.' I laughed at that. Had to. Karen applied herself to her thin glass of rosé. She was a small woman with spiky ash-blond hair, very different from Elaine.

When the conversation had moved on, I caught her eye. 'Did you mean that literally?' I asked. 'About the anti-people?'

Karen gazed uneasily at me for a few seconds. 'Have you seen them too?' she said quietly. Her face was expressionless. I bit my lip.

A few minutes later, I visited the gents'. My face in the rust-flecked mirror looked sickly and lost. On the way back, I met Karen. She touched my arm. 'Can I have a word?' she said. I nodded.

'You know I work on the Hagley Road? Addicts and prostitutes, it's not fun. The crimes people commit against themselves. Three nights ago, we found a girl who'd been beaten up. By a pimp or a client probably. We called an ambulance and I tried to give her some first aid. Her face was a mess. Later we heard she'd lost the sight in both eyes. Detached retinas, from the beating.'

Karen swayed. Her face was coated with a film of sweat. 'You've had a shock – ' I began, but she went on.

'There were two of us, me and another WPC. We were waiting for the ambulance. Just before it came, I saw something move out of the gutter. Like a surgical glove or a plastic bag blowing. But there was no wind. It slipped onto the girl's face, and I went to pull it off but my hand went through it. The blood from her face soaked into it, and I saw it was like . . . like some tiny flattened child. It was kissing the girl's eyes. She was unconscious. Then it peeled away and just melted into the pavement. I thought I was imagining it. When the ambulance came, I already knew what would happen to the girl. But Jane, the other officer, she didn't see nothing. Am I going mad?'

'I don't think so,' I said. 'I've seen two of them. We need to talk about this. But not now.'

Karen smiled. Her teeth were sharp. 'Yeah. We'd better get back. Or the others will think we're having an affair.'

Did it cross my mind, even then, that I wouldn't mind justifying their suspicions? If so, it was the drink hinting.

We swapped numbers, but I didn't feel able to call her. The anti-people were my personal nightmare, not a secret to be shared. But five days later, Karen called me at my desk in the Acocks Green station.

'I've found a nest of them,' she said. 'Where they hide. Where they take what they've stolen.'

The nest was in Harborne, she said; near the disused railway. 'I used to play there as a kid. When I was twelve, thirteen, I used to go there with boys. It's got memories for me. Yesterday, my day off, I went there for a walk. Just trying to forget about some recent things. Then I saw one of them, creeping under a railway bridge. It was carrying some . . . trophy, something it had. Then another one followed it. I could almost see through them. Made me think of . . . shrimps in a rock pool. If they didn't move, you wouldn't know they were there.

'After a few minutes, I followed them. Down in the valley . . . where there's rotten wood from bonfires, and derelict cars, and stuff. There were dozens of the things, all gathered together, surrounded by fireweed. I think they were praying, but I couldn't see what to. I ran away.'

That evening, Karen's shift ended at nine and mine at ten. We met at the Green Man pub in Harborne, and I drove her to the railway bridge near the fire station. She led me through a gap in the fence. 'This hasn't changed in ten years,' she said. We had torches, but the yellow half-moon was bright enough for us not to need them. At Karen's suggestion, I'd brought something else: a can of petrol.

The railway track was half worn away and overgrown with brambles. I followed Karen down onto the footpath and under the railway bridge, which stank of piss and decay. There were a couple of occupied sleeping bags against the brick wall, but we ignored them. Further on, trees broke up the moonlight like cracks in a window. Karen slowed down, looking ahead carefully. 'It's not far from here.'

A few rusty shells of cars were lined up at the edge of a small clearing. Beyond them, I could see an old mattress and some pillows lying on the remains of a bonfire. Karen gripped my hand. 'Wait.' She crouched behind one of the ruined cars; I dropped beside her. Ahead of us, the pale fireweed and dead bracken were trembling in the breeze. Then I realised the air was still.

I don't know how many of them were in the clearing. It was just a restless folding and corrupting of the light, and a smell like an open wound. Without blood, there was hardly anything to them. Beside me, Karen didn't move; but her breathing told me how afraid she was. I gripped the petrol can and waited. Slowly, as my eyes – or some other kind of vision – adjusted, I could make out their flattened shapes climbing over the pile of charred wood to the mattress. They all left some kind of material there: whitish streaks and lumps of ectoplasm, the ghost organs they had extracted from their human victims.

For what seemed like hours, we watched them put together two figures on the stained mattress. The moon had passed overhead and was sinking through the wet trees when the bodies first stirred. Karen drew in a sharp breath. I thought my heart would stop. The two lifeless shapes rose to a hunched standing posture and faced each other. Around them, the barely visible anti-people crept and prayed on the heap of rotten wood and among the rank weeds.

Still taking shape, the figures pressed together in a slow clinch. I thought they were fighting until I glimpsed a low swelling on one of them that was seeking the other. Kneeling on the mattress, their rough-shaped bodies locked together and shuddered in clumsy passion. Their eyeless faces grew mouths to cry out silently.

Karen snatched the petrol can from my hand, together with the oil-stained cloth it was wrapped in. She flicked a lighter to the cloth, stood up and threw the bundle onto the mound of black wood. It struck the edge of the mattress, which started to burn. The figures carried on struggling even as the fire touched them, as if this was the climax they'd worked to reach. Then the petrol can exploded, scarring my vision. A wave of heat struck me through the car's empty windows. I smelt something burning that wasn't wood or flesh; it made me retch uncontrollably.

Around us, trees and bushes were catching fire. Karen pulled at my arm, turning away. We ran together through the wet undergrowth, hitting branches, stumbling in the darkness, along the footpath, through the bridge, up to the railway line and back down to the road where my car was parked.

I was shaking too hard to drive. We sat in the car for a few minutes. Then Karen pressed her face against my chest. She was crying. I stroked her cropped hair, then slowly lifted her head until it was level with my own. As we began to kiss, I wondered if it was really our own desire that was forcing us together. But that didn't stop my mouth, or my hands.

It was a few minutes past midnight. I drove from Harborne to the Bristol Road, out beyond Longbridge to the silhouetted hills. We parked in an empty lay-by and moved to the back of the car. The radio was playing, a new song from Massive Attack. *Like a soul without a mind, in a body without a heart.* Karen breathed hard, but made no other sound, as I thrust inside her.

Neither of us spoke on the way back through the city. Karen's eyes were closed; she was shivering, though I'd turned up the heating in the car. I was thinking of an incident from my childhood: when an older boy had followed me home from school, spitting repeatedly on the back of my coat. The roads were quiet. The moon was no longer in the sky.

We should have left it there, but didn't. I needed to get past the memory of those desperate puppets and their audience. Karen wanted something from me I no longer had to give. It was hard enough managing my own life, let alone a double one.

We settled it as best we could, with a few furtive dates and a restless night at a cheap Stafford hotel. The night of the fire was the only time we didn't take precautions. We'd just about put the phantom of love to rest when Karen told me she was pregnant.

The waste ground fire had spread a little, but there wasn't much for it to harm. We'd gone back in the daytime and found nothing abnormal, except a bad smell that could have been burnt plastic. The local police had put out an alert for a teenage arsonist.

Karen decided to keep the baby. I won't presume to define her motives. But to some extent, it made the connection between us permanent. And as the foetus grew, my feelings became more complex. It might be a boy, and I'd always wanted a son. Elaine couldn't have any more children. Maybe some day I could acknowledge him. Or her. It was something to look forward to as well as fear.

One night in September, around eleven, Karen phoned me at the station to say she'd gone into labour. I called Elaine and said the station had an emergency. Hoped there wouldn't be too many more lies like that. When I came off shift, I drove straight to the hospital.

As soon as I saw her, I knew something was wrong. Her face had a shrink-wrapped look. She tried to smile when she saw me, but her eyes were focused inward. The maternity ward was uncomfortably warm. I held her hand while a nurse took her temperature and reassured her that all was well and the midwife would be along in a few minutes. 'I need more pain-killers,' she said. The nurse hurried off, and I gave Karen a gentle hug. Her breathing sounded torn. I felt sick with guilt, both at being there and at not doing more.

My daughter Julia had been born in another local hospital. It had seemed quite an easy birth – but afterwards, Elaine had lost a lot of blood. They'd had to operate. That was in my mind as I sat holding Karen's hand, watching the sweat trickle down her taut face.

'It hurts,' she whispered. Her lips were cracked. I filled a glass from the jug of water on the bedside table and turned back to her, holding it. A pale, hollow thing was crouching on her belly. I dropped the glass and lashed out at the creature, but felt only a chilly breath. Its long fingers were turning red. Karen was lying still; her eyes were shut.

At that moment, the nurse came back with a syringe. 'What are you doing?' she said to me. 'Did you spill the water?' I stood there, unable to move, as the misty creature drew a small blood-streaked mass head-first from Karen's belly. It dragged its trophy under the bed, where the pool of water was spreading. The nurse pushed me back and applied the syringe to Karen's inert arm.

The labour was protracted and terrible. Two hours later, the midwife delivered Karen's stillborn baby. It was a girl. By then, the mother was fully conscious. 'Can I hold her?' she asked. The midwife wrapped the small corpse in a strip of cloth and placed it in Karen's arms. She looked at the baby, then looked up at me. There was something worse than grief in her face. I looked down at what she was holding. Marked on the dead baby's forehead and cheeks like vaccination scars were the prints of tiny human fingers.

CONTRIBUTORS

LAURA MAURO was born in Elephant & Castle but was forced to move to Essex, where she now lives with a multitude of cats. Additional to writing, she collects tattoos, dyes her hair interesting colours and gets emotionally attached to fictional characters. Her work has appeared in *Shadows and Tall Trees* and *Black Static*.

IAN HUNTER was born in Edinburgh and is the author of three children's novels, and the alternative guide to Glasgow called *Fantastic Glasgow*. His short stories and poetry have appeared in magazines and anthologies in the UK, USA and Canada. Apart from being a member of the Glasgow SF Writers Circle, a Director of the Scottish writers collective *Read Raw*, he's also poetry editor for the British Fantasy Society, and a book reviewer for *Interzone*. Sometimes he can be found at www.ian-hunter.co.uk and right now, he's working on too many 'somethings'.

ANNA TABORSKA was born in London, England. She studied Experimental Psychology at Oxford University and went on to gainful employment in public relations, journalism and advertising, before throwing everything over to become a filmmaker and horror writer. Anna has directed two short films (*Ela* and *The Sin*), two documentaries (*My Uprising* and *A*

Fragment of Being) and a one-hour television drama (*The Rain Has Stopped*), which won two awards at the British Film Festival, Los Angeles, 2009.

She has also worked on seventeen other films, including Ben Hopkins' *Simon Magus* (starring Noah Taylor and Rutger Hauer). Anna worked as a researcher and assistant producer on several BBC television programmes, including the series Auschwitz: *The Nazis and the Final Solution* and *World War Two: Behind Closed Doors – Stalin, the Nazis and the West*. Anna's feature length screenplays include: *Chainsaw*, *The Camp*, *Pizzaman* and *The Bloody Tower*. Short screenplays include: *Little Pig* (finalist in the Shriekfest Film Festival Screenplay Competition 2009), *Curious Melvin* and *Arthur's Cellar*. Recently published short stories include: 'Buy a Goat for Christmas' (*Best New Werewolf Tales Vol.1*, 2012), 'Etude' (*This Hermetic Legislature: A Homage to Bruno Schulz*, 2012), 'Tea with the Devil' (*Strange Halloween*, 2012), 'Cut!' (*The Screaming Book of Horror*, 2012), and five stories published in *The Black Book of Horror*, volumes 5-9 (2009-2012). Anna's short story 'Bagpuss' was an Eric Hoffer Award Honoree and was published in *Best New Writing 2011*, and her story 'Little Pig' from *The Eighth Black Book of Horror* was a runner up for the Abyss Awards 2011 and was picked for *The Best New Horror of the Year Volume Four* (2012). Poems include 'Mrs. Smythe regrets going to the day spa' (*Christmas: Peace on All The Earths*, 2010), 'Song for Maud' (*No Fresh Cut Flowers, An Afterlife Anthology*, 2010) and three poems in *What Fear Becomes: An Anthology from the Horror Zine*, 2011. Anna's debut short story collection, *For Those Who Dream Monsters*, was published in November 2013 by Mortbury Press, with a novelette collection planned for release in late 2014.

The *Oxford Companion to English Literature* describes RAMSEY CAMPBELL as 'Britain's most respected living horror writer'.

He has been given more awards than any other writer in the field, including the Grand Master Award of the World Horror Convention, the Lifetime Achievement Award of the Horror Writers Association and the Living Legend Award of the International Horror Guild. Among his novels are *The Face That Must Die*, *Incarnate*, *Midnight Sun*, *The Count of Eleven*, *Silent Children*, *The Darkest Part of the Woods*, *The Overnight*, *Secret Story*, *The Grin of the Dark*, *Thieving Fear*, *Creatures of the Pool*, *The Seven Days of Cain*, *Ghosts Know* and *The Kind Folk*. Forthcoming are *Think Yourself Lucky* and *Thirteen Days at Sunset Beach*. *The Last Revelation of Gla'aki* and *The Pretence* are novellas. His collections include *Waking Nightmares*, *Alone with the Horrors*, *Ghosts and Grisly Things*, *Told by the Dead*, *Just Behind You* and *Holes for Faces*, and his non-fiction is collected as *Ramsey Campbell, Probably*. His novels *The Nameless* and *Pact of the Fathers* have been filmed in Spain. His regular columns appear in *Prism*, *Dead Reckonings* and *Video Watchdog*. He is the President of the Society of Fantastic Films.

Ramsey Campbell lives on Merseyside with his wife Jenny. His pleasures include classical music, good food and wine, and whatever's in that pipe. His web site is at www.ramseycampbell.com.

JOHN LLEWELLYN PROBERT won the 2013 British Fantasy Award for his novella *The Nine Deaths of Dr Valentine* and 2014 will see the publication of its sequel, *The Hammer of Dr Valentine* (both from Spectral Press). He is the author of over a hundred published short stories, several novellas (including his latest, *Differently There* from Gray Friar Press) and a novel, *The House That Death Built* (Atomic Fez). His first short story collection, *The Faculty of Terror*, won the 2006 Children of the Night award. His latest stories can be found in *Psychomania* (Constable Robinson), *Exotic Gothic Volume 5 Part II* (PS Publishing), *Cthulhu Cymraeg* (Screaming Dreams), *World War*

Cthulhu (Cubicle 7), *Demons and Devilry* (Hersham) and *The Tenth Black Book of Horror* (Mortbury Press). Endeavour Press has published *Ward 19* and *Bloody Angels* - two crime novellas featuring his pathologist heroine Parva Corcoran, and there is a third Parva adventure, *Suicide Blondes*, due imminently. He is currently trying to review every cult movie in existence at his House of Mortal Cinema (www.johnlprobert.blogspot.co.uk) and everything he is up to writing-wise can be found at www.johnlprobert.com. Also forthcoming is *The Little Book of House of Mortal Cinema* - a book of his film reviews from Pendragon Press. Future projects include a new short story collection, a lot more non-fiction writing, and a couple of novels. He never sleeps.

MURIEL GRAY was born in Glasgow and graduated in Graphics and illustration from the Glasgow School of Art. She was a professional illustrator and later senior exhibition designer in the Museum of Antiquities, before her playing in a punk band led her into a career in broadcasting via Channel 4's flagship music show *The tube*, which she presented with Jools Holland and the late Paula Yates.

During her many successful years continuing as a broadcaster, producer and production company director, she pursued her main passion which was horror, publishing three novels, *The Trickster*, *Furnace*, and *The Ancient*, as well as continuing to contribute many short stories to a variety of anthologies.

Muriel's first and abiding love is all things supernatural. Except for religion. Which she firmly believes could use a bloody good editor.

GARY FRY lives in Dracula's Whitby, literally around the corner from where Bram Stoker was staying while thinking about that legendary character. Gary has a PhD is psychology, but his first love is literature. He was the first author in PS Publishing's 'Showcase' series, and none other than Ramsey Campbell has described him as 'a master.' He is the author of more than 15 books, and his latest are the Lovecraftian novel *Conjure House* (DarkFuse, 2013); the short story collection *Shades of Nothingness* (PS Publishing, 2013); the highly original zombie novel *Severed* and novellas *Menace, Savage* and *Mutator* (DarkFuse, 2014). Gary warmly welcomes all to his web presence: www.gary-fry.com

ADAM NEVILL was born in Birmingham in 1969 and grew up in England and New Zealand. He is the author of the supernatural horror novels *Banquet for the Damned, Apartment 16, The Ritual, Last Days*, and *House of Small Shadows*. In 2012 *The Ritual* was the winner of The August Derleth Award for Best Horror Novel, and in 2013 *Last Days* won the same award. Adam lives in Birmingham, England, and can be contacted through www.adamlgnevill.com.

THANA NIVEAU is a Halloween bride who lives in the Victorian seaside town of Clevedon, where she shares her life with fellow writer John Llewellyn Probert, in a gothic library filled with arcane books and curiosities.

She is the author of *From Hell to Eternity*, which was shortlisted for the British Fantasy award for Best Collection 2013. Her stories have been reprinted in *The Mammoth Book of Best New Horror* (volumes 22–24) and other stories appear or are forthcoming in *Exotic Gothic 5*; *The Burning Circus*; *The Black Book of Horror*(volumes 7–10), *Whispers in the Dark; Sorcery and Sanctity: A Homage to Arthur Machen; Demons and Devilry; Night Schools; The 13 Ghosts of Christmas; Magic: an Anthology of the Esoteric and Arcane; Terror Tales of Wales; Terror Tales of the Cotswolds*; *Steampunk Cthulhu*; *Sword & Mythos; Bite-Sized Horror 2; Death Rattles* and *Delicate Toxins.*

ELIZABETH STOTT worked in industry as a scientist and is a STEM ambassador. She has published a collection of short stories, *Familiar Possessions,* and her fiction and poetry has appeared in various places. She is working on novels and collections of fiction and poetry.

KATE FARRELL lives in Edinburgh. Formerly an actress, the scope of her career spanned everything from Chekhov to *Chucklevision*. She now writes contes cruels wherein bad things happen to good people and has stories featured in the Eighth, Ninth and Tenth *Black Book of Horrors, Terror Tales of the Seaside,* and *Screaming Book of Horror*. Her first novella *My Name is Mary Sutherland* is due out this year, from PS Publishing.

STEPHEN VOLK is the writer behind the notorious BBC Halloween hoax *Ghostwatch* and the ITV drama series *Afterlife*. His other screenplays include *The Awakening* (2011), Ken Russell's *Gothic,* and *The Guardian* co-written with director William Friedkin. His first short story collection was *Dark Corners*(Gray Friar Press, 2006) and he has been a finalist for the HWA Bram Stoker, British Fantasy and Shirley Jackson Awards. In 2013 he published the acclaimed novella *Whitstable* (Spectral Press), featuring horror star Peter Cushing, as well as his second collection, *Monsters in the Heart* (also Gray Friar Press). www.stephenvolk.net.

Born in 1947 TANITH LEE began to write at age 9. Though often interrupted by school and later, various jobs, her professional writing career was launched in 1975 by excellent *DAW Books of America*. Since then she has published around 97 novels and collections, had 4 plays broadcast by the BBC, and 2 episodes of the SF series *Blake's 7* on TV. Of her 320 short stories, some get regularly read on *Radio 4 Extra*. She has won several awards including, in 2009, Master of Horror and, in 2013, the Lifetime Achievement Award. Lee lives in Sussex with her husband writer/artist John Kaiine, under the stern paw of 2 cats.

D.P. WATT is a writer living in the bowels of England. He balances his time between lecturing in drama and devising new 'creative recipes', 'illegal' and 'heretical' methods to resurrect a world of awful literary wonder. His collection of short stories *An Emporium of Automata* was reprinted by Eibonvale Press in early 2013, a recent novella *Memorabilia* was published in *The Transfiguration of Mr Punch*, and his latest collection, *The Phantasmagorical Imperative and Other Fabrications*, was published in February 2014 with Egaeus Press. You can find him at *The Interlude House*: www.theinterludehouse.webs.com.

MARIE O'REGAN is a British Fantasy Award-nominated author and editor, based in Derbyshire. Her first collection, *Mirror Mere*, was published in 2006, and her short fiction has appeared in a number of genre magazines and anthologies in the UK, US, Canada, Italy and Germany. She was shortlisted for the British Fantasy Society Award for Best Short Story in 2006, and Best Anthology in 2010 and 2012. Her genre journalism has appeared in magazines like *The Dark Side*, *Rue Morgue* and *Fortean Times*, and her interview book, *Voices in the Dark*, was released in 2011. An essay on 'The Changeling' was published in PS Publishing's *Cinema Macabre*, edited by Mark Morris. She is co-editor of the bestselling *Hellbound Hearts*, *Mammoth Book of Body Horror* and *A Carnivàle of Horror – Dark Tales from the Fairground*, plus editor of bestselling *The Mammoth Book of Ghost Stories by Women*.

V. H. LESLIE's work has appeared in *Black Static* and *Interzone*, *Weird Fiction Review* and *Shadows and Tall Trees*. She also writes academic pieces for a range of literary publications, as well as a monthly column for an online horror website, focusing on the roots of the genre. She was recently awarded a Hawthornden Fellowship and won the Lightship First Chapter Prize. For more details on her work please visit www.vhleslie.wordpress.com

REGGIE OLIVER has been a professional playwright, actor, and theatre director since 1975. Besides plays, his publications include the authorised biography of Stella Gibbons, *Out of the Woodshed*, published by Bloomsbury in 1998, and six collections of stories of supernatural terror, of which the fifth, *Mrs Midnight* (Tartarus 2011) won the *Children of the Night Award* for 'best work of supernatural fiction in 2011' and was nominated for two other awards. Tartarus has also reissued his first and second collections *The Dreams of Cardinal Vittorini* and *The Complete Symphonies of Adolf Hitler*, in new editions with new illustrations by the author, as well as his latest (and sixth) collection *Flowers of the Sea*. His novel, *The Dracula Papers I - The Scholar's Tale* (Chomu 2011) - is the first of a projected four. Another novel Virtue in Danger was published in 2013 by Zagava Books. An omnibus edition of his stories entitled *Dramas from the Depths* is published by Centipede, as part of its *Masters of the Weird Tale* series. His stories have appeared in over fifty anthologies.

MARK MORRIS has written over twenty-five novels, among which are *Toady*, *Stitch*, *The Immaculate*, *The Secret of Anatomy*, *Fiddleback*, *The Deluge* and four books in the popular *Doctor Who* range. He is also the author of two short story collections, *Close to the Bone* and *Long Shadows, Nightmare Light*, and several novellas. His short fiction, articles and reviews have appeared in a wide variety of anthologies and magazines, and he is editor of both *Cinema Macabre*, a book of horror movie essays by genre luminaries for which he won the 2007 British Fantasy Award, and its follow-up *Cinema Futura*. His script work includes audio dramas for Big Finish Productions' *Doctor Who* and *Jago & Litefoot* ranges, and also for Bafflegab's *Hammer Chillers* series, and his recently published work includes an updated novelisation of the 1971 Hammer movie *Vampire Circus* and a short novel entitled *It Sustains* for Earthling Publications. Upcoming is a new, as yet unnamed, short story collection from ChiZine Publications, a novel called *The Black* from PS Publishing, the official novelisation of the Darren Aronofsky-directed movie *Noah*, and *The Wolves of London*, book one of the *Obsidian Heart* trilogy, which will be published by Titan Books in 2014.

MICHAEL MARSHALL SMITH is a novelist and screenwriter. Under this name he has published eighty short stories, and three novels — *Only Forward*, *Spares* and *One of Us* — winning the Philip K. Dick, International Horror Guild, and August Derleth awards, along with the Prix Bob Morane in France: he has been awarded the British Fantasy Award for Best Short Fiction four times, more than any other author.

Writing as MICHAEL MARSHALL, he has published six internationally-bestselling thrillers including *The Straw Men*, *The Intruders* — currently in production as a miniseries with BBC America — and *Killer Move*. His most recent novel is *We Are Here*.

He lives in Santa Cruz, California with his wife, son, and two cats.

— www.michaelmarshallsmith.com

ROBERT SHEARMAN has written four short story collections, and between them they have won the World Fantasy Award, the Shirley Jackson Award, the Edge Hill Readers Prize and three British Fantasy Awards. A fifth collection, *They Do The*

Same Things Different There, is to be published by ChiZine later this year.

His background is in the theatre, resident dramatist at the Northcott Theatre in Exeter, and regular writer for Alan Ayckbourn at the Stephen Joseph Theatre in Scarborough; his plays have won the *Sunday Times* Playwriting Award, the Sophie Winter Memorial Trust Award, and the Guinness Award in association with the Royal National Theatre. He regularly writes plays and short stories for BBC Radio, and he has won two Sony Awards for his interactive radio series, 'The Chain Gang'.

He's probably best known for reintroducing the Daleks to the BAFTA-winning first season of the revived *Doctor Who*, in an episode that was a finalist for the Hugo Award.

He has taught short story writing at Middlesex University and for Arvon, and gives lectures and workshops on the form around the world. In 2013 he was judge for both the National Student Television Awards and the Manchester Fiction Prize; from 2011 to 2012 he was writer in residence at Edinburgh Napier University.

JOEL LANE was the author of four collections of supernatural horror stories, *The Earth Wire*, *The Lost District*, *The Terrible Changes* and the Word Fantasy Award-winning *Where Furnaces Burn*. He also wrote two novels, *From Blue To Black* and *The Blue Mask*; a novella, *The Witnesses are Gone*; a chapbook, *Black Country*; and three collections of poems, *The Edge of the Screen*, *Trouble in the Heartland* and *The Autumn Myth*. Joel edited an anthology of subterranean horror stories, *Beneath the Ground*, and co-edited (with Steve Bishop) the crime fiction anthology *Birmingham Noir*. He also co-edited the British Fantasy Award nominated anthology *Never Again*. In 2013, Joel died in his sleep, aged 50.

ACKNOWLEDGEMENTS

JEN AND CHRIS at Salt for giving me the go ahead, what an honour! Nicholas Royle for advice given before I accepted the job, Robin Ince, Charlie Higson, Simon Bestwick for his intro, Conrad Williams for saying that the *In Remembrance* section should be a yearly thing. Peter Crowther and Mike Smith for giving me the word file to Joel's story. To my family for putting up with the long stretches in my office either reading or editing, and to all of the publishers, editors and authors who made this book happen. Finally, as always, my dog Biscuit, best foot warmer in the world.